# ACE

OF

# HEARTS

# ACE OF HEARTS

MORGANE MONCOMBLE

TRANSLATED BY JENNIFER HIGGINS

AMAZON CROSSING

This is a work of fiction. Names, characters, organizations, places, events, and incidents are either products of the author's imagination or are used fictitiously. Any resemblance to actual persons, living or dead, or actual events is purely coincidental.



Previously published as *L'as de coeur* by Hugo Publishing in France in 2021. Translated from French by Jennifer Higgins. First published in English by Amazon Crossing in 2025.

Published by Amazon Crossing, Seattle

www.apub.com



EU product safety contact:
Amazon Media EU S. à r.l.
38, avenue John F. Kennedy, L-1855 Luxembourg
amazonpublishing-gpsr@amazon.com

ISBN-13: 9781662519864 (paperback)
ISBN-13: 9781662519857 (digital)

Cover design by Hang Le
Cover images: © AlexandrBognat, © Andrii Sedykh / Getty; © aekky / Shutterstock

Printed in the United States of America

# BASIC POKER RULES

The croupier deals two cards to each player, one by one. The two players seated to the left of the dealer are known as the Small Blind and the Big Blind.

The player immediately to the left of the Big Blind begins the first round of betting. Depending on the cards in their hand, this player, the Small Blind, can

- *Fold:* Put down their cards and withdraw from the round.
- *Call:* Match the bet made by the Big Blind.
- *Raise:* Bet a larger sum than the one put down by the Big Blind.

Once the first player has made their decision, the next player to the left takes their turn, and so on. The Small Blind and the Big Blind can either match the other players' bets or raise. If there is a raise, then a second round of betting begins.

When the first round of betting is over, the dealer turns over three cards in the center of the table. These are known as the *flop*.

The second round of betting begins with the player sitting to the left of the dealer. In this round, each player can choose to

- *Check:* This means not putting any more money into the pot. Players can check only if no other player in the round has placed a bet yet.

- *Bet:* The player places a sum of their choosing into the pot.
- *Raise:* The player bets a sum higher than the previous bet.
- *Call:* If another player has already placed a bet, the player can call by placing an equal sum in the pot.
- *Fold:* The player puts down their cards and withdraws from the round.

When the second round of betting is over, a fourth community card is turned over in the middle of the table. This card is known as the *turn*.

The third round is played like the second, and when it's over, a fifth community card, the *river*, is turned over. Once the players have finished placing their bets, those who are still in the game (that is, those who haven't folded) show their cards. The player with the highest-scoring combination of cards wins the round and collects the entire pot.

The player who wins a round in poker is the player with the highest-scoring hand, the hand being made up of the player's own cards and/or the five community cards in the middle of the table.

# CARD COMBINATIONS IN POKER

These are the combinations of cards a player may have in their hand, from lowest to highest scoring:

- *One Pair:* Two identical cards of different suits. Note, if two players finish a round with a pair, the pair with the higher value will win the pot.
- *Two Pair:* Two pairs of cards.
- *Three-of-a-Kind:* Three cards of the same value from different suits.
- *Straight:* Five consecutive cards from different suits.
- *Flush:* Five cards from the same suit but not in consecutive order.
- *Full House:* Three-of-a-kind, and a pair.
- *Four-of-a-Kind:* Four cards of the same value from different suits.
- *Straight Flush:* Five consecutive cards from the same suit.
- *Royal Flush:* The five highest-value cards from the same suit in consecutive order (e.g., the ace, king, queen, jack, and ten, all from the same suit).

# Prologue

## Levi

***March***
***Saint Petersburg, Russia***

*"No!" I snarl, struggling like a demon. "Let her go! She didn't do anything!"*

*Powerful arms lock around me, but I'm still shouting, tears streaming down my cheeks, the muscles of my face contorted in panic. They can't do this. They've got no right to take her away from me, not like this, not now. I need her, just as she needs me.*

*She won't last ten seconds in the place where they're taking her. I'm the only one who can protect her. I always have been.*

*But this time, I've failed at my duty.*

*"I'm the guilty one!" I bellow again, desperate now. "Stop! You've got the wrong person!"*

*Roaring with anger, I ram my elbow into the stomach of the policeman who holds me, free myself, and run to her. Everyone's shouting, and someone tries to stop me, but I manage to reach her and throw my arms around her frail shoulders. Those delicate, familiar shoulders I rode on a hundred times when I was small. Shoulders that carried all the worries I could never help her bear . . .*

*It's all my fault. I sob despairingly into her hair like I'm a child of five and not a teenager, begging her not to abandon me. I know she'd hold me tight if her arms weren't handcuffed behind her back.*

*"Levi, don't cry. It'll be all right, my angel."*

*"You need to let her go, boy."*

*No. No. But there's nothing I can do. Three police officers pull me backward so hard that I fall to my knees, my shoulders trembling. My mother smiles at me from a long way off. She isn't crying. In fact, she's completely calm.*

*"Don't do anything stupid. Do you understand?" she says firmly. "Stop crying. We'll see each other soon. I love you."*

*I shake my head, unable to hold back my tears. People I've never seen before are taking her by the arm and leading her away. She looks at me one last time, then turns her back to me. I feel as if all the light inside me were going out as the best part of me walks away and disappears.*

*What am I supposed to do now? I'm still in shock. I'm trembling like a leaf, unable to get up even when my uncle comes and stands next to me. He pats my shoulder and tells me to be a man, then takes me back home with him. I'll have to stay there until I'm old enough to make my own way.*

*He offers no words of comfort, nothing to reassure me. He acts as though nothing happened, as though my mother won't rot in prison for having killed my father.*

Mom, why did you do it?

*After the terrible day of the trial, I hardly ever see her. I'm allowed to visit or call her only once a month. She always tells me everything's fine, and that she's even made friends with some of the other women in the prison. I don't believe her, but I pretend to. And when it's my turn to tell her about my life, I do the same: I lie. I say I'm doing well at school, not drinking too much, and not staying out late. I wish that were true, but how else am I supposed to deal with all the feelings that prey on me night and day?*

I want to die.

*People keep telling me to get on with my life, not to skip school, to make my mother proud. Instead, I'm growing into an angry teenager. Angry with my father, my mother, myself. But most of all with one man. Because we always need someone to blame for our problems, don't we?*

*I see his face in the newspaper a few weeks after the incident. He's more well-known than I thought: an entrepreneur who made a fortune before he was forty (a hundred million euros, no big deal) from a music-streaming app. But he's also been photographed in casinos and at poker tournaments.*

*I stare at the page: a report about an interview he gave to Italian television. I begin to boil with rage as I read the journalist's questions to him about the "tragic death" of my father, a top poker player. Tito Ferragni, my father's rival and great nemesis, gave the following reply:*

*"It's unfortunate, naturally . . . Who could have seen that coming? But you know what they say: One man's loss is another man's gain. We must live while we can! And there's nothing standing between me and victory now."*

*I sit there, open-mouthed and indignant, staring at the Russian translation of his comments. How dare he say such a thing? He couldn't have cared less about what happened. My father dedicated his life to that rivalry. It meant everything to him. Far more even than my mother and I ever did. But Tito hasn't got a scrap of honor or loyalty. He's just thrilled that he has a better chance of winning now that my father's dead.*

*He started it. He was the one who betrayed and humiliated my father. All our problems began with him. Everything's his fault. It's because of him that my childhood is ruined, my father's dead, and my mother will be in prison for ten long years. And he's not even ashamed to say such things on television . . . while he remains free and unpunished, rich even, and admired by everyone around him.*

*Gazing at the article, I make a silent vow:* No matter how long it takes, no matter what it costs me, I will make Tito Ferragni pay.

*And after all, I have nothing left to lose now anyway.*

"Shall I repeat the question, Monsieur Ivanovich?"

I shake myself out of my waking dream, suddenly aware of the group of journalists crowding around me as I stand outside my hotel. I curse myself for allowing my mind to wander back to that dark period of my life at a moment like this, in front of a crowd of people. I knew when I left my hotel room that they would be outside waiting. In fact, I told Thomas to get them to come. I need them to pass on a message for me.

I stand lost in thought, holding the back door of the taxi open. I'm no longer the seventeen-year-old boy I was when my father died. My resentment and my thirst for revenge remain, but the feelings are quieter, tamer. I've become patient and calculating where I once was impulsive and hurried.

"I'm sorry. What were you saying?" I ask politely.

"The World Series of Poker starts in two months, and you've already said you'll be playing. You came second in the Main Event last year, so everyone's going to be watching you at the tournament. You're making a name for yourself faster than anyone, even your father, has before. What can you tell us about your goals?"

I pretend to reflect as the winter wind of Saint Petersburg whips at my coat. In fact, I've been waiting impatiently for someone to ask me this. I think back to the words Tito used in that interview, to how happy he looked at the idea of no longer having a rival. But most of all, I think about the first time I met him, six years ago. I was twenty-one, and I'd just spent all my savings on the tournament entry fee: ten thousand euros. I didn't have a single cent left. When we finally found ourselves at the same table, I made sure to shake his hand. He seemed amused by my nerve—or my stupidity—and when he asked if I was a fan, I replied exactly as I'd promised myself I would a few years earlier, stumbling over the English words. "I'm the one who'll bring you down. Levi Ivanovich. Remember that name."

I smile, remembering how quickly his arrogance melted away. He recognized my name immediately, of course—the same one as his old friend, now dead. Tito still didn't see me as a threat, though. Not yet.

"To tell you the truth . . . ," I say now to the camera as someone holds a microphone toward me, "this is going to be my last year at the WSOP."

Eyes widen in surprise, and the reporters all move closer to ask for more details. I raise my hand for silence. I take my time, fixing the camera with a stony look, hoping that somewhere in the world, in Venice or wherever he may be, Tito Ferragni is watching me and wetting his pants.

"I've decided to retire from professional poker."

There's a murmur of surprise. I revel in their astonishment, feeling drunk with excitement. *The trap is well and truly set.*

"Already?"

"But you're so young! Why now?"

One journalist catches my attention when he asks with a puzzled look, "What happened to that young man full of ambition we all know so well? I remember your first year at the Main Event. You said, and I quote, 'I won't stop until I'm number one.'"

I nod calmly. "True. And as I've decided this is my last year, I'll let you draw your own conclusions."

"Are you saying you're going to win?"

He knows the answer, but he wants to hear me say it. I don't hesitate for a second—it's not my style.

"Exactly."

My inner voice sniggers and tells me I'm an arrogant asshole. I can't deny it.

"You seem very confident. Tito Ferragni, your main rival at this point, and your father's rival in the past, has also confirmed he'll be playing . . ."

"Tito is very good, but he's sadly lacking in originality. And what with his rocky marriage and his failing business, he's showing his age!" I say. And then I add, certain that he and he alone will recognize the words, "But you know what they say: One man's loss is another man's gain."

# Chapter 1

## Rose

***May***
***Macau, China***

I desperately need some cash.

The problem is my brain thinks I need another sports car.

I've been in China two weeks now, and I'm already banned from four casinos. It seems the Chinese aren't so different from the Italians: neither of them likes me very much. But I like them, and their gambling establishments, a lot.

I like going into a casino for the first time, hearing the noise of the machines and the cries of triumph, feeling both envy and euphoria. I like sitting down at a poker table and watching all those self-satisfied men underestimate me as they size up my cleavage and my burgundy lipstick.

But the best moment is when their patronizing sneers turn into black looks as I fleece them all. Usually, they keep right on playing—too proud to stop.

"Beginner's luck, I see," they always say, loud enough for me to hear them, explaining their own defeat.

The most arrogant ones won't stop until they have no chips left. They're my favorites. I love watching them make fools of themselves.

Their money smells better than other people's, if that's possible, especially when I'm spending it on expensive shoes.

And that, in a nutshell, is my problem. I always either keep playing until I lose everything at roulette, or I blow my winnings afterward in one intense shopping session. My latest extravagance: a bloodred Ferrari F8 Tributo, bought though I know full well I won't be in China for long. I'm at the wheel of this little beauty when I pull up at the entrance of the Venetian, one of the few casinos in the country that hasn't thrown me out yet.

Night has fallen on Macau, and the building is lit up with a thousand lights. I extract myself from the car and pass the keys to the parking valet. My high heels on the steps resound like the lashes of a whip.

"Welcome to the Venetian," the doorman says in English.

The Venetian in Macau is the world's biggest casino, so I obviously had to see it with my own eyes. Taking its inspiration from Venice, it even has canals running through it, where couples share romantic moments in gondolas floating on the turquoise water. I admit it's almost like the real thing.

It makes me nostalgic for home. I was born in Florence, in Italy, but I've always felt a need to explore the world. I never stop anywhere longer than a few months. This was fun to begin with, but I'm starting to tire of it . . . I don't feel at home anywhere.

I take determined steps across the huge foyer, letting my eyes drink everything in. It always happens the same way: the adrenaline starts pumping in my veins, making my heart beat faster. It's the irresistible call of the lights and the slot machines that gets me, the bewitching urge to bet a small fortune with no way of knowing if I'll win or lose, just so I can feel *something*.

I must be weak because, once again, I'm completely incapable of resisting. I need money, and there's no way I'm selling Carlotta—yes, I've already given my Ferrari a name. That's why I can't give her back. At least, that's one of the reasons.

I cross over the rosette mosaic set into the foyer floor and take an escalator up one level. Just as I'm preparing myself mentally to enter, my phone vibrates. It's a video call from my mother.

*Shit.* She always has the worst timing.

I take refuge in a corner behind a column and answer, holding the phone up so I can see it. I can't help myself: a huge smile spreads across my face when I see my mother sitting at the piano in our house.

She's the only person who ever gets such a genuine smile out of me.

I touch my hand to my mouth and move it away again to say hello. She makes the same sign back to me, all smiles too. Though we have a close relationship, we don't call each other often. She doesn't like to talk on the phone. Because she's deaf, we have to use FaceTime, which isn't always easy.

"Where are you? It looks beautiful!" she says.

I sign with one hand. "The biggest casino in the world, the Venetian. I'll send you photos!"

I try to keep my expression neutral so she can't read it. I'm a pro at keeping a straight face, but it's impossible to pull the wool over my mother's eyes. She always knows. She's the only one who can see through my lies—maybe because she's the only one who cares enough to try. That's why it's so hard for me to keep on traveling . . . Sometimes I dream that my mother passes away while I'm far from home, and I panic. I think I'd die if that happened. Being far away from her makes me miserable, and I know I need stability and a solid foundation. Still, running away is more tempting than the idea of returning.

"We miss you. When are you coming home?"

I sigh inwardly. I miss her too . . . But I can't go back empty handed, with my tail between my legs. I came here to make some money so I can pay my debts and not owe anything to anyone.

My mother, a successful behavioral psychologist, always says that running away from my problems won't make them disappear because, according to her, problems haunt minds, not places.

As though reading my thoughts, she adds with a worried look, "We agreed it would be better if you avoided casinos, Rose. You know that. You should come home."

There it is. I try my best to give a reassuring smile, but my mouth trembles.

"I'm fine, Mom. All that's over now. I'm better."

"Would you buy a beer for an ex-alcoholic? No. And this is just the same. It's still too soon . . . Don't tempt the devil."

*But tempting the devil is my passion, Mom. I gave him my soul a long time ago.*

It's true: hanging around casinos when you've previously spent several years as a gambling addict isn't the best idea. But I really am cured! I hadn't set foot in a casino for nearly a year until two months ago. I can handle a few rounds.

I'm much better now. I've hit rock bottom before, and I know what that's like. But I've changed. I'm strong enough now . . . even if I've had a few relapses. My quitting this time is for good.

It has to be.

"I'm in control!" I reply to my mother, with hurried signs. "I'll play one round, maybe two; then I'll leave. Promise."

She narrows her eyes doubtfully but eventually gives me a smile. I know she doesn't believe me, but she's decided to trust me anyway. She's like that.

I hang up quickly and stuff my phone into my clutch bag, then smooth my clothes and walk straight into one of the gaming rooms. It's crowded. I don't know which way to look first. I keep my face expressionless and walk slowly, weaving between the tables and observing each player. What I like most about playing is that it lets me become a different person.

Or at least, that was what I used to like. Over time, though, wearing a mask has become a habit. Now I do it even when I'm not playing. Nobody except my mother can really tell who I am or what I'm thinking. Sometimes I even temporarily fool myself, but reality always manages to show through in the end. *Damn reality.*

My palms are itching. I can almost feel the weight of my chips in my bag. I haven't got as many as I'd like, though. I'm good at winning money but very bad at keeping it. That's my curse.

I see a group of older women having fun at one table, and a group of men in suits glowering at another. Casinos are full of all sorts of people. Anyone can play. Professionals, beginners, rich, poor . . . Everyone thinks just a few dollars can change a life.

The casino gives everyone a chance, sure. But it takes a lot more than it gives. In my case, it took my mental health.

My gaze suddenly lands at a table in the middle of the big room lit by chandeliers. A man has just sat down there. Poker. I take him in from head to foot very quickly. He's young, maybe thirty. He's made an effort with his clothes: a nice shirt and black trousers. There's a backpack at his feet and a timer on the table. I guess that he usually plays online, and he probably won't be here for long. I have no way of knowing if he's good or not. It doesn't matter. I already know I'm going to win.

I sit down at his table without even glancing at him, crossing my long legs. I nod to the croupier. The other man starts talking to me in Mandarin, but I signal to him that I don't understand, hoping he'll let it drop. Most of the time, they don't bother trying too hard.

"Roulette's in the other room," he taunts me in English, allowing himself a furtive glance at my breasts.

I turn and give him a cold smile in reply. A woman of around fifty joins us, and the game begins. I keep my face impassive and glance at my cards: a king of hearts and a king of clubs.

This is child's play. Adrenaline pumps through my veins and makes my heart beat faster as I bet higher and higher. I avoid the others' gazes. I hate looking directly in players' faces. Instead, I concentrate with quiet excitement on the cards laid out in the middle of the baize. *God, I've missed this!*

It doesn't take me long to win back what I bet and more. As I gather up the man's chips, I finally look him in the eye and say in Italian, with just a hint of satisfaction, *"Con le mani in tasca."* As easy as pie.

I don't hang around to see his reaction, and besides, I know he didn't understand a word I said. I grab my bag and change tables. Blackjack calls to me dangerously. I give it two rounds, which I also win. The euphoria drives me on even though I promised my mother I wouldn't do anything stupid.

After two hours, I realize I've been spotted. The croupiers have their eyes on me; I feel it the second I get up from a table and move around the room. That means I haven't got long before they show me the door.

I already have a good haul. But I still want more. Obviously. That's how it works. More, more, more. That's the danger of addiction. And yet . . . I'm also bored. I walk nonchalantly among the tables. I've always loved playing, but it's been a long time since it felt *fun*. All the players are so predictable and dull. Nothing original about them.

I order a glass of wine at the bar and continue my prowling. Should I leave? No. Impossible. I've got to . . .

*Oh.*

I stop walking and raise an eyebrow. Two tables away, three men are playing in tense silence. Nothing odd about that. Most people would pass them by without a second glance. And that's exactly what everyone's doing.

Even the croupier doesn't seem to have noticed.

I let out a little laugh and stop to watch the man with the tattoos—the one hiding a card up the sleeve of his jacket.

As soon as I see his face, I understand this is a man who has skin in the game.

Quite literally.

I eye him curiously, without embarrassment: jet-black hair, eyes the color of storm clouds, a strong jawline, and pale cheeks with tattoos under the eyes—a diamond on the left cheek, a club on the right.

He's very good looking. More than he has any business being. My mother always says that beauty is a weapon: useful for distracting people from terrible sins, or for getting those sins forgiven. This long-fingered cheat is living proof that she's at least partly right.

I drop into a chair a few meters away and sip my wine while I watch them play. Unlike me, this man doesn't avoid meeting the other players' gazes. On the contrary, he stares at them with cold eyes until they play their hands; each one in turn. Seemingly defying them to accuse him.

Suddenly, as though sensing my scrutiny, he lifts his stormy eyes to meet mine. *Mamma mia.* I have to stop myself from trembling under the intensity of his look. I don't lower my eyes. Instead, I give him a snide little half smile to show he's not as clever as he thinks. I immediately realize that he knows. He knows that *I* know.

Only two seconds pass before his calculating, impassive gaze gives way to a conspiratorial wink.

I can't believe it. The nerve! Does he even know what he's risking, cheating in a place like this?

"Flush," he announces, turning his cards over.

Naturally, he wins hands down. He gathers up the chips with dignified movements, taking his time. Nobody speaks. Nobody arrests him for cheating. I hate myself for feeling curious, but I am. Cheating in a casino is no joke. You really need to have a pair to attempt it—and I'm not talking about cards.

I bite my cheek as I contemplate his hair, long on top but shaved at the sides, the front section falling elegantly over his forehead. My whole body is on high alert: this man has *Danger* written all over him.

Of course, that just makes me want to dive in headfirst. So I only half hesitate when he leans back in his chair and, with an enticing look, extends the invitation.

"A round?"

# Chapter 2

## LEVI

***May***
***Macau, China***

There are moments, like this one, when I regret not being able to see the world in color like other people do.

I can't exactly say I miss it. How can you miss something you never had? At first, I thought I was normal. That other people saw things the same way I did. It was only when I was three that my mother realized I had a problem.

She kept telling me that my favorite sweater was blue and that it didn't go with my brown trousers. I didn't understand. To me, they were both the same color. Everything was, in fact, or nearly so. Some things were dark; others were light.

My father thought I was lying, of course. Trying to get attention, like all kids that age. It was only later, after I started school, that my mother insisted I see a doctor.

It turned out there's a name for it: achromatopsia. I can't see colors, and that's that. My perception of the world around me is a series of shades of gray, so I'm told. I suppose that's true. There's no way for me to prove otherwise.

It was hard for a while, but I got used to it eventually. You can live a very normal life with this kind of challenge: I'm living proof. I've reached a point where I don't regret being different. I've made my peace with it.

But this evening, as my eyes run languorously over this goddess with a touch of the feline about her, I feel a twinge of regret. I'd give a lot to be able to see her in all her splendor. To *really* see her.

Her short hair is dark, probably black or brown, as are her piercing eyes, which are emphasized by a long streak of eyeliner. Her skin is diaphanous and smooth, surely silky to the touch. I can't tell the color of her full lips. Rose? Peach?

She's wearing high-waisted silk trousers with a white lace corset top that inspires in me the most impure thoughts. Her eyes, almost hidden by her fringe of bangs, size me up calmly. They say, "I know what you just did." If Thomas were here, he'd be giving me murderous looks. He hates it when I cheat. I don't particularly like it, either, but the evening was becoming deathly boring.

I only cheat when I'm bored.

Is she going to turn me in? Nobody else saw what I just did; I was far too fast and skillful. But she saw me. How?

When the croupier is about to deal the next hand, I dare take another look at the young woman with eyes like a cat. She hasn't moved an inch. She's still staring at me, intrigued. The more I look at her, the more I realize how beautiful she is. I feel a strange, visceral need to know how she plays—call it professional weakness. Thomas says it's a problem of mine: this sometimes-extreme obsession with things or people who excite my curiosity.

I pass my chips from hand to hand and speak in confident English.

"A round?"

She remains impassive. I wait patiently while she hesitates.

"Given your technique, I'm not sure you're up to it," she replies in a bewitching accent. "No offense, but I like players who are worth the effort. I lose interest quickly; it's one of my worst failings."

I grin. Such an insolent mouth. Her eyes aren't cold; that's for sure. That only makes her more attractive. In Russia, we like women who know what they want.

I hold up my hands and promise, very solemnly, "I'll be good. I always adapt to my opponent."

It doesn't take her long to make up her mind. She comes and sits down opposite me, holding her head high. Someone who can't refuse a challenge: my kind of person. I observe her movements in silence. She knows I'm watching her, but it doesn't seem to bother her the way it would other people. I glance at her chips to see how much she's got.

It's a lot.

She must be a good player. This fact makes my blood pump even faster. No one speaks as the cards are being dealt. I get two eights, one of hearts, and one of spades. Not brilliant, but it'll do the job.

I watch her carefully, trying to tell what sort of hand she's got. Is she a bluffer? Does she play in silence, or does she talk to distract her opponents? Does she use her charm? Or does she, like me, prefer intimidating others with an icy look?

All that's clear is that she's refusing to pay me a single bit of attention. For some reason, this drives me crazy. Is she worried that looking at me will put her off, or has she realized that people's avoiding my gaze bothers *me*?

She's the first player to bet. She looks confident, but that doesn't mean she has a good hand. I think quickly and do the same without much hesitation. I'm there to play, after all.

The first three cards laid on the table, the *flop*, are a four of clubs, a six of spades, and an eight of diamonds. Now, the stranger finally does look at me. It's as though she's read my mind.

I don't look away. I merely rest my chin casually on my fist. We stare at one another for a few long seconds, until a thin smile spreads over her face. *Shit.*

"You probably think you're a good liar," she says suddenly.

She knows. I don't know how, and it frustrates me far more than it should, but she's managed to see through the mask. How? Impossible. It must be a coincidence. She can't have realized I was happy with those cards just by looking at me. Nobody could.

I don't lose my cool. I take a sip of lemon vodka before replying, "I do."

Her eyes shift to my hand, which is perhaps grasping my glass a little too tightly, and she smiles again. "If you were a good liar, you'd know that controlling your face isn't enough. You can be as expressionless as you like, but if you're not careful, your body will always give you away."

I nearly smile at her words. She's right. I've been stupid. I should have known better. Body language says at least as much as facial expressions. I try to control mine, but it's harder than it seems.

The next two cards are a five of hearts and a nine of clubs. I have a good chance of winning at this point. The other players have already folded. It's just me and her now.

If she really does know what sort of hand I've got, she'd do better to fold than to keep playing. I've tried to read her, but she hasn't moved a muscle the whole time. Indecipherable. We're all waiting for her to decide, when she suddenly turns to me.

"What am I going to do, do you think?"

I ponder for a minute and reply honestly. "If I were you, I'd fold."

She nods thoughtfully and leans forward a little. I hold her gaze defiantly. A single eyelash has dropped onto her cheek. I resist the temptation to blow it gently away.

"I'm going to win this round," she says matter-of-factly. "The chances of my having a better hand than yours, given the cards in the flop, were low; I'll give you that. But you've missed something."

And with that, she places a bet. I follow her lead despite my total confusion. She shows her cards first.

"Flush."

*What the hell?* She's staring at me, gauging my reaction. I should be angry. After all, she's just beaten me, a professional poker player, outright. I'm meant to be winning a world tournament within weeks, and this girl has come out of nowhere and made it clear I'm not up to the task.

Six years ago, my pride would have been my downfall.

Now, something different spreads through me. The delicious sensation of adrenaline. Curiosity transformed into pleasant excitement. Playing against Tito is the only other thing that's ever evoked this blend of feelings in me—a sense of respect but also one of envy.

"Again."

She doesn't seem surprised by my request. She hesitates, then picks up her chips to indicate she's in.

"OK. I'll give you one last chance to figure out how I did it. Keep your eyes open."

*Oh, I will. Don't you worry. Open and fixed on you and you alone.* It's not so much that she beat me that I find frustrating. That can happen. I'm a top player, but poker's still a game of chance.

I do, however, know how to read people. Having an infallible sixth sense means I never make a mistake. Except she's just proved that, apparently, my intuition isn't infallible after all. What could I have missed?

This time I have an ace and a king of hearts.

It's a good hand. I control my face and my movements while the croupier lays the flop on the table: a nine, a jack of diamonds, and a queen of clubs.

Plenty to work with there. Unfortunately, I'm concentrating more on the stranger now than on my game. I want to figure out what she meant by "you've missed something." She isn't making this easy.

When her turn comes, she takes her time. Too much time. What's she thinking so hard about? She stops focusing on me and fixes her eyes on the palm of one hand before suddenly pushing her chips forward in one confident movement, betting everything she's got.

"All in."

*All in?* Seriously? This worries me. What's she thinking? If she's hesitated for so long, it means her hand isn't very good. When you know you can win easily, you don't hesitate. So then why go all in?

Maybe she paused deliberately to make me think exactly like this.

But I very much doubt it.

She turns to me, amused. She's got a fucking gorgeous smile. Terrifying and seductive at once.

"So? Have you worked it out or not?"

"I've definitely worked out that I underestimated you."

Her mouth twitches with amusement as she crosses her long legs. The third player folds, glaring at us. We're apparently too talkative for him.

"If it makes you feel better," she adds in her crystal-clear voice, "I think you're winning."

She doesn't seem alarmed by this. It's strange. Nobody would go all in if they thought they were about to lose. Is she cheating? Impossible. She must be trying to manipulate me. And it's working.

I keep my expression relaxed, concealing my frustration as I always do. "How do you know that? You don't know what's in my hand or which cards are going to come up."

"It's easy to work out a person's chances when you really think about it. I'd say you've got about . . . a fifty-two percent chance of winning the pot."

"Is that all?"

"Those are pretty good odds."

True. What a strange young woman.

"Why have you bet everything if you've only got a forty-eight percent chance of winning?"

"More like forty-five, I'd say," she corrects me. "Counting the split. As for your question, the round isn't finished. I'm putting my trust in destiny or science, whichever answers my prayers first."

*Destiny or science.* I frown and glance once more at my hand before going all in too. There's no way I'm going to fold. I have to admit, I'm burning with curiosity to see what she's going to come up with. I almost want her to win, if I'm being honest.

The croupier turns over an eight of hearts. Good news for me. There's a good chance I'll win with a hand like that. I allow myself a quick glance in her direction, but she doesn't react.

"So? What's my percentage now?" I joke as the croupier prepares to reveal the next card.

She takes her time replying, her hands folded on the table.

"I'd say . . . about seventy-three?"

I raise an eyebrow in surprise. "That's high. Do you still think you're going to win?"

"Why not?" she says with an enigmatic smile. Suddenly, without taking her eyes from mine, she very discreetly lifts up the edges of her cards. I look down instinctively. She's deliberately showing me her hand, right in front of everyone!

An ace and a two of diamonds.

What's she up to? I look back at her, intrigued. I run through all the possible card combinations and all the scenarios that could give her a win.

"It would take a miracle," I say.

She just shrugs. We both focus silently on the center of the table. My heart beats faster as the croupier picks up the fateful card and turns it over.

A two of clubs.

My heart thuds when it hits me what she's done. I can't believe it. She's won. She's actually won. She's gone from 27 percent to 100 with that one last card. She's just won everything with one damn flush—again. It really is a miracle.

I can't help but gaze at her in surprise and admiration. She just flashes me a teasing, triumphant smile and sweeps the chips into her bag.

I congratulate her with complete sincerity and then ask calmly, "How did you know?" I can't help it. I want her to explain it to me. If she doesn't, it'll haunt me all night.

She hesitates a moment, then gives in. "I didn't *know*, exactly. There's no way to be absolutely sure. Let's just say . . . I had a feeling."

I don't believe that. It's the second time she's pulled off that kind of win. I have nothing left, thanks to her. Unbelievable. I want to ask her to wait while I withdraw some more money so we can play again . . . and again and again, all night. But she closes her bag and says, "Thanks for the shoes."

"I'm sorry?"

"The ones I'm going to buy tomorrow with your money."

I laugh and put my hands in my pockets. If only Thomas were here. He'd hate her, no doubt about it, but her barb would definitely make him laugh.

I check out the high heels she's wearing now: black, classic. Or are they blue? Brown? I can't say for certain. Strangely, I like the idea that she's going to treat herself with my money. She deserves it. I let her run rings around me as if I were a beginner, and that doesn't happen every day.

"I hope you'll get the most expensive ones," I say.

"I always do."

She gets up and smooths her silk trousers. I stand, too, and I'm about to ask her to stay, or to have a drink, when we're interrupted by two men in suits. Security guards. They come up and speak to her politely.

Seemingly unbothered by their sudden appearance, she tells them coolly that she doesn't speak Mandarin. One of them takes a step toward her, looking very serious. He says in halting English, "I'm going to ask you kindly to leave."

I frown. She asks why, still nonchalant. As though it's not the first time this has happened to her.

"We've heard all about you, Ms. Alfieri. We don't stand for tricks like yours at the Venetian."

I look back at her, concealing my surprise. Is he saying she's a cheat? And a well-known one, at that? I laugh, respecting her even more.

"Oh, I get it now! We're cut from the same cloth, you and I."

She glares furiously at me and tells the guards, "Counting the cards isn't cheating. It isn't illegal, last I checked. It's not my fault I'm intelligent."

Her answer stops me short. She counts cards? This information puts her in a new light. It's true that counting the cards isn't against the rules. It's just very much frowned upon. And not many people can do it, especially in poker.

Of course, any self-respecting player calculates their chance of winning, but some extraordinary individuals, like this girl, take it even farther. A person has to be a mathematical genius to be able to weaponize counting the way she does.

"I'll say it again. We don't accept that method here. I'm going to have to show you to the exit."

She rolls her eyes and says she can walk by herself. She winks at me, just like I winked at her earlier in the evening. I want to stop them, to say something, anything, to make it so she can keep playing.

But one of the men follows her, and before I can speak, it's too late. She disappears through the huge doors and out of the room, her heels clicking quickly against the tiles.

I should go too. I have no money left to bet, anyway. Plus I need to tell Thomas what's just happened. God knows I've already done everything I can to ensure I beat Tito this year. I promised myself: this time, I absolutely will not lose.

But maybe . . . maybe I need a little bit more help to keep that promise. A secret weapon. A plan B.

A masterstroke.

"Excuse me!" I call the other security guard, a crazy idea springing into my mind. "What did you say the lady's name was?"

# Chapter 3

## Rose

***May***
***Macau, China***

My mom keeps messaging me, begging me to come home. She must think I'm spending my time holed up in casinos, hemorrhaging money I haven't got—which, to be fair, isn't *entirely* wrong.

That's what addiction does to you. Even when you know you've had enough, even when your bank account's at zero, you still find a way to keep on playing.

Because you tell yourself the next one's going to be "the big one." And sometimes it is. One time in three hundred. Those odds are dangerous enough, but for me it's even worse, because unlike the average player, I don't just assume I'm going to win again sooner or later. I *know* it. That makes me arrogant enough to bet crazy amounts of money. Hence my debts.

My parents could pay them off for me, but I have no desire to be dependent on them. I tell myself I'll get by on my own, just like I always have.

"I'll take those," I decide, pointing to a pair of gold shoes.

The English-speaking shop assistant beckons one of her colleagues to see to my purchase. I shouldn't spend money like this, especially not on such pointless things. I travel so much, I have to be able to pack my whole life into a suitcase. The only things I always make room for are my brushes and my tubes of paint. That's the one passion I can't leave behind.

Beyond that, I need to think carefully before I buy anything, though I have been a bit careless recently. But what the hell? These shoes are divine. And I'm helping boost the country's economy by buying them, aren't I?

I pay and leave, an enormous bag in hand. I light a cigarette with my palladium lighter—an eighteenth birthday present from my father—and am just setting off toward the Café de Paris Monte-Carlo when something catches my eye.

*Oh wow.*

I'm not dreaming. It's a sublime 900-HP Ford Mustang Lithium, parked on the street. A little gem. I stop to get a good look. My eyes run along the bodywork . . . and come to rest on a man leaning against the back door, hands in his pockets. An impassive face.

Intense, stormy eyes.

"Should I be calling the police right now?" I ask.

To his credit, the poker player from last night doesn't even blink. He tilts his head slightly without taking his eyes off mine. Despite what I said to him yesterday, he is in fact hard to read. He has absolute control over his facial expressions, which annoys me.

It's a lot harder to manipulate this kind of person.

"You tell me," he says. "Do you need to be saved . . . Rose?"

I narrow my eyes. How does he know my name? And how did he find me so fast? Does he want his money back? Too late. It's almost all gone.

"The shoes, I presume?" He looks at my bag.

I give him a fake-frivolous smile. "I keep my promises."

"One of the most important qualities I look for in a person."

I raise an eyebrow. What exactly is he after? I ask whether this meeting is a coincidence, though I'm sure it isn't. He doesn't answer straightaway. His eyes wander to the cigarette I'm still smoking; then his gaze meets mine again, as if he'd gotten momentarily distracted.

"You left in a hurry last night."

"I believe it's called getting 'chucked out,'" I say.

He smiles a little at that. Just for half a second. There's a tap on the window on the driver's side, and only then do I see he isn't alone. The silhouette of a man is just visible through the tinted window. The figure doesn't move, but I know he's heard everything.

"I can't stick around long, I'm afraid," the poker player says. "Ms. Alfieri, I'm here to make you an offer. Are you looking for work by any chance?"

*Am I?* I wonder. I certainly need money. But I don't answer at first. I give him a skeptical look. Far too many rich, powerful men have asked me that question shortly before attempting to take my clothes off. I won't fall for that again.

"Why? Are you hiring?"

"Not really, but you're what I'd call an exception. I like you."

*Bingo*. The determination with which he says it makes me shiver. After yesterday, I wouldn't have thought him the type. My disappointment is real, but fleeting. I smile coldly, ready to turn and walk away.

"Sorry, but I'm no prostitute." I know we're in Sin City, where the economy feeds off gambling and sex, but still. This sort of thing gets tedious.

He takes one hand out of his pockets and waves a finger in disagreement. "I think you've misunderstood me. I don't like you in *that way*. It's more your . . . let's call it your 'gifts' that I'm attracted to."

I don't know what to say to that. I exhale a long plume of smoke, still on my guard. "Is this some kind of fetish, like people who have a thing about feet?" I ask. "I won't judge you."

He smiles again in spite of himself. Gorgeous. If I were just a little weaker, I'd already be sitting on his knee in the back of his beautiful car. But I stay faithful to Carlotta.

"I'm sure you have lovely feet, but no. I have other vices."

"Such as?"

A pause. I hold his gaze, daring him to be honest. He answers calmly, with no sign of shame. "Money and power."

I nearly laugh at this reply. Perhaps the two of us are cast in the same mold after all. "Isn't that true of everyone?"

His smile spreads over his pale, implacable face, as though my reply delights him. He detaches himself from the car and stands up straight as I get a good look at him. He's wearing a fine sweater tucked into high-waisted cream trousers. He looks classy and elegant. His smile makes him as dangerous as a snake charmer, and that smile has surely broken plenty of hearts. But it's his way of looking at . . . Oh God! The way he looks at you . . . Like Satan himself.

Obviously, this just makes him even more attractive to me.

"Here," he says. He holds out a card on which I can see the name *Levi Ivanovich*. "I haven't got time to explain it all now, but would you have a drink with me this evening? On me, of course."

I turn the card over and over, not saying anything. He's already taken the time to write something on the back. I recognize the address of the Ritz-Carlton luxury hotel. If he can afford a suite somewhere like that, it's in my best interest to listen to him. Or maybe he just wants to crash the hotel's bar?

He can't be much older than me. Midtwenties, I'd say. I look at the card again, hoping to find answers. The words are all in Russian, except for one name in English: *Rasputin*.

A club, perhaps.

"I'll wait for you in the bar at seven," Levi says.

"Sorry to disappoint you, but I don't think I'll come. You appear out of nowhere, probably because you've been following me all morning, just to tell me you like me and you want to give me a job.

Call me paranoid, but that's how women like me end up dead in an alley somewhere."

He nods as though he's thinking about what I've said and walks around the car to the rear right-hand door. His chauffeur starts the engine, and the sound is sweet music to my ears.

"What if I told you there's a lot of money to be earned?"

Unimpressed, I drop my cigarette and then crush it under my heel as I cross my arms. How did he guess that money would make me take the bait? Anybody looking at me in these clothes would think I was loaded.

*"Quanto?"* I say in Italian. How much?

It's true what they say about money being a universal language. I bet he doesn't speak a word of my native tongue, but he raises an eyebrow and replies anyway. "Enough to tempt you."

He gets into the car and slams the door. *What a pretentious asshole.* I can tell he's one of those men not used to hearing the word *no*. They're the worst kind; I despise them.

Suddenly, the back window opens, and I see him leaning across toward me, a ghost of a smile on his lips as he nods toward my feet.

"I look forward to seeing which ones you chose."

◆ ◆ ◆

The Ritz-Carlton is a beautiful hotel; I'll admit that much. My hotel doesn't even come close, though it's not too shabby either. Several people, both men and women, turn to look as I walk into the lobby.

Probably because of my clothes.

I'm wearing black trousers and a strapless satin top with long balloon sleeves and a very low V-shaped neckline. My short hair just touches my ears, which have small gold rings running all along the cartilage.

I'm wearing the high-heeled gold stilettos I bought earlier, their ankle straps gleaming with rhinestones. I feel powerful and sexy. Ready to confront this Levi Ivanovich, whom I see immediately—how could I not? He's comfortably settled in one of the Bordeaux-red armchairs, whiskey in hand. I'm late, but he's still there, waiting patiently.

I spent the whole day sure I wouldn't go, but curiosity got the better of me at the last moment. If he really doesn't like me "in that way," then I have to know what he does want from me—and how much money we're talking about, of course.

My aunt says I'm obsessed with money. I just call it being practical.

I walk over without hurrying and sit down in the armchair opposite him, crossing my legs. He seems slightly surprised to see me, as though he thought I wouldn't come.

We look at each other in silence, both of us leaning back in our chairs. After a few seconds, he empties his glass and puts it down on the table between us.

"What's your poison?"

"If only I had just one," I try to joke.

"You'll have to narrow it down for me."

A waiter appears at my elbow at that moment. Levi doesn't take his eyes from mine. He looks at me seriously.

"Where I come from, we never refuse an offer of alcohol. We have a saying: 'Only spies don't drink.' So . . . brandy? Champagne?"

I'm more than happy to play along. I don't say so, but I never turn down a drink either. Russians aren't the only ones who like to raise a glass.

"I prefer red wine."

"A bottle of Ao Yun, sir?" the waiter suggests.

Levi nods and tells me, "Ao Yun is a legendary wine. The name means 'flying above the clouds.' It's delicious, though I prefer vodka. Out of patriotism, I suppose."

I look around the room while the drinks are served. I wonder how much a night in a suite here must cost. I'd like to be able to afford that for myself. One day I'll come back. I'm certain of it.

"I couldn't have chosen better myself." Levi's voice interrupts my thoughts.

I follow his gaze down to my feet, or more precisely my shoes, and smile.

"You see my problem: I have expensive tastes, but I'm not rich."

"You could be."

I raise an eyebrow, encouraging him to go on.

"I'm not going to beat around the bush." He leans forward in his chair, his elbow leaning casually on one knee. "I've been a professional poker player a few years now, and your way of playing impressed me."

Of course. His occupation should have been obvious. Even though he lost, he knew what he was doing, and he did it well.

"I've never met anyone who could count the cards like you," he continues, not hiding his admiration. "I've always wanted to be able to do it, but I'm not what you'd call a mathematical genius."

"So you want some private coaching?"

I say this as a joke, but his serious expression stops me in my tracks. Is this what he was driving at from the start? Strange man.

"I'm competing in an annual world poker tournament in Las Vegas," he explains. "In a week's time."

I laugh without amusement. "Card counting isn't something you can learn in a week."

His deep voice turns utterly indecent when he says calmly, as though talking about something else altogether, "I'm an extremely dedicated student."

*Damn.* I feel his words all the way down to my bones.

"That may be true." I sip from my glass to hide my pink cheeks. "But it took me years to master. There's no way you can manage it in seven days."

He gives me an enigmatic smile, like I'm missing something.

"But, Ms. Alfieri, if you agree to help me, you'll be traveling to Las Vegas with me."

This comment makes me pause. Now he has my attention. I can almost see my mother telling me this isn't a good idea, that Las Vegas is the last place someone like me should even think of going.

But . . . I can already see myself there. I've dreamed of going ever since I was fifteen years old.

"OK, I'm listening. What would I be signing up to do?"

If he's pleased by my reaction, he doesn't show it. It's as though he already knew I'd agree. This annoys me.

"I'd like you to stay with me for the whole tournament and coach me. Quite a lot of players have mentors, though I never have until now. It would mean being by my side almost the whole time. You'll be extremely well paid, of course. You'll even have a share of the prize if I come out on top. I don't need all that money anyway."

So arrogant. But he says it so sincerely, so utterly without pretention, that I don't even feel the urge to spit in his face.

As I pretend to think it over, he asks, "You also have a good eye when it comes to body language, is that right?"

I pause a moment. But I have nothing to lose by being honest with him about this.

"My mother's a behavioral psychologist. A specialist in the theory of microexpressions: the idea that involuntary facial expressions can be used in lie detection. I grew up with all that."

This news seems to surprise him, in a good way. He nods slowly, absorbing it, and asks if I work in the same field.

"I studied psychology, too, yes."

"It's all starting to make sense. So . . . you can tell who's bluffing and who isn't, right?"

"It isn't an exact science, but ninety percent of the time, yes. It's my superpower." I sigh and take another sip of wine.

Levi doesn't say anything for a long time. I can tell he's thinking. His eyes remain fixed on me, but he isn't really looking at me. He's somewhere else. When he finally comes back down to earth, his smile is equal parts charming and calculating.

"Rose Alfieri, you're an angel come down from heaven."

*That's what you think.*

"I'm a lot of things," I say, "but I'm no angel."

"Then we have at least one thing in common," he says, uncrossing his legs. "Maybe we'll look back on this conversation in a few years' time when we're both in hell and wish we'd been a bit more humble. But in the meantime, let's join forces."

My decision is already made, essentially, but I take my time answering, trying to make him impatient. He waits calmly, and that's when I begin to wonder if he's reading my thoughts.

I don't want him to think I'm predictable, and I can't stand the thought of his outmaneuvering me. Still, when I think about Las Vegas . . . the bewitching sound of the slot machines, the endless poker tables, rivers of money. Day and night.

I *have* to go there.

That's why I decide to tempt the devil.

"An honest woman wouldn't give in to the lure of money," I say, "much less to a man as forward as you."

Again, he doesn't seem surprised. He takes a notebook and pen from his inside pocket and scribbles something I can't see. Then he tears out the page, folds it, and slides it over to my side of the table. I notice more tattoos on his knuckles, numbers whose meaning I don't understand.

I unfold the paper, and my heart misses a beat at the sight of so many zeros. I smile at him as I tuck it into my bra.

"Luckily for us both, I'm not an honest woman. Where do I sign?"

# Chapter 4

## Levi

***May***
***Macau, China***

Rose Alfieri is an interesting case.

I've only known her a few days, but she's already impressed me thoroughly. Yet I still don't know anything about her. And, my God, does she know how to hide everything I'm trying to discover. Her face is a clean, blank canvas. A locked safe, impossible to crack. Even her smiles are a false front.

I'm not too surprised to realize I'm pleased by all this. Not because I like safes, but because what's inside them is usually worth the chase.

Thomas keeps telling me I'm making a mistake, says I'm blinded by my desire for victory and revenge. Back in our hotel room, I just smiled at him as I took off my tie, like the overconfident prick I am, and said, "Have you ever known me to have a bad idea?"

My friend, sprawled comfortably on his bed, seemed unimpressed by my act.

"You mean like those stupid tattoos you have plastered all over your face?"

I stopped short, annoyed. Thomas's Swedish accent is very strong and sometimes hard to understand, but that little dig was impossible to miss. "You said they were cool!"

"We were pissed that night, Levi. I can't wait to hear how you feel about them when you're eighty."

I didn't answer because, drunk though I may have been, I've never regretted my tattoos. Getting them wasn't a whim; it was a homage to the cards. A reminder of all they've taken from me, and of what they've done to me.

◆ ◆ ◆

Rose signed the contract she insisted on us having, then disappeared for two days after, complaining that she'd have to "sell Carlotta." I don't even want to think about what she meant by that.

We've been waiting for her at Macau International Airport for ten minutes now. Thomas is muttering to himself, completely furious. He's not a patient person. And he's not used to working with anyone but me.

"One more minute and then we're leaving without her."

"She'll come," I reassure him from my seat in the airport lobby. "She just wants to show us she doesn't take orders from anyone."

"What is she, fifteen?"

I don't reply, because at that moment I catch sight of Rose, wearing high-waisted jeans and a dark-colored camisole underneath an oversized jacket probably meant for a man. She finishes her cigarette outside the sliding doors without hurrying, then crushes it under her heel. I shake my head at this bad habit. Seeing her one and only suitcase, I wonder how on earth she's managed to fit in all her shoes. It's enormous, but I'm pretty sure she must have a lot of pairs.

Not wanting to give her the pleasure of seeing me annoyed because she arrived late, I make the introductions with an expression that's just as neutral as hers.

"Rose Alfieri, Thomas Kalberg."

She looks him over indifferently, taking in his neat beard and long blond hair pulled back in a man bun, then narrows her eyes behind her vintage sunglasses.

"Oh, you're the chauffeur from the other day."

Thomas looks so horrified, it's comical, and I can't help smiling. He notices this, of course, and glares at me. A lot of people make the same mistake, and it's starting to annoy him.

"I'm not his chau—"

"Has anyone ever told you that you look just like Chris Hemsworth? Well . . . a lot like him, anyway."

At least two hundred times, yes. It's Thomas's nightmare, and there's nothing he can do about it. If he didn't have that vicious scar running over his mouth, he'd be the man's doppelgänger.

I smile and give him a teasing pat on the shoulder.

"You have a good eye, Rose," Levi says in a teasing voice. "He's actually Chris Hemsworth's official Swedish double. He does events, including bachelorette parties. For fifty extra euros, he'll take off his shirt. Isn't that right, Tommy?"

Strangely, my affectionate nickname doesn't win him round, and he turns to me and hisses through gritted teeth, "You promised you'd drop that joke. After three years, it's not funny anymore."

"I find it hilarious," Rose says.

Thomas doesn't look at her as he says to me in a cool voice, "I don't like her. Let's leave her here."

He doesn't like anyone—except me, of course. But who wouldn't like me?

"Thomas isn't my chauffeur. He's my bodyguard and associate," I explain to set the record straight. Then I add in a low voice, "And he hates being compared to Chris. We're not allowed to mention it."

All this is true, except my best friend does act as my chauffeur when we need to get around. I'm not allowed to drive because of my achromatopsia—my vision isn't good enough.

"Are you a poker player too?" Rose asks him.

Thomas just nods as if to say, *I'm answering you, but I don't have to like you.*

Rose turns to me, looking serious, and says, "I thought you said you were a professional?"

"I am."

"Only a beginner would think he could have 'friends' at a big competition," she retorts. "Especially at a world tournament worth a few million dollars."

I resist the temptation to smile. She's right, and I know it, but she doesn't know me. She doesn't know anything about my life. I lean dangerously close to her and, intoxicated by her perfume, murmur my response.

"When I want your advice, I'll ask for it."

I grab my suitcase and approach the airline check-in counter. I don't need to turn around to know she's fuming with indignation. Thomas walks next to me, fighting back a triumphant grin.

Later, on the plane, he pretends to sleep to avoid having to make small talk. Rose would probably have preferred to do the same, but I don't let her.

I haven't explained my plan to her yet. I haven't even told her why winning is so important to me. Thomas would prefer that I not, but I think it's vital that she know. We need to trust each other a little if this is going to work.

"Tell me about yourself, Rose."

"How did you learn to play poker?" she asks instead of replying. "I thought it was illegal in Russia."

I cock my head, surprised that she's chosen this avoidance tactic. So she doesn't like talking about herself. Interesting.

"That's true," I say, "Betting games are against the law. But in Moscow, there are secret rooms in clubs and high-end restaurants. You have to pay to go in, though."

"How very James Bond. I like it. Do you organize illegal games in your own club, then? That's what I'd do."

"Maybe . . . My love of the game comes from my father, who was a well-known player."

Rose laughs at a joke only she gets. "I'm guessing he must have been either a nasty piece of work or a genius."

"The former. What about you?"

She hesitates a second, then looks straight at me and says, "What do you mean? Are you asking about my father? Or about how I learned to play poker?"

"Whichever you like."

She smiles wickedly and stares over my shoulder, out of the window.

"I had a mentor," she murmurs after a long pause. "At the beginning, it was all about teaching me what he knew. Then, when he realized I was gifted, he used me. I was a godsend for him. A way of getting rich. I liked him too much—so I let him do it."

I must not be much better than that man, because I understand what he did. I suppose I'm doing the same thing. I wait for her to go on, but unfortunately, she turns the conversation back to me again.

"What exactly do you want me to do for you? Teach you to count the cards? Help you pull off the biggest cheat of the century, *Ocean's Eleven* style? Fine by me, but only if I get to be Matt Damon—he's the best looking and the most intelligent."

I lower my voice and begin a condensed explanation of what I have in mind. I tell her about Tito and my thirst to win. She asks what I have against him. I say he's always beaten me and not always honestly. I'm not being entirely forthcoming, but at least what I have said is true.

"Oh, so he cheats."

I nod. She takes off her jacket, revealing silky, slightly tanned shoulders. Her perfume floats across the row of seats, peach and sandalwood, like the flutter of a distant memory from a sunny olive grove in a remote countryside.

"You should just report him. Problem solved."

I'm dead set against that. "That would be too easy, and much less fun. I want him to lose, and I want to be the one who beats him."

She seems surprised by my determination. Thomas is of the same mind. Reporting Tito was the first thing Thomas advised me to do when I talked to him about it three years ago. I repeat now what I said then.

"I'm a man of honor."

"Says the guy who was cheating the first time I met him," she shoots back, raising an eyebrow.

I have to smile at that. "That's different. I wasn't cheating to win. I was going to win anyway."

"I thought you couldn't predict those things?"

"The other guy was sweating like a pig," I explain patiently. "I didn't need to be an ace lie detector to know he didn't have anything more than a pair. He was a terrible bluffer."

"Then why cheat at all?"

I pause and look at her, intrigued. I'm sure she knows the answer, maybe even feels the same way. Why ask me, then? I play along, shrugging my shoulders.

"For the adrenaline, of course."

She nods, not saying anything. I explain that we'll be staying at Caesar's Palace where the series of tournaments that make up the World Series of Poker are held: fifty-one days, all expenses paid by my sponsors. We'll train together when I'm not playing, and she'll help me while I'm playing too. She makes a face when I say that.

"I'm no expert at tournaments . . . but I don't think spectators are allowed to wander around in the gaming rooms, are they?"

"No, they're not. But I've thought of everything. You'll be able to walk around the tables as much as you like, so you'll be able to watch the other players and report back to me on their techniques."

She still looks unconvinced, but I promise I'll explain properly at the hotel.

"Sounds an awful lot like cheating to me," she says. "But OK."

I don't reply to that. We spend the rest of the flight sleeping—or rather, she falls asleep, and I spend the time thinking through everything that could go wrong when we get to Vegas.

I know that hiring Rose is madness. I'll never be able to learn to count the cards like she does in such a short time. I couldn't even if I spent the rest of my life trying, to be honest. But why not give it a try?

What I'm most interested in, though, is her gift for observation and analysis. If she can help me decipher the code that is Tito, I have a much greater chance of winning.

And if achieving that means I have to pay a lost, unstable, and arrogant girl a small fortune . . . ? So be it.

◆ ◆ ◆

It's obvious that Rose has never been to Las Vegas before. As soon as we land, she clams up and surveys her surroundings. Her expression is curious, hungry, even a little admiring. Though I've only known her a few days, I was sure she'd like it here.

When Thomas opens the trunk of the rental, a magnificent shining black Audi R8, Rose strokes the bodywork with something approaching reverence. I already knew she liked cars. That probably explains "Carlotta"—thank God it wasn't a dog, or something worse.

"Can I drive?" she asks.

"No," Thomas replies for me as he lifts our suitcases into the trunk.

Rose glares at him, offended. I wouldn't play this game with Thomas if I were her. There's a good chance she'll get her feathers ruffled. But watching them tussle is fun, so I leave them to it.

"Why can't I?" she asks.

"A: because I always drive," Thomas says. "And B: because we've known you for what . . . five minutes?"

She mutters something in Italian that I don't understand but then flashes him a mocking smile.

"Sorry, Chris. I'd forgotten it's your job."

She leaves him to load up her suitcase and climbs into the back seat like a princess. I stand there with my hands in my pockets, unable to suppress a smile. She plays the role of the spoiled brat magnificently.

Thomas clenches his jaw, trying to control himself, and gives me a black look. He's near his boiling point.

"I'm going to leave her fucking suitcase on the pavement, Levi. I'm not touching it."

I should probably let Rose know that she should really think twice before teasing him . . . Thomas's god complex makes him too proud for his own good, and we're still working on his grasp of empathy. But in every other way, he's great!

I walk over and pat his shoulder, lowering my voice to say, "I'd pay a lot to see what happens if you were to do that . . . but I need her."

"You don't need anybody."

*I wish that were true.*

"Be nice, will you?" I say. "The poor girl doesn't know what she's got coming."

He frowns and asks what I'm plotting. I just grab Rose's suitcase and put it in the trunk. I smile as I think of the idea that came to me on the plane, and as I imagine her face when she hears about it.

I'm so exhausted, I don't say a word for the whole drive. Rose is staring out of the open window, the warm wind ruffling her short hair. The heat is suffocating. I hadn't missed the forty-five-degree Las Vegas heat: it's a world away from what I'm used to in Saint Petersburg.

When we reach the hotel, there's already a swarm of people outside the entrance. As we get closer, I recognize a few well-known players. Caesar's Palace is the ideal base for a visit to Las Vegas. It also happens to be where a lot of loaded players hole up during competitions.

"The whole world's turning up at the same time as us," Thomas mutters.

*Exactly as I planned.*

Rose follows my gaze, which is fixed on Tito's back. I'd know him anywhere. A huge man, with powerful shoulders, salt-and-pepper hair combed backward, and a square jaw that women seem to find attractive.

As though sensing my presence, Tito turns around just as Thomas is pulling up. His gaze meets mine as if our eyes were irresistibly attracted magnets, and he gives me a wolfish smile.

It seems to say, *I've been waiting for you.*

My stomach is in knots, and I feel as though my insides are turning over. I hate this feeling of rage and fear that takes hold of me every time I see him. He scares me.

"Shall we come back later?" Thomas eyes the little crowd buzzing around Tito like wasps around a honey pot. It's only then that I realize they're journalists.

Absolutely perfect. Even better than I'd imagined.

"It's not worth the hassle," I say. "Come on."

Thomas gets out first. Rose sizes up the situation in silence, seeming to sense that something isn't right. I undo my seat belt and lean toward her, a little closer than strictly necessary, but she doesn't draw back. I lower my face to her ear and murmur, "You see the guy just to your right who looks like Mads Mikkelsen? You know, that Danish actor who plays Hannibal Lecter on television?"

She follows my gaze, her catlike eyes hidden behind her sunglasses, and nods ever so slightly.

"Tito, I presume?"

"Exactly. Remember that face."

I open my door as Thomas is unloading our suitcases. I ask him to go inside and check us in. One of the journalists near Tito seizes his chance while I'm defenseless and comes over, brandishing his camera, quickly followed by several others.

Rose stays behind me, trying to avoid the limelight for the first time since I've met her. I'd have thought she'd enjoy being in front of a lens, but I guess even her self-love has its limits.

"Levi, fancy seeing you here! How does it feel to be back, after yet another defeat last year?"

Twisting a knife in the wound: the classic technique used by hacks like him. I don't let him ruffle me, though. I'm very aware of the cameras and of Tito's intense stare. He's loving this.

"I'm delighted, as ever. Looking forward to meeting my future opponents."

Several journalists speak at once. I can barely make out what they're saying until one raises her voice and holds her microphone right up to my face.

"Three months ago, you dropped a real bombshell. Can you confirm that this will really be your last WSOP?"

Silence falls on our little group. I play it cool.

"That's right."

"So you haven't had second thoughts?" she presses.

"Having second thoughts isn't really my style."

"May we know why?" someone else asks. "This is quite surprising news from you. Especially since you've lost so many times in a row."

I resist the temptation to say that being one of the top three players in the world isn't exactly losing. Not winning doesn't make someone a loser. Instead, I leave a dramatic pause. My secretive smile seems to heighten their curiosity.

"Let's just say that I've recently realized there are more important things in life."

"Meaning what? Have you got other plans?"

"I have. I love poker, but now I'd like to start building something completely different."

Tito is still listening, and I sense rather than see his eyes narrowing. I'm already trembling with excitement when I announce with a smile, "You're looking at a man who's soon to be married!"

Ignoring the fact that Rose is quietly choking behind me, I turn to take her hand. Her skin is cold but soft against mine. I don't dare look her in the eye, knowing that she'll be looking daggers at me as I add, "Allow me to introduce you to my beautiful fiancée, Rose Alfieri."

# Chapter 5

## Rose

***May***
***Las Vegas, USA***

I've never wanted to hit someone so much in my life.

Levi gives the crowd a proud smile, the very picture of a devoted young lover, and in a flash, I imagine myself flooring him with a punch right in the mouth. As though reading my thoughts, he tightens his grip on my fingers to tell me to behave myself. He planned all this right from the start, the bastard.

I remain silent and avoid looking at the cameras. I'm not a good actor. I know how to lie, and I can hide my feelings from people. But playing a role is entirely different.

"Sorry, but we've had a long flight," says Levi, picking up my suitcase like a true gentleman. "We need to rest, don't we . . ." He says something in Russian that I don't understand.

I have no idea what he's just called me. I fight the urge to knee him in the groin as he gazes at me in adoration.

*Oh, I'm going to kill him.*

What's got into him, exactly? This wasn't in my contract! He keeps his grip on my hand as we make our way to the entrance, and it hits me: he's trying to hide the fact that there's no ring on my finger! Has he been planning this sham engagement from the start? Or is this some kind of impromptu punishment for something I've done? He trapped me into this moment, knowing I couldn't call him out in front of all those people.

But he has no idea whom he's dealing with.

I stay calm as we rejoin Thomas in the hotel foyer. He raises an eyebrow in surprise and annoyance when he sees us holding hands, but he doesn't say anything, just gives us the keys. Levi pockets them and tells Thomas to meet us in an hour.

My blood's boiling. I can feel people looking at us, and that's the only thing keeping me from exploding. We get into the lift, and I try to look normal. As soon as the doors close behind us, it's Levi who lets go first, as though my hand were burning him.

I grab his shirt collar and push him back against the wall of the lift.

*"Cazzo!"* I shout in Italian. Fuck! "What's your problem?" I hiss, furious, my face a few centimeters from his.

He remains impassive, as though he'd anticipated I'd react exactly like this. He just blinks at me with those beautiful lashes of his. Despite his apparent calm, he clearly doesn't like my tone.

"I don't particularly like being touched. Let me go," he orders curtly. "Now."

"And I don't like people taking me for an idiot. I guess we'll both just have to deal with it."

His smile has completely disappeared now, replaced by an icy stare. He's handsome and terrifying at the same time. I probably shouldn't get on the wrong side of a man like this, but my pride won't let me back down.

All he says is, "Walls have ears."

The lift doors open, and he quickly yanks on my wrist to make me release his shirt. He then smooths it down with a nonchalant gesture and walks out into the corridor, without checking to see if I'm following.

I don't bother to stop and appreciate the beauty of the corridor, or even the suite—a suite?—once we're inside. I just cross my arms and stand in the middle of the room by the pool table, waiting for an explanation. Levi takes his time, dropping onto a purple velvet sofa with a little sigh. He runs his hand through his dark hair, exposing his forehead for a second, and undoes his tie.

"This little lie is part of my plan to weaken Tito," he explains finally. "I want to make him think he's going to win, that I'm gradually losing interest in poker, so he'll let his guard down."

At least the lie was part of a plan, not just a way of annoying me . . . but "little" lie? Really? This is marriage we're talking about! Where I come from, marriage is sacred. I'd like to up and leave this minute, to punish him for tricking me, but the call of his money is too strong.

Instead, I ask, "What do you mean?"

Levi looks up with a smile that could only be described as devilish. It's almost enough to make me tremble.

"Tito knows me. He knows I'll never give up, not after I've sworn to beat him one day. The only thing that could possibly distract me from my objective is love," he adds, tapping his heart with two tattooed fingers.

This takes me by surprise. He wants to convince Tito and everyone else that love is distracting him from poker? That he's resting on his laurels and has lost the drive to win?

It's a far-fetched plan, but a smart one.

Levi crosses his long legs and gives me a meaningful look. "Men are weak, Rose. You'll be my weakness."

"I never agreed to this kind of masquerade. Besides, we're *not* engaged. We hardly even know each other."

He smiles maliciously at that. "We're in Las Vegas, Rose. Everything's possible."

This man is mad. Much madder than I thought. What the hell have I got myself into?

"I'm not going to marry you."

He waves his hand as if to dismiss what I've said and replies as though stating the obvious. "Of course you're not. It's just a cover."

Am I really considering doing this? Pretending to be engaged will be a lot more work than what he initially described. I'm not an actor. More importantly, the game he's proposing is a dangerous one. Especially when played with a man like this.

On the other hand . . . this gives me the perfect excuse to make more demands. And it's only for six weeks.

"I don't even know what you do for a living," I say. "You could be part of the Russian mafia for all I know."

He rolls his eyes and answers casually, "What a cliché. I'm the owner of a nightclub in Russia. The Rasputin. Happy now?"

I'm actually astonished by this revelation. He owns a nightclub? On top of the poker playing. He must really be loaded. I can't give up at the first setback.

"OK, I'll do it. But I want more money."

"Naturally." He explains that he's reserved a suite so we'll each have our privacy, but people will assume we're sharing a bed.

I can't believe I'm doing this . . .

"We don't even need to see each other when I'm not training. We don't even need to like each other."

Message received, loud and clear. I agree and ask if fun-sized Thor is going to be staying in the room next to our suite.

"No. Thomas will be staying here with us. Somebody else is staying in the next room."

I raise a questioning eyebrow.

"Guess," he says.

I can hardly believe it. "Tito?"

He just smiles even more widely, as if laughing at a silent joke. I don't get where he's going with this. Taking the suite next to Tito's room is risky. That's too close. One false move and he could realize what we're up to. I don't know what Levi's got in mind, but this all seems too complicated to me. I've had enough for today.

"Levi."

He looks at me, listening.

I say very seriously, "The next time you blindside me like that, you'll get my fist in your face."

His silence is cold and dangerous. I hold his gaze to show I mean business. I need him to know I hate being taken for a ride: I'm his ally, not his employee. I'm his equal or I'm nothing.

Not expecting a reply, I take my suitcase and start climbing the floating staircase to pick out a bedroom. Just as I reach the top, his cool voice floats up the stairs.

"Seeing as we're in the business of making threats . . ."

I turn and see his eyes fixed on me, his face unsettlingly calm.

"You'd better not ever grab me again like you did in the lift." His tone is icy.

Silence falls between us. Who does he think I am? Thomas? Does he think I'm going to fall in line and obey just because he's paying me? If so, he's got some surprises coming. I smile at him and keep on walking.

"Then you had better behave yourself, Levi Ivanovich."

◆ ◆ ◆

The suite is amazing.

My bed's enormous, with a mattress so soft I'm afraid I won't want to get out of it in the morning. Levi's room is on the ground floor near the big bathroom, which has a Jacuzzi and a Roman shower.

It's the ultimate luxury, yet I feel a pang of melancholy at the thought that I'm traveling yet again. Despite the adventures I'm having and the luxurious places I'm staying, I miss having a normal life. I haven't got any furniture of my own, or special sheets I've chosen myself, or plants . . . I'd like to hang my favorite paintings on the walls somewhere, but that's impossible.

It's as if I don't own a thing. It's exhausting.

I tour the suite without once bumping into Levi. I take a shower, then curl up on the sofa, my feet on the table, a glass of wine in hand. The calm doesn't last as long as I'd like.

"I see you've made yourself at home."

I don't need to look up: I can tell from the harsh accent that Thomas has just barged in. He'll be frowning, as always, and looking condescending, as always. A person doesn't have to be a mind reader to see he thinks he's better than everyone else. Under different circumstances, we might've been friends.

"I found this in the fridge," I say, raising my glass.

"It's midday."

"It's six o'clock somewhere."

He stands right in front of me, blue eyes glaring. He's got an unusual face. Attractive in his way, but mainly he looks terrifying. He tells me Levi's waiting for me in the foyer. I ask why.

"To work—that's what you're paid for, isn't it? The tournament starts tomorrow."

I gulp down the rest of my wine, put my glass down on the low table, and stand up. Still feeling stifled by the heat of the desert, I leave my jacket behind and follow Thomas out of the suite. I ask him why he's staying with us.

"So I can watch your every move."

That's it. My patience runs out, and I turn to him, arms crossed.

"What exactly is your problem with me?"

He doesn't hesitate for a second. Speaking coldly and collectedly, as though he's been waiting for this moment all morning, he says, "You're mercenary, capricious, bad tempered, selfish, dishonest, and manipulative. I know this because I am too."

Whoa. Is he sweet-talking me? Such flattery! And we've only known each other twenty-four hours! He ain't seen nothing yet, poor guy. I smile approvingly.

"Bravo. You've understood more about me in one day than my old shrink did in six years. What's your point?"

"Levi is the brother I never had," he says as the lift doors open on the ground floor. "I'd do anything for him, but he's got very bad taste in women. He's an idiot, not to put too fine a point on it. And this isn't a great time for him to find a new way to destroy himself."

I point to my chest, as if to say, *Who, me?* but he ignores me beautifully.

"So find some other sucker to prey on, if that's what you're looking for."

I ignore him because I don't give a damn what he thinks of me, and go join Levi over by the entrance. Thomas disappears, who knows where, probably a dark corner somewhere to pour out his angst into his diary. I bet he was one of those emo teenagers who used to write depressive poetry on Tumblr in 2010. My worst nightmare.

"Where's he gone?" I ask Levi, who's staring at my left hand. He doesn't take my hand in his; he simply pretends to touch my back with his hand to guide me forward, but never actually touches me.

"Thomas has other things on his plate," he says, then changes the subject. "The lack of a ring could be a problem."

True, that could raise a few eyebrows. But buying engagement rings would be taking the joke too far. Still, I lower my sunglasses and tell him, "Just in case you're serious, diamonds are my favorite."

"Good to know."

We cross the foyer, passing the Roman statue in the middle. I nearly suffocate when the outside air hits us in burning waves. I love the sun. I'm Italian, so I'm used to it. But this is something else. The air is so hot and dry, I can barely breathe.

Levi takes us to the swimming pool—one of six at the hotel, according to him—and I whistle my admiration at the classical décor: columns, statues, and sculptures inspired by Greco-Roman art.

I gaze longingly at the huge domed cupola and the fountains. What I wouldn't give to dive into the cool water. I make a mental note to buy myself a swimsuit ASAP.

"By the way," I say, "what was it you called me earlier?"

Levi gives me a puzzled look as we sit down on a pair of deck chairs. He takes off his shoes and socks, exposing slim, elegant ankles. Somehow, I get the impression he takes care of himself. It's sexy.

"You called me something, in Russian I guess, in front of the cameras."

"Oh." He says the word again. It sounds like *lyubimaya.* "It means *my love.*"

I force myself not to visibly react, but I can't stop a little shiver from running through me. The word is pretty. It sounds so natural coming out of his mouth too. I think back to Thomas's words in the lift. "I'd do anything for him, but he's got very bad taste in women."

And yet, Levi doesn't seem particularly interested in me. He seems like a man so completely taken up with his rivalries that he's otherwise emotionally absent. He might look like the perfect gentleman, but I can't imagine him taking care of a woman—or another man, for that matter.

"What should I call you? The same thing?"

He moves a little wooden table so that it's between our two deck chairs and pulls a pack of cards out of his shirt pocket.

"Levi will do."

Like I said, not interested.

"We're here to work," he reminds me.

"And I'm taking my role very seriously. If I'm meant to be madly in love with you, I'm not going to call you Levi, just like everyone else. It's boring and unoriginal. Using an affectionate name in Russian is more intimate. It shows I'm interested in my lover's background."

He finally looks at me, seemingly blasé. I hold his gaze, still serious. I don't know myself what game I'm playing, and I'm probably going to get my fingers burned doing it, but I press on regardless, like I always do. Because apparently, I flirt when I'm bored, specifically with people I hate or who make me jealous.

He deals the cards, then softly says something that sounds like *lyubimiy.* "It's the same thing, but for a man."

I close my eyes and repeat the word over and over so I won't forget it. After about the sixth time, I notice Levi looking at me. His face is still impassive, but his eyes are different. I raise an eyebrow. He looks away, and it's as if I only imagined it.

"Let's get down to work."

# Chapter 6

## Levi

***May***
***Las Vegas, USA***

Rose spends the afternoon explaining all about how to count the cards and calculate probabilities. I'm not a complete beginner, of course: all poker players count their outs—that is, the cards that can improve their hands—to some extent. But I've never used that method much. I've always thought it too hard and a waste of time.

"You have to remember it's not an exact science," she reminds me when we start, shuffling the cards next to the swimming pool. "You can never know exactly what's in your opponent's hand."

"I'm not stupid, Rose. Just explain."

And that's what she does; very clearly, I must admit. It's as though she becomes a completely different person before my eyes. She seems . . . fascinated by her subject. It's a huge improvement over her ridiculous, clichéd flirting act.

"We'll start with the 'rule of two and four,'" she explains, dealing us each a hand. "You only use it to calculate your chances in the turn and the river." She looks at me, as if checking to see that I'm following. Of course I am. The turn is the fourth card to be turned over, introducing the third round of betting. The river is the fifth and last card to be turned over. I couldn't be a professional poker player, or any kind of player, if I didn't know that much. "After the flop, you multiply your number of outs by four to calculate your equity. For the river, you multiply by two."

I've never been very good at math, but I catch on quickly. Contrary to what lots of people think, counting the cards doesn't help you guess exactly which cards will be dealt, but it does help you calculate the chances of getting the cards you want.

"So, if I have twelve possible outs on the flop, I multiply that by four?" I say, just to be sure I understand. "Which gives me . . . a forty-six percent chance of getting the right cards and getting the hand I want."

"More like forty-eight. And if you've got twelve outs left to come, you'll have a twenty-four percent chance."

The basic concept isn't *too* hard to understand, but the more rounds we play, the more complicated it gets. Poker's mainly a game of chance, so playing while relying on probabilities turns out to be tricky. Even Rose, who counts like a pro, doesn't manage to win every time. The main thing is to know when to keep going and when to fold.

And tomorrow's the first day of the tournament. Nobody will be eliminated that day, but it's still important: we only have one chance to make the right first impression on the other players.

I won't be on my own, at least. Thomas will be there, at another table somewhere. Who knows—we might even play against each other. Rose will be there, too, albeit under cover.

"You still haven't told me how I'm supposed to get into the playing rooms during the tournament," she says.

I give her a mocking smile, and she immediately narrows her eyes. She's getting to know me. That's good.

"You won't be there as Rose. People will recognize you as my fiancée now. At the tournament, you'll need to be someone else."

"Meaning what?"

"One day you'll be a journalist, the next day a massage therapist, then a server . . . basically, anything that allows you to get into the room and walk around. You'll just need to avoid making eye contact with anyone."

"How are you going to manage that?"

"I know people."

Rose says nothing for a moment. She isn't stupid.

"You've been bribing them," she says at last.

"Exactly. Your role is to watch the players, mainly the ones on the same table I'm at, and report back to me during the breaks. The primary aim, of course, is to focus on Tito."

She nods.

We go back to our suite. Pretending I need an early night so I'll be in top form tomorrow, I tell her to make the most of the mini bar and room service, and excuse myself.

After a shower, I sit down in my room to practice. Again and again. I'm forced to switch off the light and use the bedside lamp due to a thumping migraine. My eyes are worse than usual, maybe because the jet lag's making me tired. This happens more often than I like to admit.

The other problems I have with my eyes cause me to also suffer from photophobia, or abnormal sensitivity to light. That's why I almost always wear sunglasses during poker games. Tournaments allow it, and some people think I do it to help me bluff, or to look cool. The truth is much less glamorous.

Without them, there's no way I could last ten hours at a poker table.

◆ ◆ ◆

The next morning, I find Rose in the suite's living room, looking completely transformed. She's wearing a long curly wig, a form-fitting pantsuit, and a pair of cat's-eye glasses. The only way I can recognize her is by her murderous glare.

Yep, it's definitely her.

*"Uffa,"* she grunts. I'm fairly sure that's *ugh* in Italian. "I hate yellow."

So the pantsuit is yellow. I see. I resist the temptation to ask why she doesn't like it. Isn't yellow the color of the sun? The sun's beautiful, isn't it? Why would she hate the color of the sun? Strange.

"It's just for a few hours," I assure her. "You'll survive."

Just then, Thomas walks in, wearing his usual gray suit, his blond hair just touching his shoulders. Rose whistles appreciatively.

"Wow . . . the thunder god himself!" Levi says. "Where's your hammer, Thor?"

He ignores that comment and passes her something.

"Here—your pass."

She turns it over curiously, then makes a face.

"Margaret Fisher? Seriously? That's so boring . . ."

I can't hold back the grin that rises, but I quickly hide it when I see Thomas looking at me.

"Ready? Let's go."

◆ ◆ ◆

I'd been missing the atmosphere of a big tournament. This euphoria, this feeling of adrenaline in every fiber of my body, the hum of conversation, and the faces of people looking excited and anxious . . . As soon as I get into the room where I've been assigned to play, the mask goes on.

I'm not Levi anymore, but Levi Ivanovich, son of Jacob.

I sit down casually at my first table, recognizing a few familiar faces. Some WSOP regulars, but also two newcomers I don't know. I put my chips on the table and get ready to play, pretending not to pay them any attention.

We start off slowly. Nothing too exciting. The players at my table don't seem particularly creative, but I'm not surprised. When a tournament has a ten thousand dollar entry fee, one can't expect much. I don't mind—it'll keep me from making any silly mistakes.

I don't know where Thomas is, but I'm not worried about him. Rose, though, is a different matter, and she's nowhere to be seen either. Forcing myself to resist distraction, I keep on playing.

The most interesting player at the table—I think his name is Wittelsbach—is studiously avoiding my gaze, fiddling with the neck of his *Jurassic Park* T-shirt and pulling it up to his mouth like a baby. I fold twice, mainly so I can analyze his technique and his reactions. He doesn't seem to know how to bluff, and he often checks—that is, passes without calling, folding, or raising. He doesn't seem to want to fight to win the pot either. I make mental notes.

After an hour, just as I'm about to make a raise, I pause. Rose is behind me; I can sense it. I know it. I can't see her, but the faint scent is unmistakable. It's the soft perfume she wears every day that leaves its trace everywhere, even on the bra she abandoned on the bathroom floor this morning.

I keep playing without batting an eyelid, but I watch her pass by out of the corner of my eye. Nobody pays any attention to her. She wanders among the tables but always comes back to mine, her eyes focused on the game.

After a while, I'm told to change tables. This essentially means moving up a level. I win more than I lose, so this comes as no surprise, but it's still reassuring.

"Well, well, well!" drawls a soft voice as I sit down at the new table. Then the person adds, in Mandarin, "Long time no see."

I look up expressionlessly to see Li Mei, a poker tournament regular. According to the media, Li Mei is the definitive rich daddy's girl: twenty-four years old, with more money than she knows what to do with. Naturally, she spends it on luxury hotels and poker—a game at which she turns out to be surprisingly expert. She's also obsessed with a singer whose name I always forget, and she speaks largely in quoted song lyrics. People find her exhausting, but I like her.

I don't let that show in public, of course.

"I saw on Weibo that you've just got back from China," she says, citing the Chinese social network. "You should have told me. We only just missed each other!"

Li Mei was born in Shanghai. I take in her perfect skin, her laughing eyes, and her pure white hair, cut into a mullet. She's wearing a long-sleeved top that covers her neck and shoulders, paired with an extremely short, flared skirt. She's a real beauty; I can't deny it.

"We're not friends, as far as I remember."

She's used to my brush-offs and isn't discouraged. Her sad pout doesn't reach her twinkling eyes.

"Ouch," she says. "I'll be crying into my pillow tonight."

We play for another two hours. There's no denying that Li Mei gets better every year. Unlike the other, passive players, she's not afraid to make aggressive moves. I like that. Li Mei presents a real challenge. Others, like the man to my right, don't seem up to the fight. Her only weakness is that she makes ridiculously high bets, as though to show everyone she's got money to burn.

"Congratulations on your new fiancée," she says with an amused look when we all take a break. "What's the theme for the wedding? Please don't say 'rustic.'"

"That's funny—you seem to think you're invited."

She whistles, crossing her arms. "I just want to make sure this poor girl isn't being forced to marry you. She didn't *look* insane. Naturally, I'm intrigued."

"She's perfectly willing, I assure you," I retort coldly.

"Given that face of yours, I believe it. In fact, I'm tempted to invite you to dinner, but Taylor Swift tells me I'd be pushing my luck . . ."

I raise an eyebrow, feeling completely lost. "Is she a friend of yours?"

"If only! No, she's my inner voice."

*Okaaay. Not weird at all.*

"In that case, Taylor Swift is right. See you."

I step outside with one hand in my pocket; the other hand keeping a firm hold of my bag. I don't follow the other players, preferring to sit by myself in a corner near the pool, in the shade of the Greek statues.

As I wait, I conduct an inner debriefing. Li Mei always acts needy in front of everyone. Other than that, things are working out so far just as I thought they would. One of the players at my first table, not someone I recognize as part of the usual cohort, particularly caught my notice. He hardly moved, just seemed to keep his attention focused on his earphones. He must have been a pro—and judging by his appearance, a pretty competent one. I know it sounds stupid, but a person's looks convey a lot.

Rose finally appears, minus the wig and glasses. She runs her hand down the length of my arm before sitting next to me with a winning smile. "Hello, *Lyubimiy*. So, how was the first morning? Did you make some new little friends?"

A shiver runs through me. I should never have let her call me that. I bitterly regret it now that I know how it makes me feel. I ignore her playacting and ask what she's managed to observe during the first session. The breaks aren't as long as I'd like, so we don't have time to waste.

"That gorgeous girl who kept flirting with you," she responds, serious again now.

"Li Mei Qian."

"She doesn't know how to hide her emotions. Every time she has a good hand, her eyes narrow just a little and crease up at the corners. You can also see her mouth opening as though she's about to smile."

I frown, intrigued. "I've been observing all the players, but I've never seen her smile when she looks at her cards."

"That's why it's called a microexpression," she shoots back, clearly annoyed that I'm questioning her analysis. "It only lasts half a second. Often, a person's expression is completely neutral immediately afterward. It's hard to see."

I know she's right. I nod slowly, impressed, and ask what else she's got to report.

"The guy on your right at the first table: he thinks he's better than everyone else. He's very confident. You can tell by the way he clasps his hands behind his head, leaning back in his chair and stretching out his legs under the table. He looks down on everyone, especially you."

I already knew all that, because I beat him in the semifinal last year, but I'm curious to know what Rose thinks of him. "How can you tell?"

"His attention was completely focused on you. Disdain is the only asymmetrical microexpression: only half the face moves. I could see the right-hand side of his mouth twitch slightly."

"I guess that means he's not much of a threat."

"On the contrary. The level of disdain is disproportionate to the twitch. If it's just a slight twitch, that means he's trying to hide it, and the disdain is actually quite strong. It's likely he's got a grudge against you, but I don't know why. He's getting too comfortable, though, and forgetting to pay attention to what the other players are doing."

"Meaning?"

She stares into the distance, thinking. A drop of sweat runs down her forehead.

"I'd describe his game as 'tight-passive': that is to say, if he decides on something, he really goes for it; on the other hand, he doesn't take risks with his bets. He only raises if he's sure of having a winning hand, which makes his strategy too predictable. I think he'll slip up before long."

I was right: Rose is going to be a godsend. I smile inwardly and murmur, "Not bad, Alfieri."

She confirms that none of the players I've come up against so far has been terribly good, except maybe Wittelsbach, the guy in the *Jurassic Park* T-shirt. Like me, she can't quite work him out.

I ask if she's seen Tito, but she shakes her head.

"Or Thomas either. I think they're in the other room."

I nod, then glance at my watch and get up. Rose does the same, fanning her face with her hand. It's sweltering outside, and has been since the early morning, a sharp contrast to the hotel's air-conditioned rooms. Every year I come here, I manage to get ill.

I remind her to stay hydrated, and add in a low voice, noticing a few other players sneaking looks at us, "It's time to go back in." I drop a kiss on her cheek and head off without allowing myself the pleasure of seeing her reaction.

The first day's play lasts ten hours, a sweet form of torture. I spend the afternoon with my sunglasses on, noise-canceling headphones covering my ears. I lose all sense of time. That's the risk in places like this: you could spend days here and never once go outside.

In the evening, I find Rose slumped on the sofa in our suite, barefoot, her wig tossed on the floor. I notice some marks, probably red, on her heels. Sweat makes her bangs stick to her forehead. I feel a bit sorry for her.

"Everything OK?"

She doesn't answer, just covers her eyes with her arm. I go get a bottle of cool water and leave it next to her. She's worked hard.

"This isn't a walk in the park. You need to go to bed early and drink plenty during the day," I advise her. All I get in reply is a grunt.

I take a shower, and by the time I've finished, Thomas is back. He tells me he's seen Tito but hasn't played against him yet. They're in the Amazon Room, whereas I've been in the Pavilion Room all day.

I tell him about my own encounters, and about what Rose has observed. When I get back to the living room, my fake fiancée's water bottle is already empty. She's standing next to the television, hand on hip, staring at one of the paintings on the wall.

I watch her for a while before going over. The picture in front of us is incomprehensible to me: a mixture of colors I'm incapable of seeing, and shapes that look like the scribbles of a three-year-old child. "Do you like it?"

"It's a Joan Miró," she says. "A surrealist Catalan artist. I don't like it; I *love* it."

I wasn't expecting that. She looks as though she knows what she's talking about. I suppose she must love art. I like this idea, and I hate it all at the same time. I'm immediately overcome with jealousy. I resent her for being able to appreciate art and colors when I can't.

"Do you like art?" she asks.

I can't help replying brusquely. "No. Come on. We're going out for dinner."

At least that gets her attention. She looks at me with a fiendish grin. "OK, but I'm driving."

I agree without admitting I'm not allowed to drive anyway.

She quickly showers and changes into a little backless black dress and Louboutin stilettos. She hasn't made a huge effort, but she looks incredibly seductive, all in black like the wife of the devil. I guess it fits with the act.

In the lift on the way down, I ask what she wants to eat. She spends ages trying to decide after we step out, so I notice Tito long before she does.

I freeze at her side, quickly slipping my arm around her slim waist. She stops midsentence and raises her dark eyes to look at me in surprise, but I just smile down at her tenderly.

It's the way my father used to smile at my mother.

A long, long time ago.

"The choice is yours, *lyubimaya*," I say. My love.

She seems to realize we're being watched, and I take her hand and kiss her fingers lightly. She shivers and smiles back at me, resting her other hand near my heart. She can certainly react quickly when she wants to.

"That's my favorite sentence," she says.

He chooses to interrupt us just at that moment. "So here's the woman who's managed to turn the head of the great Levi Ivanovich . . . ," he says in English.

We both turn, feigning surprise at seeing him there. Tito looks at us with a calculating smile. He's alone. I drop my lovesick expression and greet him politely, but he seems much more interested in Rose.

"I'm Tito Ferragni. Pleased to meet you."

"Rose Alfieri."

Her tone is icy. She's making it obvious that she doesn't want to talk to him. I smile inwardly, making a mental note to buy her whatever she wants for dinner.

Not seeming to get the message, Tito exclaims with fake enthusiasm, "Oh, you're Italian! *È un piacere conoscerti.*" He lapses into English again, presumably for my benefit. "Where are you from?"

I speak only a few words of Italian, but I gather he said he was pleased to meet her. I turn to Rose, who replies, head held high, *"Per me no."* Did she say she's not pleased? I'm not sure. She continues in English. "I was born in Florence."

Whatever she said to him, he doesn't look pleased about it.

*"Non importa,"* he says firmly. I caught that much: It's not important, or something along those lines. "Anyway, I'm rather surprised. Levi getting married . . . It's unexpected. And so sudden too! It almost doesn't seem real."

I anticipated he wouldn't be fooled that easily, of course. Tito isn't stupid—he suspects I'm not in love with this woman. The goal of the masquerade is to convince him that I am.

I tighten my arm around Rose's waist and assume a protective air, replying calmly, "We need to be on our way."

Before we can leave, he adds, "Dear Jacob probably wouldn't have approved."

I stop dead, a horrible shiver running through me. Rose watches, noting my reaction. My blood boils as I turn very slowly toward him. How dare he mention my father at a time like this? How dare he even say his name, after everything he did? After all the plotting and, worse, after having insulted him after he was dead?

Rose touches my arm delicately, trying to prevent me from flying into a rage. She doesn't know yet that losing my temper isn't my style. My anger isn't hot and explosive, like hers or Thomas's. It's cold and deadly. Silent. Patient. As calm as the surface of a lake.

I smile at Tito once again, but there's nothing friendly in my expression, and we both know it. "And that just makes me love her all the more."

I take Rose's hand, and we continue toward the door. She walks beside me and calls back, *"Arrivederci, perdente!"*

I don't need to be fluent in Italian to know what she's said: Bye, loser. Or something to that effect.

I smile as we walk down the hotel steps hand in hand, but let her go as soon as we're out of sight, eager to hide my trembling fingers in my pockets. Before I do, I throw her the car keys.

"I'm starting to see why you hate him," she comments, catching them as they fly. "But there's one thing I still don't get. What have you got against him, apart from the fact that he's a patronizing asshole?"

I get into the passenger seat, serious now. I think about Tito, my father, my mother . . . and instantly my good mood evaporates like snow in sunshine.

"Just that he ruined my life."

# Chapter 7

## Rose

***May***
***Las Vegas, USA***

Today I'm a massage therapist.

I'd have reconsidered if I'd fully understood the implications of Levi's proposition. Or I'd have at least tried to negotiate even more money. I'm not being paid nearly enough for my efforts.

I hide my disgust, barely managing not to make a face as I massage one of the players at Levi's table. Levi doesn't give me a second glance, but I'm sure he's thrilled by my discomfort. The heat is making my short wig unbearably uncomfortable.

"More to the left," says the man I'm massaging, and I eventually realize he's talking to me. "Have you never done this before, or what?"

I grit my teeth and keep my expression cold. I bet he's been asked the same question plenty of times, in a different context . . .

"That's what they all say," I murmur under my breath, pressing harder into his shoulders.

"I'm sorry?"

I smile in reply and babble a few things in Italian to make him think I don't understand what he's saying, and he quickly forgets about me. Levi is still impassive, but when I look up, I see his cheek tremble, which means he's listening.

*The prick.*

"He ruined my life." I've been turning that sentence over and over in my mind since yesterday. I could tell this wasn't a straightforward case of two players being competitive, but I never imagined that Tito could have affected Levi that much. If this Jacob was Levi's father, it's clear that he and Tito must have known each other, perhaps even been friends. What could have happened to make Levi react the way he did?

I tried to make him tell me the whole story in the car, but he kept his mouth shut. He took me for dinner in a chic restaurant and didn't say a word for the whole meal. I recognized a few other players there with their partners, and they were all looking at me pityingly. As if I were the future wife of a wealthy man who cared nothing for me.

For some reason, this annoys me more than it should. Which is why I decide to have a little fun today. If I have a fiancé, fake or not, it's unacceptable that he should be anything but crazy about me. Never once has a man invited me to dinner and then ignored me for the whole evening. In Italy, it's just not done. And I won't let Levi Ivanovich get away with it in Vegas either.

Today, he's wearing his vintage sunglasses again. His eyes don't wander from the other players at his table, but I can tell his mind is elsewhere. When I arrived this morning, I saw straightaway that Tito was playing in the same room. Thomas is here, too, though he's a more discreet presence.

The tense atmosphere makes me both excited and anxious. But the two men don't end up at the same table even once.

I spend the lunch break training Levi in our suite, and Thomas is there too. He doesn't say anything but watches and listens carefully as he eats his salad. I don't know why Levi lets him stay since, friendship aside, Thomas is still a rival. But that's what happens.

"Can I ask you a question?" Levi suddenly bursts out.

His curiosity makes me a little apprehensive, but I nod anyway. He looks at me with his head tilted as I shuffle the cards.

"If you're so short of money, why aren't you playing in the tournament?"

Thomas looks up—clearly, he's been asking himself the same question. It's true that it doesn't make sense. I could have put my name down and tried to win the big prize.

The problem is that I don't trust myself. I'm already finding it difficult to walk among the tables all day and not play. My hands tremble more than I'd like them to at the sight of the chips. If I took part . . . I'd be sure to have a relapse. But I can't tell them that, so I lie.

"I can't be bothered."

He doesn't look convinced. But I'd rather be seen as capricious and lazy than weak. He gives me an intense stare and replies, "Rose, you're gifted. I've worked like a dog for years, day and night, to get to this level. But you . . . you were born with this ability. The fact that you don't take advantage of it doesn't make any sense."

No, it doesn't. I knew he'd eventually ask about this, but I don't have an answer ready. I shrug and do what I do best—change the subject. "Don't you feel threatened?"

He looks surprised. "Threatened by what?"

"My talent."

Thomas shakes his head with annoyance and ignores the rest of our conversation.

Levi looks amused, which I hadn't anticipated. "Why should I feel threatened?"

"Because I'm better than you. Lots of people would want to simply use my abilities . . . not learn from them. But not you."

I hadn't intended to say that. It just came out. The first time I saw Levi, I thought he was one of those men I detest. Rich, arrogant, and thirsty for power, with an inflated ego. But he isn't like that. He asked me for help. He admits his weaknesses. He never tries to crush me or prove he's better. I'm not used to this kind of behavior. It throws me off-balance, and I don't know how to react.

He watches me for longer than I'd like, and finally says, "Only cowards try to take advantage of people they perceive as better than they are, instead of learning from them. I know I can't always be the best. When I'm not, I want to figure out what I can do to improve. There's no weakness in admitting that."

I have no response to that statement. My question had just been a selfish joke at first, a way of distracting him, but his honest reply gives me goose bumps. I wish everyone were like him . . .

I must have been wrong about him. Just a bit. Still, that doesn't mean I like him.

"Thinking you have nothing to learn from other people only leads to failure," he adds, standing up gracefully. "I'd have liked to play against you in this tournament. Too bad."

As he carries our plates into the kitchen, I realize that the feeling filling my chest is disappointment.

*Too bad, indeed.*

◆ ◆ ◆

Levi gets two rest days this weekend. We spend the first holed up in our suite with the air-conditioner on full blast. He's starting to understand how to apply what I'm teaching him, but he still thinks too much, which leads him to make clumsy errors.

In the evenings, I fill the living room with a canvas I've bought and with the paints I take everywhere with me. Levi, on the other hand, spends his evenings analyzing his opponents' techniques. He studies their ways of playing, their habits, the ways they bluff, and adapts his own game accordingly. I have to say I'm impressed. Despite his saying he wasn't born with talent, he's quite ingenious. And above all, he's devious.

Levi is the kind of player nobody but masochists want at their table. His game is loose-aggressive: he's always active and raises often, which can make him seem completely crazy; and that's what he would be if he were an amateur. But his experience makes him formidable. He's in control of every situation and hits the right rhythm at every stage of a round, easily confusing his opponents with the way he reads them like a book.

I've noticed that everyone avoids him like the plague, and I can see why.

I get back from the sauna one evening—yes, this hotel has its own sauna—planning to suggest we go out to eat. The sound of heavy metal being played at full volume reverberates from his room, as if he were having a party.

"What's going on?" I ask Thomas, who's eating by himself in the kitchen.

He acts as though I weren't here. I ask again, not happy about being ignored, but this time he pretends he can't even see me. I give him the middle finger. "Hilarious, Chris. Almost as funny as the first *Thor* film."

I just manage to dodge the teaspoon he throws at me. *This guy is insane.*

I find Levi alone, sitting on the floor and leaning against his bed, focused on the cards laid out in front of him. He doesn't hear me come in, even when I shout his name at the top of my lungs. I switch off the music, which finally gets his attention.

When he sees my legs in front of him, his eyes widen in surprise, and he pulls off his earphones. "Oh, it's you."

"What the hell is this?" I ask, my ears still ringing, "And before you answer, you should know I could never marry a Marilyn Manson fan, not even for show."

He probably thinks I'm joking, but I'm deadly serious.

"To tell you the truth, I prefer opera," he says. "My mother loves Sergei Prokofiev. Do you know his music?"

I shake my head, surprised to hear him open up like this. I'm struck by the nostalgic look he has as he smiles faintly and murmurs, "He's a Russian composer and conductor. He composed a ballet of *Romeo and Juliet* in the 1930s. I've always wanted to take my mother to see it."

"Why don't you?"

He's silent for such a long time that I change the subject.

"I thought you didn't like art?"

Levi shrugs. "I prefer the kinds I can listen to rather than look at."

"I get that. But why have music on full blast when you're wearing headphones?"

He gives a triumphant smile. "They're noise-canceling headphones, so I can't hear the music. That means I can still concentrate."

I frown, still lost. This all seems completely absurd and surreal. "You could just . . . switch the music off, you know? Do you want our neighbors to hate us, or what?"

He smiles again, very patiently, and that's when the penny drops. "Ooooohhhh . . ."

What a proper bastard he is. On the other side of the wall, Tito is undoubtedly being driven crazy by the noise. If he wanted to get to bed early to be on top of his game tomorrow, he'll be furious.

"Why do you think I chose this room in the first place?" Levi gets up. He's wearing only a T-shirt and pajama bottoms.

"So your plan is to ruin his sleep and weaken his game? How Machiavellian," I say with a smile. I love it.

"That, and he'll think I'm partying at all hours. Which will lull him into a false sense of security . . ."

Like the whole thing about us being engaged, I guess.

"Meanwhile, you're actually spending your evenings practicing like a maniac," I add, nodding. Ingenious, though a bit dodgy from someone who claims he's above cheating to win.

"It's not cheating," he says as if reading my mind. "Just a bit of manipulation. Besides, I have no pity for dirty thieves like him."

*Dirty thieves?* I want to ask what he means, but I can see by his look that he won't be disclosing anything tonight. I say instead, "You'd better get changed."

"Why?"

"There was a note stuck to our door. Apparently, Li Mei's having a party in her suite, and we're invited."

He makes a face and mumbles something in Russian as he looks back down at his cards.

"Excuse me?" I say.

"I said, *I'd rather die*. The party will have to go on without me."

"No excuses! I need to get out, and there's no way I'm turning up without my fiancé."

I leave his room, closing the door behind me. I'm not giving him a choice. I came to Las Vegas to have fun, not to spend my evenings alone in my room.

When he walks into the suite's living room an hour later, Levi's wearing black trousers and a white shirt with the sleeves casually rolled up over his forearms. His hair is still damp from the shower, which adds to his charm. Despite his reservations about going to the party, I see he's listened to me.

When Thomas asks where we're going, Levi tells him to get changed and join us later at Li Mei's room. He doesn't give Thomas time to object, which elicits a wicked laugh from me.

"We still haven't agreed on our head-over-heels love story," I remind Levi as we walk down the corridor.

"I prefer to improvise."

"At least tell me what Russian women are like," I insist. "I know people's ideas about marriage are different in other cultures. Should I nod and smile at everything you say, or am I allowed to have a personality?"

He doesn't say anything for a while. We get into the lift, and he leans back against the mirrored wall, looking at me with his piercing eyes.

"Marriage is a very important thing in Russia. Women tend to marry young so they can start a family. Things are changing gradually, but it's still a very patriarchal society. Women do the cooking, the housework, and the childcare while the men work and bring home the money."

I raise a teasing eyebrow, eyeing him from the other side of the lift. "Very 1950s."

"I guess you're right . . . but that's not how we see it," he adds calmly. "You can't judge my culture without knowing it or understanding it."

He's right about that. So I ask him to explain.

He seems to be searching for the right words, then says, "You women don't want us men to provide for you because you refuse to be seen as weak. You see this dynamic as yet another way of dominating you."

"And isn't it?"

"I can't speak for others, but in my case, no, it isn't. I was brought up to be a gentleman, that's all. A 'head of the family.'"

I smile mockingly.

He seems amused. "It's just a turn of phrase."

"Words are important, Levi. They're what gets passed down through the decades and make history and shape society."

He looks at me for a moment, then nods. "You're right. My mistake."

"Did your father hold the same view?"

"Not really," he replies, looking away, seeming lost in his memories, "It was my mother who always taught me to respect women. The things I do that you see as bad are well meant. Men like me pay in restaurants because we like it, because we want to take care of the women we're with. We carry heavy things, not because we don't think you can but because we want to save you the trouble. I know my way of seeing things can seem old-fashioned, but I still don't really see what's wrong with it."

I want to tell him there's nothing wrong with wanting to take care of the person he loves, as long as it doesn't mean she has to play a role she's not comfortable with, but I stay silent.

He continues. "In Russia, men have a certain attitude toward women. We pay their bills in restaurants; we hold the door for them; we buy them flowers on a first date; we open the car door for them . . . But we don't see that gallantry as an attack on their independence. It doesn't mean we think you're weaker or less competent. On the contrary, we do it because we love you and respect you."

I think I get what he's saying. Times have changed. Criticism of what was wrong in the past has altered people's mindsets, but unfortunately, some people have tried to go too far, too fast, and have got everything mixed up.

Personally, I like men to be gentlemen. I don't see it as an insult to my strength as a woman or my ability to earn my own money. It's as if he and I really were made for one another!

"Shall we just do what feels right to us?" suggests Levi. The lift doors finally open, and he moves to let me out first. "Not overthink it?"

"Sounds good to me."

His hand automatically moves to the base of my bare back as we walk side by side. I'd rather die than admit it, but ever since I've been in Las Vegas, I've been feeling . . . well, less alone.

Traveling all the time means managing for myself, not making lasting friendships, waking up alone, and going to sleep alone. But for the first time in ages, I've been spending my days with the same people. We see each other first thing in the morning; we eat together; we come back to the same place in the evening . . . and it all makes me nostalgic, somehow. Suddenly aware that being part of something, of a group—even a strange one—has been missing from my life.

"I should warn you," Levi says as he knocks at the door, "Li Mei is quite . . . special. But I think the two of you will hit it off."

The woman in question doesn't keep us waiting. She quickly opens the door, dressed in a tiny apple-green dress and transparent high heels. Seeing Levi greet her, I realize that he genuinely likes her. His face immediately relaxes, as though the mask were coming off. Strange.

"Here you are at last! I've been waiting for you. Come in."

Her suite is similar to ours, so I'm not at all disoriented. I'd been expecting an intimate gathering, but it looks as though she's invited the whole floor. She focuses all her attention on us, though.

Leading us into the kitchen, she offers us drinks and raises her voice above the music. "I'm finally meeting the future Mrs. Ivanovich! Pleased to meet you. I'm Li Mei Qian. With a man like that, you've won the jackpot."

I smile as sincerely as I can and joke, "I'd say he's the lucky one, but I guess that depends on whom you ask."

She bursts out laughing and says I'm probably right. Levi wasn't wrong: I already like her. She has a calming aura. My fake fiancé is just opening his mouth to say something when someone taps him gently on the shoulder.

He turns around and faces a man standing right behind him. The stranger is much shorter—he can't be more than five foot nine, like me.

"Er . . . good evening . . . ," stammers the man, looking like a deer in the headlights. "Wow, I'm super impressed. Can I have an autograph? No, even better, a photo! The guys at my fishing club won't believe this." He drops the name of a well-known female porn star and says he once got his photo taken with her, but proclaims this will be even cooler.

The man giggles like a groupie and pulls a gigantic camera out of his backpack. We watch him in silence. Levi seems rather annoyed by his appearance, or maybe by the familiar way the man is speaking to him. I find it hilarious.

"Let me introduce myself. My name's Lucky. I'm Aquarius and Leo rising, and my perfect evening would be spent watching *Bridget Jones*."

"Thanks, but we didn't need your Tinder profile," says Li Mei.

I look at him, amused, from his Hawaiian shirt open over a white vest to his fine gold chain. If you ignore his dodgy fashion sense and his manner of speaking, he's a good-looking guy. His flawless dark skin is glowing, and his curly hair is cut very short. His eyes, especially, sparkle with life.

"Hi, Li Mei," he adds with a little wave, giving her a dazzling smile. "Will you dance the next one with me?"

She frowns. "This isn't a high school prom, you know."

Just then, Thomas appears and whispers something in Levi's ear. My fake fiancé nods and looks at Lucky coldly. "I don't do photos."

"Oh. OK. Thanks anyway." He smiles sheepishly.

"But this guy does," I say, seizing Thomas's shoulders enthusiastically. "Ta da! He's the official Swedish double of Chris Hemsworth!"

I ignore Levi, who's struggling not to smile, and Thomas, who looks as though he'd like to stick a fork in my eye. Lucky opens his mouth wide and covers it with his hand, as though to keep himself from shouting.

"Oh my God . . . Really?"

I nod, and tears appear in his eyes.

Li Mei looks at him in disbelief. "Wait. Are you actually crying?"

"I'm so emotional," he says, touching Thomas's arm. "Oh, you're much less muscly in real life. Shorter too." He's talking as if Thomas were the real Chris Hemsworth.

This is too much—Levi snorts with laughter.

"I have to tell you, I sometimes fall asleep thinking of you and Kristen Stewart," says Lucky, squeezing Thomas's hand. "Sometimes, Natalie Portman is with you. Other times I'm there too. It depends."

Li Mei looks as though she's had enough. She seemingly swears in Mandarin and then tells him to go share his sexual fantasies elsewhere.

Lucky looks horrified. "What are you talking about? In my fantasies, we spend the night watching films and eating popcorn, while wearing matching pajamas. It's wholesome!"

No one says a thing. Levi's expression shifts from amusement to pity.

"To be honest, I don't know which of those options is worse," I say, making a face.

"Yeah, that escalated from *disgusting* to *tragic* quickly," agrees Li Mei. She taps Lucky on the shoulder.

I tell him to take his photo quickly, and he doesn't waste any time, posing next to Thomas, who's still giving me a black look. When it's done, Lucky is delighted. I feel bad lying to him, but I can't resist saying, "Don't forget to put the photo on your socials with the hashtag #therealchris, and mention his next film!"

Lucky smiles and looks as though he doesn't want to leave, but Li Mei waves him away with an air of condescension and invites us to sit on the stools around the island in the middle of the kitchen.

Next to me, Levi whispers, "You're a genius. But if I were you, I'd take care . . ."

"You think I should lock my bedroom door tonight?"

"Probably."

"And if I apologized? Would he take pity on me?"

"Not a chance." He looks over at Thomas who still seems furious. "He really does detest you."

I open my mouth in surprise. I can't tell if he's joking or not. I promise myself I won't tease Thomas so much from now on, hard as it is to resist.

Li Mei sits down opposite us and starts bombarding us with questions.

"So, how did you two meet?"

Levi doesn't reply. I look at him, appealing for help, but he just gives me a wicked smile.

"You tell it so much better than I do, *lyubimaya.*"

The coward. Fine, if that's how he wants to play it . . .

I snuggle up to him and put my hand on his thigh in what's meant to look like an intimate gesture. He doesn't bat an eyelid, which only improves my estimation of him.

"Levi owns a nightclub in Russia," I explain cheerfully. "I was one of his new strippers."

Thomas snorts into his glass, and Li Mei's smile evaporates. My talent for improvisation makes Levi look up from his phone at long last. He gives me an intrigued glance, but I ignore him and just keep going.

"That's how I got the job, in fact! Of course, it was just sex at the beginning, but when his lordship got me knocked up, I told him it was time to face facts; hence our engagement."

I relish their astonished faces. In the background, behind Li Mei, I glimpse Lucky listening reverently to everything we're saying, his hands cupping a glass of Coca-Cola that he's sipping calmly.

"Wow, a baby?" he exclaims. "Where's the ring? And you're still drinking alcohol? Have you already chosen a godfather? I'm available . . ."

"Are you still here?" groans Li Mei.

Levi still doesn't say anything. He lets me ramble on, as if he couldn't care less about his reputation. When I tighten my grip on his thigh, he freezes and draws in a deep breath.

"It doesn't show, I know," I say, stroking my belly. "It's a girl, and we're going to call her Carlotta."

This time Levi does laugh a little. He puts down his glass, glances down at my hand, and gives me an enigmatic smile. "What an incredible life we have."

I shrug, fighting the urge to let my eyes wander to his indecently tempting mouth. "Don't we, though? Sometimes I can hardly believe it myself."

He looks at me with detached interest and lays his hand over mine. I smile contentedly, enjoying my little game. Who said I couldn't have some fun? I promised to be his fake fiancée, not to be perfect.

Finally, he draws my hand away from his thigh very gently. Lucky asks me if I'm still doing stripteases now that I'm pregnant, and Li Mei gets mad at him. While she's distracted, Levi leans over and whispers coldly in my ear, "What game are you playing?"

"I don't know what you're talking about," I say, feigning innocence. I try to suppress the shivers that run up and down my spine when his warm breath touches my neck.

"*I'm talking about* your hand on my thigh, for example."

"What, don't you like it?" I don't know what's gotten into me. The truth is, I'm bored, and I find Levi unbelievably attractive. We're consenting adults, so what's wrong with flirting a little?

My fake fiancé doesn't move for several moments; then he leans back a little and smiles at me. At first I think he's going to kiss me, right there in front of everyone, but my whole body stiffens with humiliation when he kisses my forehead and says, "Sorry, *lyubimaya*, but you're not my type."

# Chapter 8

## Levi

***June***
***Las Vegas, USA***

Everything's going exactly according to plan.

Thomas and I are still in the game. Rose is still coaching me whenever I have time off. In the evenings, I practice alone in my room with music playing at full volume while she disappears who knows where. Probably blowing her first paycheck.

Every time I bump into Tito, I play the role I assumed at the start of the tournament. I'm usually with Rose, and I've taken her hand so often now, it's becoming a habit. We act like the perfect couple, both sickeningly sweet and semi-indecent. Tito might have had his doubts before, but now I notice his expression changing. He's starting to believe it.

In his defense, we're playing our parts so well, I'm almost starting to believe it myself. And that's saying something.

I doubt Tito gets much sleep before 3 a.m., which is when my music switches off automatically. My noise-canceling headphones have saved my life. I bought some for Rose, too, even though her room is on the other side of the suite. Thomas doesn't need them—he falls asleep in three minutes flat whether the music's playing or not. I've paid the staff well to ignore the noise.

Given the bags under Tito's eyes every morning, I think this tactic must be working. I also make sure I have a drink in my hand every time our paths cross. He looks down his nose at me, but I ignore him, enjoying a private laugh. I'm having a great time.

"Careful!" Rose cried out yesterday, catching hold of me as I stumbled on the hotel steps. *"Amore mio,"* she said. The Italian version of *my love.* "You should stop drinking so much . . ."

"I'm fine."

Tito was standing nearby. "Perhaps you should listen to your wife," he interrupted with a nasty sneer.

Rose gave him a murderous look that almost made me laugh. But I merely straightened up, swayed on my heels, and flung my arm around her shoulders.

"Everything's under control," I mumbled.

As Rose helped me toward the escalator, I could feel Tito's eyes boring into my back. Once the doors were closed behind us, I stood up straight with as much dignity as I could muster.

"How was my performance?"

Rose rolled her eyes, failing to hide her amusement. "I don't understand why you're wasting so much energy on something like this. It's stupid."

"I've got to have a little fun, you know."

The more Tito thinks I'm letting myself go—drinking too much, having sex, and partying—the more he'll drop his guard. Rose asked me if I really needed to do all this to beat him.

"I thought you were a man of honor."

That remark hit home. My smile faded, and I replied curtly, "Honor is a two-way street."

I don't owe it to that lunatic to behave honorably. A man who betrayed my family, and then destroyed it and left it in ruins, all the while boasting about what he'd done. I owe him nothing. I'm acting honorably enough. I refuse to cheat in order to beat him, if only to prove to my dead father that I'm worth more than both of them put together. But as for the rest . . . I don't give a fuck.

This morning, I'm doing a required photoshoot. I hate photoshoots. I don't like posing while twenty pairs of eyes inspect me from all angles. The photographer asks me to smile about twenty times, but the whole thing is a humiliating failure. After an hour and a half, Thomas intervenes, bringing me my phone.

"You need to take this call."

"I'm busy."

"It's Berezniki."

I freeze. Thomas didn't say it loudly, but I understood. It's a call from the prison.

I rush over, take the phone from him, and walk away. The photographer tries to stop me, but I'm not listening anymore. I go outside and find a quiet spot by the pool. I take a deep breath in before lifting the phone to my ear.

"Hello?"

"Hello, Son," says my mother in Russian. "I hope I'm not disturbing you?"

◆ ◆ ◆

Even after ten years, this remains the hardest thing I've had to bear. Not a day goes by when I don't wonder how she's doing, if she's OK, if she's surviving. Every time my phone rings, I'm afraid it's to give me news of her accidental death.

I hope she can hear the smile in my voice as I talk to her, happy to speak to someone in my mother tongue. "Not at all. It's good to hear your voice. How are you?"

My father always used to say I was a "mama's boy," and he didn't mean it as a compliment. He knew I loved her more than I did him.

He hated that . . . and I think he wanted to make her pay for that more than for anything else.

"I'm fine. I'm keeping on the straight and narrow," she jokes weakly. I can tell she's trying to reassure me, as always. "I can't wait to get out."

"I can't wait either. Only two more months."

I'm counting the days. I've been counting them for ten years.

"Are you eating well?" I ask, worried at how weak she sounds, "Nobody's treating you badly?"

She gives a little laugh, which doesn't convince me. I know she makes light of things, that there's nothing she wouldn't hide if she thought it would help me sleep better at night . . . It drives me crazy.

"Always the same questions! Stop worrying! Your mother's a tough cookie. I've held out this long. Two more months don't scare me."

It's not exactly surprising that I worry, though. She paints a rosy picture of things, says everyone treats her well, that she eats enough and that she's made friends. I know it's not true. I'm not seventeen anymore. I've read about what it's like.

Conditions in Russian prisons are horrendous. Barely any light or fresh air, thirty prisoners in a cell designed for six, all sharing one toilet. They get a shower once a week—no shampoo. I try not to think about the quality of the food or about the mice and cockroaches that infest the cells.

But the worst thing is the prison guards who are only too happy to use their cudgels, or even their dogs, on so-called "uncooperative" prisoners. I could easily kill any one of them if I ever heard they'd laid a hand on my mother.

All because I didn't protect her. I'll blame myself for my weakness and cowardice all of my life.

"And you?" she asks. "What are you up to? Are you at work?"

It must be nearly 5 p.m. in Russia. I lie, as always, and tell her how things are going at the Rasputin.

My mother knows almost nothing about my life. I've hidden as much as I can from her. She doesn't even know I play poker; she thinks the tattoos on my cheeks are the result of a bet I lost while drunk. The truth is, she'd be devastated to know I waste my time on such a pointless thing. She'd think I'll end up like my father.

But I didn't have a choice. Besides wanting revenge, not just on Tito but also on Jacob, I've been obsessed by one idea ever since they took my mother away: I will do everything in my power to guarantee that when she gets out, she has the life she deserves. The one she abandoned when she gave herself up to the police.

All the money I have now, that's taken me so long to build up, is for her. Safe and sound in the bank. The reason this is my last year at the WSOP is quite simple: my mother is finally getting out of prison.

Once she's out, I'll be done with intrigue, poker, and bad memories. I swear.

"Take care of yourself, all right?" my mother says just as I'm about to hang up. "I know you. You're your father's son."

*Ouch.* I know she didn't mean to hurt me, but that goes straight to my heart.

"Please, don't say things like that."

She apologizes in a low voice. I promise I'll see her soon and hang up.

It takes me a few minutes to blink back my tears before I can go back and pretend everything's fine. I find Thomas bickering with Rose, as usual. She sees me and crosses her arms, throwing me a look of exasperation.

Maybe it's the call from my mother, but for some reason my heart suddenly feels lighter. I stop next to her, eyeing the fluid silk of her dark shirt—not black, but surely blue or red?—and her high-waisted trousers. I can clearly see that she isn't wearing a bra underneath.

I think back to the delicious sensation of her hand on my thigh and almost regret the way I rejected her.

"Levi," she begins, "can you tell your chauffeur that . . ."

"You're looking beautiful today."

I don't know what's gotten into me. I wanted to tell her that; that's all. And it's true. She's always beautiful, but I guess I'm feeling bad about being an asshole the other evening.

She appears slightly unnerved by my comment. Her mouth closes, and she blinks a few times and clears her throat. Thomas sighs wearily.

"Please. Are you actually blushing?" he says.

I raise an eyebrow, surprised, and look back at my false fiancé's face. Her embarrassed expression makes me smile. I can't see any difference in her coloring, though. She appears as pale as ever. The idea that I'm incapable of distinguishing something Thomas is lucky enough to see fills me with melancholy, a sense of regret I thought I'd left behind years ago.

"I'm not blushing," she says bluntly.

"She's lying," Thomas says.

I smile even more broadly. I wonder why a woman like her would blush at such a banal compliment. I bet people say that kind of thing to her every day, ten times a day.

"Fascinating. In the future . . . can you tell me every time you're blushing?"

Rose looks at me as though I'm crazy. "You've got eyes, haven't you?"

"They don't work all that well, I'm afraid."

She must think I'm joking, because she tells me it won't happen again and storms off, making the excuse that she's hungry. I can't help laughing.

I'm still gazing at her disappearing back as I ask Thomas, "What color was her shirt? And her trousers?"

"Emerald green. And beige. She wears a lot of beige."

I catch a suspicious look in his eyes. I ask him what he's thinking, even though I already know the answer. He pauses long enough to tell me it's something serious.

"You never take your eyes off her, Levi."

"And?"

"And that worries me. You're not superhuman, you know. I might find her unbearable . . . but unlike you, I have a pair of eyes that work. She's very attractive. And you don't need to be able to see colors to see that."

I don't resent him for saying this. Thomas is here to make sure I don't mess up.

"If you're going to cave in to the first sexy woman who . . ."

"It's nothing like that," I assure him, smiling warmly. "She's very beautiful, it's true, but she's not the first pretty woman I've ever met. I'm stronger than that."

He looks at me, unconvinced, and asks what's going on, in that case. To be honest, I'm not sure myself. I like Rose in a way I find hard to explain. She probably knows that, given that she flirts with me at every opportunity, despite my attempts to discourage her.

I told her she wasn't my type, but she took the rejection with dignity, which only made me feel guilty.

"I don't know yet . . . but it won't take me long to find out."

◆ ◆ ◆

I'm exhausted by the time I get back to the comfort of the suite at the end of the day. I did Rose a favor and said she didn't have to come today, as I wouldn't be needing her. I still haven't gotten a chance to play Tito yet, which is starting to get frustrating.

I'm piling up the victories, but it's never enough.

For now, though, I've earned a hot shower. I walk into the living room and then down the corridor to my room, unbuttoning my shirt. I'm walking past the bathroom when I hear noises coming from my bedroom.

Not just any noises.

Moans.

I stand stock-still, completely taken aback. They're female moans. I'm completely thrown, for once in my life. Should I turn around and go back? But it's my room!

"Rose?" I call out.

No reply. Filled with curiosity, I push the door open very slowly, wondering who on earth I'll find.

*Oh.*

I frown in surprise, taking in the sight before me: Rose, sitting cross-legged on my bed, leaning back against the headboard, wearing a silk nightgown, a magazine in one hand and a glass of wine in the other . . . Moaning loudly.

Staring at her in astonishment, I cross my arms and lean against the doorframe, observing her in silence for a good minute.

"Any chance you could tell me what you're doing?" I say at last.

She looks up, finally realizing I'm there, and stops for a few seconds to reply calmly, "Oh, there you are. How was the tournament this afternoon?"

She starts moaning again as she waits for me to reply, adding a few *"Oh, si . . . Oh, Levi, si . . . per favore . . ."*—Oh yes, Levi! Please! I want to laugh at the absurdity of the situation, but hearing my name in her mouth suddenly has an entirely indecent effect on my body. I swallow, trying to hide my embarrassment.

When I don't answer, Rose looks up from her magazine, wondering why I haven't answered. Finally realizing I asked her a question, she says, "Oh, nothing special. Just reading a magazine and taking a rest."

"On my bed?"

"I saw Tito go into his room just as I was coming back. So I thought someone should take over in your absence," she says, shrugging.

I finally understand what's going on. I laugh, still feeling shocked. It's a very good idea, actually. If this doesn't drive Tito completely mad, nothing will.

Rose continues to moan, the sounds now happening faster and faster. When I give her a questioning look, she whispers conspiratorially, "We've been in phase one for fifteen minutes now. I think we can speed things up a bit."

I shake my head incredulously as she bangs the wall behind her with her elbow and starts to cry out. I smile despite the wave of warmth running through my body.

"Am I that good?"

That gets her attention. For some stupid reason, I wonder if she's blushing again. Not knowing fills me with more disappointment than it should.

"Actually, I feel a bit let down," she says, answering me.

"What about?"

"The life of a bride-to-be," she says, making a face. "I was expecting more."

"Such as . . . ?"

"I don't know . . . Breakfast in bed at the very least. Poems about my beautiful hair. Anything, really!"

I raise an eyebrow in amusement. I can't tell if she's serious or if this is still a joke.

"I see. You must be *very* disappointed."

Suddenly, Thomas appears, looking in to see what's going on. When he catches sight of Rose in my bed, he turns to me, puzzled.

"Do I even want to know?"

I shake my head, but Rose jumps right in. "My fiancé is neglecting me. I suggested couples therapy. Even our sex life is going wrong . . ."

"We're not married, Rose."

She rolls her eyes. Thomas sighs and goes away, muttering to himself, "I knew I shouldn't have come in here."

I know what he means, only too well.

"I could do with some help here," Rose says, scooting over to make room for me. "I don't like silent lovers."

"Not a chance."

I wish her luck and leave to go take a shower. I can't help thinking back to Tommy's words earlier. I was telling him the truth, but he's right to worry. Because that night at Li Mei's party, I lied to Rose.

*"You're not my type."*

That's not true. Far from it.

And that's exactly what makes her so dangerous.

# Chapter 9

## Rose

***June***
***Las Vegas, USA***

By the time Levi arrives at his allotted table, the other players are already in their seats.

Tito is one of them.

I shoot a nervous glance in Levi's direction, but he's managing to look as though he doesn't give a damn. I stay near the door, dressed in my server uniform and an itchy wig, while he sits down and acknowledges the player to his right with a nod.

I notice Lucky's there too. He's wearing yet another patterned shirt—flamingos this time—and a bucket hat. I usually can't stand sentimental buffoons like him, but for some reason I like Lucky.

"Don't go too close," Thomas whispers as he walks past. "Tito might recognize you."

I nod discreetly, and he goes back to his own table with a determined look on his face. My stomach tightens. I don't know why I'm so stressed. I can't take my eyes off Levi's face, and I find myself scrutinizing his every expression.

He's impassive, as always, but I know him well enough now to realize he's tense. His body is stiff, and his ankles are crossed under his chair. He's in defense mode, but his eyes are still fixed on Tito.

I circle their table as soon as the round begins, curious to see what will happen. The air is electric. Tito seems confident even though he looks tired, which doesn't entirely surprise me. Lucky appears completely oblivious to the rivalry playing out right in front of him.

"Wow, playing next to you is a dream come true!" He smiles at Levi. "Can we take a selfie?"

"No. A daiquiri, please," Levi asks me without looking around.

A daiquiri? At eleven in the morning? In the middle of a game? I hesitate, but he ignores me completely. He should keep a cool head and not let himself be distracted by alcohol. What's gotten into him?

I turn around, feeling annoyed, and order the drink at the bar. The bartender seems to hesitate and asks me whom it's for.

"Levi Ivanovich."

He nods, as though he already knew, and disappears for a moment. When he comes back, he's carrying a glass. I put it on my tray and head back, wondering whether I should lie and tell Levi they're all out of daiquiris.

Wondering how strong it is, I take a sniff of the drink. It doesn't smell at all. When I'm sure no one's looking, I take a little sip.

*What the . . .*

It isn't rum. Just fruit juice.

I consider going back to the bartender and asking what he's playing at, but then I think twice. This is probably for the best. I wipe the edge of the glass, go back to Levi's table, and put the cocktail down next to him.

"Thanks."

At that very moment, he folds, which makes Tito snigger. I hover nearby, doing my best to melt into the background.

"I've known you to play more aggressively," Tito comments, sneering.

Levi doesn't take the bait but only leans back in his chair.

"A good player knows when he needs to bow out."

He grabs his glass and swallows half the contents in one gulp. I expect him to turn around and glare at me because it's so weak, but he just makes a face as though the drink burned his throat. A moment later, he downs the other half in the same way and hands me back the glass with an arrogant gesture.

"Same again."

*Oh.* I get it now. He never had any intention of drinking alcohol. Tito's got no idea, and he gazes at Levi in disgust.

"What a fall from grace . . . I guess the apple really doesn't fall far from the tree."

"I'm sorry?" Levi says.

"That's what brought Jacob down in the end." Tito continues speaking as I take Levi's glass. I have to pry it out of his hand because his fingers have tightened around it. "Or one of the things, anyway. There was love, as he called it. Money. Parties, and of course, his true soulmate, the bottle. That didn't end well for him, though. Don't you think?"

At that moment, while Levi is blinded by silent anger, and the other players are exchanging embarrassed glances, I see it happen. I watch Tito glance quickly to my left, where a journalist wearing dark glasses is standing, then look back at the game. But now a triumphant smile is spreading over his face.

I make the connection immediately. Lucky is sitting just in front of the journalist in question, feeling overconfident and not paying attention to his cards. That asshole in the dark glasses is spying on the players' cards and telling Tito what they are with one flick of his fingers.

"What I think," Levi says in a quietly careless tone, "is that you're far too fond of the sound of your own voice."

Tito shrugs and places a high bet. I'm waiting to see what Lucky will do. He takes another look at his hand and calls, a big smile on his face. Levi remains silent, his jaw clenched.

I don't know what cards Lucky and Tito have, but judging by Tito's expression, it would take a miracle for Lucky to win the hand. I find myself holding my breath as the croupier turns over the last card.

An eight of clubs.

Tito's smile evaporates immediately, and Lucky whistles as he gathers the chips into the middle of the table. This one card has allowed him to win with a weak flush.

"Don't take it personally," Lucky chirps to Tito, his face glowing. "I've always been a lucky bastard. I think it's something to do with my name—thanks, Mom!"

Levi is smiling openly now. He toys with his chips, eyeing Tito mockingly. "See? You should focus on your game instead of gossiping."

The day drags on in a strange, tense atmosphere. I continue to bring glasses of orange juice to Levi, and he continues to pretend they're alcohol. I have to say, he's a good actor.

Eventually, Tito changes tables, and my fake fiancé drops the act.

When we get back to our suite, he heads into the shower without saying a word. I take the opportunity to go out as soon as I've changed. But first, I check to make sure Thomas isn't following. For a while now, I've noticed that he's always keeping an eye on me, whatever I'm doing, wherever I'm going. It's a pain.

I meet Li Mei by the slot machines.

"So?" I ask.

She smiles at me, lifts her sunglasses up into her white hair, and pulls a wad of notes from her handbag. "Check it out. I bet on twenty-four, like you asked me to."

I can't suppress a smile, and my heart starts to beat faster. Li Mei and I have become . . . I wouldn't say friends, exactly, but it's fair to say she's the only person I speak to other than Levi and Thomas. We had a drink together the other night in one of the hotel bars, and that's when the idea hit me.

"It didn't work the first few times," she says. "But the fourth time was the charm!"

I thank her and hand back the money, which seems to surprise her. "Tomorrow, bet everything on three."

She frowns and asks why I don't do it myself. "After all, your fiancé spends all his time playing poker. You must be dying of boredom, all alone!"

I mumble some excuse and beg her to do it for me. I'm trying to be strong and avoid the tables, but the temptation is too great. That's why I sent Li Mei to play roulette on my behalf. I figured I could play indirectly without getting sucked in.

Except it's having the opposite effect. I spend the whole day thinking about gambling. Every time I can get away from our suite, I venture down to the slot machines and the poker tables. Yesterday I nearly cracked. I'm weakening; I can feel it.

"OK, on one condition." Li Mei smiles, taking my arm. "The vultures are circling, and if I have to face them alone again, I think I'll die."

"Huh?"

I don't have time to ask what's going on. She fixes a false smile on her face as a gaggle of older women comes up and greets us enthusiastically. I recognize one or two of them, Alice and Lin, both players' wives.

"Li Mei! I didn't know you were friends with the future Mrs. Ivanovich . . ."

Her eyes shine with ghoulish interest. Li Mei introduces me, and I play along and smile politely.

They tell me their names one by one, and I nod, immediately forgetting them all. I think the blonde is called Judith, but I'm not sure.

"You will come and have tea with us, won't you? I saw your fiancé going upstairs, and I'm sure he could use a rest."

*Weird,* I think, then dismiss it.

"I should go and join him . . ."

"Come on. Leave him in peace for a while!" she cuts in, taking me by the shoulders, "You seem very young. Come have tea with us, and we'll all get to know each other."

Li Mei glances at me as if to say, *You owe me one.*

I sigh and follow them reluctantly.

◆ ◆ ◆

It quickly becomes clear that Judith, Alice, and Lin are gossip queens. They tell me they meet in Vegas every year and make the most of living the high life for two months. Li Mei apparently joins them sometimes, but I get the feeling she's more of a hostage than a friend.

After we've been at the bar a few minutes, Judith starts bombarding me with questions about Levi. One glance at them craning eagerly forward, eyes wide open in avid curiosity, tells me the real reason for this little ladies' get-together: they want to interrogate me about my fiancé. But are they just curious and envious, or are they spying on behalf of their husbands? After all, Levi is the one to beat.

I really don't like this way of going about things.

"Where are you from, exactly?" one of the ladies asks.

"Italy."

They blink, as though they'd never heard of such a place.

"That's . . . in Europe, right?"

*Seriously?* I shoot a furtive glance at Li Mei, who's trying not to laugh.

"Yes. It's in Europe."

*"Hola!"* one of them says, with a proud smile.

"That's Spanish."

Li Mei splutters into her tea, trying to disguise her laughter as a nasty cough. While they're all distracted, I pull out my phone under the table and quickly tap out a message to Levi. Come and save me, quick!

"Haven't you gotten engaged rather quickly?" asks Judith. "It seems quite sudden."

"It was love at first sight," I explain with a sigh.

*"Love at First Sight in the Rasputin,"* says Li Mei with a smile. "That would be a great film title. Something like *Pretty Woman*. I'm sure Lucky would love it."

Oh yes . . . I'd forgotten that Li Mei thinks I'm a pregnant stripper.

"What do you see in him? I find him so . . . intimidating! I don't think I've ever seen him smile!"

I frown, strangely annoyed. It's true; he does always look sulky, but I don't find him intimidating. He's just . . . intense. And incredibly sexy.

"I heard that Russians don't like to smile."

"That's rubbish," I say defensively, "They just don't smile without a reason. They would find that insincere. And, actually, Levi is very handsome when he smiles."

*Even if I'm not his type*. Wow. I'm surprised by those words popping into my head. I thought I'd gotten over that, but apparently my ego is still bruised. What does that even mean, *not his type*?

The women spend the next hour telling me, at great length, how rich, handsome, and powerful their husbands are. I hate it. What are they trying to do? Make me jealous? I bet their husbands never pay them any attention. My fiancé is just as good as their husbands—even if he is fake!

"But tell me . . . where's your ring?"

*Shit*. Taken by surprise, I resist the temptation to touch my ring finger. I think fast and don't let my smile drop as I say, "Levi has given me an old ring, his grandmother's. It was slightly too big, unfortunately, so we're having it resized."

They nod in unison, so I guess my excuse must have been convincing. I glance at my phone, which vibrated a few minutes ago with a text from Levi.

No time. You're on your own.

So ungrateful. I'm sure he's enjoying leaving me to my fate. It would serve him right if I spread some rumors about him as payback. But Judith's nosy stare changes my mind immediately. *Plan C!*

"Well," I say, sipping my tea, "I'm lucky. Levi is amazing. He works hard to earn all this money, it's true, but I'm still his number one priority."

"Really?" Judith sniggers. "How nice. Enjoy it while it lasts."

*Bitch.*

"Men are all the same," Alice confirms dramatically. "Once the honeymoon period's over, he'll give you his credit card to shut you up and smile absently whenever you tell him about your day."

"Doesn't sound too bad to me . . . ," murmurs Li Mei.

I give her a high five, delighted to find we're on the same wavelength. The others shift their attention to her and ask when she's "finally" going to get married. And yet a few minutes ago, they were saying I was too young, the malicious gossips!

"'It's possible for a woman to be a romantic and also to be single and happy,'" says Li Mei so solemnly, I can't help smiling. "That's what Taylor Swift says."

"Oh yes. Your inner voice?" I say.

"No, no. The real Taylor Swift. Try to keep up."

I apologize, and then laugh at the sight of their incredulous expressions. Li Mei tells them that her last relationship didn't work, and since then, she's preferred to stay single.

It's clear that they have absolutely zero interest in what she's got to say. They suggest a brunch together, with our husbands, tomorrow or another day. I hate Li Mei for getting me into this.

"I'd love to, but . . . I sleep a lot," I say. "All day, in fact."

Judith purses her lips disapprovingly. "Can I give you some advice, as someone who's been married for twenty years? You won't keep the flame alive by being lazy."

I give her a hard, arrogant smile in return. I'll show her flames!

"The truth is, I'd never get any sleep if I didn't sleep during the day." I enjoy watching my meaning dawn on them gradually. "You wouldn't think it, but Levi's got a lot of stamina. He's very passionate. I feel sorry for the person in the room next door to us. He can't be getting much more sleep than we are."

I laugh aloud at that because it's probably true. Li Mei hides her smile behind her hand, her eyes wide.

"Every night?" Lin breathes, intrigued, before Judith silences her with a murderous look.

I nod, feeling proud. I hate these women who think they can say anything they like just because they've made a "good match."

I'm about to add more details when they all suddenly turn pale. I sense a presence behind me and stiffen as Levi bends over me and places his hands on either side of my armchair.

I'm just turning my head as he takes my breath away by dropping a light, gentle kiss on my bare shoulder. I can't suppress a shiver. He lifts his eyes to mine. His expression is tense, dangerous. He's very close. Too close in fact.

"Here you are," he murmurs softly. "I was looking everywhere for you."

"Oh?"

I hate myself for not saying something cleverer. He's taken me by surprise, in front of witnesses. I don't know how to react. My cheeks redden, and I realize I'm blushing like a teenager. I suddenly remember Levi's words: *"In the future . . . can you tell me every time you're blushing?"* Ugh, I hate him.

"The bed was empty when I came out of the shower," he explains in a low, tired voice, ignoring our little audience.

Does he have to be so sexy? He has no right to say things like that! In the middle of the day, no less. Then again . . . I was asking for it. I gather myself and put my hand over his, like a woman in love.

"Sorry. I bumped into some friends."

He raises an eyebrow at the word *friends*, which amuses me. He takes me by surprise again by kissing the corner of my mouth, before saying, "Shall we go?"

*Fuck*. Since when has he been so into role play? Usually I do the work for both of us. Did he hear everything I said about sex just before he arrived?

Still feeling the tingle of his lips on my mouth, I get up and entwine my fingers with his. He's changed into less-formal clothes, swapping black for white and beige. He looks like an angel.

But his devilish smile betrays his true nature.

"I'm going to steal her from you," he says. "Good evening, ladies. Li Mei."

I give a nod goodbye and leave without a word. The women don't try to prevent me, not even my friend, who just gives me a triumphant smile and a wave. Levi doesn't let go of my hand as he slips his arm around my waist, drawing both our arms behind my back.

"What was all that about?" he asks as we cross the foyer. "I have a lot of stamina, have I? I'm . . . 'passionate'?"

So he did hear everything I said.

"There's no way I'm letting people think I've chosen an average man. I have my reputation to think of."

He smiles calmly at that. We enter the lift with a few other people and move straight to the back. I try to keep my cool as he leans down to my ear and whispers, "You're right. And you know what? Everything you said about me was true."

*Oh God*. I look up at him defiantly. He doesn't move an inch, so his mouth is now only a few centimeters from mine. It would be so easy to kiss him. He couldn't even refuse because we're not alone.

I don't know what gets into me, but I begin to move my hand up his chest, over his T-shirt, until I touch his neck. The lift stops, and everyone else gets out as Levi looks straight into my eyes and says, "Now what? Are you going to back me up against the wall and threaten me again?"

We're alone now. The lift begins to move once more. The air is electric. My eyes drop to his mouth, the same mouth that kissed my shoulder so tenderly but has also told so many lies today. I breathe my next words into his lips. "I only believe what I see."

He doesn't say anything for a long time. I've been thinking about it, and I've decided I need to get this obsession out of my system—I need to know. I need to have him, so I'll stop thinking about him day and night. I need to prove to myself that I can seduce him.

He's so self-contained that I have no idea if he's interested in me or not. He says I'm not his type, but he keeps flirting with me, looking at me when he thinks I can't see him, and telling me I'm beautiful. I don't understand.

Suddenly, his hand comes up to my cheek. His thumb caresses me once, then twice. My skin warms under his cool fingers. A slight smile tugs at the corner of his mouth.

"I knew it . . . You're blushing."

My heart's beating so hard, I feel it might jump out of my chest. What does that mean? I'm about to ask that when he drops his hand and sighs.

"Believe me, Rose; you don't want to get caught up in this."

*What?* I blink, humiliated by this second rejection. Am I not good enough? What's going on with this self-absorbed man? Or for that matter, with me?

"You don't know what I want," I fume through gritted teeth.

He raises an eyebrow, his face still very close to mine. My lips are tightly closed.

"Tell me, then. Be honest for the first time in your fucking life, and tell me what you want."

I wasn't expecting the conversation to take this turn. Ever since the start of our arrangement, I've been flirting with him, trying to elicit some reaction. There are lots of reasons for this: boredom, wanting to provoke him, curiosity . . .

I open my mouth to reply, feeling ruffled, but I can't think of a single thing to say. Because I have no idea what the answer is. And he knows that.

He nods, unsurprised, as the lift doors open on our floor.

"I don't know what you want, Rose, but I know it's not me. So stop wasting my time."

# Chapter 10

## Levi

***June***
***Las Vegas, USA***

*I'm seventeen years old, and I've just gotten back from a party. It's 2 a.m., and I should have been back hours ago. I weave my way to the door, slightly drunk.*

*I hear cries before I even open the door.*

*That sobers me up right away. I forget my euphoria, my friends, and Anika's warm thighs, between which I was busy only an hour ago.*

*"Jacob, no! Stop!" my mother screams as I burst into the living room, my heart pounding.*

*I freeze, rooted to the spot as I take in the scene before me. My mother is on her knees with my father standing over her, grasping a fistful of her hair. Her lips and nose are bleeding. I notice scratches on his arms, proof that she's tried to defend herself. One of his eyes is already starting to turn black.*

*"M-mom?" I stammer like a child.*

*My father gives me a look full of resentment. Alcohol slurs his words as he barks, "What time do you call this, you filthy little brat?"*

*I ignore him. My eyes are riveted on the tears running down my mother's face. She manages to smile with difficulty, her shoulders trembling. I know I wasn't meant to see this.*

*"It's nothing," she says. "Go to bed, OK?"*

*My father shouts something about her being too soft on me. I'm not even listening to him. My heart's breaking at the sight of the expression of shame contorting my mother's face. But it's not the first time I've witnessed this kind of thing. It's not the first time I've tried to defend her against my father, either, and it's not the first time I'll get a beating for my pains.*

*Every time this happens, I tell her we should run away.*

*Every time, she promises to think about it.*

*But we always stay.*

*"Leave her alone." My words come out like an animal's snarl.*

*My whole body's trembling with an uncontrollable anger. He sees this, and it enrages him. He can't stand the fact that I'm growing up, or the idea of my challenging him. In his eyes, he's the master of the house, and his weird offspring—handicapped from birth, mama's boy—should learn to keep his trap shut.*

*He lets go of my mother and storms out, shouting that I deserve a good beating. I rush over to help her up, and she apologizes and tells me she's fine. I can't speak. I'm too afraid, too drunk, too much of a coward to know what I should do.*

*"No!" my mother suddenly shrieks.*

*I don't even have time to turn around before I'm knocked to the ground by a dizzying blow. The pain in my back is unbearable. I can barely open my eyes, but when I do, I see my father standing over me, armed with a broom handle. What happens next is a blur.*

*I remember struggling to my feet and trying to fight him, thinking my time had come. I remember seeing his hands around my mother's neck, and then feeling them around mine, and finally hearing her desperate sobs as she begged him to let go of me. And fear tearing my heart in two.*

*Then a shot. An explosion.*

*Blood. My ears ringing.*

*Then the gun, still smoking in my mother's hands as the police break the door down and shout at her to drop it.*

*"Levi."*

*Somebody says my name. I cry, begging them to arrest me instead of her, telling them it's my fault, but nobody listens.*

*I'm lost.*

"Levi!"

I jerk awake, my heart thudding. I'm in bed, my neck and chest bathed in sweat. Thomas is standing over me, his eyebrows furrowed. I feel tears in the corners of my eyes and realize with shame that I've been crying in my sleep.

"Another nightmare? Here."

He hands me a glass of water, but I shake my head. I'm fine now. It's over. I'm here, safe and sound. Far away from Saint Petersburg.

Wanting to change the subject, I adjust the duvet and ask what he's doing up at this hour.

"Just contemplating doing away with your dear fiancée. I figured I should let you know."

I raise an eyebrow, still half-asleep. "Mm. Understood."

"Good."

"It would be inconvenient, though."

He considers that, then replies, "I'm not so sure. More positives than negatives, surely."

I smile and ask what she's done this time. I'm not surprised that Thomas and Rose don't get on. I often feel like a harried father caught between the two of them, but I let them fight, curious to see which will kill the other first.

"I keep telling her to keep a low profile and not go out at all hours. She doesn't get it."

"You told Rose Alfieri to 'keep a low profile'?" I laugh and make a face. "That was just asking for trouble, my friend."

"It's not funny."

"She's not our prisoner, Tommy. Let her do what she wants."

"What if she bumps into Tito and ruins our plan?"

I sigh and rub my eyes.

"She barely knows anything about what we're up to, really. Relax. And even if Tito finds out she and I aren't really engaged, he can't possibly know what's in store for him. Now, go run a bath, and take some time to calm yourself."

He snorts and comments that baths are a waste of time and water, and then leaves the room.

"I'll say it again, just to make it clear: Don't kill my fiancée, OK?" I shout after him.

He pretends not to hear me, but I'm not worried. I know Thomas like the back of my hand. I'm not saying he's harmless . . . that would be a lie. He's convinced he's better than everyone else. He's stubborn, calculating, clever, aggressive, and impulsive. Dangerous if provoked.

And yet he's the person I trust most in the world.

◆ ◆ ◆

My head's killing me. And my eyes.

Rose and I are spending the day training. She explains several things over and over, with remarkable patience. But I'm still in a terrible mood. I slept badly because of the nightmares, and the lack of sleep is affecting my eyes. Daylight is proving to be an assault I can barely survive.

"Why do you wear your sunglasses even when it's just the two of us?" Rose teases me. She can't help herself.

I stay focused and don't rise to the bait. She must realize it's not a good day, because she doesn't try to provoke me any more after that. She doesn't flirt, either, which is a first. Even though she pretends not to mind my endless rejections, I know they must drive her crazy. Part of me finds it funny.

I suggest going down to dinner, and she accepts, saying she wants to change first. I'm sipping my first beer of the day when the sound of her stilettoes draws my attention.

I'm so surprised, I almost choke. I cough as subtly as I can, desperately hoping my cheeks aren't as red as I think they are. *Holy shit.*

"Well, well!" She smiles and stops in front of me. "Am I finally getting a reaction?"

I don't manage a reply. I just look her over from head to toe. In many respects, Rose looks like she always does: same dark eyes with a long flick of eyeliner, same sublime lips accentuated by a thick layer of transparent gloss, same short hair, perfectly smooth.

But this evening, she's put on trousers and a suit jacket with . . . nothing underneath. A golden pendant dangles from her neck, its triangle shape falling directly between her breasts. I swallow, taking in the long earrings hanging from her earlobes, and the smaller cuffs higher up around the top of her ears.

She's utterly stunning. I'm overwhelmed by my own feelings. I've always found her beautiful and sexy, from the moment I first saw her in the Venetian. But now . . . words fail me.

I don't want her to go out. I don't want other people to see her like this. I want to lock the door, lay her down on the kitchen island, and run my tongue along that alluring strip of skin . . .

"Let's go," I say instead.

We go down to the hotel restaurant, her hand on my arm. Of course, everyone stares at her. I keep my sunglasses on, but she doesn't tease me. As we eat, we talk about the tournament and the players I'll be sharing a table with tomorrow afternoon. Little things, nothing serious.

I ask what she's been doing with her free time, but she answers vaguely, saying she's been sleeping and painting. I only half believe her.

"Shall we go back up?" she suggests.

"Why?"

"I need a cigarette."

I go to settle the bill. As we leave the restaurant, Rose is walking backward, talking to me, when all of a sudden someone bumps into her hard, knocking into her shoulder. I try to hold on to her arm but too late; she staggers, catching hold of my wrist to steady herself. The man turns back to us in surprise and apologizes.

"Excuse me, I didn't see . . ."

He stops short when he sees Rose's face, and she goes pale, trying to hide her own surprise.

"No problem."

She pulls on my sleeve, signaling to me to move on. I frown and look at the man. He's still focused on Rose, but then he obviously realizes I'm scrutinizing him and looks embarrassed. In the end, he smiles and moves away.

I may not be an expert in human behavior like Rose, but I'm not a complete idiot either. They know each other.

"Who was that?" I ask in the lift.

She refuses to meet my eyes, and it's clear she's an excellent liar, because I almost believe her when she says unconcernedly, "How would I know?"

I don't insist, and I realize it wouldn't do any good if I did. Besides, it's none of my business. Everyone has secrets, me included. I'm still curious, though.

An ex-boyfriend, perhaps? Strange to bump into him in Las Vegas, but not impossible.

"Can I get you a drink?" Rose asks when we're back in our penthouse.

I accept her offer and drop into the sofa, taking off my shades. She comes back with two glasses and sits on the floor by the low table. I look at her in silence, but I'm itching to say something. She already drank at dinner. Like she does every evening.

I haven't seen her drunk yet, but she does drink a lot. And she smokes a lot. I don't like it, even though it's nothing to do with me. I haven't got any influence over her.

Still . . .

"Don't you think you've had enough for today?"

Tact isn't my forte. Besides, tact wouldn't work with Rose. I know that because we're similar in that way—like we are in so many ways. That similarity's what scares me.

"No, I don't think I have actually," she shoots back. She pours herself a whiskey and smiles straight at me as she takes a swallow.

I turn my glass round and round in my hands, my elbows resting on my knees. I can't resist saying what I'm thinking. "I don't like alcoholics."

That's an understatement. I hate them.

"And I don't like drop-dead gorgeous men who stick their noses into other people's business."

*Touché.*

"Thanks for the compliment," I say.

I can tell that gets under her skin. Her cheeks don't change color, but I'm sure that if I were to touch them, they'd be as hot as they were last time she was blushing. Her eyes appear less focused, her pupils dilated, her movements slow.

She holds her liquor well, but she's clearly smashed. I've known lots of drunks, not just my father. Some can hide how much they drink; others can't at all. Either way, no good comes of it.

She deserves better. But there again, it's her problem, not mine. At the end of the day, she needs to make her own choices, and I need to live my life without getting involved.

*Yes, but . . .*

"What are you punishing yourself for, Rose?" I hear myself say.

"Excellent question," she says with a jaded smile. "What about you, Levi?"

I keep my face neutral. I want to reply that I have no idea what she's talking about, but I also don't want to lie to her. Even though lying's my specialty.

"What makes you think you don't deserve better?" I insist, and she laughs bitterly.

"You've got it all wrong," she retorts. "You think I'm a tragic figure with no self-confidence, but you know what? I think I'm wonderful. I'm beautiful, sexy, funny, and intelligent."

I do my best to look unimpressed. "As a rule, the more someone boasts, the less they like themselves." I know what I'm talking about.

She acts as though she hasn't heard me and picks up the pack of cards we always have on hand, then shuffles them with her slim fingers.

"Shall we play? If you win the round, you get to ask one question, and vice versa. We each have one joker. One free out."

I shouldn't agree to this. The odds won't be in my favor, but Rose is tipsy, and curiosity gets the better of me. I accept and take off my jacket. Judging by the look on her face, I'd say she's determined to win. Mostly, she looks angry.

We play a first round. I manage three of a kind, but her diamond wins. She tells me to have a drink while I think about her question. Annoyed, I obey.

"What would you say is your passion? Poker?"

I'm surprised. I was expecting worse. That said, she's the first person ever to have asked me that.

"No. At least, I don't think so."

"So what is it, then?"

"Poker?" I repeat. I think about it for a long time. "My prison. My punishment. My personal hell." I give her a smile that doesn't hide the bitterness in my voice.

She's taken aback and doesn't speak for a moment. "I was asking about your passion, but OK."

"I haven't got one. Photography, maybe, but I guess that's stupid."

She frowns. It's been a long time since I talked about photography with anyone . . . At one time, I considered doing it professionally. Before everything blew up in my face.

"Why would it be?"

I keep my eyes fixed on hers, studiously ignoring that strip of naked skin exposed by her jacket. It's a miracle no one's seen her breasts yet.

"That's more than one question."

She doesn't say anything to that, and we keep on playing. She wins again and asks how I met Tito. She's cunning. I'm sure that's the question she would have liked to ask first, but she waited so as not to be too obvious.

I pause. Thomas wouldn't want me to discuss it, but I can't see why I shouldn't. As long as I don't go into detail.

"He and my father were friends." I sigh, leaning back against the cushions. "They met here, at the WSOP. Then they gradually became bitter rivals."

"Why?"

"Because money corrupts everything it touches."

She doesn't reply, but I can see the questions forming themselves in her dark eyes. We continue to play and drink. I end up winning a few rounds, evidently to her annoyance. I'm able to learn that after studying psychology, she worked as a nude model for art students. And that she loves to paint, although I already knew that. When I ask whether being naked in front of people bothers her, she shrugs.

"Metaphorically, yes. Literally, no. The second is always easier than the first, don't you think? And why should it bother me? It's the way I was born."

I nod and sip my whiskey, then offer her the glass, which she accepts. Her eyes are warm, and her pupils are dilated by the alcohol.

She throws the question back at me. "What about you? Does nudity bother you?"

"Only other people's."

She nods as though she understands this.

I know I need to win another round before I ask her, but I can't wait. "Rose."

*"Cosa?"* she answers in Italian. What?

I hesitate for a second before asking. "What's your favorite color?"

She raises an eyebrow in surprise. She could refuse to answer, but she must think the question is inoffensive enough, because she says, straightforwardly, "Beige."

I could have guessed. "Beige . . . ," I mutter to myself, trying to work out what that means. She asks me the same question, which makes my bad mood return.

"Black, I guess," I say flatly.

She drains her glass before giving it back to me. Then she deals another round, and I win again. She groans, but I smile in triumph.

"Why do you need so much money?"

"Because you can never have too much!"

"You're not playing fair," I scold her, finally feeling the alcohol going to my head. "Be honest, or I'm going to bed."

She sighs and rolls her eyes before replying. "Debts. I owe too much money to too many people. My parents could help me, but I want to sort things out for myself. I don't want to owe anything to anyone, much less drag my family into problems I created."

Rose refuses to go into detail, but I get the picture. I realize that in spite of the selfish act she puts on, she's got a big heart. She isn't perfect, that's for sure, but she takes responsibility for what she is. All her failings, all her mistakes.

"You're not a bad person, Rose," I say quietly. "You just pretend you are so you don't have to feel guilty for the bad things you do."

My analysis stops her in her tracks. At first, I think she's going to lay into me, but she doesn't say anything. She lights a cigarette, and we continue drinking and playing. I tell her that my family is very religious, hence my biblical name. She raises an eyebrow when I tell her I love the movie *La Dolce Vita* and hate people who hurt those weaker than themselves.

"Aren't betting games banned in Orthodox Christianity?" she asks, clearly knowing the answer.

I shrug. "At this point, one more sin isn't really going to matter . . ."

She just smiles and says her favorite film is *ET*; she loves taking baths; and the last time she cried was years ago. I could go on all night, but I'm afraid my defenses will come down altogether and I'll reveal things I shouldn't.

"It's late," I say, glancing at my watch. "We should go to bed."

"One more," she insists.

It's obvious that she has a very specific question in mind and intends to ask it no matter what. I'm not sure I want to know where she's going with this, but deep down I'm curious.

She wins the round with a beautiful flush. I drop my cards on the table and look straight into her eyes.

Rose moistens her lips and asks straight out, "What is your type, exactly?"

I blink in surprise. I wasn't expecting something so trivial. But she looks as though she really wants to know. I realize that my comment the other evening must have hurt her more than I meant it to. Part of me regrets it. *If only she knew.*

"Men? Women? Both? Neither?" she says, crossing her arms. "What kind of people do you like, and why aren't I one of them?"

"That's a lot of questions."

"Answer, Ivanovich!"

If I answer honestly, she'll know that I've been lying. That the mere fact of her being here in this suite with me poses a threat to the revenge I've spent years planning.

I can't risk that. Not just for sex. Because if I give in, that's what it'll be. A fling with no future. I'm not sure either of us is capable of anything more.

And even that might be a form of double suicide.

"Joker."

I avert my eyes as though I'm offended and get up to leave. I wish her good night and head for the door, leaving her sitting alone on the floor.

I haven't gone more than a few steps when something hits my head. I shout in pain and spin around. Rose is standing next to the sofa, looking furious. One of her stilettos is now lying at my feet.

"Are you completely insane?"

I already knew that while I'm ice, Rose is flame. And God knows I'd like to see her catch fire.

*"Ti sta bene!"* she shouts. Something about my getting what I deserve, I gather. "It's the simplest question I could have asked, and you don't even bother answering!"

A tantrum, that's what this is. Because Rose Alfieri isn't used to people saying no to her. I bet her father gave her everything she wanted. Well, I won't do the same.

"Why are you so interested, *lyubimaya*?" I smile maliciously, hands in my pockets. "Scared I'll go looking elsewhere?"

She marches over to me without hesitation. I can almost make out the color in her porcelain cheeks, and that little detail makes me smile even more. She must take my smile for arrogance, because she plants her hand on my chest and pushes me back against the marble column, her alcohol-tinged breath tickling my mouth.

"You're a pretentious asshole."

Whether it's her vulnerable expression, her words, the alcohol, or the stifling scent of her perfume that changes things, I'm suddenly very aware of her body close to mine. Apparently sensing this, she lifts her chin ever so slightly.

"I don't believe you, you know," she breathes, lowering her gaze to my mouth.

I don't know if she's moved closer without my noticing, or if she's been this close all the time. Suddenly, I feel her knee between my legs. My blood is pumping through my veins, reaching places it really shouldn't be going right now.

I keep my hands buried in my pockets, not moving a muscle. But her knee rises higher, brushing against my thighs. I'm struggling to keep my breathing even.

Thomas was right. I'm not superhuman.

I'm weak, weak, weak.

I keep my hands where they are, clenched into fists, as I lower my face toward hers. My eyes are still looking into hers as my nose grazes her cheek. It feels red-hot, as I'd guessed, but incredibly soft. Is the rest of her body the same? I imagine the skin of her thighs against my face and lose control completely.

I lower my face farther, letting my nose travel down along her jaw. I can almost feel her heart pounding against my chest. When I can't hold out any longer, I answer her question.

"Women who will inevitably break my heart. That's my type."

She shudders at the touch of my lips. I should stop, but I'm completely incapable. She smells much too good. Not just her perfume, but the wonderful scent of her skin! She must taste divine.

Her knee rises higher and higher as my nose runs down her neck, light as a feather. She sighs almost inaudibly. Just as her knee is about to touch my erection, I react and catch her leg in my hand.

Would it be so bad if I took her into my room for the night? Just this once?

"You really know how to pick them," Thomas always says to me. "They're always spoken for, emotionally unavailable, or not interested. It's as if you do it on purpose."

Rose is no exception.

I raise my head, rest it against the column, and take a deep breath. I have to bring the temperature down. Lock myself into my room as if none of this ever happened.

"Don't fall in love with me," she murmurs.

I smile, and she moves closer to kiss me on the mouth.

"Same to you, Alfieri."

I'm closing my eyes to receive her kiss, my heart turning over, when an explosion rocks the suite.

# Chapter 11

## Rose

***June***
***Las Vegas, USA***

At first, I don't understand what's happened.

A second ago, my lips were almost touching Levi's. Now he jumps and pulls me roughly to the ground as a sound like a bomb going off rips through the suite. My heart pounds in fear as he protects my head between his trembling arms.

We stay like that for a few seconds. Nothing happens. We're still alone. I prop myself up tentatively on one elbow and hear a second crash, which is followed by a flash of blue light on the walls.

Levi jumps again, his hands like a vise around my shoulders, but I realize it's just a storm. Nothing more.

"Levi . . . you're hurting me," I groan.

His eyes are wide in his pale face, full of some unknown terror. I've never seen him like this before. Did he think he'd heard shots? Puzzled, I reassure him, telling him it was only thunder.

He closes his eyes and lets go of me, slumping back against the wall. He puts two fingers on his wrist, as though to take his pulse. His face is calm but extremely pale, as if he might faint. I wonder if he's trying to control himself because I'm there. His hands are still trembling, and he's struggling for breath.

Is he having a panic attack?

"Are you OK?"

He opens his eyes but avoids my gaze. His eyes are cold and serious.

"Fine. Can you bring me my jacket from my bedroom please?" he says through clenched teeth. "Quickly."

His jacket? I don't know why he wants it, but I rush to do as he asks. The warm, sexy atmosphere of a few minutes ago has completely evaporated. I've sobered up too. In his room, I see at least four jackets draped over the chair. Two black, one blue, one gray.

He didn't say which, so I bring them all. As I'm walking out, I see something lying on his bed and grab it too.

"I didn't know which one you wanted," I say, kneeling in front of him, "The gray, the blue, or . . ."

"I don't have a gray jacket, and I definitely don't have a blue one," he says crossly. "I only wear black." He looks at the jackets in confusion.

"Are these not yours?"

A pause, then, "Yes, they're mine."

OK . . . I purse my lips, silent.

"I see. Which color, then? What are you looking for?"

He hesitates, looking lost. His breathing is even more irregular now, and he shakes his head, closing his eyes.

"There's a box of Afobazole in one of the inside pockets."

"Which one, Levi?" I start to rifle though all the pockets.

"The black one . . . I think . . ."

I start looking in the pockets of the first black jacket, trying not to stress out, but he stops me. "Not that one."

I search the other one, but he interrupts me again.

"That one, with the white buttons." He points at the gray jacket.

I frown, pausing to look at him properly. Is he really that drunk? I don't stop to ask, not when he's trembling like that. I just grab the gray jacket and find a box of tablets. I open it and put a pill on his tongue.

He closes his eyes and swallows it. I don't say anything for a while. There's another clap of thunder, and Levi grimaces, so I pull out the thing I took from his bed; he seems surprised.

"Look."

He keeps his eyes fixed on mine as I put the noise-reducing headphones over his ears. Within seconds he looks grateful and calmer. Lightning is still flaring in the sky, but now he seems totally immune to the noise.

Once the storm has passed, I gently take the headphones off him and whisper that it's all over. He's stopped trembling now, and his cheeks have a little more color in them.

"Levi . . ."

He opens his eyes again and looks at me. I can tell by his expression that he already knows what I'm about to say, and that he would give anything to avoid it. I still hope I'm wrong.

"This jacket is gray, not black," I say quietly.

He's silent and impassive, still staring at me. After a long pause, he sighs. "I'm going to have to have a word with Thomas about that."

What exactly does that mean? I point to my own jacket and ask him what color it is.

"It's late . . ."

"Answer me, Levi."

He clenches his jaw and looks at me, annoyed, before resigning himself to answering. "Green?"

*Shit.*

"It's brown."

He nods, betraying no surprise, and gets up as gracefully as possible. I do the same, feeling shaken. Is he color-blind?

More importantly, what just happened? A panic attack caused by a storm? Surely that's a symptom of something much worse.

"Levi . . . Can you not see colors?"

He bends down and picks up his jackets in one swift movement. He looks at them carefully as he walks toward the kitchen, then takes the two I said are gray and blue and puts them in the bin.

"Good night, Rose."

And that's it. He goes back into his room as though nothing had happened. No explanation. I stand there alone like an idiot for a long time, trying to process it all.

Back in my own room, I sit on my bed and ponder. Details I didn't notice before begin to float to the surface of my memory, like bodies from the bottom of a river. His sunglasses, which he wears even when it's just the two of us. The fact that he never uses colors to describe things: it's always their shape, texture, or size. Even the poker chips he has to look at carefully, as though their color alone isn't enough to tell him how much they're worth.

Have I just discovered one of Levi Ivanovich's secrets? There are plenty of people who'd kill for that information. Most would use it against him, of course. I thought all this was "just poker," but I was naive. When there's money involved, it's never "just" anything.

There are so many rumors going around about him; some nasty, perverted, fetishist, or even gory. I've heard them as I've been walking around among the players, but I've read them on the internet too. My fake fiancé seems to inspire as much fear as he does respect. Some say he's part of the Russian mafia. Others say he's a cheat.

I don't believe any of it. Especially after this evening. But I'm sure he's hiding more than I thought.

My mobile vibrates on my bed. I glance at it and sigh. It's two in the morning, and I'm exhausted and still a bit drunk. But I change and leave the suite as quietly as I can. I take the lift down and get into a taxi in front of the hotel.

I let my tired eyes run over the view of Las Vegas at night, still lit up everywhere. Ten minutes later, I get out opposite a bar that's still open.

"Keep the change," I tell the driver.

I push open the door, feeling downcast, and walk toward the bar, urging myself on. Everything'll be fine. I'm strong. I won't let myself be walked all over, not this time.

I sit down, pick up the glass of wine that's already waiting patiently for me, and look up at Tito, who's sitting next to me and smiling.

"Hi, Dad," I say.

◆ ◆ ◆

When my father heard he had a daughter, he reportedly sighed.

My aunt told me, doubtless wanting to wound me, that all he said was, "Next time we'll get it right." But after I was born, my mother didn't have any more children. I personally think that was karma.

My father adapted quickly, though. It was quite simple: if my mother couldn't give him a son, he would create one himself. He put me in every boys' sport he could think of: basketball, football, tennis, handball, boxing . . . He even initiated me into hunting, which is one of the things I hate most in the world. He watched me burst into tears at the sight of a dead boar, and that still didn't stop him. I was six at the time.

When he found me kissing my first boyfriend, he looked at me with disappointment and said one word.

"Disgusting."

I think that was when he finally realized I was a girl, and there was nothing he could do to change that. Still, he insisted on teaching me poker. That was probably the only time he was impressed by something I did. He told me I had a gift. Said that, in the end, I really was my father's daughter.

He took full advantage of my talent, naturally. I thought it would be something that could bring us together, finally, and allow us to become close. I spent my whole life thinking that, accepting everything he put me through, in the hope that he'd be proud of me and show me he loved me, but it never happened.

Poker was no exception.

He soon began to boast about my gift and show off to his friends over talents that weren't even his. I brought him money, lots of money.

Until that wasn't enough anymore.

"How's Mom doing?" is the first question I ask.

"All right, I guess. She's still in Venice. She doesn't suspect a thing."

Good. I'd hate for her to know. She'd worry about me and try to stop my father from dragging me into his schemes. I hate myself for lying to her, but I'm doing it for us. She asked him for a divorce six months ago. He still thinks he can talk her out of it, but I know her mind is made up, and I'd do anything to help her stick to her decision.

I love my father as much as I hate him. That's the problem.

"So," he says, eyeing me intensely, "it seems congratulations are in order . . . Mrs. Ivanovich?"

I roll my eyes and cross my legs.

He adds, "That wasn't part of our plan."

"I was as surprised as you were," I say, hoping he believes me. "But it's not such a bad thing in the end. It means I can get closer to him, which serves our goal."

He nods, still scrutinizing me. I force myself to stay calm and ignore the glass of wine in front of me. I've had enough for one evening.

"I'm curious. Now you've gotten to know him . . . what do you think of him?"

I ponder this for a while, not knowing what to say. When I went to the Venetian in Macau, I already knew Levi would be there. It was all part of my father's plan. Catching Levi cheating was a lucky break: a perfect excuse to start a conversation. And when I left him hanging, knowing only my name, I knew he'd come looking for me. Tito figured he'd be interested in me romantically.

"Levi can neither resist a challenge nor ignore a mystery when it's right in front of him," he said.

I thought Levi would just flirt with me, nothing more. For a few weeks, we'd act out a version of *Pretty Woman*—with him in the Richard

Gere role, me as Julia Roberts's heart-of-gold hooker Vivian Ward. For some reason, I have that power over men. After that, I'd follow him to Las Vegas.

But I wasn't expecting him to ask me for help. I accepted, of course, since I was already going to follow him here. My father had described him as cold, antisocial, calculating, and arrogant. He's wrong.

*Levi is . . . endearing.*

"I wasn't expecting this," I admit, running my finger around the rim of my glass. "He's very intelligent. Clever too. He has eyes and ears on everything. He's always thinking, even in situations where you have to react fast. He's much more considerate than everyone says. He smiles a lot when he's with Thomas. He protects him too. He's honorable, fair, polite, charming . . . the complete opposite of a criminal. That's what makes it so hard to hate him."

"And he doesn't suspect anything?"

I shake my head confidently. "I'm almost sure he's done some background research on me, but he won't have been able to learn much. His friend's keeping a close eye on me, though."

"Why?"

"He thinks I'm a gold digger."

Tito sniggers to himself and sips his wine.

He's never wanted my mother and me to be in the public eye. We've always been kept in the shadows. I was even given my mother's last name, as though he's been embarrassed by me ever since I was born. Every year, I ask him to take me to Vegas with him, but he always flatly refuses to take me anywhere near a casino. He says gambling is my weakness, and that he didn't bring me up like that.

I begged him this year, promising him I was cured. He accepted on the condition I do him one favor: I never guessed it would be to spy on Levi Ivanovich.

The guy who stole my father from me.

He never stood a chance against me. I hated him before we even met, simply because my father has spent the last six years pursuing a vendetta against him—and comparing me to him. Everything has been "Levi this" and "Levi that."

"So," he says, leaning toward me. "Tell me all."

I give him my first report. I tell him about our training sessions, about Thomas and his suspicions, about Levi's attempts to pretend he's losing interest in poker.

"Clever," he comments. "I'll admit, I nearly fell for it."

"He's very convincing."

"So the noises keeping me awake at night . . ."

My cheeks turn warm. I'd completely forgotten about that. "That was just a ruse. We sleep in separate rooms."

He looks pensive. "Rose . . . That little shit is up to something. He's got a plan; I know it. If he didn't, he wouldn't look so confident."

"I've just told you what his plan is. He wants to make you think . . ."

"No. That's not enough. You're just a distraction, another layer of whatever it is he's plotting. He's got something else in mind that he hasn't told you about. I've done everything I can to find out what it is. I've even had him followed! But I've had no luck. It's getting irritating."

I know I shouldn't, but I feel a great sense of satisfaction flow through me as I see the light of fear in his eyes. Tito Ferragni scared stiff—that's a first! I may hate Levi (and his father) for having stolen my childhood, but I must say . . . I admire him too. Just a little.

I don't know what Levi is cooking up, and I don't really care. He's nobody to me. A pawn on a chessboard, a means to an end. All I want is to settle my debts and get away from my father for good. To get away from poker. Away from my weaknesses.

My father thinks we're a team, but he has it all wrong. I've never been on his side. I work solo. I have my own plan: betray Levi first, then my father. I'll make Tito win, because that's what he's set his mind on; then I'll steal his winnings and run away with them.

My mother will come with me, of course. There's no way I'm going without her. I'm sick of rich, arrogant men who think of nothing but poker, revenge, and power. Their little games don't interest me. They're pathetic.

"What if we beat him at his own game?" my father says.

"Meaning what?"

"Make him fall in love." He sits up straighter in his chair, his tone implying an order rather than a suggestion. "Get him to trust you, confide in you. Levi is strong, but he must have an Achilles' heel."

I shake my head. "I've already tried. I flirt with him all the time, but he brushes me off—and believe me, it's terrible for my ego. He has zero interest in me."

"He's just making sure you're interested; that's all," Tito assures me, rolling his eyes. "You're a pretty woman; you'll manage. And it's not as though it's the first time you've done this."

*Oh, so I'm a woman now, am I? Since when?*

I glare at him, teeth clenched. But what he says is true. This isn't the first time he's sent me off to seduce someone, this man who's normally too reluctant to face the fact that I'm no longer a child. I've never gone as far as sleeping with any of them, but still, it doesn't feel all that different from being prostituted. It makes me sick. But I still do it. Because I'm a fool who's scared to do anything he won't like.

I get up to go. I don't want this to last any longer than it needs to. "Actually, one of your associates recognized me—Robert."

My father groans and promises he'll take care of it. It's not a big deal, but I'm sure Levi noticed my reaction when we bumped into one another leaving the restaurant.

I'm about to leave when he calls me back.

"Rose."

"Mm?"

"Is that really all you have to report?" His arms are crossed over his stocky chest "There's nothing else I should know?"

I think back to this evening, to the storm and my discovery of Levi's secret. I should tell Tito about that. It would be a huge advantage, for all sorts of reasons.

And yet my heart is begging me not to.

In the end, I decide I can't be absolutely sure what I know. And although I used to do anything I could to please him, I can't even stand to see my father smile anymore. There's no way I'm giving him this gift.

I'll keep it to myself a little while longer. Who knows what I'll do with it? For once, I'll use my knowledge to my own advantage. Mine and nobody else's.

I shrug and draw on all my meager stock of talent as an actress.

"No," I tell him innocently. "Not a thing."

# Chapter 12

## Levi

***June***
***Las Vegas, USA***

"Levi . . . can you not see colors?"

I still can't believe I was so stupid. I've managed to keep my secret for years, and then the minute Rose comes on the scene, I make a schoolboy error.

"I told you," Thomas says wearily. "You're an idiot."

"In my defense, I wasn't quite myself."

It's true. I heard the thunder, and in an instant, I saw myself, ten years earlier, in the living room of our little house, my father's body still warm on the floor. Ever since that night, every sound like a gunshot has taken me straight back to that moment. I detest this weakness that leaves me petrified with fear, but there's nothing I can do about it. I tremble; my heart contracts; I'm afraid. I've been offered antidepressants, but I always refuse. I get by with antianxiety pills that calm me down whenever I have a crisis.

"She won't say anything," I say.

"Not if you pay her enough."

I shake my head, amused. "You underestimate her, Tommy."

I spend the next quarter of an hour telling him off for having let me buy blue and gray jackets when he knows I always want black.

"They were all out of black!" he says defensively.

"So you let me make a fool of myself? You know I always want to look impeccable. I must have seemed like a buffoon to her."

"Nobody says *buffoon* anymore, boomer."

"OK, Chris," I reply, copying Rose.

He rolls his eyes and leaves me alone with my thoughts. They keep circling back to *her*. It strikes me now that the storm broke at just the right moment. If not for it, Rose would probably have woken up in my bed this morning, and that would have been a terrible idea; the worst, in fact.

She's still asleep. Given the amount of alcohol she drank last night, her head's probably spinning.

I decide to prepare for tomorrow's return to the tables by watching the finals of previous tournaments, especially those featuring Tito and my father.

The two men I hate most in the world.

I've spent a long time analyzing my father's technique, which, unlike Tito's aggressive game, draws on patience and caution. He was a very good player, back in the day. He only beat Tito once, though that was once too often. Tito couldn't bear the insult. I'm convinced that he was also scared. He recognized my father's potential and saw it as a threat.

And shortly after that, he betrayed him.

My revenge isn't just about pride and honor. Tito is at the root of all my problems. Perhaps if he hadn't cheated my father for the sake of his own ego and lust for power, my father would have taken a different path. I'd probably have had a decent childhood. I wouldn't wake up sweating every night. And my mother wouldn't be in prison, forever altered.

So many ifs. I have no way of knowing what would have happened. The uncertainty torments me.

"Who are they?"

I turn around, surprised. Rose is standing next to the sofa, her feet bare and her hair ruffled. She's wearing denim shorts and a sleeveless T-shirt that she's tucked up underneath a bra that can't be very thick, because I can make out a lot more than I should. She hasn't put her makeup on yet, so her eyes are without their usual heavy eyeliner. She looks different. Very pretty. Too pretty.

"Hello," I say softly, before looking back to the screen. "My father. And Tito, as you can see."

"Wow. Jacob was an attractive man."

I raise an eyebrow, amused.

"You're very like him," she adds. She sits next to me, crossing her legs.

That little phrase is enough to pour cold water on my mood. I reply that I'm only like him in appearance. In every other way, I'm more like my mother. She doesn't answer, just watches the game with me in companionable silence.

When my father wins, she says, "I bet he's proud of you. Doesn't he play anymore?"

"He's dead."

She looks at me, her face impossible to read. She doesn't say sorry, which I appreciate. I never know how to reply when people say that. Instead, she asks me what he was like.

I stop the video and snap my laptop shut.

"Horrible. Are you hungry?" I ask, to change the subject. "I called room service about an hour ago. There're still some waffles and bacon if you want."

She makes a face and pulls her cigarettes out of her pocket. I watch her extract one and put it between her lips, which are still puffy with sleep.

"No thanks. I'll just smoke a . . ."

She snorts with indignation as I grab the cigarette and stand up calmly.

"It'll kill you," I say.

"You mean, like my fist in your face will if you don't give that back right now?"

"You're not fifteen anymore. You should be well past your rebellious phase by now."

She gives me a murderous look and pulls the cigarette from my fingers, her face a few centimeters from mine. "What business is it of yours?"

"I don't like the smell of smoke . . ."

"I won't smoke near you, then."

"Or smokers' breath," I whisper against her cheek.

She smiles maliciously. "I won't kiss you, then."

I smile, but I can taste bitter disappointment on my tongue when I say, "Perfect."

I'm heading toward Thomas's room when she says my name. I stiffen, sure she's going to mention what happened last night, but she just takes a drag on her cigarette, crosses her arms, and says, "Be ready at two. I have something planned for us."

◆ ◆ ◆

"How's business at the Rasputin?" Thomas asks on the other end of the line.

We're both having a coffee on the terrace . . . at different tables. Las Vegas in daylight is a bleak vision that I've never really gotten used to. The streets are almost deserted, and even with the casino in the background, the town looks completely dead without its neon lights. As if in suspended animation.

*Shit, I'm sweating!* I wonder how Rose stands wearing a wig all day in this heat. I hadn't really thought of that before. I've only been sitting here for an hour, under a hat, glasses, and a fake mustache.

No, I'm not joking.

Since I can't employ someone else to do this dirty work for me (we're already bribing enough people—it's getting expensive), I've had to come with Thomas to keep an eye on Tito today. Thomas says Tito's been spending most of his free time meeting with businesspeople. Potential investors. Tito is extremely influential, despite his business having recently seen a downturn following the launch of a rival app.

"It's going OK. I spoke to Victor last night. He seems to have things in hand."

I look away from Tito to focus on the documents I'm reading on my laptop. Tito's business appears to be in a slow but constant decline. He must be working all hours behind the scenes to protect this venture that means so much to him.

"Damn, this thing itches."

"Stop complaining," Thomas mutters into the phone. I see him touch his wig in disgust. "Did I really need to wear this?"

I glance at his false black curls, resisting the urge to smile. No, he really didn't. I just wanted to annoy him.

"He must not recognize us," I say. "Do you know who he's with?"

He looks over at Tito's table and shakes his head in disbelief. "Only Giulia Moretti. She's on the board."

"Is she up to speed?" I ask, guessing the answer.

Though I word my question vaguely, Thomas knows exactly what I mean. "She's his right hand. She has to know."

I think fast, committing her face to memory. "I want a full report on her. What about the *New York Times*?"

"Already on it," Thomas replies with a hint of pride. "I managed to swing a phone interview with the editor. He'll call you this week."

"Perfect."

I study the schedules on my computer screen pensively. My plan seems to be working so far, but it's still too weak. One little hitch could bring it all crashing down. And if . . .

"Am I disturbing you?"

Thomas and I both jump and hide our faces behind our menus. Rose is standing over me, squinting against the sun, a suspicious expression on her face. She catches sight of Thomas a few tables away.

"Can someone tell me why you're both here hiding, disguised as Starsky and Hutch? Very badly disguised, I might add."

"We're not hiding," Thomas retorts into the phone.

Rose rolls her eyes and turns to me.

"We had a date, remember?"

*Oh shit.* I force myself not to look over at Tito, hoping he hasn't noticed us. Thomas and I have many talents, but tailing a person admittedly isn't one of them.

"You're right; sorry. Let's go, in that case."

I get up and slip my computer and my USB key into my bag hurriedly. Rose frowns and says, "What is all this?"

I see my friend giving an almost imperceptible shake of his head, but I ignore him. I want to trust Rose.

"Things to do with Tito," I murmur into her hair, pretending to kiss her. "I'll explain this evening, in private."

She doesn't reply. I pick up my bag and offer her my arm. "Shall we go?"

"OK, but first . . ." She rips off my mustache with one quick movement, making me wince with pain. "I prefer you without this."

I lead her away, signaling to Thomas that I'll see him later, and ask her if she wants to drive. She accepts eagerly.

I take off the rest of my disguise once I'm in the passenger seat, sweat trickling down my forehead. Rose watches me, and I sense she's about to start asking questions, so I start talking first.

"Where are we going?"

She smiles enigmatically and explains that she's put our names down for a couples' activity. My face immediately falls back into its neutral expression.

"If it's a pottery course or cookery class, I'm warning you I won't get out of the car."

She doesn't even bother to reply, but simply carries on driving in silence under the Nevada sun, through this city that feels like an abandoned amusement park. After ten minutes, she parks in front of a row of shops, and she turns to me.

"Do you know what color your eyes are?"

Oh. I get it now. My smile completely disappears. I knew she wouldn't let the subject drop. Rose isn't the type to ignore things or pretend they don't exist. She meets them head on.

I reply casually, "Gray."

"OK. Mine are brown. Chocolate brown, I'd say."

I nod, but my heart beats a little faster. I've been longing to know what color her eyes are! I could never have asked Thomas—he'd have taken my question the wrong way. Brown . . . Chocolate, to be precise. Chocolate, but which kind? Now that I think of it, they do look the same shade as dark chocolate. Like my morning coffee.

"What are you driving at, Rose?"

"Nothing. I just want to talk about it."

"It's not a big deal, this thing with colors. You can see that for yourself."

She gives me a piercing look, refusing to back down. "You don't have to lie. Not to me. You shouldn't be ashamed either."

This time, anger rises inside me. Why is she poking her nose into this? I didn't ask her to. I've gotten by perfectly well without her interference. "You think I'm ashamed of it?"

"Aren't you?"

"No," I say curtly.

I used to be ashamed when I was young, because other children kept reminding me of it; adults too. The whole world kept reminding me I couldn't see things the proper way. I couldn't understand why I was the one with the problem. Why was my world the wrong one, not theirs? Was it just because there were more of them? I rejected their reality. In time, I learned not to give a damn.

"Why hide it, then?" she asks.

"Because until I've beaten Tito, he'll use my weaknesses against me. Also, I don't want to be treated differently, like you're treating me now."

"But you *are* different. You'd do better to accept it."

With that, she grabs my laptop bag, shoves it toward me, and opens her car door. I hesitate but then join her on the pavement, maintaining a resolute silence.

Her interrogation continues as we walk. "Is it that you can't tell the difference between colors, or that you can't see them at all?"

I give a deep sigh and resign myself to the conversation. She's already guessed most of it anyway. "I don't see them. My world is made up of shades of gray, from white to black. At least, that's what I was told when I was four."

"Like an old film, then," she says with a slight smile.

"I guess so. All films look the same to me."

After a few seconds, she says, "Yesterday, I asked you what your passion is—remember? Well, mine is painting. I've always painted, ever since I was little—mainly abstract. And almost always self-portraits. It sounds very narcissistic when I say it like that." She laughs softly. "But I can't manage to draw anyone else. I don't even understand myself."

I suddenly wish I could see her paintings. I'd like to give her a canvas and spend a whole day watching her work. I ask her why she didn't study art.

"I didn't think my work would stand up against the rest."

We stop in front of a boutique. Rose pushes the door open and lets me go in ahead of her. As I look around the room, my fake fiancée informs me she made an appointment for us earlier this morning. The woman in charge asks us to follow her, then leads us into a room behind the shop and down a narrow spiral staircase.

We step out into a large, light, air-conditioned room, where several people are already gathered.

"You can choose a spot wherever you like," says the woman in a southern accent I find almost impossible to understand. "The teacher will be here right away."

I suddenly realize what's going on. My eyes take in blank canvases on easels, tubes of paint, and a platform in the middle of the circle.

All of a sudden, my arms are covered in goose bumps. People are looking at us, smiling shyly, and I feel an urge to run away as fast as I can. I'm about to turn around when Rose's hand takes mine. I want to shake her off, but she holds on tighter.

"I want to leave."

"It's only for an hour," she says, looking pleadingly at me. "Please, give it a try. For me."

"Why should I do it for you when you've tricked me?"

My tone is more cutting than I meant it to be, but I can't help it. Why has she brought me here? To mock me? Torture me? Because it feels a lot like that. I'm surrounded by works of art, but I can't appreciate their true beauty. I examine the tubes of paint in front of me, unable to know what they hold.

"It's not a punishment, Levi," she counters quietly. "I can't possibly imagine what it's like not being able to see the world as others do. I'm sure a lot of people have told you that you can't paint. But you know what will never judge you? Art."

I calm down a little, but my teeth are still clenched. She looks at me without blinking, very serious. Her hand warms mine.

"In art, anything's possible. Everything's subjective. In painting, colors don't matter. Who cares if they don't go together? The important thing is what you put into your work. What you bring to it. In the end, somebody will see themselves in it, and that will touch them so much that they won't be able to see anything else."

It's a nice speech, but I'm still not convinced. I've already tried, but attempting to use colors only increases my misery, because doing things other people do makes me hope I can be like them. See what they see. Then I remember I'll never be able to, no matter what I do.

"That's why you gave up photography, isn't it?" she asks.

I sigh, feeling uncomfortable. "When I was ten, I told my father I wanted to be a photographer. He burst out laughing as though it were a joke, then said, 'That's not for you.' And he was right."

"Rubbish. A photographer captures moments and emotions, not just colors. It's the same with painting." Then she asks, "Do you know Jay Lonewolf Morales? He's a famous American painter, but he has achromatopsia, like you. I just want you to . . . try something different. Instead of trying to see colors, why not try to feel them?"

I look at her, drinking her in for several seconds, and my heart beats faster. I hate what she does to me. I love what she does to me.

"OK."

That's all I manage to say. The teacher arrives, and we take our places in front of our easels. I look at the brushes and tubes of paint like they're an army ready to fight me, as the teacher explains how the hour will go.

He arranges objects on a table on the platform: a tray of grapes next to a vase, flowers, and a glass half-full of wine.

I spend a good ten minutes just thinking. Rose whispers to me, telling me not to think about the colors, and to get started. But I'm lost. What if I use orange to paint the grapes, when I know in theory that they're green?

"Don't overthink it."

I follow her advice, a little timidly at first, and force myself to begin. I'm grateful to her for not trying to steal a glance at what I'm doing, and for giving me the privacy I need.

I choose a tube that looks as though it could be the same as the grapes in front of me—a light gray to me, but not too light. Obviously, I'm working completely at random. I have no idea how to draw.

"You can do something abstract if you prefer," says Rose. "That's what I'm doing."

I glance enviously at her canvas. It's true that she's departed a long way from the still life in front of us. The colors are mixed up wildly. It's wonderful. How could she have ever thought her work wouldn't stand up against others' work?

I decide to follow her example and let inspiration guide me. The more time that passes, the more I let myself go. I stop worrying about the colors I'm using and focus instead on the shapes, the lines, and the spots I make with my fingertips. I feel energized by adrenaline and by the urge to create something, to express my feelings on canvas.

Suddenly, Rose daubs a line of paint onto the back of my hand with her finger. I look at her in surprise. She smiles, tilts her chin up at me, and whispers, "That's the color of my cheeks when I blush. I thought you might like to know."

I swallow, struggling to keep my face expressionless. I'd rather she didn't see how much I want to smile right now. I glance down at my hand and take in the color, nodding absently.

*I'll try to remember that.* Eventually, I smudge some of the paint onto my thumb and dab it gently onto her cheeks. She lets me do it without objecting, her eyes gazing into mine. When I've finished, I pull back to look at her.

I may not see colors, but I'm not blind. She's . . .

"Stunning," I say. I imagine her blushing again and laugh quietly.

The hour passes quickly. I contemplate my work with a mixture of pride and wonder. I never thought I could do something like that. I have no idea if the colors work well together, but I don't care. I don't even want to know. I like what I've done.

"I love it," Rose says, smiling too. "It's very you."

"Yours isn't bad either."

That's an understatement. She thanks me, although I don't think she shares my opinion. We take the canvases back to the car with us. Rose asks me if I want to drive, but I finally admit I'm not allowed.

"Oh, of course. I should've realized."

We drive back to the hotel in peaceful silence. I'd never admit it, but this little outing has done me a world of good. For the first time since we arrived in Las Vegas, I've thought about something other than poker or Tito.

Walking into the suite, I feel like a little boy eager to show off his messy drawings to his mother. Thomas has to see this!

"Also . . . ," says Rose as I'm closing the door behind us. "Do you want to talk about what happened last night?"

"Not really, no." I keep walking toward my room, bag in hand, but she grabs it and puts it on the kitchen counter behind me.

"I do."

"And since when do I have to do what Rose Alfieri tells me?" I joke, putting my hands in my pockets.

She comes dangerously close, taking me by surprise. Why does what happened mean so much to her? It's none of her business.

"I hate secrets, Levi."

"Oh, and you haven't got any of your own, I suppose?"

She doesn't bat an eyelid. I appreciate what she did for me yesterday, and what she's done today. But she isn't my mother, or my girlfriend. This isn't her place.

"I don't owe you anything. Now, let me past."

"Not today."

I'm about to turn around and pick up my bag, but she suddenly grabs my shirt and pulls me toward her, and urgently presses her lips against mine.

# Chapter 13

## Rose

***June***
***Las Vegas, USA***

Levi stiffens at my touch, his eyes opening a little wider. For an instant, I congratulate myself on having overcome his defenses, if only for a second.

I know he's going to push me away, so I hurry to find what I'm searching for in his bag. His lips are soft against mine, to my surprise. Warm too. I'd have liked it to go on longer, but don't want to be rejected yet again, so I let go of him, ignoring the desire growing inside me. But just as I try to move away, his hand seizes the back of my neck. I barely have time to look into his eyes, darkened by passion, before he pulls me toward him and begins to kiss me wildly.

I moan with a mixture of surprise and pain but don't draw back. Goose bumps cover my arms as he holds me firmly against him, one hand buried in my hair, the other low on my back.

My body reacts automatically, catching fire as his hands pass over it. I feel his tongue imploring me, and open my mouth to it, wrapping my arms around his neck. Our tongues meet and intertwine. His kiss may be wild, but his hands on my body are gentle and attentive, gliding indecently along my spine.

*Oh shit. Levi is actually kissing me.*

Finally.

The silence in the suite is broken only by the sounds of our kiss and our shuddering breathing. I arch myself against him, my breasts pressing against his powerful torso as he devours me. I feel as though I'm drowning, suffocating, gasping for air.

A familiar ache throbs between my legs. I want him so badly. Of course I want him. Levi is unbelievably sexy, and he kisses like a god.

And he's not actually interested in me—what could be better?

*I'm such a masochist.*

My fingers stroke the shaved hair high on the back of his neck, then grasp the longer hair above it. I give it a little tug, forcing him to pull back from my mouth. His eyelids are heavy, and his panting only excites me more.

He looks at me, his mouth half-open, his tongue just touching his lower lip. I slide my other hand all the way down his stomach, stopping at the bulge in his trousers. He swallows but doesn't say anything.

"Not your type, you say?"

Levi seizes the opportunity to come closer again, as close as I'll let him. Having him under my control in this situation, even though I know he's letting me do it, makes my legs tremble with excitement.

He inches his face closer to mine, his eyes fixed on my mouth, and soon he's leaning down so far that I let him have what he wants, letting go of his hair. He kisses me again, even more sensually now, and I groan when he captures my lower lip in his teeth and bites into the forbidden fruit.

I begin to tremble, my cheeks burning. I forget all about the USB key I'm clutching, even though that was the reason why I kissed him so unexpectedly in the first place.

"Your room," I implore him, feeling his excitement pressing against me.

He sighs against my mouth, his thumb caressing my chin and moving down over my throat. I ask in a whisper what's wrong. His tongue teases my lips, tantalizingly slow, and I imagine it coaxing its way over my whole body, to even more sensitive places.

"I'm not going to sleep with you, Rose," he murmurs hoarsely. "Sorry."

It's like a bucket of cold water has been dumped on me. Suddenly I remember who I am, who he is, and what I'm meant to be doing. "Seduce him" is the mission my father gave me. This isn't the first time I've felt angry following a rejection by Levi. Before, it was for purely egotistical reasons, but now, at this precise moment, it's disappointment that's running through me. Because as much as I hate to admit it, I really like this asshole.

"That's not what a woman wants to hear from her fiancé."

He looks at me without blinking, his expression cold and distant. His fingers brush a few strands of my bangs back into place as he replies, "You won't be the first wife to be disappointed by her husband in the bedroom. I'm sure you'll get over it."

He gently takes hold of my arms, which are still around his neck, and disentangles us. I manage to keep the USB key hidden in the palm of my hand, anger still surging through me. I'm a ball of frustration.

After a kiss like that, how dare he reject me again, like a piece of rubbish? Who does he think he is? I'm not his toy. I don't care what my father says—I won't lower myself to the level of Levi's little games again. I have my dignity.

"That's the last time I'm going to make a fool of myself with you, Levi. I'm warning you." I can hear the pain in my own voice, and that makes me even angrier.

He turns around, looking indifferent despite his dilated pupils. "OK. So?"

"So don't come begging when it's too late; that's all."

"May I remind you which one of us threw themselves at the other?"

"You didn't seem to be hating it two minutes ago. And I've seen the way you look at me."

He raises an eyebrow, intrigued. "And how do I look at you, Rose?"

"Like all men do."

He takes his time answering, and I realize he's wondering whether to answer honestly, probably fearing that he'll hurt me.

"It's true. I look at you because you're beautiful. Perhaps beauty is all that counts in your world, but not in mine. Appreciating a woman's beauty doesn't mean I want to go to bed with her."

*Ouch.* That was harder to take than I would have imagined. I ask him if that means he doesn't want to go to bed with me. He doesn't reply. I nod and then keep on nodding as a triumphant smile spreads over my face. It's stupid, but I still have some hope. Because he didn't answer my question.

"Oh, I can't wait . . . ," I laugh to myself. "I can't wait for that moment, Levi Ivanovich."

I move back toward him, and he asks me what I'm talking about.

I whisper my reply. "I'm talking about the moment when you beg me to go to bed with you. Because that's what's going to happen. And the day it does . . . you'll regret that you rejected me so many times. I'm going to have you crawl, grovel, and beg until you can't beg any more. And when I give in, you'll thank me as though I were the Messiah."

He doesn't even bat an eyelid. Just stares at me and shrugs. "If you say so. I'm going to go take a shower. Good night, Rose."

My pride absorbs this additional hit, and I tighten my grip on the USB key and head straight for my room.

As soon as the door's closed, I stop pretending and give in to the frustration that's devouring me. I think back to his fingers in my hair, his hand on my back, his tongue against my lips . . .

The bastard.

What's his problem? He returns my kiss, then humiliates me? Is he playing hard to get, like Tito said? Or does he genuinely feel no attraction toward me? But . . . he was excited; there's no doubt about that.

I shake my head, trying to rid it of these pointless questions, and open my computer to investigate the USB key. My heart is pounding. Levi and Thomas are hiding something from me. They were spying on my father across the terrace; I'm sure of it.

And that spying had nothing to do with poker.

Two files come up on the screen, both with ridiculous names: "Mom's recipes" and "Nephew's birthday." Bizarrely, they're password protected, confirming that the names are only a ruse. Who would password protect his mother's recipe for beef stroganoff? And anyway, Levi's an only child. It makes no sense.

I wonder what the password could be, but no ideas come.

Should I send this straight to Tito? He'll know someone who can break into the file.

No. No chance. I want to know what it is first, then decide whether to share it with him. I look through my contacts and email a guy I know in Florence: Andrea, a computer science student. I ask if he can help me get around a password. The bastard says it'll cost me fifty euros. I agree.

I copy the files onto my computer and delete them from the USB key. Whatever they are, it can't be good for them to be in Levi Ivanovich's hands.

I tiptoe out of my bedroom, wanting to replace the stolen goods unnoticed while he's in the shower. I make my way stealthily past the closed bathroom door. The shower isn't on. Has he already finished?

His bag is still on the kitchen counter. Quickly, I slip the USB key back inside and head back toward my room, but just as I'm passing the bathroom, the door opens.

I freeze, caught in the act. My heart performs a somersault. Levi stops short too, looking surprised. He is disheveled, with pink cheeks and a strange light in his eyes. Even more astonishingly, he seems . . . embarrassed? Levi Ivanovich uncomfortable! Who'd have thought it?

"I was thirsty," I blurt out.

I'm about to ask if he's finished when I realize he's still wearing the same clothes. He doesn't say anything as he slips past me, just avoids my gaze, and heads down the corridor.

Very odd. He looked as guilty as I felt. I frown and go into the bathroom, expecting to find some illegal substance in there. There's no sign of him having taken a shower. But the room is strangely warm, a muggy heat that's got nothing to do with the Las Vegas climate.

What on earth could he have been . . .

Oh.

*Oh.*

I feel myself blush as all sorts of images form in my mind. My beloved fiancé isn't so indifferent after all . . .

Now all I have to do is feign indifference until he gives in first. And if sex isn't enough to trick him, make him trust me, I'll just have to make him fall in love with me.

◆ ◆ ◆

We spend the whole next day at the tournament. I'm pretending to be a journalist again. Levi acts as though nothing happened the day before, and that suits me fine. When the lunch break comes, he says he needs to rest and leaves me to eat alone.

I take the opportunity to head to the hotel restaurant and check my emails. Andrea replied to me early this morning, sending me the unlocked documents. I open them on my computer, but it takes me a few minutes to work out what they're all about.

One of the files is full of charts and tables containing information about my father's business. Numbers, turnover rates, lists of investors, and so on. My throat tightens with anxiety. How did he get his hands on all this? More importantly, why?

If I weren't already worried enough, the second file makes my blood freeze. Dozens of documents appear before my eyes, all of them with the potential to incriminate my father. Most are evidence of bribery.

It appears Levi is taking his revenge very seriously. I underestimated him. "He ruined my life," he once told me. This thing between them goes much deeper than a straightforward poker rivalry.

And yet I still don't really understand. I don't know all the details, of course—Tito has never talked to me about any of it. I just know that when I was a child, he was obsessed with Jacob Ivanovich. Then, after I thought all that was in the past, he became obsessed with Jacob's son, Levi.

The whole thing is beyond me. I agreed to do this for one reason: money. But is it worth all the sacrifices? I might hate my father, but I don't want him to lose his business. I don't want him to end up in prison. I don't want his problems to hurt my mother.

*Oh Christ.*

*Sorry, Levi,* I say to myself as I attach the files to an email to my father. *I have to protect myself.*

# Chapter 14

## Levi

***June***
***Las Vegas, USA***

"They're gone."

Thomas looks at me and frowns. I keep my expression calm and relaxed, not taking my hands out of my pockets as other players file past us to their tables.

"What do you mean, gone?"

I can guess at the questions in his eyes, but I don't have answers that will satisfy him. Yesterday, the proof was there on my USB key. This morning, it's not.

"I had it on me the whole day."

"Really?" he insists, and I sense a hint of mistrust in his voice. "Even when you went off with Rose?"

I stiffen and raise my eyes to look at him. I don't like the question, even though it's not unreasonable.

"I know you don't want to hear this, but . . ."

"It wasn't Rose. I didn't take my eyes off her all day."

Thomas is silent. I can hear his thoughts, though. He's never trusted Rose. I tell him to relax and put my hand on his arm.

"We've made copies. Nothing's lost. And even if it was, it's not a problem. This is only plan B. We've got the whole alphabet ahead of us."

I don't give him time to reply. I sit down at my place, pull out my sunglasses, and greet Li Mei with a nod as she sits down next to me.

"Fancy meeting you here." She smiles. "Things are heating up, aren't they?"

"I don't know what you're talking about. I'm bored to death."

She bursts out laughing. But she's not wrong. The games are getting harder. The ordinary players are making way for the more experienced ones. No one I haven't beaten before, though.

"Arrogant as always. Your fiancée doesn't seem to have cured you of that unattractive fault."

"My fiancée must like it," I say, getting out my chips.

Just then, Rose walks past us, dressed as a massage therapist, and gives a tiny wave. I struggle not to smile. I'm pleasantly surprised to see her being friendly, given yesterday's events. Can she have forgiven me already?

She wouldn't say a word to me this morning. I guess I deserved that. The fact is, I should never have kissed her in the first place. It was stupid. But the way she arranged the afternoon, the concerned way she took care of me—it all lowered my defenses . . .

Her first thought after discovering my weakness was to take me painting; to share her passion with me. Who else would have done that? She's . . . surprising. Rose walks a tightrope between good and bad. She's too broken to be an angel and too good to be a demon.

Despite all her faults, I'm attracted to her in a way I've never been attracted to anyone before. I don't know what it is yet: obsession, admiration, curiosity, or just plain physical attraction? Whatever it is, I have to keep on pushing her away. Rose was meant to be my secret weapon. But the more time passes, the more I worry that she'll become my one and only vulnerability.

"You'll be my weakness," I said to her on the very first day. I must have jinxed myself.

"I meant to tell you—a journalist friend of mine heard that you and I are friends . . . ," Li Mei says.

"We're not friends."

"She's interested in you," she continues, ignoring me. "She wants to do a profile of you and Rose."

"No thanks."

"It would be good for your image."

I don't answer for a long time. A profile of us is a terrible idea. The farther away from the public gaze we are, the better. Anyone who looked closely would see that Rose and I aren't in love.

"I don't need to work on my image."

"It would be a video interview for the *Glamour* YouTube channel."

I make a face, finally giving her my full attention. Isn't that a women's fashion magazine?

"*Glamour*? Since when have they been interested in us?"

Let's face it: poker only interests poker players. This isn't the Olympic Games or the Oscars, or even the Grammys. The world of poker tournaments is a lot less sexy than people think. The only reason things have been a bit different over the last few years is Tito. Love him or loathe him, he's well-known and very influential, so journalists follow him wherever he goes.

Happy to have piqued my curiosity, Li Mei smiles and smooths her skirt over her knees. She lowers her voice as she sees the croupier taking her seat, a sign that we're about to start.

"Poker is super fashionable right now. Haven't you seen the series *Cards on the Table* with Anya Taylor-Joy? It was a huge hit."

"I don't watch television."

"Of course you don't." She sighs and hands me a business card. "Look; these are the journalist's details. You might attract some sponsors."

"I'm already sponsored. Forget about it, Li Mei; it's a no."

She knew it would be and only shrugs. Not only are my tournaments all-expenses-paid; I also get a monthly income for allowing my sponsor to use my image.

I put the business card into the inner pocket of my jacket and promptly forget about it. I have other things on my mind. I need to focus, but I can't help thinking about it all: the missing files, Thomas's suspicions about Rose, Tito's provocations, and the sham fiancée who haunts my nights. I can't even control myself; I had to finish myself off like a horny teenager after our kiss. I don't like what's happening to me.

"What's up?" I ask Rose when she joins me for lunch in our usual spot next to the pool.

She's seemed preoccupied since we left the gaming room. I noticed her staring at Li Mei. I ask if she's noticed something about her.

"I don't get it."

"What?"

"Her mouth. Her eyebrows. She was showing signs of anger during your game. But . . . I don't think she was angry."

I watch her carefully, intrigued and quite impressed, I must admit. "What do you mean?"

She looks into the distance, and shakes her head a little. "She wanted people to think she was angry."

"Why?"

"No idea. To tell you the truth . . . I still can't figure her out. Lucky's the same. He tries to come across as naive and uncool, but there's something not quite right. The effort isn't always natural."

I allow myself a little smile. She's good, very good; there's no denying it. She promises to keep an eye on them, and we eat and play cards. She congratulates me when I beat her twice.

Meanwhile, I can't stop thinking about my conversation with Thomas earlier regarding the USB key. I wonder, could the disappearance of those files have some larger significance than I've acknowledged? Maybe it's a sign. After all, who am I to judge? I'm playing God, trying to punish Tito for his sins, but maybe it's not my place. I should mind my own business.

*I'm no better a man than Tito.*

"Do you think people are born good or bad?" I ask.

Rose looks up from her plate, one eyebrow raised in silent interrogation. "They say it's society that corrupts people," she says thoughtfully, "and that there's no such thing as original sin." I like that she answers naturally and doesn't find my change of subject absurd.

"But society was created a long time after humans appeared on the scene. People created it, didn't they?"

She tilts her head to one side, chewing slowly. Today she's wearing cropped jeans and a flannel shirt open over a white crop top. I love it.

"So you think people have it in their nature to be bad?" she says.

I sigh. "I think they're capable of terrible atrocities. They use war to win their arguments. And then there's slavery, rape . . . murder."

"And yet," she says with a shrug, "people are still capable of doing good things. Some spend their lives helping others. Some who find themselves in the most dangerous situations manage to find a path to solidarity, even sacrifice. Most people would die for someone they love."

"Or kill." I said it quietly, but her glance shows me she heard. My face doesn't give anything away. My chest hurts. I think of my mother, my father, and the terrible evening I can't manage to put behind me.

Rose gazes at me for longer than I'd like. Finally, she puts down her plate and wipes her mouth with her napkin.

"I think the binary opposites of good and evil are too extreme a way to look at it," she says. "Nothing is black and white. People are capable of both. And still . . . I do think we have more good than bad in us. In general, people don't want to kill, do they? And even when someone does, they usually feel guilt and regret."

She's right. It's a question with no answer. The greatest philosophers are still working on it. I smile at Rose, suddenly feeling very tired.

"I wouldn't have taken you for such an optimist."

She stands up and holds out a hand to help me up too. I take it, and she rolls her eyes as she answers me.

"What can I do? We all have our faults."

◆ ◆ ◆

Rose still isn't back when I come out of the shower. That's not unusual; she often disappears for a few hours without my knowing where she's gone. But she always returns.

I pull on a T-shirt and black joggers, and sit down on the sofa with a glass of red wine. I leaf through a book about poker, underlining parts that interest me. The silence does me good. It doesn't last long, unfortunately.

"Levi."

I keep reading as Thomas comes into the room. He repeats my name, and this time I look up. I'm surprised to see Li Mei with him. Her expression is reserved.

*Something's wrong.*

"What's going on?"

"Where's Rose?" asks Thomas irritably.

"Interesting question. Why do you ask?"

He glances at Li Mei, who is uncharacteristically silent.

"I already thought it was weird the way she kept on disappearing without telling us where she was. But since this morning, I've been paying more attention."

"Tommy," I groan. I get up, anger beginning to worm its way into my heart. "I told you not to do anything. You need to trust me."

There isn't a flicker of regret or remorse on his face. I'd forgotten that regardless of how much he respects me, Thomas does whatever he likes and always thinks he's in the right.

"I'm not sorry. Because the verdict is in: I've been searching for her for two hours with no success."

"OK. And?"

"I bumped into Li Mei in the foyer. Apparently, they saw each other earlier."

I glance at Li Mei, and she nods.

"Something's not right," she says. "Rose asked me a favor earlier. When I said I couldn't do it because I didn't have time, she . . . completely lost it."

"What kind of favor?" I ask, trying to ignore the foreboding rising inside me.

She bites her lip, hesitating, and sighs.

"She wanted me to place some bets for her. When I said no, she hurled insults at me and stormed off in a rage. That was an hour ago."

I can hardly believe it. I know Li Mei wouldn't lie, but this doesn't sound like Rose. She's got a short fuse, it's true, but she'd never lose complete control like that. Except to throw a shoe at me, of course. I look at Thomas, trying to gauge what he thinks, but he's stone-faced.

"I'll take care of it. Thank you," I say to Li Mei.

She nods, and I can see that underneath her calm expression she's worried. I suppose she and Rose must have gotten close without my noticing.

I get changed and tell Thomas not to mix himself up in this any further. I go downstairs, trying to call her mobile, but it goes straight to voicemail.

I go through all the gaming rooms, starting with the slot machines. Now that I think of it, Rose hasn't come into the public part of the casino once since we've been here. Why not, if she loves it so much? Why has she never suggested that we go there together for an evening of fun?

Why ask Li Mei to place bets for her? Did she want to hide it from me?

"Looking for your 'fiancée'?"

*Shit.* I grit my teeth and turn around. Tito is smiling cruelly at me, a bottle of water in one hand. He must have only just finished playing.

I look him up and down, and not in a friendly way. Then I turn to walk away.

"Mind your own business," I say.

"I know where she is."

I stop and turn around slowly. He's savoring the moment, his arms crossed over his muscular chest.

"She was in the process of pissing your money away at blackjack an hour ago." He sighs. "Then when she ran out of chips, she laid into the croupiers. It wasn't a pretty sight . . ."

I know he might just be saying this to hurt me, but I can see in his eyes that it's the truth. His eyes narrow as he says, more seriously, "You shouldn't let her go near the tables."

My first instinct is to spit in his face. My second, more reasonable one, is to force a laugh. What right does he have to give me advice about my fiancée?

"It's true that you're an expert when it comes to relationships." I smile, keeping my cool. "How is your wife, by the way? Still asking for a divorce?"

Tito is far less gifted than I am in the art of hiding his emotions. He clenches his jaw in fury.

"You're playing a dangerous game, Levi."

"Is that what you said to my father before you stabbed him in the back?"

"Your father didn't have the strength of character you have. I admit that. But you're picking the wrong fight. I have nothing against you."

He's terrified. He knows what I'm capable of, and he's afraid. This simple fact gives me the strength to keep going. I shake my head and raise my hands, lying shamelessly.

"I've told you: this is the last time I'll play against you. If I win, so much the better. If not, I'll get over it. I've found love. That's far more important than an old quarrel that doesn't even concern me."

With that, I leave, and he shouts at my retreating back, "Have fun while it lasts!"

The asshole. I try to forget him as I make my way to the blackjack tables. I'm afraid Rose might be spotted counting cards and get herself kicked out of the hotel. That would be bad. Especially since they'll make the connection between her and me.

I scan the room, feeling frustrated. I'm about to call Thomas to help me when someone puts a hand on my shoulder. I jump and turn to see Lucky behind me.

"Are you looking for Rose?" he asks.

"Have you seen her?"

He nods and scratches his head. "I bumped into her just after a croupier told her to leave the table. She looked a bit wired. I asked her if she was OK, and she asked me to lend her some money."

I frown in confusion.

Lucky runs his hand through his hair. "She saw me hesitate and swore she'd pay me back double."

"Did you give it to her?"

"I didn't get the chance. She came to her senses immediately and told me to forget it. Then she left in a mad rush."

I ask which way she went, and he points toward the fire exit. He offers to come with me, but I decline and thank him for his help. I have no idea what's going on, but whatever it is, it's nothing good.

None of this makes any sense.

I cross the room and walk through the fire exit into a silent, deserted stairwell. I call her name, but there's no reply. I go down a few floors, and just as I'm about to give up, I stop dead.

A small form is hunched on the floor near me. Her back is against the cold, white wall. Her head is in her arms, leaning on her knees, but I recognize her dark hair.

"Rose?" I murmur gently, *"Lyubimaya."*

She looks up at me miserably. I notice scratches on her left knee. She's bleeding. She doesn't look like herself. My heart pounds.

"What happened?"

# Chapter 15

## Rose

***June***
***Las Vegas, USA***

I haven't felt this way in a long time. I've been worse, but I know this looks bad enough. I'm kicking myself for letting Levi see me like this.

I'd promised myself I'd never let him see the three-headed monster inside me. I thought I could do it. It would seem I overestimated myself. My mother was right—recovery is never permanent. If you drop your guard, if you tempt the devil, the illness returns.

"What happened?" Levi asks me in a voice that's surprisingly gentle and patient.

He came looking for me. I guess my absence aroused his suspicions. And he's right to be suspicious. I really am betraying him.

"Nothing. I wanted to play one game; that's all. It was a mistake."

My voice is no more than an exhausted whisper. I despise the weakness it betrays. Levi crouches in front of me, one knee on the ground, and takes my calf delicately in his hands. His skin is like silk on mine, his touch light as a feather.

"What's this?" he says, pointing to the graze on my knee.

"I misjudged the height of the steps," I admit, avoiding his intense gaze, ashamed.

I don't add *because I'm drunk*, but I think he's guessed as much. Levi doesn't make fun of me. Instead, he bends down and blows gently on my broken skin. Even this little gesture is enough to make my spine tingle.

"Have you drunk any water today? Your lips are dry."

"I'm fine."

He's still gazing at me, his face impassive. All the signs in his face tell me he's angry, but his voice is soft, and the way he's touching me shows he wants to be gentle.

"Let's go."

Abruptly, he slips one arm under my legs and another one under my shoulders and lifts me up with no effort at all. I'm about to protest, but he holds me close to his chest, and words fail me. What's he playing at, exactly? Just because I have a little cut on my knee doesn't mean I can't walk.

I want to tell him this as we exit the stairwell, but for some reason I stay silent. Instead, I join my hands around his neck, surprised by his strength. His closeness calms me down. I feel . . . protected. It's not a feeling I have often, so I embrace it greedily.

When we come out into the foyer, I understand why he's behaving so affectionately. My blood freezes when I see Li Mei, Thomas, and Lucky deep in conversation near the fountain. They break off as soon as they spot us.

"Was this really necessary?" I whisper into his neck.

He raises one eyebrow as though he doesn't know what I mean. I'm about to explain when my eyes fall on Tito, standing with his arms crossed near the escalators. I stiffen, ill at ease. My father narrows his eyes and walks away.

I hide my pink cheeks against Levi's T-shirt until we reach our suite. There, he puts me down carefully on the sofa and fetches a first-aid kit from the bathroom. He hands me a bottle of water, and I let him sit down on the coffee table opposite me; then I take off my shoe and put my foot up on his leg.

I don't like the way my heart beats faster when he touches me. I wish I could slow it down, but I can't. He disinfects the wound and puts a bandage on it, and I tremble every time his fingers brush my skin.

"It's not as bad as all that," I protest.

"I didn't say it was," he says simply.

When he's finished, he puts the first-aid kit down next to him and takes my foot in his hands. His eyes devour me, full of questions that I'm sure he's struggling not to ask.

I down half the bottle of water he gave me. I know that I never hydrate enough, but I'd forgotten that you can't get away with that in Las Vegas. And alcohol doesn't count.

"Li Mei told me you asked her to place bets for you."

*He certainly doesn't waste any time*. I sigh inwardly. Of course, that sneak ratted on me! The truth is, I don't resent her for it. She agreed to help me without asking anything in return, and the minute she couldn't do what I asked, I bit her head off.

I hate the person I become when I'm craving a game.

"I should never have come here," I say.

That couldn't be more true. Levi waits attentively, saying nothing and giving me space to go on. But should I? Of course I shouldn't. But . . . I want to talk to someone about it, anyone. In my heart, I know he'll understand. That he won't judge me. He might even be able to tell me what to do.

"In Macau, you asked what my poison was, remember? Well, this is it," I say with a sad smile. Fuck, I really want to smoke right now. The idea makes me laugh inside, and I add, "Or I should say, it's one of my poisons. Because one addiction usually leads to others."

I see him connecting the dots in his mind. Gambling, alcohol, cigarettes . . . I'm completely broken. My mother always tells me I'm too young to say something like that. My father says I'm weak-minded, and that I get that from my mother. Ever since my recovery, he hasn't let me go near a casino. I embarrass him in front of his friends.

"You're addicted to gambling?" Levi murmurs, with no trace of judgment in his voice.

I nod. He asks me how long this has been going on. Now that I've started confiding in him, I can't stop.

"I started playing when I was a teenager, with my . . . mentor. More for fun than anything else. But when I turned eighteen, I celebrated by going to a casino for the first time." I smile at the thought of that memorable evening. "At first, it was fun. I don't know exactly when it started to get out of control. Falling into addiction is a bit like falling in love; you don't realize what's happening until it's too late."

His silence is strangely comforting. He makes me want to tell him everything, to reveal more of myself, and God knows that's risky.

"You realized that with your talent, you could get rich," he says quietly.

"Exactly. Before I knew it, I was caught in the spiral. I spent all my time playing, either in casinos or online. I had no more social life. To be honest . . . it's why I dropped out of school. I lied before. I never managed to finish anything. I was skipping my college classes, wasn't sleeping at night—all so I could spend more time gambling."

Memories float to the surface of my mind, and I confront them bitterly. I remember the adrenaline, the feeling that I was all-powerful, then the disappointment whenever I lost all the money I'd won. "I'll win it all back," I'd tell myself every time. "I just need to bet twice as much!"

The classic vicious circle.

"I used to steal money from my parents when I had none left to bet," I admit, hanging my head. "Or sometimes I'd borrow it from other people. My mother looked at my computer and discovered my online gambling habit. She and my father did everything they could: changed my passwords, took away my money and hid theirs, confiscated my computer, grounded me, everything."

"And that didn't work?"

I bite my lip, laughing softly. If only it were that simple. Addiction can overcome any obstacle. It always finds a way of getting what it wants, even if that involves taking extreme measures.

"When I discovered my father had changed all the passwords on the computer so I couldn't play, we had a huge fight. He and my mother were about to go somewhere, to visit my aunt, I think. They got in the car and told me we'd talk about it that evening. I thought they were abandoning me, so I . . . I threw myself into the road in front of the car and said they weren't going anywhere, that they'd have to run me over.

"I realize as I say this how messed up it is. How sick I was back then. I could think of nothing but gambling. After that day, my mother made me get help. I agreed to do it because even I could see that things were going wrong, and I had no control over the situation.

"It took time and a lot of relapses, but I managed it. Now, a few years down the line, I'm in recovery. But it's a fragile recovery. Picture a dandelion in the wind. And today the wind was too strong for me."

"The debts you mentioned . . . are they because of this?"

I nod. He sighs deeply, gazing into the distance. I can't tell what he's thinking. Is he disappointed? Not that I'm interested. I don't care what he thinks of me.

At least . . . I wish I didn't. But deep down, I know I do. I want him to think well of me. I want him to think I'm beautiful, intelligent, talented, funny, and wonderful. I want his attention. Not just anyone's attention—*his*.

"But . . . you're fine now?"

"Would you ask that of an ex-alcoholic who'd got a job as a wine merchant?"

He grimaces at the irony of the situation. "Rose, I'm sorry . . ."

I ask him why, surprised by this admission. This time I hold his gaze. His expression is guilty and sincere. He sighs again and looks away, shaking his head.

"I was the one who asked you to come. I don't regret it, but . . . if I'd known, I wouldn't have done it."

"Really?" I say teasingly, not believing him.

"What do you think?"

"I think there's nothing you wouldn't do to win the tournament and humiliate Tito. Other people's problems aren't *your* problem."

He looks at me without saying anything for a long time. He knows I'm right. I'm starting to know him. We share a selfishness that turns us both into lost children. I'm not judging him. Far from it. I know I'd have done the same.

Levi lowers my foot back to the floor and rests his elbows on his knees, giving me a piercing look. I've obviously touched a sore spot.

"That's true. But there's a difference. I've seen the damage addiction can do. I wouldn't wish it on anyone . . . So yes, I'm sorry."

Oh. I fold my legs underneath me on the sofa, suddenly feeling very vulnerable. I've just handed him the perfect weapon with which to destroy me. But then again, I know his biggest secret. We're even now.

"Are you talking about yourself?" I ask.

He shakes his head and stares into the distance. "My father."

Suddenly things begin to fall into place.

*I don't like alcoholics,* he said to me. And he told me smoking would kill me. And then there were Tito's taunts when they met the other day. I should've realized sooner. Did his father die because of an addiction? I know it's wrong, that I'm supposed to hate him, that he's my worst enemy, etc., but I feel a wave of compassion for him.

Tito's never told me about any of this. I jumped in headfirst without asking any questions. I only knew Levi's name, but that was enough. I didn't want to know anything about him because I didn't want to feel any attachment to someone I wanted so badly to hate.

"Did your father ever recover?" I ask.

"He never got the chance," he says simply.

"And your mother?" He never mentions her. Has he even got one?

"In prison."

*Holy fuck*. At first, I think he must be joking, but he's deadly serious. I sense his sadness too: his face has softened, and his eyebrows furrow as he looks at the floor.

"Involuntary manslaughter. She pleaded self-defense."

Oh wow. So his father's dead, and his mother's in prison for murder. Coincidence? Could his mother have . . . killed her husband? But that's awful! Why didn't I know about this? I thought I was broken, but Levi must be living with far worse things than I could even imagine. He smiles faintly at my shock, then puts a reassuring hand on my knee.

"I think you'd be better off going home, Rose."

I can feel myself go pale. Go home? No, no, no. That's not part of the plan. I can't. My father would kill me. He'd know I'm useless, that I'm weaker than my demons.

*And I wouldn't see Levi again.*

"Why? We haven't finished."

"Rose, you're in a casino. A casino where there's a world tournament taking place, and you're walking around among the players all day. It couldn't be much worse."

"I'm fine!" I assure him as I stand up. "Believe me. And anyway, I need this money."

He gets up, too, looking thoughtful. I know what he's going to say before he even opens his mouth. He's going to say he'll pay me anyway, and in that case, I'd have no excuse to stay.

"I can give you . . ."

"Please." I cut him off.

He looks at me in silence.

He can't send me home. I need to stay here. Close to him.

For Tito, of course.

"I don't know. If it happens again . . ."

"Levi," I say, taking his hand and smiling reassuringly, "I'm not going to have another relapse. I promise. I'm strong. Look. I haven't played since I was in Macau, and I'm fine! I only turned to Li Mei because I really need to repay my debts. I could have gambled myself earlier, but I took the precaution of asking someone else to do it for me. Today was . . . a one-off. OK?"

He doesn't blink once as he looks at me. I look right back at him, praying he'll believe me. I almost believe myself. In the end, he nods and says he'll trust me.

"I'm going to order some food," he says. "Why don't you take a bath while I'm gone?"

He doesn't need to ask me twice.

◆ ◆ ◆

I wander back into the kitchen, wrapped in a white towel, makeup-free with my hair still wet. Levi's waiting for me by the island, which is covered in bags.

"I didn't know what you wanted, but I remembered you like sushi."

I open the bags and to my surprise find the same order I got a few days ago. I'll admit he has a good memory. I thank him with a smile.

My bath has done me a world of good. Just after I got out, I found a new message from my father, saying, "How's it going?" I'm glad he didn't see me at the blackjack tables . . .

I look up at Levi, guilt clouding my vision. The more I get to know him, the more I feel a bond between us. He's not what I'd imagined, and I regret what I have to do to him.

*Technically speaking, you're under no obligation,* my conscience replies. I silence it with a swig of water. He asks me if my knee still hurts, and I shake my head. I tell him I want to apologize to Li Mei and Lucky, innocent victims of my crisis, and he agrees that it would be a good idea.

When all the sushi's gone, I disappear into my room and come back with a little gift. I sit down and hand it to Levi. He raises his eyebrows, his mouth full.

"I didn't have time to give it to you today, but . . . I bought you something."

"It's not my birthday."

"So what?"

"I didn't know we were on gift-giving terms."

"We're engaged, *amore mio*."

He grins and accepts the gift. He tears off the wrapping but pauses when he sees what's inside. He doesn't say anything for a while, his expression unreadable.

"What is this?" It's not really a question. He knows very well what it is. I refuse to be deterred.

"It's a color chart."

He gives me an icy look.

"No need to get your claws out!" I say, rolling my eyes. "I thought you'd be pleased."

"Rose, in case you haven't got this yet, I *can't see* colors."

"I get that, thanks, but I've had an idea. Give it to me, and I'll show you."

I take it out of his hands, feeling confident now, and take a sheet of paper and a pen from a drawer. Then I fan out all the color strips in front of him.

"There are two hundred thirteen colors here. On this side," I say, showing him the right-hand strips, "are all the colors you probably don't recognize. On the other side are all the nuances of white, gray, and black: the ones you've told me you can see as well as I can. Are you with me so far?"

"So far, yes." He sighs, not understanding what I'm driving at.

"I know it's not very precise, and maybe it's a stupid idea, but I thought it might help you." I point to a shade of dark gray and show him the other colors as a comparison. "Out of all these colors, which are the same shade as number 9004?"

Now he looks surprised, as though he's getting the idea. I explain to him that for all the colors on the chart that he can't see there are other colors that he *can* see—and that it's possible to notice which ones are similar and use that knowledge to narrow down the possibilities.

He plays along, examining the different shades. In the end, he points to several, and I write them down.

"6012, 5022, 3007, 4007, 3011 . . ."

He's pointed to red, brown, green, purple, and orange, all the darkest tints. We follow the same process for all the colors, which takes us over an hour. Once we've finished, I admire our detailed table.

"Ta-da!"

Levi shakes his head without saying anything, but I ignore him.

"OK, we're going to do an experiment. Don't move. I'll be right back."

I go and put on a different shirt and pair of trousers, choosing the colors at random; then I come back. I point to my reddish-brown shirt and ask him what color it is. He looks at it, and for a second, I get the distinct impression he's scrutinizing my breasts, but then he turns to look at our chart.

"It looks like that tone," he says, pointing to 9007. "So, by process of elimination . . . it's one of these eleven colors. Great. That really helps."

I glare at him. Sarcasm, really? When all I'm trying to do is help?

"Give it a try. It's a process of elimination."

He has zero interest in doing what I'm asking him to do, I know, but he does it anyway. He manages to eliminate half the corresponding colors. I hide my smile when I see that auburn isn't one of them. He can grumble as much as he likes, but my method works.

I'm a genius.

"And now, you can think about it in context. Which of these colors do you think I might be wearing?"

To be honest, it's quite easy. The other choices are yellow—he already knows I hate yellow, burgundy, and navy blue. He points to auburn almost straightaway, looking at me with an expression full of hope, like a child.

My stomach turns over as I look at him. I'm pretty sure that even if he'd got the answer wrong, I'd have lied just to make him happy.

"Bravo!"

"Really?" he says, amazed but skeptical.

"Really. Of course, it won't work every time, but it might help, don't you think? OK, now my trousers. Which col . . ."

"Beige."

I don't even have time to finish my sentence. I stop, open-mouthed. He didn't pause for a second before answering. I ask him how he knows, and he just smiles and shrugs.

"It looks like beige."

"You're lying. You cheated; admit it."

"How could I have cheated?" he asks me innocently.

I don't know, but I'm still convinced he did. I let it go and clear the things off the table. He watches me, a strange light in his eyes. It's probably the wine. His eyes always shine when he's had a little too much to drink. It's adorable.

*Adorable? Since when has it been adorable?*

I decide I'd better leave before I do something stupid, so I tell him I'm tired.

"Rose," he calls me back, his chin resting in his hand as he looks at me.

"Mm?"

"A journalist from *Glamour* wants to do a video interview with us."

I stop walking, amazed. *Glamour*? Did I hear right?

"What do you mean, 'with us'?"

"With us as a couple. What do you think?"

I want to ask why he hasn't already turned down the offer. It's a terrible idea, after all. And let's be honest; we both know he doesn't need the publicity. The readers of *Glamour* aren't a potential source of business. Besides, Levi couldn't care less about his reputation.

What's behind this, then?

"Why not?" I say.

"OK, I'll call them."

I nod. He's still looking at me, a little smile on his lips, probably waiting for me to leave. The mood has shifted. Is it because he's had a drink, or because of what happened today? Whatever it is, he's not looking at me in the same way he did this morning.

"You know . . . ," I murmur awkwardly, "Levi Ivanovich is very different from what people say he is."

He raises an eyebrow. "And what do people say?"

I think of the rumors I've seen on the internet, the whispers I've heard in the hotel corridors, and my father's warnings about him even before I met him.

"That you're a bad boy. That you're a selfish, manipulative, greedy, cruel, dangerous womanizer."

For a moment, there's only silence. He doesn't stop smiling, far from it. His smile widens as he suppresses a sigh whose meaning I don't understand.

"You should probably still watch out, Rose," he tells me at last. "You know what they say. Where there's smoke, there's fire."

# Chapter 16

## Levi

***June***
***Las Vegas, USA***

I can't sleep.

It's stupid, but I can't get Rose out of my thoughts. She's gone to bed, and here I am lying awake, my arm over my closed eyes, still dressed. First the painting lesson, now the color chart. It's crazy, but I feel more touched than I should by these gestures. Because they mean she thought of me. She came up with a way of helping me. I don't know how to take that. The very idea softens my heart, and that worries me.

I'm already too attached to her. I like her and am infuriated by her in equal measure, and she only infuriates me because I like her.

I even agreed to this *Glamour* interview because I thought it would interest her.

I'm weakening. But how can I not when she looks at me with those eyes? How can I resist when she smiles at me like that? When she touches me at every opportunity.

I feel like I could explode at any moment. Because wanting to go to bed with somebody is one thing, and I know how that feels. But this . . . this is different. The things I dream of doing to her almost make me blush. And worse, when I'm not fantasizing about tying her to my bed and ravishing her, I'm imagining taking her hand . . . holding her in my arms all night . . . stroking her hair and kissing her shoulder.

"What are you, crazy?" I curse to myself, sitting up on my bed.

And now I'm talking to myself.

Suddenly, there's a knock at my door. I assume it's Thomas, who must have returned since I came into my room. I tell him to come in but am surprised to see Rose's silhouette outlined in the doorway. She looks at me, her hand on the door handle, and I try hard not to let my gaze wander over her body.

"I wanted to know what time we need to get up in the morning," she says quietly. "I thought you would still be awake. Nightmares?"

I swallow at the sight of her short, pale nightdress and her magnificent bare thighs. I'm ready to bet she's not wearing anything underneath. She must have just taken a shower. *Fuck*.

I undo another button of my shirt, feeling like I'm burning up despite the air-conditioning.

"I'd have had to be asleep to have a nightmare."

She doesn't say anything, just continues to lean against the doorframe. I don't like knowing she's there, but at the same time, it's what I've been hoping for—for longer than I'd like to admit.

"What's stopping you sleeping? The present or the past?"

I force a laugh. "Both. Sometimes I feel like there's no difference."

"Because you're still living in the past," Rose says, crossing her arms. There's no trace of judgment in her voice.

I ask what she means. She sighs, seems to hesitate, then shrugs.

"You might not like hearing this, but I think revenge is stupid and childish. And the reason you're here now is for revenge."

I don't much like the turn this conversation is taking. But I like talking things through with her too much to stop; I love the way her mind works. It's incredibly sexy.

And I admit, I also want her to stay longer.

"But it can bring satisfaction," I say.

"True . . . but for how long?"

I don't say anything to that.

She shakes her head. "Getting revenge doesn't achieve anything. It only makes us more miserable, because we hang onto something instead of letting it go. We remain obsessed with a wound that we should let heal."

That's easy to say. I already know all that.

"What if the person deserves it? Imagine a man murders your mother," I say as casually as I can. "Wouldn't you want to do everything you could to find him and make him pay?"

She thinks about this very seriously. I realize that although we're very like one another, Rose's character is still quite different from mine. She has fire inside her, but she never uses it against others. She destroys herself without hurting another living thing, whereas I get the whole world involved in my quest for revenge, with no concern for the consequences.

"Yes . . . but that would make me just the same as him, wouldn't it?" she murmurs. "And once it was done, would it bring my mother back? Would the man regret what he'd done? His death would have been easy and quick, but I'd be condemned to a miserable life, full of suffering and guilt. The only person who'd end up punished would be me."

I look at her, shaken. This is the first time I've ever doubted what I'm doing, and all because of a few remarks made by Rose Alfieri. Thomas has always gone along with my desire to make Tito pay, simply because he doesn't care. He's incapable of putting himself in my shoes, of imagining how I might feel, or how anybody might feel, for that matter.

He does it because I asked him to, and that's that.

Will the result of all this be worth my efforts? The sweat and tears, the sense of guilt, putting my life on hold for several years to focus all my attention on this one man? A man who probably couldn't care less about me.

Rose sees me thinking and adds, in a softer tone, "We think revenge will set us free. But in the end . . . it puts us in a cage. I don't want to live like that. Do you?"

I think about that as I plumb the depths of her sublime eyes. It's like a revelation. I think about all the years I've wasted brooding about Tito and how to destroy him. Time I could have used to focus on myself and build something that would make me happy.

In the end, I'm the one I've made miserable.

But after all, perhaps that was what I always meant to do, at least unconsciously.

*"What are you punishing yourself for, Rose?"*

*"Excellent question . . . What about you, Levi?"*

I laugh to myself, feeling unsettled, then sigh and rub my eyes. Rose couldn't be more right. I should stop while I still can. I could lose the tournament on purpose, go back to Russia, pick up my mother when she's released from prison, find love, and live a happy life with my past safely behind me.

Except I'm nearly at the end now. I'm almost there. If I abandon this now, it will all have been for nothing. I have no choice but to keep going.

But right now, I don't want to think about that. I want to feel invaded by her. Nobody else.

"Rose?"

She raises one eyebrow, on her guard. I smile at her ever so slightly before getting up and slowly walking over to her. I see her stiffen as I move toward her, her eyes darkening. The words flow from my mouth before I can stop them.

"What do I have to do . . . to be forgiven?"

My voice is quiet and deep. The desire I feel for her is impossible to contain. Even more so when she plays the innocent and murmurs, "For what?"

In front of her now, I look at her but don't touch. Instead, I reach over to the door . . . and close it behind her. She opens her mouth as though to take a breath, but it catches in her throat.

I lower my head, my nose grazing hers, and pretend I can't remember, whispering, "What was it? 'I'm going to make you crawl, grovel, and beg until you can't beg any more'—was that what you said?"

Her chest heaves, and she trembles violently as I trace one finger, light as a feather, down her spine.

"What else?" I breathe against her ear, my own pulse accelerating. "Ah yes . . . 'And when I give in, you'll thank me as though I were the Messiah.' Was that it?"

My lips brush her ear innocently, imprisoning the lobe for a fraction of a second before moving down her jawline. She told me once that she'd never try anything with me again, and I thought it was for the best. I thought I was too proud to ever make the first move.

I was wrong. Thomas was right. I'm just a man, and Rose is an enchantress straight from the underworld. The forbidden fruit, so very tempting.

My blood thunders in my veins as my hand moves to the back of her neck, stroking her hair where it meets the skin, and then I pull her closer in. The desire to kiss her is stronger than anything else in me. Her gaze is indecency itself—intense, seductive, and defiant.

"Open your mouth," I say, my lips against hers.

"You're not begging."

A smile escapes me as I drop a chaste kiss on her heart-shaped mouth. I promise her in a whisper, "I will soon."

She tries to reply, but I cut her off, covering her half-open mouth with my own. I plunge my tongue inside, meeting hers wildly. She groans against my lips, the sound echoing within my chest. Her lips are warm and moist, like her skin, which is burning at the touch of my hand on her waist.

I push my hips against hers, backing her against the door with a thud. Her hands burrow into my hair as she returns my kiss with violence and passion. *God, it's good.* I didn't know kissing could be like this.

I almost want to take my time.

Almost.

I've already waited too long; I need to touch her now, quickly, before one of us changes our mind. I'm about to break away from our kiss when she suddenly begins to suck my tongue. I groan, my body aching with impatience. Rose pulls on my hair as I nibble her lower lip.

My mouth makes its way over her chin and along her neck, which I bite, suck, and lick with devotion. She's sure to have a mark tomorrow, but that doesn't seem to bother her, because she tilts her head back to give me better access, her fingers exploring under the collar of my shirt.

"If you stop again after this, I'll kill you," she warns me, her breathing growing more and more uneven.

*Oh no, this time I'm going all the way.* I'd give a lot to see the color of her cheeks right now. They must be glowing, surely. Her whole body is red-hot, to my great satisfaction.

Rose pushes my head down, making me go lower. I let her do it, more excited than ever, and groan as I kiss her stomach through the silk.

"Savor this, Rose."

She stares at me as my hands slide over her hips, then her thighs, down to the soft skin of her calves.

"I only ever get down on my knees to pray . . . but I'll make an exception for you."

I get down on one knee, then both. I move more slowly now, more gently, too, the exact opposite of the speed and urgency of my beating heart. I don't break our eye contact as I beg her, with a little smile. "Please . . . Rose . . ." I murmur in Russian, which she doesn't speak, that she is beautiful. "Let me taste you."

Thank God, she doesn't make me grovel any longer. She bites her lip and nods, trembling under my hands. I run them back up her legs, passing underneath the hem of her nightdress to her bottom. Then I pull on her lace G-string, draw it down to her ankles, and toss it away.

"Such a beautiful color . . . ," I whisper, lifting her delicate nightdress up over her hips.

"You can't even see it."

Pause. I flash her a wicked smile. What does she imagine? I'm a model student. And if I'm not mistaken, it must be . . .

"It's rose-colored, isn't it? Like you."

She has no answer to that. She looks at me, open-mouthed, as I lift the nightdress still farther, up to her stomach. She's so beautiful. So soft. At my mercy.

Or am I at hers?

I put my hands on her buttocks and kiss her where her thighs meet. Her nightdress falls over my hair, where Rose's fingers are already entwined. I almost let out another groan just as my tongue makes its first contact with her skin.

I've fantasized about this moment, dreamed of this closeness, for so long . . . I've wondered so often how she'd taste . . . and now I know. Her essence is pure honey on my tongue. I lick her skin with short, delicate strokes, lingering over the place that elicits her first groan. She swears out loud, an obscenity that almost makes me laugh, and tightens her fingers in my hair.

I grab her buttocks and pull her toward me, galvanized by her reactions, and push my tongue into her.

*"Dio mio!"* she cries out, stiffening immediately.

I whisper to her to relax, but as soon as I speed up, she tenses again. I kiss her thigh tenderly, then stand up and, taking hold of the hem of her nightdress, pull it up and over her head.

Oh Jesus. Her breasts are absolutely perfect.

"Why are you tense?" I whisper, kissing her cheek. "Let yourself go."

"I want to touch you."

"You have to wait your turn," I murmur, shaking my head.

I resist the urge to take off all my clothes and take her hand, leading her to the bed. I lay her down on her back and sit astride her, caressing her hips, then her waist, then her breasts, which I take in both my hands.

"You're magnificent," I say. "Absolutely perfect." The words come out in my native Russian.

She takes my face in her hands as I bend down to give her a long, sensuous kiss. When I break away, I imprison her nipples with my lips, one by one. I lick and suck them until she's panting heavily. Finally, she begs me to move lower.

I don't need to be asked twice. I touch her with my fingers first, to help her relax. Then I kneel on the floor again, pass my arms under her thighs, and pull her toward me hard.

I taste her again, tenderly, my fingers moving inside her. The sensation is nothing short of divine. She's warm and moist all around me, and I have just one desire: to enter her. Rose's moans are getting louder, and she's lifting her hips toward my face.

I can't hold on any longer. I get up and join her on the bed, lying on my back so she can climb on top of me. I catch hold of her thighs again and continue licking her. Rose seems just as impatient as I am, moving back and forth against my lips.

*Shit.* Rose Alfieri is fucking my mouth. Unbelievably well too. It's the sexiest thing I've ever seen.

"Admit it," she pants. "The other day, in the bathroom . . ." I groan against her, my cheeks burning. She clearly realized. Anyone would have guessed, seeing me come out of there.

"Were you thinking of me while you were getting off?"

I nod, moving my fingers inside her again. My erection is pushing so hard against my jeans, begging for release, that it hurts.

"Were you imagining that it was my hands around you?"

*Oh fuck.* If she carries on, I'm going to come while I'm still fully dressed. I shake my head, my heart ready to explode.

"My mouth?" She tries again, straddling me sensually.

I nod as her thighs begin to tremble. And not with fear. She swears again, tightening herself around my fingers. I take that as a sign to accelerate. She moans again and again, her eyes closed, and trembles more and more violently against my tongue.

Rose explodes against my mouth with a symphony of erotic sounds, and for an instant—a wonderful instant—everything is perfect. Then, the next instant, a totally different sound tears through the room.

I clamp my hands over my ears, memories hurtling at me, then try to shield Rose with my body. Taken by surprise, she pushes me away.

"Levi . . . Levi . . . It's just fireworks!"

I don't see her or hear her. I'm caught up in a tornado of sounds that leave me terrified. The explosions don't stop; in fact they get faster and faster. I feel as though I'm about to burst.

I see my father again, his hands around my mother's neck. His crazy eyes. It's as if he were here again, right next to me, ready to strangle me for having dared challenge him.

*No, no, no. Please. Calm down.*

Rose disappears for a moment and comes back, holding my noise-reducing headphones. She puts them on me and rests her warm hands on my neck.

I open my eyes again, paralyzed with fear, and see her worried expression. She's pulled her nightdress back on, as though nothing happened, but the sheen of sweat on her forehead confirms that I didn't invent it all. I've just ruined a supremely perfect moment.

I grow calmer, but my throat is still tight with tears I can't shed. Her face is clearly asking the question I fear most: "What's going on?"

I don't know what gets into me at that moment. I don't know if it's because of what we've just shared, the vulnerability I'm feeling, or the fear that's gripping my heart.

Or maybe it's the fact that I can't hear myself that causes me to murmur the words, painfully.

"I killed my father."

# Chapter 17

## Rose

***June***
***Las Vegas, USA***

I don't stop to think for long.

My hands still trembling, I hurry to Thomas's room to wake him up. I have absolutely no idea what to do, but he'll know. I knock, but nobody answers. He must be asleep.

I can't wait—I open the door.

"Thomas? Sorry to disturb you, but Levi isn't well . . ."

I stop short. Thomas isn't asleep. He's sitting cross-legged on his bed, and Li Mei and Lucky are sitting next to him. The three of them look at me wide-eyed, as though I've caught them red-handed.

"What's going on?" Thomas asks. He's already jumped up. "Where's Levi?"

I'm still shaken, but I reply, "In his room. I don't know what happened. I think he's having a panic attack. What are those two doing here?"

Thomas doesn't reply. He heads straight for Levi's room. I have no idea what's going on. Li Mei gives me a weak smile and puts her hand on my arm, murmuring, "Don't worry. Come with me."

OK . . . Lucky doesn't say anything, but he looks worried. We all follow Thomas. When we get to Levi's room, he's just where I left him, sitting on the floor and leaning back against his bed. He's still wearing the noise-reducing headphones. Thomas squats down in front of him as Li Mei and Lucky follow him into the room. I'm the only one who hangs back.

I feel strangely uneasy, as though I don't fit in here. As though I'm not welcome.

"Levi, are you OK?"

His eyes are still closed, but his breathing is calm. I'm almost sure he hasn't heard. Thomas turns to me and asks what happened.

"We . . . were talking," I lie, trying not to draw attention to my thin nightdress. "Then all of a sudden, he started panicking. I think it was the fireworks. They scared him."

Thomas's furrowed brow relaxes as if in sudden understanding. He takes the headphones off Levi, who slowly opens his eyes.

"Tommy," he says weakly, seeming surprised.

"Are you OK?"

Levi gives him a tired, lopsided smile. "I'm perfect."

He refuses to look at me. He registers the presence of Li Mei and Lucky but doesn't seem very surprised. More like resigned.

"He's lying. He's not OK," I say to Thomas. "He . . . he said something. I think he's delirious."

"I'm not delirious." He laughs softly, then heaves a deep sigh. "I wish I were."

"What did he say?"

I glance at Thomas, then at the others, unable to open my mouth. I can't say it, not in front of them. I'm about to tell them to forget the whole thing when Levi looks up and urges me in a low voice, "Go on. Tell them."

I still hesitate. What if he isn't delirious? After all, I haven't known Levi for long. But I can't help trying to deny his claim. I don't want to believe it. Because I have to know him. To like him. Levi isn't a murderer.

"He said he killed his father."

Nobody says a word. But they don't seem surprised. All three look at me, then turn to Levi, who shrugs.

"Well, this isn't embarrassing at all . . . ," Lucky says.

"This is the kind of thing you're meant to confess once you're *actually married*, Levi," jokes Li Mei. "Definitely not in the middle of a roll in the hay, for God's sake."

Thomas frowns at her. "Huh?"

"Oh, come on! That's obviously what they were doing. 'Talking' is code for 'fucking.'"

*Oh my God.*

"Even less embarrassing now!" says Lucky.

I look at them, dazed, not knowing how to react. What the hell is all this? Why are they joking about something so serious? More to the point, why does Li Mei seem to know this is a fake engagement?

"Levi?"

He finally looks me in the eye and nods. "Yeah, I know. I owe you an explanation."

I cross my arms as he gets up, his shirt half-unbuttoned over his chest.

"Rose, my love, let me introduce you to Thomas, Li Mei, and Lucky, my one and only family."

◆ ◆ ◆

All five of us are sitting on the sofa in the living room in silence. Lucky has made coffee, and I've pulled on a bathrobe over my nightdress. What happened between Levi and me seems strangely distant already.

I glance furtively at Li Mei and Lucky, who've started squabbling about something. They look like totally different people. The poker queen has swapped out her colorful girly clothes for an oversized tracksuit, and her acolyte is wearing a plain T-shirt and jeans, a far cry from his retro shirts and fishing hats.

"So . . . you know each other? Outside of the tournament, I mean?"

"We've known each other for years, yes. We're his only friends—no offense, Levi," says Li Mei.

He forces a smile at this, but his eyes immediately return to me. I don't know how to react. I'm way out of my depth. I guess Li Mei and Lucky must also be in on the act, helping him with his stupid revenge against my father; it's the only explanation.

"Tell me everything," I say firmly. "From the start."

He agrees readily. I cradle my coffee in my hands as he begins in a low voice.

"My father was Russian, and my mother's Spanish. They met when they were very young . . . and it was love at first sight. Everyone in the neighborhood knew Jacob and Paloma. My father had already started playing poker before I was born. It was his life; much more important to him than his wife, who preferred her child, her handicapped runt of a son, to him."

Ouch. This is painful to hear, maybe because I know what it means to have a father who puts his passion over his family. I guess that was the reason our parents were friends; they had that much in common.

"He would often leave us to go and play cards, especially after he got to know Tito. My father became his new best friend," Levi says mockingly, shaking his head in disgust. "He admired Tito, I think. Too much—he became jealous. He wanted to be like Tito, and he ended up hating his life with us. I think there was a part of him that resented us for not being rich, too, but he resented himself the most."

I'm not too surprised to learn that Levi doesn't come from a rich family. Even though he has money now, he hasn't got the attitude that usually comes with it. I've seen how he tips waiters and car valets, and it's clear he does it not just because it looks bad not to. He doesn't spend money carelessly either. He's very aware of the money going in and out of his pocket, but he's never stingy.

"I wanted him to teach me to play poker, mainly so I could get closer to him, because that was the only thing he loved, and I sort of . . .

wanted to be part of it. He said a dope like me could never understand all the subtleties." He smiles bitterly at me.

Li Mei rolls her eyes, mirroring my own reaction. Levi ignores us and carries on in the same detached tone.

"Then one day, Tito made a proposition: he wanted my father to invest a huge sum of money in his business. He promised my father he'd be rich, like him. It was . . . a lot of money. My father agreed right away, thinking our lives would finally change for the better. He borrowed money, more than he should have, convinced he'd be able to pay it all back once he hit the jackpot."

I listen carefully, confused. My father never told me about this. Levi must be lying, or misremembering. And yet I feel my heart tighten because it knows; it knows I'm burying my head in the sand.

"My father never saw a penny of his money again, of course." Levi gives me an ironic smile. "He was stupid to have believed a thing like that. Tito stole all the money we had, and the money we didn't have."

I resist the urge to hang my head in shame. My cheeks are burning with guilt. How could he have done something like this? It's not as though he needed the cash!

"But why?" I gasp.

"Because he was scared, I guess. Just like he's scared again now—of me. And he's right to be scared."

I know exactly what he means by that. My father is a megalomaniac and a proven narcissist. He was happy to be friends with Jacob Ivanovich as long as he wasn't a threat, but as soon as Jacob came close to beating him, Tito couldn't handle it. So he found a way of keeping Jacob down.

I hide my trembling hands under my legs as Levi goes on.

"We were poor. My father could still play in tournaments because he was sponsored, but that didn't bring in as much money as it used to; not enough to repay his debts. He started drinking. A lot. And he got nasty, of course . . ."

He doesn't say it in so many words, but we all understand what he means. His father's alcoholism made him violent. I clench my teeth as I imagine a man taking out his anger on a sweet little boy with beautiful eyes. It makes me sick.

"You told me your mother was in prison for murdering your father . . ."

"She is."

"But . . ."

"I told you she was sent to prison. Not that she was guilty."

*Oh.* That changes everything. I open my mouth, stunned. Everyone watches me, wondering how I'm going to react. All I can do is return Levi's unflinching gaze. Did this man really kill someone?

"What happened?" I ask in a voice that I hope sounds stronger than I feel.

"I was seventeen. I got back from an evening out, and I saw my father hitting my mother. He was blind drunk. I went and fetched the gun to scare him; that usually worked. But that evening . . . I don't know. It was different. He was determined." For the first time, Levi allows his pain to show. "He jumped on me, shouting about how ungrateful I was, and we fought. He was stronger than I was. He was throttling me. It wasn't the first time he'd done that, but this time his eyes were different. I knew he was going to kill me. He wasn't himself. I managed to push him away, but he lunged back. So . . ."

I steel myself for what's coming. His gaze remains level as he says the rest.

"I got scared. My survival instinct kicked in, and I fired."

*Oh God.*

Levi sighs, his face bleak, and tells me that after that single shot, his father collapsed, an expression of shock and fury on his face.

"I was in a state of shock myself. I never thought I'd dare to do it. I didn't mean . . . I didn't mean to kill him, of course. I just panicked. I didn't want to die."

*I didn't want to die.*

I know I should be panicking now. I should be frightened. I should get as far away as possible, go to my father and tell him I'm bailing out.

But . . . but, there's only one thing I want to do: send everyone else out of the room and take Levi in my arms. Stroke his hair and tell him it will be all right. Kiss him on the mouth until he forgets everything else.

How has he managed to live with that on his conscience?

"I was stunned after it happened," he continues. "My mother immediately grabbed the gun and ordered me to keep quiet. I realized she was going to claim responsibility. I started to cry and said I wouldn't obey, but she told me there was no way her son was going to prison for something that was her fault."

"But it wasn't her fault, or yours! It was self-defense. If you hadn't fired, you'd probably both have ended up dead."

"She's right," says Li Mei. "He was hitting you. All that physical and psychological damage over so many years . . . It's impossible to imagine. Anybody in that situation would lose their head."

"But it's not that simple," says Thomas, "especially since Russia decriminalized any acts of domestic violence that don't lead to hospitalization. Jacob wasn't armed, so self-defense would have been difficult to prove."

It would have indeed. I hadn't thought of that. In that case, I guess his mother was lucky to get away with just ten years in prison.

"When the police arrived, my father was taken to the hospital," Levi says, "but he died on the way."

He explains that his mother immediately "confessed" to the police. He tried to tell the truth, not wanting his mother to take on his guilt, but the case was soon closed.

"They had my mother's confession, and all the signs pointed to the same thing. Everyone thought I was lying to protect her . . . when the opposite was true. She got ten years. I went to live with my uncle until I turned eighteen."

All at once, the jigsaw pieces fall into place. Levi is traumatized. That's why he has panic attacks every time he hears a noise like a shot. First the thunderstorm, then the fireworks. Every time it happens, he relives that terrible night and the act he still feels guilty for. I'm sure of it.

That's what he wants to punish himself for. For having killed his father to save himself. For having let his mother pay for his crime.

"I inherited my father's debts. I dropped out of school. A few days later, Tito gave an interview to the Italian media. He boasted that my father's death meant he could win more easily from now on."

I close my eyes, pain swelling in my chest. *That bastard.*

"I started playing poker myself, first to pay back the money I owed, then because I realized I was good at it. I had ten years ahead of me before my mother would be out of prison, and I vowed I'd use it to destroy the man who fucked my father over."

"It's all his fault," I whisper, almost to myself.

A sad smile flickers briefly across his face.

"I don't hold him responsible for what I did. I had a choice. I chose wrong. That's *my* mistake. But . . . I'll never forgive him for having fleeced my father. That's what ruined him. That's what cost me my childhood. Our family life. Everything."

He's right. Even though Levi is responsible for what he did, he'd probably never have found himself in that situation if Tito hadn't brought his father down. Bringing people down is exactly what he always does. And then, he lies. Like he did with me. He carefully avoided telling me all of that because he knew. He knew if he did, I'd never have followed him into this.

"Which brings us . . . here. Now," Levi says, opening his arms to indicate the room we're all sitting in.

I look at him with a mixture of compassion and anger—at Tito, at myself, at Levi's father. I know what I said before, and I believe it: revenge is never the right answer. But I understand Levi's reasons.

Levi Ivanovich is a victim of our parents, just as I am. Instead of hating him for stealing my father from me, I should have suspected he was going through something like I was. He didn't choose to be in this situation either. He was just in the wrong place at the wrong time.

In fact, he should be the one hating me for what his family went through. He lost everything because of Tito. If he knew my secret, he wouldn't be looking at me with such tenderness and blind trust. The thought makes my stomach turn over.

"So what are you planning to do?"

There's a long pause before he replies; then he nods to the others and says, "Introduce yourselves to Rose. For real this time."

"I'm Li Mei. I'm thirty, not twenty-four. I was born in Shanghai. I'm a Buddhist, and I've done a few years inside for burglaries—but in my defense, I only stole from the obnoxiously rich who have more money than they know what to do with."

At the mention of her age, my eyes widen, which makes her smile with pride, and I'm even more amazed when I hear the second part.

*In prison? Burglary? Who are these people?*

"I'm Lucky. I'm twenty-five, from Los Angeles, and I'm an architecture student. Oh and I'm also an escort. Li Mei is my ex . . ."

"What's that got to do with anything?" she butts in. "She didn't need to know that. *Ugh*, please."

"It's an important detail, OK?"

He blushes furiously, folding his hands shyly as Li Mei mouths to me that I should forget everything he's said. I'm speechless. So everything was . . . fake.

I'd thought I was tricking Levi with my dual identity, but he's been the one who's been pulling the wool over my eyes from the start. He and his friends aren't who they said they were. Every single thing he's told me could turn out to be a lie.

"You already know the truth about me," Thomas says, interrupting my thoughts. "I'm twenty-seven, I'm from Sweden, and I'm a bodyguard. None of us is a professional player. We all learned on the job from Levi."

"But why?"

"The goal is for all four of us to make it to the final table, along with Tito."

"And then?"

"Win, of course," Levi says. "It doesn't matter which of us it is, though obviously I'd like it to be me."

Yes . . . except he's still hiding something very important from me. All the things I found on his USB key had nothing to do with poker.

Almost as if he's read my thoughts, he adds, "It's simple. There are two stages: first, we win the tournament; then we turn his investors against him."

I think back to the proofs of bribery, and I get what he means. My father really is rotten to the core, isn't he? And because of me, Tito has destroyed the evidence they had against him. Even worse, he's on his guard now because he knows Levi's after him.

I've messed up his plan, like an idiot.

I can't help gazing at him in admiration. Levi is an absolute genius. He's planned everything to perfection, or almost—he just didn't factor my arrival into the equation.

Resentment gnaws at me, for having been betrayed by my father. All my life I've tried to make him proud, and for what? He doesn't deserve my efforts. He isn't the respectable man I thought he was.

And God knows I'd give a lot to see the look of horror on his face when Levi wins the tournament.

I make my decision there and then. I want to be part of this. It's time to switch sides.

"So . . . if I have this right," I say, looking from one to the other of them, "this is your team?"

"Yes, why?"

"A color-blind killer, a sociopathic Chris Hemsworth look-alike, a Swiftie ex-con, and an escort addicted to rom-coms. Plus me, your fake fiancée with a gambling problem."

Levi smiles at me. "That's us!"

I nod.

"Fantastic. Count me in!"

# Chapter 18

## Levi

***June***
***Las Vegas, USA***

"You have such beautiful skin!"

I smile politely in reply, not knowing what to say. In the mirror, two seats farther along, Rose grins mockingly at me, and I instinctively smile back.

We haven't really had an opportunity to discuss what happened before . . . everything. The two of us, on my bed, half-naked. Her coming against my mouth. We haven't had any time alone to talk.

At first, I thought she was avoiding me. I was worried she'd be scared off by my revelations from that night. But it seems I underestimated her yet again. She took everything in, digested it, accepted it all.

"Have you done an interview on camera before?" the makeup artist asks as she retouches my lips.

"This is our first official appearance together."

Our *Glamour* interview, which is going to be called "Levi Ivanovich and his Fiancée Take a Love Test," has been moved up because of my busy schedule. This is the only day when I'm not playing. The adjustment means that we haven't had time to prepare our replies, but

Rose assures me it'll be fine and reminds me we've managed fine so far just by improvising.

"Something tells me we're going to have fun!" she cackles, rubbing her hands together as the team leads us to the studio.

"That isn't exactly reassuring."

I rest one hand in the curve of her waist, trying to push away memories of her naked body arching over me. I still can't believe it really happened; the memory seems strangely like a dream.

In the studio, a crowd of people bustles about. Technicians, stylists, makeup artists, camera operators, interpreters . . . it's a lot of people to have all in one place.

I glance at the backdrop: a plain white canvas. No other décor. The journalist Li Mei mentioned gives us an enthusiastic wave and comes over, smiling broadly. She briefly explains how it's all going to work.

"Try to be as natural as possible. Look straight at the camera. And above all, avoid turning your back on us. And thank you for being here today; we can't wait to see how it turns out! You look so good together!"

I glance at Rose and raise my eyebrows, but she rolls her eyes. They give us microphones, which we hide under our clothes; then someone sits me down alone in the middle of the white backdrop. Rose remains standing near the camera, her arms crossed and laughter in her eyes. Suddenly, I feel very ill-at-ease. Too many people staring at me. I don't like it.

I fix my eyes on Rose and don't look away. I concentrate on her and nothing else as the interview begins.

"Tell us about the moment you first met. What was your first impression of Rose? How did your relationship develop after that?"

They're plunging straight in. A grin starts to appear on my pretend fiancée's face. I don't even have time to invent a lie, so I choose honesty.

"The first time I saw her was in a casino," I say, completely naturally. "She was watching the game going on at my table. I looked up and saw her, and I was immediately struck by her beauty, of course. I asked her to play a game with me, which she did. And she beat me hands down."

I smile at her pleased expression. It feels so long ago . . . but it was only a few weeks.

"My first impression? I found her intriguing. Intelligent. Conceited too. I thought . . . I'd found someone like me. A twin soul, maybe? Unfortunately, she slipped through my fingers that evening, but I did everything I could to find her again. I thought it was fate."

Her smile fades as she drinks in my words from the other side of the room. I realize I don't even need to lie. I believe every word I'm saying.

"It wasn't easy at first. I think we were both on our guard, scared of getting hurt. But we tamed each other in the end. Now . . . ," I say, looking straight into her eyes, "she's one of only five people in the world who know everything there is to know about me. I trust her completely."

I would have thought that would be difficult to say, but strangely it isn't. I think . . . I really believe it. Rose blinks, thrown off-balance, and looks away. They ask her to swap places with me and answer the same questions.

I watch her from a distance, stunning in her flowered corset. She tells them that she wanted to bleed me dry at poker so that she could buy herself a pair of new shoes, which makes everyone laugh.

"My first impression of him . . . ? To be honest, I didn't like him," she says, making a face. I raise an indignant eyebrow. "He was too . . . rich. Too handsome. Too arrogant. Every time I was near him, I felt I was losing control. I think . . . he annoyed me because he seemed better than me."

Oh. I frown in surprise. I'd never have guessed she felt that way, or that she'd admit it in front of the cameras.

"But as time went on, I realized I was wrong, and that we were equals. Being near Levi . . . makes me feel safe. When I'm with him, I can drop the mask. I can be myself without fear of judgment. He makes me feel . . . important."

*Boom boom.*

I resist the urge to put my hand to my heart, which is suddenly beating faster. What she just said . . . is exactly how I feel.

When she's finished, they ask me to join her. I smile serenely as I go and stand opposite her. The next exercise is to embrace each other for a full minute.

"Come here," I say, opening my arms wide.

She shakes her head teasingly, but I move closer and lift her up in my arms.

"That's not hugging," she complains, her hands on my shoulders.

I release her, letting her body slide down mine, and her smile fades as her feet touch the ground again. Her body is glued to mine. Images from the other evening in my bedroom flash through my mind. If her face is anything to go by, she's thinking about the same thing.

I smile and put my arms around her. She matches my movement and wraps her arms around my waist, her cheek against my pounding heart.

I think it's the first time we've ever embraced like this. It's . . . far more intimate than I'd ever imagined. I can feel her heartbeat, in harmony with mine. I nestle my mouth against her neck, hidden under her hair, which has a faint scent of almond, and whisper, "You smell good."

She shudders against me but doesn't say anything. I calm her with a kiss on her neck and shift my position so I can join my hands at the base of her back.

We're turning round and round, as though slow dancing without music, which makes her laugh. The sound resonates against my heart and calms me down too. I don't know what gets into me, but I lift one of my hands to cradle the back of her head.

"You wouldn't know it to look at you, but you give great hugs," she says as I stroke her hair gently.

"Of course. Your future husband is perfect."

"My future husband wears blue jackets without even realizing."

I nibble her ear in retaliation, which makes her laugh.

The minute is up too soon for my liking, and we pull apart as though everything that just happened was completely normal. I immediately wish I could be close to her again. I'm dying to kiss her, but the journalist interrupts us.

The next exercise is harder than the first two. We're each given a sheet of paper and a pen, and they ask us to write a list of compliments, things we like about one another.

I think for a few seconds, then start to write, the words flowing easily. Rose doesn't move, her pen suspended in midair. I see her leaning toward me, trying to see what I'm writing, but I hide my paper with my hand. "Hey, no cheating."

"But this is hard . . ."

"Thanks a lot! You'd better invent something, fast. I expect to be hit by a wave of compliments about my incredible physique and awesome intelligence, understood?"

She glares at me, wrinkling up her adorable little nose into an angry expression. "You're so stingy! You could at least slip me a few hints . . ."

"I've just given you some ideas!"

"All things intended to feed your ego! No way," she laughs, rolling her eyes.

After several minutes, she finally manages to write down a few words. My sheet of paper is so covered with ink, my wrist hurts. When the journalist tells us it's time to read them aloud, Rose closes her eyes in despair.

I volunteer to go first, to help her out, and she thanks me with her eyes.

"Rose . . . The truth is that I admire you," I say, unable to keep the warmth from my gaze as I look at her. "I genuinely think you're a force of nature. You're aware of your faults, but you never impose them on other people. You don't use them as excuses. You overcome them, alone and bravely. I love your determination. Your independence. The way you tackle life with honesty and courage. You look as though you aren't afraid of anything, even though you sometimes are afraid. You make me laugh, especially when you think I'm not watching you. You understand me like hardly anyone does. You've got a great sense of style too. My friends adore you. You're smart. Mature. My equal."

It's a lot more than I'd written. I'm afraid I may have gone a bit too far. I clear my throat, holding my hands behind my back. Rose was biting her lip as she listened to me, avoiding my gaze. She looks embarrassed. I'm sure she thinks this is all part of our act, and that irritates me.

She turns to the camera, a half smile on her lips, and whispers in a conspiratorial voice, "I paid him to say that."

Several people burst out laughing, but I shake my head in reply.

"Your turn."

"Don't get too excited."

I wait, amused. She glances over what she's written, clears her throat, and then reads, not daring to look at me.

"My mother always used to say, 'You can tell a lot about a person from the way they treat the people around them.' And that's what I love most about you—the way you treat people. I've seen how much you inspire them. How much they rely on you and listen to you and trust you. You're a born leader." She looks at me and adds, without looking down at her paper, "You're kind. Loyal. Honorable. Perhaps too honorable. You're not afraid of trying new things; in fact, you like taking on a challenge. You're not afraid to admit your weaknesses, because you're willing to find ways of doing better, of being better. You never give up."

*Boom boom.*

There it goes again, my treacherous heart, pounding crazily against my ribs. Rose continues to improvise, her intense gaze giving me goose bumps.

"You say kind things without expecting anything kind to be said in return. You've got this amazing charisma that makes people want to follow you to the ends of the earth. You never cease to surprise me. Oh, and I love your smile. That's it. I think."

She looks down, embarrassed, and crumples up the paper. I nod silently and look at the camera with a half smile. "And all this time, I thought she was marrying me for my money."

That earns me a punch on the shoulder.

The final exercise is very simple: we have to mirror each other's movements. Standing face-to-face, we raise our hands to begin. She starts to move first, very slowly. I imitate her movements in perfect synchronization, anticipating every move.

She makes me rotate my hips, to my embarrassment, and I get back at her by making the most grotesque faces I can. She does the same, struggling not to laugh. We look like a pair of idiots, but my face hurts from smiling. I've never felt so good in my life.

There's only one other person on earth who ever sees this side of me: my mother.

I'm stunned by this realization. So much so that my smile evaporates, and I relapse into my usual cold, impassive state. This takes Rose by surprise, and she gradually loses her smile, too, clearly embarrassed.

"Thank you! That was fantastic!" the journalist tells us when our time's up. "You've got an unusual relationship, I have to say, but it's clear how much you care about each other."

We nod silently. I'm suddenly aware again of all the eyes fixed on us, sizing us up and judging. I need to get out of here and be alone with Rose. Now. Somehow she understands, and she grabs my hand and entwines her fingers with mine.

"We've got an important meeting right after this," she says, "so we'll go now, if there's nothing else you need."

"Oh sure! Thanks again for playing along! And say hi to Li Mei from me."

Rose waves to the team and leads me toward the dressing rooms, where we collect our things. There's a taxi waiting for us outside, and I climb with her into the back seat, feeling exhausted for some reason. Maybe it's all the playacting. But were we really playacting?

Because it all felt very real to me.

"That was nice," says Rose as the car begins to move. "And funnier than I thought it would be."

"True."

Her hand is still in mine. I look at her out of the corner of my eye, not sure where I stand. After a few seconds' silence, I pluck up the courage to stroke the palm of her hand softly with my thumb. At first she doesn't react, but then, ever so slowly, she returns the caress. It's a tender, intimate gesture that drives me wild. I touch my forehead touching hers and murmur, almost inaudibly, "Sorry about . . . what happened the other evening."

I wish it had turned out differently. I wish we could have carried on for another hour, or more, then called room service and had dinner, naked on my bed. After that, we'd have picked up right where we left off, probably in the living room or the kitchen, or maybe the Jacuzzi?

"You scared me," she says simply.

I have no answer to that. I rest my head against the seat back. My eyelids are growing heavy. I realize how tired I am. After a few minutes, as I'm starting to drop off, I hear her whisper, "Why?"

"Why what?"

"Why the sudden change toward me that evening?"

I shrug weakly. "Because I wanted you so much."

Silence.

"But not before?"

"Yes, before too."

"So why now? What's changed?"

I think about that, but no answer comes to me. "I don't know. Something."

She seems satisfied, because she doesn't say anything else. Soon I hear her breathing becoming more regular, and then she's asleep. I brush a strand of hair gently out of her eyes, then dare to rest my head against hers and close my eyes.

My heartbeat slows immediately, and I gradually drift toward sleep, my hand still in hers. Then a cruel thought flits into my mind: the touch of her skin against mine is something so special . . . I might never tire of it.

And then I remember.

Rose is nothing more than a dirty liar and a traitor who's come here to destroy me on her father's orders.

# Chapter 19

## Rose

***June***
***Las Vegas, USA***

The more time passes, the harder it is for me to resist.

The lure of gambling is too strong. I can tell I still haven't recovered enough to get away with tempting fate, so I limit myself to playing only with Levi, and never for money. Predictably, that isn't enough for me. When I'm not painting, I spend my time watching people play and wondering what choices I'd have made in their place.

It's driving me crazy. Luckily there are always people with me, which stops me giving in to temptation. Li Mei and Lucky have essentially moved into our suite. Now that I know the truth, they spend all their time with us, which means I've had to give them my room . . . and start sleeping in Levi's bed.

Not that we've done anything in it. Yet.

"How did you two meet?" I ask Li Mei when we're alone at the bar.

I don't even know what time it is. The truth is, spending all my time in the hotel, immersed in the shadowy, frenetic atmosphere of the tournament, makes me lose all sense of time. That's one of the dangers of a casino: once you're there, you never have to leave.

"Levi, you mean? It wasn't long after I got out of prison," she tells me, twirling the paper umbrella in her cocktail. "In a bar in Shanghai. I'd come for a job interview, but I ended up arguing with the boss. He wasn't happy when he discovered my prison record, naturally. Levi saw what happened, and as I was leaving, he came over and asked if I was looking for a job."

I laugh. He makes a habit of this, apparently. Does he think he's some kind of good Samaritan?

"I was lucky." Li Mei smiles. "I think he was touched by my story because of what happened to his mother. There's a part of me that's always wondered if he helped me because he blames himself and wanted to make amends."

Which he couldn't do with his mother. Because he does blame himself; of course he does. How could he not? I ask Li Mei what kind of job he offered her.

"He'd opened up another Rasputin in China and asked me if I'd manage it."

I'm amazed.

"Seriously? He didn't even know you!"

"God only knows why he trusted me. But Levi never does anything without a reason. The fact that we're so close now is proof of that."

It's true. Levi has the knack of surrounding himself with good people. I start to wonder if that's because he likes them, or because they're useful to him.

"What about your family?" I ask.

She makes a funny face and looks away.

"I have an older brother. He's the only one I still speak to. My parents . . . they never got over the shame I brought them. I have only myself to blame. I shouldn't have burgled a luxury home with my friends . . . especially since I only did it so I could buy clothes. My mother thinks I'm a kleptomaniac."

She's right; that wasn't a good idea. I ask her if she is a kleptomaniac, and she laughs before thinking for a moment.

"Who knows?"

I burst out laughing too. What a team we make! I get the feeling Lucky is the most stable member of our group. I'm not entirely sure what that means, but it's not a good sign.

"Also, I still can't believe you and Lucky used to be an item. Tell me all—I need to know how, where, and mainly *why*."

"Tell me about it," she sighs, hiding her face in her hands. "In my defense, he's very different from the image he projects in public. It's just an act, like mine. In fact, he's . . . sweet. Romantic. Kind. Funny. He won me over."

"Did it last long?"

"Four months."

"That's not long. What happened?"

She rolls her eyes, looking exasperated.

"He's too young! Too sensitive too. It's awful. I'm the kind of person who's never bothered too much by anything, who never stops in one place for long. Lucky is the exact opposite: he cries every time he watches *Titanic*; he's incapable of saying no; he's a coward; and he's obsessed with the idea of getting married and living happily ever after. I freaked out!"

I'm amazed. Didn't he say he was an escort? Li Mei must guess what I'm thinking, because she explains.

"His parents fell in love at first sight. Forty years of marriage. He wants to do the same . . . but he couldn't pay back his student debts. Hence the escort job. He never stopped, except when we were together. He likes it. He's not ashamed, and he gets on with his clients. I'm almost certain he thinks one of them might turn out to be the love of his life, which just proves what a dope he is."

"Who knows? It could happen! So . . . there's no chance it could ever work out between the two of you?"

She's about to say no when she stops short, narrows her eyes, and looks at me suspiciously.

"Why? Are you interested?"

Her tone has changed. It's colder now, more brusque. I suppress a smile. Whatever she says, she's still crazy about him.

"Not at all. I have enough on my plate already . . ."

She relaxes, then laughs to herself.

"You can say that again. Do you like Levi?"

No. Yes. I don't know. Physically, yes definitely. I like the kind of person he is, too, but I'm not romantically interested. He's become a good friend. I like being with him. That's all it is. Isn't it?

An image flashes into my mind: Levi's hair between my thighs, imprisoned in my fingers as they curl with pleasure. I remember the wave of emotion I felt as I came against his mouth.

I take too long to reply, which makes Li Mei smile. I pout, blushing, and mutter my answer.

"Oh, he's OK."

◆ ◆ ◆

When I get back to the suite, Levi's there waiting for me, lying on the sofa with his arm over his eyes.

"Where were you?" he asks casually.

"Having a drink with Li Mei. Are your eyes hurting?"

He doesn't answer immediately. Eventually, he sits upright, his legs apart and his elbows resting on his knees. I sit in the armchair opposite him, and he looks straight into my eyes. I'm surprised by how pale his face is. He doesn't look right.

"I'm fine," he lies. "I was thinking."

"What about?"

"Tito."

I pray he won't notice how my body tenses at the name. My father called me earlier this morning for an update, but I lied to him so he wouldn't realize I've had a change of heart. I even managed to give him a few false leads.

I change the subject as naturally as I can. "You should eat something."

His intense gaze lowers slowly and slides purposefully over my body . . . coming to a stop between my thighs. *Oh Jesus.*

I close my legs and answer his look, raising an eyebrow. "In your dreams."

He flashes me an arrogant half smile. I get up and head into the kitchen to survey the contents of the fridge. Some fresh pasta and cutlets that I bought earlier, which I put on the counter. That'll do nicely.

"What are you doing?" Levi asks in a tired voice, coming into the kitchen after me.

"Making dinner. On the menu tonight: chicken piccata with lemon and fettuccine. A family specialty—watch and learn."

He doesn't need to be asked twice. He sits on a stool and watches as I coat the cutlets with flour.

"Tell me about your family," he says, crossing his arms.

I'd rather not. I want to avoid the subject, fearing I'll let something slip. I also want to avoid telling him too many lies. He might get suspicious, though, if I refuse.

"My mother is the purest person I've ever met," I say, warming the olive oil. "She just had the bad luck to fall for the wrong guy when she was very young . . . She got pregnant—with me. Their two families were very conservative, so there was no way they could break up at that point, and abortion was out of the question. My father took responsibility and asked her to marry him."

I sense Levi's scrutinizing gaze on me. He asks if they're still in love, and I shake my head.

"My father cheated on my mother for years. He had a daughter from that relationship . . . but I've never met her. My mother finally asked for a divorce."

"I see. I'm sorry."

I look at him, surprised by the sincerity in his voice.

"And you?" he asks. "What about you? Are you close to your father?"

That's the million-dollar question . . . I don't even know myself. I peel and chop the shallots sadly.

"I've spent my whole life trying to make him love me. My old psychoanalyst used to say that sometimes you have to stop trying and just . . . make your peace."

Levi gives me a hard look that's impossible to decipher. Finally, he nods.

"Your psychoanalyst is right."

"You say that, but look at you. You've spent ten years of your life obsessed with a guy who betrayed your father. When are you going to make *your* peace?"

His jaw clenches, and there's a glint in his eyes as he answers, in a voice trembling with anger.

"I have no pity for traitors. I can't stand liars. And hypocrites who pretend to be your friend and then stab you in the back are even worse."

*Oh.* I suppress a shiver of horror. Guilt worms its way into my heart, but I ignore it. I can blame myself all I like; what's done is done, and I can't turn the clock back.

When Levi finds out the truth . . . I hope I'll be far away.

"Luckily, I have supportive people around me," he adds suddenly, his eyes less hard. "I trust you as much as I trust Thomas and the others, Rose. You're one of us."

I swallow, my throat tight. If I weren't so certain he didn't know, I'd swear he was doing this on purpose. I smile at him uneasily.

"So I'm part of the gang of crazies with warped priorities? Great. We should make badges . . . or better yet, personalized T-shirts! Have we even got our own battle cry?"

"We're friends, not a bowling team."

I smile. He finally relaxes and offers to help me cook. I show him what to do, and soon the room is full of the scent of Italian cooking. Once it's ready, he sprinkles parsley on the chicken while I add a few slices of lemon.

"Thank you for this," he says, ready to dig in.

"Wait! It's sacrilege to forget to put the sauce on the pasta."

Levi looks surprised at the passion in my voice. He asks me if the sauce is as important as all that. I pour sauce onto his pasta before replying.

"In Italy, pasta can reflect different passions. There's a dish called *pasta del cornuto*, which means 'cuckold's pasta.' It's pasta without sauce. It's got that name because sauce is always prepared at the same time as the pasta, and doing that takes time."

"OK . . ."

"In cuckold's pasta, there's only a bit of butter and pepper. Maybe a little cheese but definitely no sauce. The idea being, if the woman hasn't prepared the sauce, what has she been doing, and with whom?" I ask mysteriously.

He gets the idea because he smiles as he takes his first mouthful, then puts his hand on his heart.

"My wonderful fiancée is faithful to me, then. What a relief."

"You should thank your lucky stars."

We eat in silence. I think back to our conversation—about Tito, about betrayal, and about our group of friends. Each one of us has been involved in dodgy, even illegal, activities. I know Levi's family is Orthodox, like mine, so I pluck up the courage to ask my question, feeling sure he'll understand.

"Do you think you'll go to hell?"

"I certainly hope so. I have a few questions for Oscar Wilde. What about you?"

"It's a serious question."

He looks up from his almost empty plate in surprise, but this question has been worrying me more and more. Levi finishes his mouthful and wipes his mouth before replying, with complete seriousness.

"I killed my father, Rose. Yes, I think I'll go to hell."

OK, so it was a stupid question. I think I wanted him to say something reassuring, idiot that I am.

"And does that scare you?"

He takes his time to reply, looking sad, as though he's already spent too much time thinking about this.

"No," he says eventually, staring into space. "The more frightening thing would be if it didn't scare me. Because if it didn't, how could I live an honest life?"

# Chapter 20

## Levi

***June***
***Las Vegas, USA***

I was raised by a father who constantly accused me of lying. It started with the achromatopsia—even after I was diagnosed, he said I was exaggerating to get his attention. It never got any better, so I ended up feeling as though I always had to justify myself. To this day, I assume nobody will believe me, and I collect evidence in every situation, just in case I need it.

The irony is that I never lied when I was accused of it, but it's since become my survival instinct. Even though I hate liars.

That includes Rose Alfieri Ferragni, the biggest liar of them all.

I admit she had me at first. I fell for her poor-little-broke-girl act. She even made me feel sorry for her for a second . . . But then, the evening she discovered my secret, she went out immediately afterward. I found that odd, so I followed her to the bar where Tito was waiting for her, all smiles. I connected the dots immediately, of course. I'd been blind not to see it sooner, and I kicked myself for having told her about something I'd worked hard to hide for so long.

The anger soon gave way to questions I couldn't answer. I couldn't figure out why she was doing it, so I kept my distance. She flirted, and I rejected her. I wanted to see how far she was prepared to go to help her father. Was it their plan for her to seduce me? It seemed so flimsy and unoriginal. I did everything I could to drive her crazy, knowing that an ego like hers wouldn't be able to stand it. It was fun.

But the next day, at the still-life class, something changed. What she did seemed genuine . . . and I liked it. That was why I kissed her when we got back to the hotel. Then she ruined everything again by taking my USB key. I could have caught her in the moment and told her to get out of my life for good.

But I wasn't strong enough. Despite her lies, Rose attracts me like nobody ever has before. I hate myself for that—for wanting to insult her and screw her in equal measure.

So I let her keep it up, because if there's one thing I love, it's watching someone lie when I know the truth. I let her destroy the evidence of bribery—after all, I'd put it on the USB key on purpose to see what she'd do with it.

I've given her plenty of chances, and she keeps on disappointing me. Up until recently, that is. I don't know what's changed, but after I gave in just a tiny bit . . . and went down on my knees in front of her, I got a glimpse behind the mask. What I saw was a different person, a more humane, vulnerable one. A person who wasn't just Tito's daughter . . . but Rose, just Rose.

Confiding in her about my past was a huge risk. I couldn't be certain she wouldn't go and blab to her father about it. I took the risk anyway because I hoped she wouldn't. I hate liars, yet it seems I'm incapable of hating this woman.

She revealed a lot about herself to me too. Why would she make herself so vulnerable if she was planning to betray me? It makes no sense. Maybe I'm an idiot . . . but I still hope that not everything she's told me is lies. I still hope there's some truth to who she is when she's alone with me.

I haven't said a word to Thomas about all this, of course. God only knows what he'd do if he knew. Saying, "I told you so," would be just the beginning.

A voice inside my head won't stop asking, *What if she betrays you?* I don't think she will. But if I'm wrong . . . I'll betray her first. I'm always one step ahead of her, after all.

I return to the hotel after my phone call with the editor of the *New York Times*, feeling famished. I'm surprised to find the suite plunged into darkness.

"That Rose is so ungrateful," I hear Li Mei say in the living room. "Seriously, could she not have shared? There was plenty of room on that door!"

Rose? *My* Rose? I raise my eyebrows when I see Li Mei, Lucky, and my fake fiancée snuggled up on the sofa. They're sharing a blanket and a carton of Ben & Jerry's.

Opposite them, the tragic scene from *Titanic* is playing on the television. Ah. Now I get it.

"That's not fair!" the real Rose exclaims. "She gets so much flak for that, but if you think about it, they could never both have gotten onto it. They'd have been too heavy—the door definitely would have sunk. It's obvious."

Li Mei thinks about that and nods. Lucky waves at them to be quiet, tears rolling down his cheeks.

"True, but couldn't they have taken turns? I guess you're so selfish, you'd have probably done the same. Must be a Rose thing . . ."

Li Mei sticks her tongue out at Rose as she says this, and my pretend bride shakes her head, looking unbothered.

"Of course I wouldn't! I'd have swapped places if he was the man I loved . . ."

She glimpses me out of the corner of her eye, and her words trail off. She blinks and looks away, turning her focus back to the television. *Interesting.*

"I'd have let you stay on the door, Li Mei," says Lucky, his eyes glued to the television as though he hasn't already seen this film at least a hundred times.

Li Mei wrinkles her nose in disdain. "No thanks. Besides, knowing you, you'd have jumped into one of the lifeboats with the women and children."

She's not wrong. Lucky has plenty of good qualities, but he's a coward. He opens his mouth to protest but evidently can't think of anything to say. I take the opportunity to jump in and ask them what they're doing.

"We were waiting for you!" says Li Mei, getting up and trailing the blanket across the floor. "One of the players rented the indoor pool for a party this evening. There's even going to be a wet-T-shirt competition."

Lucky turns to her quick as a flash, his eyes lighting up. "Are you going to compete?"

"Do you want my parents to lose their last bit of faith in me? Of course I'm not. I'll enjoy the show; that's all." She looks at me. "Are you coming?"

I lower my eyes and look at Rose, who returns my gaze. She shrugs and smiles so seductively that my resolution never to touch her again instantly evaporates.

"Just try to stop me!"

◆ ◆ ◆

"Er . . . you didn't tell me it was a wet-T-shirt competition for *men*."

Lucky looks crestfallen as we reach the pool. He's barefoot, with towels in hand. Music reverberates, bouncing off the walls, making the dancing bodies around the pool move as one.

So that was why Rose insisted I wear a white T-shirt with my swimming shorts.

"Well played," I murmur into her ear. "But I'm not planning to swim."

"We'll see."

That sounds like a promise. She winks at me and goes to find us some deck chairs, her sarong doing little to hide her sublime body.

Lucky stands beside me sulking while Li Mei phones Thomas in the hope that he'll join us.

"The last time I felt this betrayed was when Zayn left One Direction," Lucky says grumpily.

I turn to him. "Are you serious?"

"Obviously not." He rolls his eyes.

I nod—it was a stupid question.

A few seconds later, I hear him mutter, "I always preferred Harry."

Rose quickly finds us somewhere to sit, thank God. I should probably be in my room perfecting my game, but when Rose unties her sarong and pulls it away from her body, I feel no regrets.

I admire her openly, seized by sudden desire. She's wearing a simple black swimming costume that looks a lot like her underwear. It shows off the luscious contour of her thighs to perfection, and I immediately imagine them wrapped around my waist.

My gaze travels upward, and the bewitching sight of her breasts has me erect in an instant.

"Are you coming?"

Rose holds out her hand to me, oblivious to the admiring gazes of both the men and the women around her. I understand why they're staring—who wouldn't? But I resent them too. I'd like to be the only one to see . . . all this.

I get up, subtly trying to hide her with my body. I'm about to take my T-shirt off when she catches my hand.

"Keep it on."

I don't have a chance to object. Her tiny fingers slip through mine and pull me toward the pool. Li Mei and Lucky are already in the water, bickering as usual.

Rose gets in first, the change in temperature taking her breath away. I jump in, too, glad of the cold. I'm grateful that the foamy water covers both Rose's magnificent body and my growing erection.

At first, I stay where I am, my mouth just at the surface as I watch the others. Rose, Lucky, and Li Mei are dancing to a song by Ariana Grande. Then Rose is trying to climb onto a pool float, a cocktail in hand. Her failed attempts make the others laugh.

Suddenly, she looks at me, and I realize I'm grinning like an idiot. I pull myself together, but it's too late. She downs her drink in one gulp before putting the glass down and swimming over to me like a stealthy crocodile.

"Are you having fun?" I ask when she reaches me, her nose almost touching mine.

"So much fun. It's been ages since . . . I laughed so much."

"I'm glad."

It's true—I am glad. I look her over, my gaze lingering over the droplets of water that cling to her eyelashes. She's glowing. In moments like this, I refuse to believe she's a mole. Perhaps I have it all wrong. Perhaps it's all a huge misunderstanding.

"It would be even better . . . if my fiancé danced with me."

"Your fiancé isn't dancing with you?" I feign indignation. "Dump him. You know you should."

"I should, shouldn't I? He doesn't know how lucky he is, the loser."

"They're all losers. You should find yourself a lover to make him jealous."

"Oh really?" She laughs. "Are you applying for the role?"

"Naturally."

I move closer and put my arms around her slim waist. Nobody can see us under the foam, and I wouldn't care if they could. She half opens her mouth, her eyes focused on my lips, and runs her hands over my soaking wet T-shirt.

"You were right. You should have taken it off."

I don't know what gets into me, but I breathe against her mouth, "This evening, in our room, you can do that yourself."

Her eyes look straight into mine, as if to ask if I'm serious. I don't even know that myself. I suppose I must mean it, given that I'm physically incapable of resisting her charms.

I hold her closer, pressing my erection against her stomach, and she starts to breathe more deeply. I'm sick of only fantasizing about her, and even more sick of masturbating in the shower as I replay the one intimate experience we've shared.

"On one condition."

I raise an eyebrow, swallowing as she runs her hands underneath my swimming shorts. She presses my buttocks, her pupils dilated.

"That you take a photograph of me just afterward, for a souvenir."

*For a souvenir*, as though she already knows it can only happen once. As though she's planning to run away soon. I'm about to ask what she means when a familiar shape appears behind her, distracting me.

I grow tense in her arms. Tito is walking along the side of the pool, his eyes fixed on us. Rose follows my gaze and freezes too.

"Hey," she murmurs to get my attention. "Relax."

She puts one hand on my cheek and turns my face back toward hers, forcing me to look away from him. I look deep into her eyes, just as she leans forward and kisses me. My heart catches fire. I entwine my tongue with hers, my hand resting tenderly on the back of her delicate neck.

I know I shouldn't, but I hope Tito is burning with anger at the sight of us. I hope he hates seeing me with his precious little daughter. And I hope he knows I wouldn't hesitate for a moment to use her against him if I had to.

But after a few seconds, I forget all about Tito. There's only her, me, and my excitement, pulsing painfully against her thighs.

"Feel this," she whispers, seizing my hand and putting it on her breast.

I moan involuntarily, first from desire and then in despair as I feel her heart beating frantically under my fingers. Is this really happening? Is this more than a game to her? I find myself hoping against hope that it is.

"You know," I say, whispering against her moist lips, "I don't think it's got anything to do with Rose, or about how much room there is on the goddamn door."

"Oh yes?"

"Yes. I think it was all about Jack and the fact that he would have done anything for the woman he loved. He wouldn't have risked taking turns on the door. He would have kept her on it no matter what, to make sure she survived. He wouldn't have accepted any other option."

She stares at me in silence. At just that moment, Li Mei calls my name from over by the deck chairs. She's got my phone in her hand. Someone's calling, probably Thomas. I pull away from Rose reluctantly, placing one last kiss on her delicious mouth.

"I'll be back. Don't do anything crazy while I'm gone."

"That's *exactly* what I'm going to do," she jokes with a wink.

I shake my head in amusement as I climb out of the pool, then dry my hands on my towel and take the phone. Thomas asks if he's disturbing me, and I make my way to the exit to find somewhere quiet, still keeping my eyes fixed on Tito.

He's staring at his daughter with a menacing expression on his face. I don't like it one bit.

"What's going on? Can't it wait?"

"I just wanted to know how the call went earlier."

I stay in the corridor, dripping water, and tell him all about it. It takes me a good five minutes. The editor was reticent at first, but the evidence convinced him in the end.

"He's interested, then?"

"Of course he's interested. This is Tito Ferragni we're talking about. He wanted to publish the article next week, but I talked him out of that, and he's going to wait."

I know Thomas is probably nodding his head at that.

"You did the right thing. The timing needs to be perfect."

I ask him why he didn't come down to the pool with us, and he says he's not interested. That makes me laugh. I didn't think I'd be interested, either, but I surprised myself. Rose makes everything fun.

"No worries. See you later."

I hang up and go back to the pool, where I'm taken aback to see a little group forming around our deck chairs. I slow down, frowning, and stop when I see Rose standing in the middle. She's drawn up to her full height in front of a young man, water still dripping off her bare skin, and she's shouting and gesticulating. *"Ci fai o ci sei? Pezzo di merda! Cazzone! Figlio di puttana!"*

I look at her in shock, recognizing enough of the words to know they aren't good. Something about the guy being crazy. A piece of shit, a dickhead, a son of a bitch. The man's face darkens, and I see his lips moving but can't hear what he says.

Whatever it is, it enrages Rose. I don't have time to react before she rams her knee into his groin, hard. He groans with pain and doubles over, grabbing roughly at her arm, but she jumps onto his back, shrieking, her hands yanking his hair.

Li Mei and Lucky throw themselves into the fight with a piercing war cry. A woman, the man's girlfriend by the look of things, shoves Li Mei, but Li Mei grabs her ponytail, and they yank on each other's hair while Li Mei shrieks that she's fought worse in prison. Lucky assumes a boxing pose but doesn't actually join in the action.

"Help me out, you useless piece of shit!" Li Mei shouts at him before her adversary silences her with a punch in the chest. "Ow! Not the breasts! That's cheating!" Reverting to Mandarin, she calls the other woman a slut.

"I'm coming, Li Mei!" Lucky calls, throwing punches into empty air. "It's just that . . . Oops, sorry, miss . . . My mother always told me not to hit girls . . ."

"Lucky!" Slipping into Mandarin again, she threatens to hit him next.

I cross my arms and frown at this infernal spectacle. Everybody watching is laughing—that's how ridiculous it is. I should probably intervene. Rose seems to be holding her own, though. In fact, she's wiping the floor with the guy.

"I'm engaged to her," I say to the man next to me with a proud smile.

He looks at me with an expression of deep compassion. "Good luck."

Rose hangs on as the man spins around, trying to shake her off. She bellows at him to apologize, but he calls her a nutcase.

I walk over casually, intending to separate them. All eyes are fixed on me as I stop in front of them, my face expressionless, and say to him coldly, "That's my future wife you've got on your back. I'd appreciate it if you'd put her down. *Now.*"

The man's eyes widen, and he tugs on Rose's hands, which are still buried in his hair.

"I'd like to, I swear! Get down, you crazy witch!"

"*Lyubimaya?* Would you mind leaving this poor guy alone?" I ask Rose tenderly, my head tilted to one side.

She grunts, her cheeks flushed dark—crimson, I assume.

"He said something really rude about Li Mei, and when I told him to apologize, the bastard told us to 'go back where we came from'!"

"I said I was sorry," the man whimpers.

"Once I'd kicked you in the balls you did!"

One look from me, and the man gives another groveling apology. I decide that's enough and reach up to Rose to lift her down. She sets her jaw as her feet touch the ground, her back against my chest.

"OK, let's go."

I take her hand and pick up our towels with monumental calm. Li Mei loosens her grip on the poor girlfriend, who's probably lost quite a lot of hair by now, and releases her. Lucky is panting as though he's run a marathon.

"That was intense . . ."

"Shut up," Li Mei snarls, her cheeks red and scratched. "You were useless as always."

We leave together, our departure followed by amused gazes. Near the exit, I sense Tito watching us and instinctively hold more tightly onto Rose's hand. I want to leave without any trouble, but as we pass in front of him, I hear him murmur, so only I can hear, "She's a fiery one. You need to train her better."

I stop short, my heart pounding. Rose looks up at me questioningly, but I'm completely focused on Tito. I can hardly believe he'd talk about his own daughter like that.

"She's not an animal."

I'm about to leave when he adds, in a vicious whisper, "I hope so, for your sake. If she's anything like your mother, you'll suffer the same fate as your father."

My anger, always cold and implacable before now, bursts into flames, blinding me with its force. Without pausing even for a second, I let go of Rose's hand and jump forward like a tiger, grabbing Tito by the collar and hitting him in the face as hard as I can. He staggers under the force of the blow as Rose pulls me backward, shouting my name.

"Say that again, you piece of shit!" I bellow, my throat constricted.

Tito regains his balance, touches his bleeding mouth, and smiles triumphantly at me. The effect is like a bucket of cold water. I retreat, still looking wildly at him. I can barely hear what Rose is saying as she drags me toward the exit.

Tito's words won't stop echoing in my mind. He knew that mentioning my mother would drive me over the edge. It's exactly what he wanted. I'm trembling violently, regretting having lost my cool.

"Are you OK?" Rose asks when we get to the changing rooms. "What got into you?"

My three friends look completely taken aback. Lucky murmurs what everyone's thinking.

"Woah . . . that's the first time I've ever seen you lose your shit. You scared me. I thought you were going to . . ."

He doesn't finish his sentence. Li Mei stands on his foot, very obviously, to shut him up. My chest tightens.

*I thought you were going to kill him*. That's what he was about to say. And who could blame him? Because that's what I do, isn't it? Kill people. *Fuck*. I need some air. I need to be alone. I need to ground myself somehow.

I turn away abruptly without replying, ready to make my escape, but Rose catches hold of my arm. I pull away, more roughly than I meant to.

"Leave me alone."

"Why?" she says, walking by my side.

What exactly doesn't she understand? I don't want her there; that's all! "Because I'm angry."

"Well, that's fine, because I'm angry too. Let's be angry together," she says, trying to joke.

I clench my fists and stop, turning to face her. I stare right into her eyes. "No, Rose, I'm angry with *you*."

"Me?" she exclaims in surprise. "What did I do?"

"I got into a fight because of you! Couldn't you just stay out of trouble for five minutes, for God's sake?"

This time, she opens her mouth wide, on the defensive. She's not used to seeing me angry, even less so to me talking to her like that. I feel bad for lashing out at her when it's Tito I'm really angry with, but still I'm not ready to back down. I'm angry with her for being that man's daughter. I'm angry that I can't trust her. I'm angry because she makes me feel all these things that make me miserable when I'm with her.

"Because of *me*? But I didn't ask you to do it! I was getting on fine until you came along. And what's Tito got to do with that, anyway?"

"I hit him because of what he said about *you*. I haven't lost my temper like that for years, because I hate fighting, because you *never* know what could happen, and then you fucking show up and . . ."

"Stop!" she interrupts, furious. "So it's my fault if someone insults *me*? It's my fault if you see red? You know what I think? I think you're in denial because you're angry, but that doesn't give you the right to take it out on me, just because what he said touched a nerve."

She hands me my towel and turns to join the others. But as she walks away, she stops once to look over her shoulder and add one more thing, still fuming.

"Oh, and we both know that what you just said was a lie. What Tito said that made you so angry . . . has absolutely nothing to do with me."

# Chapter 21

## Rose

***June***
***Las Vegas, USA***

Are you OK?

Of course I'm OK. You didn't have to say those things you said.

You're not feeling sorry for your fiancé, by any chance?

It could have turned nasty. Those comments were really below the belt.

My father doesn't reply for several minutes. I hesitated for a long time before sending him a message, but in the end I decided I had to. What he did was mean and nasty.

I'll never forget the pain in Levi's eyes at that moment. It turned my stomach.

*I hate fighting, because you* never *know what could happen . . .*

That comment destroyed me when he said it because I realized what he meant: the last time he fought someone, he killed his father. And it appears he's a lot farther from coming to terms with that than he lets on. Which is completely understandable.

If I were him, I'd have fallen into depression.

Your acting's improving all the time . . .

Because it is still just an act, isn't it?

I sit staring at my phone, cross-legged on the sofa. My chest tightens. It's a fair question. I ask myself the same thing every day.

I'm not sure that I am still acting. Levi and I haven't really talked for two days now. We say the bare minimum, mainly for the purposes of the tournament, but at night I sleep in our bed without even acknowledging he's there. He doesn't try anything.

That was the first time he's ever been angry with me, and . . . it hurt. His silence these last two days has hurt too. I thought he'd apologize, but apparently I'm more upset by all of this than he is.

Of course it is.

I delete the conversation and switch off my phone just as Li Mei and Lucky burst into the room, all dressed up to go out.

"Why is a half beer a quarter of a liter, not half a liter?" Lucky is asking her, looking puzzled. "I don't get it."

"Do I have 'Google' written on my forehead? Oh, there you are!" Li Mei smiles when she sees me. "We're going clubbing. We've placed bets on who'll drop out from exhaustion first. We've even managed to talk Thomas into coming, and, believe me, that doesn't happen every day! Are you staying here?"

I nod. I haven't the heart to go out partying tonight. I don't really relish the thought of being alone with Levi either, but he seems to be holed up in his room for the evening. He must be practicing.

"Don't wait up!" Lucky says, giving me a knowing wink.

I have no idea what he means by that. I tell them to have fun, and then silence falls again. After a few minutes of drinking and staring into space, I get up and fetch the canvas and tubes of paint I left stored in the bathroom.

I stand in front of the big windows in the living room, throw on a paint-spattered white shirt, and start painting. This is what I always do when there are too many thoughts swirling around my head. Instantly, my mind empties. I paint without thinking about what will appear on the canvas. I'm completely calm, until the warm colors begin to take shape into . . . a portrait. One that, for once, isn't of me. The result is chaotic but unmistakable: it's an abstract version of Levi's face.

Hardly believing my eyes, I look down at the other abstracts I've done over the last few days. *Oh right* . . . I hadn't noticed, but it's him I've been painting the whole time.

I'm so shaken that I barely notice him come out of his room, hands in pockets. At the same moment, the doorbell rings, and we look at one another in surprise.

Levi opens the door, and I watch, full of curiosity. It's a delivery guy. He hands the parcel to my bogus fiancé, who takes it and closes the door.

"What is it?" I ask.

"A package for me. It's from . . . you?"

I gasp, suddenly panicking. I'd completely forgotten! My mouth opens, but nothing comes out as he watches me, eyebrows raised.

"It's a mistake. It's for me!" I lie, dropping my brush.

I walk toward him, my heart beating fast. I ordered this before our argument. I should never have done it. I hold out my hand to take it from him, but he lifts it up out of my reach, unmoved as ever.

"Is your name Levi Ivanovich? I don't think so."

"Give that back!"

It's too late—he manages to open it before I can reach it. I sigh in frustration and go back to my canvas without giving him another look.

I'm going to look like a fool. I keep my eyes fixed on my painting, my cheeks burning. Out of the corner of my eye, I see him take the present out of its box. I don't need to look to know what it is.

It's a top-of-the-line camera. I don't even dare think about how much it cost—not much less than my last paycheck. I thought he'd be happy, maybe take up photography again. I couldn't have predicted what would happen between then and now.

Levi comes over, still silent. My heart beats faster with every step he takes. He stops just behind me. I hold my breath as he sighs, lowers his head, and rests his forehead against the back of my neck. I shiver in spite of myself.

Having him so close hurts me. I want him to go away, but I also want him to come even closer, to touch me and never stop.

*"Mi dispiace,"* he breathes, his mouth next to my skin. I'm sorry.

Shit. I close my eyes, my hands trembling. I wasn't expecting him to apologize, much less speak Italian.

*"Avevi ragione. Sono stato uno stupido."* You were right. I've been stupid.

His broken Italian is even more irresistible than his English. It does all sorts of things to me, in my heart and between my legs. His lips touch my neck in a chaste kiss. How could I not forgive him after that? I turn to face him, gazing right into his eyes.

"Will you be my model?" he asks.

I smile weakly. "I do have a bit of experience there, as it happens . . ."

"Perfect. Take off your trousers and keep your shirt on."

I do what he asks and pull off my trousers, then remove my bra from underneath the shirt. He looks at me with serious eyes. I ask him what he wants me to do next.

"Keep painting. You're beautiful when you're concentrating."

I do what he asks without asking any questions. He watches me without doing anything at first. I try to forget everything and paint. Finally, he hides his face behind the camera.

When I see him grimace, I ask what's wrong.

"I have no idea what the pictures look like. It's all . . . monochrome. It feels like a waste of time."

"Do you remember the painting lesson? You weren't thinking about the colors you were using. You followed your instinct. This is just the same."

He doesn't look convinced. I wonder how to counteract the frustration that's plainly visible on his face. I tell him to put down the camera and then hand him a brush.

"Paint."

"Paint what?"

"Me."

I put the tubes of paint in front of him and slowly start to unbutton my shirt. I see him swallow, his eyes following the tantalizing movements of my fingers. His face remains impossible to read, but his eyes darken when the shirt falls to my feet.

Then they look back up into mine.

"You're making my job extremely difficult . . ."

I ask him if this makes him feel uncomfortable. He's already told me that other people being naked bothers him. He's very reserved in that way, whereas I'm not at all. I don't want to do the wrong thing.

To my relief, he shakes his head. "I'm just afraid of being distracted by my model, that's all."

"Shocking," I tease. Then I quote from the movie. "'Jack, I want you to draw me like one of your French girls.'"

Levi laughs and moves closer, devouring me with his eyes. I let him take his time before making his first mark. He dips the brush in the blue paint and traces a line between my breasts. I shiver. God, it's cold.

His smile is devastating. He continues his masterpiece in silence. I hope to God the others don't come back suddenly. "Don't wait up!" Lucky said as though he knew. I guess we can take our time.

"What have you painted?" I ask, when he finally stands back to admire his work.

"A rose."

I look down at the midnight-blue rose now blooming on my skin. It's wonderful.

"Keep going. All over."

He's hesitant at first but soon loosens up. He draws the brush over my collarbone, then my nipples, which harden at the touch. The air is warm and electric. I pretend not to notice the growing bump in his trousers, and instead fix my eyes on his as he works.

Soon, he casts the brush aside and begins using his fingers instead. The whole of my upper body is covered in paint. His hands are covered, too, but that doesn't stop him from wrapping them around my neck and kissing me hungrily.

"You drive me wild," he whispers between kisses. "I hate it."

"You haven't seen anything yet."

I slip my hands under his T-shirt, touching his warm, smooth chest, and pull it off over his head. His torso is a work of art. I stroke it with my hands first, before letting my tongue run over one of his nipples. He lets out a shuddering sigh—it's clearly a sensitive point. That excites me even more.

My tongue wanders lower and lower, and I unbutton his trousers. He clenches his teeth as I unzip them and kneel in front of him.

"I've wanted to do this for so long."

He swears softly in Russian as I take him in my hand and begin to lick. He throws his head back as my tongue slowly caresses him, teasing.

Levi lets out a sound of pure pleasure when I take him into my mouth and start to suck.

He moans something in Russian, sounding like he's crying out to heaven. Then he cups my face in his hands. "You're going to kill me."

"I hope so," I say, pausing for a moment. "Did you know that orgasm used to be called 'the little death'?"

My mouth can't take him in completely, but I play my tongue over his whole length. His hand rests on my cheek, his thumb stroking the lump there. He slides it over to my lips, which are closed around him, and buries his other hand in my hair.

"I'm not going to last long; I'm sorry." He grimaces, looking ashamed. "Oh God, what are you doing to me?"

I take my cue from the excitement growing inside me and increase the speed, my hands holding his buttocks. Suddenly, he grasps my hair with both hands and begins to move back and forth more quickly. He fucks my mouth, looking me right in the eyes, as though he can't believe what's happening.

"You're so beautiful . . . I'm going to come."

I feel him tense, and I suck in my cheeks to grip him tighter, pushing him over the edge at last. He swears again and comes with a groan. His hands grab my shoulders and pull me up to him, his mouth claiming mine in an urgent kiss.

"I need to calm down," he gasps, "or I'll make a fool of myself by coming again as soon as I'm inside you."

*Oh God.* I pull away reluctantly and tell him to go get a condom. While he's out of the room, I try to pull myself together, in vain. I'm about to have sex with Levi. Levi Ivanovich. My worst enemy. My best friend. My fake fiancé.

This has to be a mistake, but I plunge in headfirst anyway.

The paint on my body has almost dried now. He returns wearing only a pair of black boxers.

"Can I paint you now?" I ask.

He raises an eyebrow and nods.

"I want to leave my mark on you too."

I dip my fingers in the paint and set to work. His arms grow covered in goose bumps, and I let my fingers wander all over him, mixing the colors into a chaotic mass that, strangely, makes total sense.

A bit like us.

He grabs my wrists and kisses me before I can finish, the whole length of his body touching mine. The wet paint transfers itself onto my breasts, a detail that makes me shiver.

His hands, which he must have rinsed before he came back in, catch hold of my thighs and lift me up effortlessly. I can't help devouring his mouth as though we were running out of time as he lays me down on the sofa and kneels over me. He kisses the few parts of my body still untouched by his brush and slips my panties down my legs.

His boxers soon meet the same fate, and he throws them across the room.

"How do you like it? Slow and gentle? Fast and wild? Should I make love to you like a husband to his wife? Or fuck you until we're both breathless? Tell me and I'll do it."

*Dear God.* I want to say, *All of them.* But the way I want him here, now, has nothing to do with slow patience or devoted sentiments.

"The last one," I breathe as he opens my thighs and caresses my clitoris with his fingers.

"Fast and wild, then. Perfect."

His fingers continue their stroking as he kisses me lingeringly on the lips. My chest burns almost unbearably. I tense and move my hips against his hand. The more I moan, the faster his fingers move.

I'm in a state of being unlike anything I've known before.

I bite his lip and beg him to enter me. He puts on a condom, and I catch hold of the back of his neck to draw him close. Our noses touch, and his eyes connect with mine as he penetrates me in one swift movement.

He groans without opening his mouth, his fingers pressing into the flesh of my hips. I wrap my legs around his waist, my feet pushing against his buttocks. It's . . .

"Unbelievable," he whispers, his face nestling against my neck. "It's so good. I'm never going to be able to do without it."

*Me neither*. That's just what I'm afraid of. He moves back and forth inside me, harder and harder, his fingers entwined with mine on the sofa near my head. His body is amazing. The feeling of him deep inside me blows a few more of my neurons.

"Lift up your bottom, *lyubimaya*."

I'm only too happy to obey. He puts his hands under me and draws me toward him to the cadence of his thrusts. I moan, my arm covering my closed eyes. My pulse grows faster by the second as I grow more and more excited by the sound of his skin hitting mine.

Suddenly, he withdraws, leaving me panting.

"Are you joking?" I cry. "Why did you stop?"

Levi sits on the sofa, legs apart, seizes my chin, and kisses me languorously.

"Get on top of me."

My heart leaps. I remember having wanted to climb onto his knee in the back seat of his car in Macau. This was only a matter of time, in the end.

I crouch over his bare thighs, and he lies still as I lower myself onto him. It's an utterly divine sensation. I've never felt anything like it. He throws his head back against the arm of the sofa and lets out a gasping sigh. Can he feel how deep it is in this position?

I feel as though I'm going to burst.

I straddle him without breaking eye contact. He looks at me with almost disconcerting intensity. As though he has something to tell me but doesn't dare. I wrap my hands around his neck, stroking the hair at the back of his neck. His hands find the sensitive skin of my breasts, and he spreads the paint with his palms.

I move against him more and more quickly, and he starts to lift his hips in response. Suddenly he places his hand low down on my stomach, over my belly button.

"Can you feel me? Just here?"

I nod, moaning, and quicken the pace. Nobody has ever been so deeply inside me before. It's driving me wild. He quickly loses patience and penetrates me harder, making us both come at the same time. In the space of that one second, his mask falls away.

I lean my forehead into his shoulder, spent. My skin is damp with sweat and paint, just like his. He stays inside me a few seconds longer, breathing hard, his arms wrapped around my back. I close my eyes, savoring the feeling of his fingers stroking my hair.

"Show me your face," he says softly. "Please."

I draw back to look at him. He must like what he sees because he pulls away and tells me not to move. I stay sitting on the sofa, my face burning and my muscles throbbing, while he disappears into the kitchen. I hear water running.

When he comes back, I'm holding a cushion over my belly.

"Don't move," he says again. "Don't change a thing."

I look at the camera, my skin electrified at the realization that he'll have a photo of me naked and covered in paint, my cheeks pink and my pupils dilated after our first time. Then again, that was my one and only condition.

*For a souvenir.*

He looks in the camera screen at the photo he's taken, his face expressionless.

His smile is strangely melancholy as he sighs and utters one word.

"Breathtaking."

# Chapter 22

## Levi

***June***
***Las Vegas, USA***

Another nightmare rips me from my sleep in the middle of the night. Once again, my face is wet with tears when I wake. My heart is pounding, and I feel as though I'm suffocating.

Even the warm, comforting feeling of Rose's body curled up against me isn't enough to make me relax. I pull myself from her arms and sit on the end of the bed, hanging my head.

For ten years, in my dreams, I've been reliving the moment when I pulled the trigger. Always the same scene: the moment when I saw the shock in my father's face. When I almost saw a glimmer of regret in his eyes, maybe a hint of fear.

But tonight is different. It wasn't a nightmare. It was a happy memory.

When I was five, my father and mother organized a surprise birthday party for me at McDonald's. My father dressed up as Mickey Mouse. I wasn't meant to realize it was him, but when he put his arms around me and asked what I wanted for my birthday, I recognized his smell. Isn't that strange?

It was one of the best days I ever spent with him.

*It's too cruel. I almost prefer the nightmares.*

I can't stand this. It reminds me what a terrible person I am. I killed someone. I killed my father, the man who brought me up, the man who helped give me life. He wasn't a good person, but he didn't deserve to die. He loved me. And I loved him.

Because of that terrible act, my mother had to abandon me to my sad fate. I had to endure it alone, so consumed by guilt that I often wanted to die. But I didn't die.

I can't stop the tears from falling. I cry like an idiot in the darkness of my room, my heart heavy. I want to disappear. I hate myself.

Suddenly, I feel a warm hand on my shoulder.

"Levi?"

I try to stop, ashamed of being caught in a moment of weakness, but the concern in her voice tells me she's already heard.

"I'm here," she whispers, putting her arm around my bare waist.

Then there's nothing I can do. I let it all out. I hide my face in my hands, my elbows propped on my knees, and cry without stopping.

"I'm sorry . . . I'm so sorry . . ."

She knows that my apologies aren't meant for her. So she doesn't say anything, just rests her cheek against my back and strokes my chest in a motherly gesture.

"I didn't mean to . . ."

"I know; I know," she repeats.

Rose draws me toward her, whispering things in Italian. The sound of her voice calms me straightaway. I lie down with her under the covers, my head nestled against her chest. She strokes my hair and keeps talking to me even though I don't follow what she's saying.

I fall asleep before my tears have even dried.

◆ ◆ ◆

Thomas, Lucky, and Li Mei are already sitting around the small table when Rose and I join them for breakfast. We haven't talked about what happened during the night, and I'm grateful to her for it.

"So?" Rose asks with a malicious grin, "Who dropped from exhaustion first?"

Li Mei points discreetly at Thomas. "Who do you think?"

I don't know what they're talking about, and I don't feel like asking. I'm in a terrible mood. I slept very badly, despite the presence of Rose's reassuring arms around me.

Even the memory of our steamy night doesn't set me to rights. Even though it was paradise. I was almost ready to tell her to choose me over her stupid bastard of a father.

Because I've got it bad. Very bad.

Me, Levi Ivanovich, crazy about the only girl I'm not allowed to love.

"What about you two . . . Did you make up?" Lucky asks.

Rose and I exchange glances. I just smile in reply, feeling calmer. Shit, she's so beautiful. I have to play poker this morning, but all I want to do is spend the day in bed with her. We haven't done that yet.

"Yes," Rose says, sitting down near Thomas on the sofa.

"We all heard," he mutters.

Thomas must have come home earlier than the others . . . Thank goodness we moved to the bedroom after the first time. I feel uncomfortable and am about to apologize, but Rose seizes the opportunity to tease him.

"Just be thankful we cleaned the table after we finished," she lies, nibbling on a chunk of watermelon.

Thomas freezes, his expression cold. "You did it on the table?"

"Yeah."

"We *eat* off this table!" he roars, grabbing his plate and balancing it on his knees. "There's no way I'm eating off a place where Levi put his ass, even if you did clean up afterward!"

"It was my ass, actually . . . But if you're worried about asses, you shouldn't sit there either." Rose nods toward the sofa with a grimace.

I do my best not to laugh at my friend's horrified expression. Li Mei and Lucky burst out laughing, and Thomas gets up and moves to the beanbag, but Rose's words bring him up short.

"Or there."

He glares at me, breathing through his nose, and sits down on the floor as a last resort. A heavy silence falls. He gives us a questioning look, and Rose raises an eyebrow. His expression says it all.

Everybody bursts out laughing except Thomas, who leaps up and shouts, "My God, what are you—animals? We have beds for a reason, you know! Do I have to avoid everything except the walls now?"

I feel as though I should tell Rose to stop tormenting him, but it's so funny, I let her keep going. She pouts and pours herself a glass of orange juice.

"I'd avoid those, too, if I were you."

Thomas turns and leaves, while we all cackle at this bad joke. Rose looks proud of her victory.

"He's right, though," Lucky says. "It's like hearing your parents making love. Disgusting."

"Am I the only one who got turned on?" asks Li Mei.

Lucky makes a face and tells her she ought to see a shrink. We continue eating and discussing the tournament. Only Thomas, Lucky, and I are playing today. Li Mei begs Rose to spend the day with her away from the hotel. Rose asks me if I need her, but I tell her to go have fun.

"Are you going to dock my salary?" she jokes.

"Oh, you want paid holidays now, do you?"

"Naturally."

I roll my eyes in mock horror and head to the bathroom for a shower. It's not long before Rose joins me, but I'm running so late, we have to content ourselves with a few kisses.

"Rose?" I say afterward.

Dressed in a black bra and a pair of cropped jeans, she turns to me. I walk over to her, holding a velvet-covered box in my hand.

"I have a gift for you too. But I didn't really have a chance to give it to you yesterday."

She waits, looking wary. I don't know what I'm doing. Or perhaps I know exactly what I'm doing. I'm giving her my heart. Because I can't deny it anymore, not after last night . . .

I'm falling in love with this woman.

Is it too soon? Is a phase of denial supposed to come before falling in love? All I know is, I can't be without her. I'm even prepared to trust her despite everything she's hiding from me. She must have changed her mind, surely? There's no way she could have faked the emotion that was on her face when I was inside her.

"Give me your hand."

She holds it out, understanding what I'm about to do. I open the box and carefully lift out the jewel.

"My grandmother didn't really leave me a ring, I'm afraid," I say, slipping it onto her finger. "I chose this one myself. If you don't like it, we can always change it . . . but it made me think of you."

It's exactly the right size, thank goodness. Rose stares at it, at a loss for words. I have no idea what she's thinking. The ring is sublime, though—dark, mysterious, otherworldly. The central stone is a magnificent salt-and-pepper diamond, set within two crescent moons made of diamonds, six additional small brilliants. The band is twenty-four karat rose gold.

"It's the most beautiful thing anyone's ever given me. But . . . it isn't for real," she murmurs, almost making it sound like a question.

My heart thumps in my chest. I want to tell her that it is, but I don't want to drop a bombshell like that just as I'm about to leave. So I reply, "We'll discuss it tonight. In the meantime, make sure to show it off."

Rose holds her hand out and gazes at it, her face reminding me of the emoji with hearts for eyes. "I fully intend to."

She hurries off, undoubtedly to show it to Li Mei. I'm almost ready to follow when I hear something vibrate on the bed. At first, I think it's my phone, but when I look down, I see that it's hers, and there's a message on the screen . . . from "Papa."

My blood freezes. I don't want to look. I swear it. But I can't avert my eyes from the message that flashes up, seeming to mock me.

Thanks for the tip.

I knew I could count on you.

Oh.

◆ ◆ ◆

I was already in a bad mood, but after seeing Tito's message, I'm off the charts. I know she probably has a good excuse. She'd *better* have one. Which tip does he mean? What can I have missed?

Could she have guessed what we're cooking up with the *New York Times*? If she has . . . everything could go up in smoke.

I tell myself I'll talk to her about it this evening and then try to put her out of my mind while I'm playing. Every day, fewer players remain. The competition is also getting fiercer. Today I find myself at the same table as Thomas for the first time since we arrived, which helps improve my mood.

We play for several hours. Everything's going well when somebody suddenly pulls up a chair opposite me. It's Tito, his face looking puffy and red. He gives me a murderous stare that probably looks just like the one I'm giving him.

Resisting the temptation to look at me, Thomas concentrates on his game. We play in silence at first, but Tito starts to talk once Thomas and I are the only two left in the game.

"You look tired. Slept badly, did you?"

I don't deign to look at him, preferring to act as though he doesn't exist. Unfortunately, he presses on.

"You can stop putting yourself to so much trouble, you know. Pretending to drink and party and screw all night just to keep me from sleeping. It's pathetic."

I stiffen, and I sense Thomas doing the same. I realize he's referring to last night, and to the sounds he must have heard through the wall. So he knows. Rose must have told him I'm just pretending, like the good little spy that she is. How far has she gone with her treachery? Does Tito know I'm color-blind? Worse, does he know I'm guilty of killing my father?

Is he just waiting for the best moment to bring it up?

I can't help it. I start to panic. I shouldn't reply, but I'm having a bad day. I smile wolfishly and lick my lips.

"Actually, everything you heard last night was real," I say, fiddling with my chips. "I guess you must be proud of her?"

He clearly wasn't expecting that. He stares at me in silence. Thomas frowns, not understanding what's going on. I don't care about keeping up the pretense. I just want to wipe that fucking smile off his face.

"You did send her to seduce me, didn't you? Your own daughter . . . I didn't see it coming, I must admit."

Thomas turns his head suddenly to look at me, his eyes wide.

Tito has let his mask fall, and he looks disappointed but not particularly surprised. I place my bet and then focus my attention on him, leaning forward so the croupier can't hear me.

"Don't worry, Tito. Mission accomplished. And I really . . . and I mean *really*, made the most of it."

I wink at him to make absolutely sure he knows what I mean. Fury spreads over his face, and his fists clench on the table. *Touché.*

As I expected, he doesn't move. He wouldn't dare attack me in the middle of the tournament, for fear of getting himself disqualified.

"You're going to regret that, Ivanovich."

I don't even take the trouble to reply. The croupier warns us that it's against the rules to talk about anything except the game, and that we'll be sanctioned if we don't stop.

I'm distracted for the rest of the day. I change tables after two hours and meet up with Thomas later at the entrance of the hotel. He takes me firmly by the arm and walks me outside, murmuring in my ear, "What was all that crazy stuff about? Don't tell me . . ."

"That Rose is Tito's daughter? Yes, she is. And she's also a spy."

He looks at me as though I've gone crazy, then swears to himself and scratches his beard. "How long have you known? Why didn't you say anything?"

"For a while now. I wanted to give her a chance to change her mind. To realize her father's a bastard . . . To switch sides."

"You're out of your mind, man," he fumes. "You should have gotten rid of her as soon as you found out. He's her *father*, Levi. And you served up all your weaknesses to her on a silver platter!"

"It doesn't m . . ."

"I warned you!" he goes on, furious now. "I told you to be careful, and said that she was dodgy and you were stupid! I knew she was going to wrap you around her little finger. Shit!"

I tell him to calm down. He falls silent, running his hand through his blond hair in frustration. I want to tell him she's changed, that her feelings are sincere, that we're in love.

But the truth is, I have no idea if any of that's true. She might be using me, for all I know. The message I saw this morning flashes before my eyes, and I sigh in frustration.

"Don't tell the others. I absolutely forbid you to do that, do you understand?" I say firmly, "Tonight I'll tell her I know her secret. We'll see what she says. I want to give her one more chance to explain."

He shakes his head disapprovingly but accepts my conditions. Before long, Lucky joins us and starts complaining about the heat.

"Shall we go for a swim? Li Mei and Rose are getting massages. Maybe we could join them."

"I need a drink more than I need a massage," Thomas grumbles, avoiding my gaze.

I can tell he's still angry with me. It's rare that I keep anything a secret from him. I put my arm around his shoulders.

"I wouldn't mind a drink," I say. "What about you, Lucky? Shall we have guys' night out, like in the old days?"

He smiles, throwing his shoulders back. "Sure! I could ask the girls if they want to . . ."

"I said *guys*, Lucky! Which part of that didn't you understand?"

His smile fades, and sadness spreads over his face. "Not even Li Mei?"

"Is Li Mei a guy?"

"No."

"Then that's your answer," Thomas cuts in, starting to walk more quickly.

I pull Lucky after him, promising to give him some advice on how to win back his ex. I'm not going to lie; it could be difficult. But I know Li Mei well enough to be sure that she's still madly in love with him.

She's just ashamed to admit it.

We head toward the bar at the end of the street as Lucky complains about their evening out last night. I'm hardly listening, and the truth is, I'm completely lost in my thoughts when I cross the road.

*"Watch out!"*

At that exact same moment, I hear the squeal of tires.

But it's too late.

# Chapter 23

## Rose

***June***
***Las Vegas, USA***

There's only one thing I want: for this day to end so I can see Levi tonight.

I know; it's pathetic. Since when have I been so addicted to a guy? After yesterday, something's changed. The way he looks at me isn't the same. The gentleness of my hands when I touch him isn't the same. It's *real.*

I glance for the millionth time at the ring on my finger, and my chest tightens. Am I truly falling in love with Levi? That would really be the greatest irony yet.

"That's a pretty rock," Li Mei observes. "Your man's got taste."

"He's not my man. Not really."

I hate hearing the note of regret in my voice. Li Mei hears it, too, because she smiles mockingly as we walk past the Bellagio fountains.

"Are you sure about that?"

I don't reply, and I avoid her gaze. I've only ever lost my heart to one man in my whole life, my first boyfriend, Marco. We lost touch after we finished school, and since then, I've only had brief encounters. I've had other things on my mind. Things that don't leave room for love. And anyway, I've had other priorities. I suppose it's true what they say: it happens when you least expect it. I thought Levi was my ticket to freedom—a cash machine, or at least a way to pass the time. Karma just happened to catch up with me. Now here I am, caught in a game of my own making, unable to tell the truth for fear of everything I'll lose.

"The problem with Levi . . . is that we're too similar," I say, screwing up my eyes against the sun. "We're both too selfish, too manipulative, too emotionally unstable . . . We'd destroy each other."

"That's not true. I've known Levi for a few years now, and I know this is going to sound like a cliché, but . . . I've never seen him like this."

I'm not convinced. And anyway, that's not my biggest problem. There's a much bigger reason I can't be with him.

My lies.

I can never be with Levi, because the moment I tell him who I am, he'll end it without thinking twice. And there's no way I'm starting anything without telling him the truth. That I'm an imposter.

"What about you?" I say, to change the subject. "I've seen the way you look at Lucky."

"Pff, rubbish."

I stare at her, raising one eyebrow, and link my arm with hers. "Oh please! You know what I think? I think you love him, but you don't want to love him. Because he's young, and sensitive, and high strung, and all those other things you hate. But . . . our hearts do their own thing. Believe me; I know what I'm talking about."

She groans, proof that I'm right. I ask what she plans to do, but she just shrugs.

I envy her. Her problem is so straightforward compared to mine. I'd like to talk to her about it and ask her advice, but Levi has to be the first to know. I owe him that much, at least.

We do a little shopping—I even find a souvenir key ring for my mother—then head back to the hotel.

"Oh my God, there you are!"

We turn to see Judith, one of the gossip queens, running toward us and looking horrified. I'm about to pretend I don't see her and turn away, but she's already reached us, and she's grasping at my arm.

"How is your fiancé? I was just coming back to the hotel when I heard the ambulance, but it was already driving away! One of the valets told me Mr. Ivanovich was inside!"

I turn white, and my smile vanishes. At first I think there must be some misunderstanding, but when I ask what she's talking about, she frowns.

"Oh Lord, you didn't know? Your fiancé's in the hospital!"

My heart stops. "What?"

"What happened?" Li Mei asks.

"A car ran into him as he was crossing the road. So tragic . . ."

I don't stop to think. Li Mei calls me back, but I'm already off, my heart pounding. Fear seizes my throat. My friend catches up with me and grabs my hand.

"Come on. We can take my car!"

Oh. Yes. She's right. She has a car. I follow her like a robot, utterly stunned. I'm trembling with fear. I should have asked Judith for more details before running off. Is he OK? Did the car run over him, or did it knock him down? What state was he in when they put him in the ambulance?

"I'm sure he'll be OK," Li Mei reassures me, but there's a tremor in her voice. Levi would never fail to notice a car. He sees everything.

I don't say anything, because I'm too afraid of what will come out if I open my mouth. I try to call Levi, but it goes straight to voicemail. I try Thomas and Lucky, but they don't answer either. The fact that none of them answers frightens me even more. Li Mei drives so fast that we reach the hospital in five minutes. There are lots of people milling around, but I make a beeline for the reception desk.

"Hello, I'm looking for Levi Ivanovich. He was brought here after a car accident, I think?"

The woman types something into her computer and asks me a question I don't understand. I'm so confused and disoriented that the English words mix themselves up in my head. I know all the words she's using, but I'm completely incapable of remembering what they mean. I ask her to repeat what she just said, but I still don't get it.

Just as I'm starting to get angry, Li Mei intervenes.

"She's asking if you're family."

I don't hesitate for a second.

"I'm his fiancée."

◆ ◆ ◆

Thomas is pacing up and down outside the room, looking at his phone. I feel a little relieved to see him safe and sound.

He hears us coming and looks up. His tone is hard as he says, "I was just trying to call you . . ."

"How is he?" I cut him off abruptly. Maybe I'm paranoid, but I get the sense there's real anger in his eyes. He puts his phone in his suit pocket and replies coolly, unmoved by our anxiety.

"Fine. They're both out of danger."

Li Mei startles at that. "What do you mean, *both*?"

"What happened?"

Thomas explains that they were heading to a nearby bar for a drink. As they were crossing the road, Levi got distracted and didn't see the car coming straight for him.

"Is it serious?" I breathe.

I keep my cool despite my fear. Thomas shakes his head, keeping his eyes on Li Mei. He studiously avoids looking in my direction. What's he hiding, exactly? Why does he look so furious with me?

"No. Lucky jumped in front of him. He took most of the impact."

Li Mei gasps and claps her hands to her mouth.

"He's OK. He's broken an arm and a few ribs. Probably has a concussion, too, but he was lucky. Levi came away with only a few scratches."

Before I've even had time to register my relief, Thomas opens the door to the room, and we crowd in. I see Lucky lying on the bed, wearing a hospital robe, one arm in a cast. My heart leaps when I see Levi standing near him, his arms folded. All in one piece.

He turns to look at us, and his eyes meet mine. I tremble, resisting the temptation to throw myself into his arms to reassure myself he's really alive. His face is expressionless, as usual.

"Lucky!" Li Mei exclaims, rushing past me and taking her ex's hand. "What were you thinking, you clumsy idiot?"

I look away from my pretend fiancé to make sure Lucky is all right. He looks shaken but in good form despite the cast. He's smiling as though everything were going brilliantly.

"I saved Levi," he says delightedly.

I raise my eyebrows. Thomas explains that Lucky's been high on adrenaline for a while now. Li Mei asks him what happened, and Lucky gives us his version of the story.

"Levi crossed the road and didn't see the car until it was too late."

"Weren't you looking?" I ask, turning back to him.

This comes out sounding more like an accusation than I mean it to. Levi just smiles and looks at me, still not showing any emotion. I guess he must still be a little in shock. It's Lucky who replies.

"In his defense, the car came out of nowhere. The road was clear when we started to cross. The light was red. Then all of a sudden . . . there it was! It was a completely instinctive reaction—I jumped toward him, trying to push him out of the way."

"Were you both hit?"

"Yes. But not badly, to be honest. We were already almost out of its path, so it was just the front light that hit us. We were lucky!"

Thomas nods, his jaw clenched. He's standing near Levi, who still hasn't said anything. I notice the scratches on his face, and a Band-Aid on his left cheekbone.

"Levi fell over because Lucky knocked into him," Thomas says.

I can't believe it. If Lucky hadn't been there, Levi would probably be in a far worse state. If I'd known that one day I'd be thanking Lucky for saving my fiancé . . . I'd never have believed it.

"You were . . . really brave," Li Mei admits, holding both his hands.

"Me, brave?"

"Yes. You acted without thinking."

"Anybody else would have done the same," he says with a shrug.

"That's not true."

Li Mei smiles and shakes her head, her eyes wet. Lucky looks lost, as though not understanding the importance of what he's done.

Levi speaks up for the first time since we've been there, looking directly at his friend. "I owe you one. I really do. Thanks, man."

I can see he really means it. He's incredibly grateful.

I step forward and ask the question that's been nagging at me for a few minutes now. "What about the car? Did it stop?"

Thomas shakes his head grimly. "Hit-and-run. We spoke to the police, but I didn't even have time to get the license plate. I was just . . . scared." He says that as though the very idea comes as a surprise to him. The whole story seems completely crazy to me.

Thomas murmurs something into Levi's ear, and Levi nods. His eyes meet mine again and don't look away. I don't feel good. I need to touch him, to feel sure he's really there. I go over to him, still holding his intense gaze, and wind my fingers around his.

"Are you OK?"

Thomas draws back, still looking straight ahead.

Levi looks at me and nods. "I'm OK."

Li Mei asks Lucky when he can be discharged, and he explains that the doctor was more than happy to sign his release, but Levi insisted on his staying another night so they could keep an eye on him. Li Mei decides to stay too.

"We'll go, then," Levi says.

He tells his savior to get some rest, and the three of us leave, closing the door behind us. The silence is bizarrely heavy. The two men are talking as we get into the lift, but I don't listen. I feel groggy.

We take a taxi back to the hotel, riding in silence all the way. Levi is completely ignoring me. When we reach the door to the suite, he surprises me by slipping his hand into mine. I glance at him in surprise, but he's looking at Thomas.

"Can we have some time alone?"

Thomas seems unwilling, but he purses his lips and nods, before heading back down the corridor. Levi leads me into the suite, his fingers still entwined with mine. As soon as he closes the door behind us, I feel as though I might fall apart.

I follow him to the living room, my legs trembling and my heart beating incredibly fast. I don't understand what's happening to me. It must be the stress taking its toll, because I suddenly break down. I can hardly breathe, and I hide my face in my hands, sinking down onto the floor.

*He's alive. Safe and sound. Everything's fine.*

I collapse completely, my throat seizing up. For a while I really thought . . . I thought . . . It was as though the world were crashing down around my ears. For a nanosecond, I thought, *If I haven't got Levi anymore, what* have *I got?*

"I was so afraid," I mumble into my hands. "I thought you . . ."

I can't finish my sentence, or stop the tears running down my cheeks. I'm probably more surprised by this than he is. I haven't cried for years, but here I am bawling, paralyzed with relief.

That's when the truth hits me.

*I can't deny it any longer. I love Levi Ivanovich.*

I knew it already, deep down, of course. I realized I loved him when his face became the only thing my fingers ever painted.

I hear him come over and crouch next to me, and I finally uncover my face. He's directly opposite me, as beautiful and perfect as ever.

He smiles ever so slightly and tilts my chin upward with his long fingers. His touch is extremely gentle, as though he wants to reassure me, but his eyes, just like his words, are icy.

"You can drop the act now, *lyubimaya*."

# Chapter 24

## Levi

***June***
***Las Vegas, USA***

Rose furrows her brow in confusion, her face bathed in tears. That doesn't soften my resolve one bit. The anger is cold and hard in my heart. I stroke her cheeks tenderly, lovingly, wiping away the crocodile tears that die on her lips.

Those lips that have told so many horrible lies. Those lips that kissed me, just so she could more effectively betray me.

"What?" she stammers, and I've never seen her look so vulnerable.

I glide my fingers over her cheekbones and brush away a stray strand of hair from her mouth. My movements couldn't be gentler, but the fire inside me is fierce and deadly.

"It was Tito's men who did this."

She turns a shade paler, looking for all the world as though she didn't already know. What an actress! I analyze her every expression, admiring her mastery at lying. I watch her shake her head, only slightly at first, then more decisively.

"Impossible."

"Oh really? Why?"

"He'd never do a thing like that," she claims confidently. "He's a bastard, but not a murderer."

"You mean, not like me?"

She blinks, confused. I don't know why I'm so very angry. I already knew what she was. I already knew she was taking me for a ride. But I never thought she'd go as far as to . . . I was stupid enough to think that maybe, just maybe, she'd really fallen for me.

"How can you possibly know what he might or might not do? You don't know him very well, after all," I say, putting my head on one side.

She doesn't have an answer to that. I tell her I recognized the make of car as belonging to one of the stooges who follows Tito everywhere. Not just the make, but the exact vehicle. At least all that time I've spent spying on Tito wasn't completely wasted.

Rose pretends to be shocked. It makes me sick. Just this morning, I was persuading myself I could trust her. I was about to tell her I loved her, for fuck's sake. She played me for a fool, and that's something I can't tolerate.

She toyed with my feelings for the sake of a goddamn poker game. Not just my feelings but my life, and my friends' lives.

"Rose."

She looks fixedly at me, her eyes shining, as I take her chin in my hand, my thumb on one side of her mouth, my fingers on the other. I pull her gently toward me and press a soft kiss onto her lips.

She closes her eyes and doesn't resist, but I press harder, and she eventually moans in pain. I pull back without letting go of her, my eyes shooting daggers, and whisper, "I know everything, my love. Tito, your father, your false identity . . . I've known it all right from the start."

Rose stiffens under my touch. She does her best not to show it, but thanks to her lessons, I can read the signs of fear in her face.

"Was it fun?" I ask. I feel a false smile contort my face. "Is he paying you more than I am? I bet you're rich now. That's why you did it, isn't it? Or was it to please Daddy? To make him love you?"

I can see in her eyes that these last questions have hit home, but her sadness quickly transforms into anger, and she smacks my hand to make me let go before she jumps to her feet. I sigh dramatically, still crouching on the ground, and take my time standing up.

"The truth hurts, does it?"

"It isn't what you think."

I almost laugh. Of all the stupid things she could have said, that's the worst. When someone says that, you can be pretty sure they're lying. And now that I know her talent at that, I can see it coming.

I dig my hands into my pockets, my defense systems activated. Rose has known me for only a few weeks. She doesn't really know who I am yet, or how I operate. But the fact is, nobody cons me. She's been the exception to the rule, until now. But when I'm angry, I fight back. And I have no pity. If you hurt me, I'll use your worst insecurities to hurt you twice as badly.

Even if it means lying.

Even if it means making myself suffer.

"Oh, so you're not Rose Alfieri, daughter of Tito Ferragni?"

She hesitates, her fists clenched at her sides. "Yes, I am," she admits reluctantly.

I smile and turn away, then start to pace up and down the room.

"Let me guess. He asked you to spy on me? To find out what I was plotting? No, even better: to seduce me and then destroy me, without him having to even lift a finger. Was that it?"

Her silence speaks volumes. *Ouch.*

"He likes others to do his dirty work, it seems."

"It's not as simple as that," she insists. "I fucked up; I know. I was about to tell you everything."

"Of course you were. What convenient timing."

Rose scowls at me but doesn't speak. I know she's dying to tell me to shut up, but she knows she's in the wrong. I guess she's still hoping to save her skin. Didn't her father bring her up to speed?

"How long have you known?" She bats away her tears with an impatient gesture. Her expression is cold and closed. Her chin is high. The person I see is a million miles from the Rose who held me in her arms last night while I cried over my father's death.

*I've been so stupid. I've only got myself to blame. Thomas warned me.*

I sit on the sofa, crossing my legs coolly. "Ever since you've known about my color blindness."

Her mask drops for a second. She looks dumbfounded. "But . . . that was ages ago."

"So?"

"Why didn't you say anything? You've known all this time . . ." She doesn't finish her sentence.

I shrug nonchalantly. I want her to think I don't care and that she hasn't managed to wound me. It's my only chance to save whatever shred of dignity I have left.

"I didn't say anything simply because it was easier not to. You amused me. My father used to say, 'Keep your friends close, and your enemies closer.' No doubt Tito taught you the same thing, or you wouldn't have slept with me at the first opportunity."

It's as though I've shot her. I force myself to keep the vicious smile on my face. Can she see the suffering in my eyes? I hope not. Thanks to her, I'm an expert in hiding my emotions now. That's one way she's helped me, at least.

I get up and stand directly in front of her, holding her murderous gaze. I feel the urge to lay things on even thicker, wanting to see her suffer at least as much as I have. It's not fair for her not to.

"It was funny . . . seeing you acting your little heart out and knowing none of it was true. I used it all to beat you at your own game, of course. I was curious to see how far you'd go."

"You're lying."

"Am I?" I say mockingly. I lower my head toward hers, a nasty smile on my face. "Are you sure about that?"

Her eyes search mine, looking for the real me underneath my iron facade. I can see my words have hit their mark, but I can't tell if she's still acting or if her ego really has just shattered.

"So you told me all your secrets just for fun? You weren't worried about where that might lead? I don't believe you."

"Why not?"

"What if I went to the police and told them you killed your father?"

My whole body stiffens. I hide my anxiety and pretend to think about this, before replying offhandedly, "Who'd believe you? There's no proof, and my mother has already served her time. Plus I already tried to confess when I was a kid. There's no way they'd bother digging up an old case from ten years ago. But go ahead and tell them, by all means. Be my guest."

"I never said I'd actually do it." She sounds annoyed that I might think her capable of such a thing. "I know I lied. And I did accept your offer with the aim of helping my father. But . . . things changed. I mean it, Levi. I switched sides a long time ago."

*A convenient excuse*. She really must take me for a loser if she thinks I'll fall for that again. Women like her are dangerous, especially ones who've been raised by Tito Ferragni.

"Really?" I ask.

She blinks, and nods hesitantly. I can't stand seeing that damn ring on her finger, proof of my stupidity.

"Really."

Silence. I nod once, then twice, and sigh. "I'm afraid I can't say things changed for me, unfortunately."

The lie is bitter on my tongue. It hurts me, but I go on, satisfied to see her expression grow increasingly miserable as I speak.

"It was all a game. The sex was good, I won't deny that. Now that I think of it, you know what I find amusing?" I give a bark of laughter. "When I offered you this job, back in Macau, you told me you weren't a prostitute. I guess that was a lie too."

Rose slaps me hard in the face. I was expecting it, so I'm not completely caught off-balance. But the strength behind the blow does astonish me, and I welcome the burn of the mark she leaves on my cheek.

I look at her again, no longer smiling, and see she's ready to explode.

"What?" I ask in a venomous whisper. "Isn't that what your father does? You must mean a lot to him. After all, you've spent your whole life accepting whatever he dishes out, hoping that maybe one day he'll love you . . ."

"Shut up, Levi. I'm warning you."

"You must think I'm pretty pathetic, with my dead father and my mother behind bars. But you know what? I pity you even more, Rose," I murmur, right into her ear, like a lover. "Because unlike me . . . you've got nobody else."

I don't have the chance to say more, because she shoves me away with all her strength, yelling wildly, "You piece of shit! I forbid you to pity me!"

At first, I think she'll stop there, but she grabs my shirt and tries to hit me again. I take her by the wrists to stop her and push her backward, hard enough that her back hits the wall. The books on the shelf fall off with a crash.

Rose seizes one and hits me on the head with it. I groan and stagger backward. I don't want to hurt her, but I'm overtaken by a sense of terrible injustice. I want her to suffer as much as I'm suffering. I want to shake her and ask her why she did everything she did. Why she doesn't feel the way I do.

Why did she have to ruin everything, just when I thought I'd finally found a reason to live, and to leave my guilt behind?

"You make me sick!" she shrieks. She reverts to Italian, spewing what I assume is a flood of insults.

"I warned you at the start, my love. I'm not a nice boy. You wanted to play the game, and you lost. Now get out of here."

She blows a falling lock of hair out of her eyes angrily. She's still incredibly sexy despite the fury of her expression. I watch her walk quickly into our room, presumably to go pack up her things.

As soon as she's gone, I let my mask fall and draw in a deep breath. My hands are trembling. I run my fingers feverishly through my hair. I can't believe what's happening . . .

When she doesn't come back, I go to look for her.

I find her standing in the middle of the bedroom, holding a huge pair of scissors, surrounded by my clothes. She's cutting them into pieces, garment by garment, and throwing them on the floor.

I leap toward her and snatch the scissors out of her hands, hardly able to believe my eyes. "Oh my God, you're actually crazy!"

"Yes, I'm fucking crazy! You should have done your homework before choosing me to be your fiancée, *amore mio*."

She starts grabbing random objects and throwing them at my head. I manage to dodge some, but not all of them. Finally, she takes hold of my computer, which was on the bedside table, slams it to the floor, and stamps on it. I push her away, but it's too late.

Jesus Christ. She's smashed my computer. I watch her march out of the room, obviously pleased by what she's done, then follow her. Her hips sway enchantingly, I notice to my shame. How can I be thinking about that, when at this moment I hate her with every shred of my being?

"You can tell your father it's not a good look, sending his daughter off to prostitute herself!" I shout after her as I follow her into the hallway.

She doesn't turn around as she retorts, "You can say hello to yours from me, in hell!"

Something explodes in my chest. I see red. I take her by the shoulders, utterly beside myself, and back her up against the wall.

"What did you just say?" I hiss menacingly.

"So the truth hurts, does it?" Her rigid smile is full of cruelty. Devious, nasty, irresistibly beautiful.

My eyes stray to her lips. I'd like to wipe off her triumphant smile that makes me want to throw up.

"I *hate* you," I breathe, my lips against her mouth, my hand on her shoulder. "I really hate you, Rose . . . I can't tell you how much."

Her gaze is defiant, somber, and devastating. It strays down to my lips, and she whispers, "Say it again, and maybe I'll believe you."

She doesn't give me time to repeat it, and I couldn't even if she did, because she presses her mouth hard against mine. My brain tells me to push her away, but my burning desire and my wounded heart seem to think I haven't suffered enough yet.

My hands take possession of her hips and lift her up. I devour her mouth, my excitement pressing so painfully against my jeans that our tongues start to fight where our words left off.

I've never experienced anything like this. I feel as though my heart could explode. Adrenaline prevents me from stopping to think about what I'm doing. I'm gasping for air. I'm suffocating. I want her, but I also want her to suffer.

"You drive me crazy," she whispers, breathless, as she runs her teeth down my neck and bites into my skin.

"Welcome to the club. You drive me fucking *insane.*"

I can't hold back. I need to be inside her right now. She seems to feel the same, because she's wrestling with my belt buckle as I'm tearing her dress away and pulling off her underwear.

I haven't got a condom. I don't stop to think, consumed by the need to possess her. As soon as my belt's undone, I don't even bother to pull off my trousers. I enter her without pause, the act causing us both to groan with pleasure.

Her hands wrap themselves around my neck, then pull my hair as I hold her thighs tightly against me. There's nothing gentle or romantic about what we're doing. It's all urgent violence, revenge, and wounded egos. I take her brutally and fast, my pulse accelerating with the speed of my movements.

We hold one another's gaze defiantly. I breathe harder, and she sinks her nails into my shoulder blades and moans loudly as I grab her buttocks, pulling her toward me with every thrust.

We don't speak. I'm afraid of what I'd say if I did. She comes first, and I'm not far behind. My orgasm is like a fireball, and I can barely hold up Rose's trembling legs.

Once she's got her breath back, I let her go. As soon as her feet touch the ground, she pulls up the straps of her dress and scowls at me. The silence is heavy with meaning. I feel excited, exhausted, sad, angry, and ashamed. My head is an insane mess.

All I want is to keep her near me.

But I break the silence, saying calmly, "Go away."

I know I seem like a total bastard who's just taken advantage of her, but the truth is it's the other way around. I just don't want to give her the satisfaction of knowing it. Not when she's already taken so much from me.

She looks at me without a word, clearly wounded. I watch her take off the ring and throw it at my chest. I don't catch it, so it falls to the floor with a dull thud. The symbolism of the gesture hurts me more than it should.

"Keep it or sell it," I say, zipping up my trousers with as much dignity as I can. "It means nothing to me."

I don't wait to see what she'll do. I turn my back on her and go into my room, my hands in my pockets. I should feel relieved. After all, the whole point was to say all those horrible things to her.

And yet I've never in my life felt more like a piece of shit.

# Chapter 25

## Rose

***June***
***Las Vegas, USA***

I spent the night in a bar.

I'm absolutely hammered. I thought alcohol would dull the pain in my heart, like it usually does, but it's not working this time.

Levi has completely messed me up. It turns out he's a total asshole. It's my own fault. My father told me what he was. I'd heard the rumors. Levi even warned me himself. I was stupid to think there was anything different hidden behind his image as the devil incarnate.

I stagger to a bench by the side of the road, sit down, and close my eyes. The sun is already starting to show itself. I haven't slept a wink. I hate Levi, but I hate myself even more. This is all my fault.

I started it; it's true. I was going to explain it all to him. I wanted to tell him I haven't given any really important information to my father. I wanted him to know I'd fallen for him, and that I'd never have slept with him if I hadn't.

*I'm not really a prostitute, am I?*

But when he admitted to having used me, the words died on my lips. He's known everything right from the start. He let me keep on going so he could manipulate me even more. So that he could seduce me right back and make me change sides. He's completely twisted. The person I love doesn't even exist.

The memory of how I let him take me against the wall comes flooding back, and I almost vomit on the pavement. The worst thing is, I enjoyed it. Somehow, I don't regret it. It was my way of saying goodbye to him. Everything else was a huge mistake. I shouldn't have begged my father to let me come here; I shouldn't have agreed to spy on Levi; I shouldn't have followed him here . . . All for what? Some money and a broken heart?

My phone buzzes in my pocket. I stiffen, almost expecting to see Levi's name appear on the screen, but it's just my mother. I take a deep breath, tidy my hair as best I can, and answer the call.

Her face appears on the screen. I see the garden of our house in Venice behind her, with its vines and oleanders. She gives me a beaming smile and signs to me, "Hello, sweetheart. I'm not disturbing you, am I?"

I shake my head, not trusting myself to open my mouth. But it's my mother, and my mother knows everything. Her face falls slightly, and she asks if I'm OK.

That tips me over the edge. I don't know what happens, but I burst into tears through my smile. That hasn't happened in years. My mother is taken aback, and a look of panic appears on her face. Everything's blurred through my tears, so I can barely understand what she signs to me.

"What's going on? Where are you?"

"I've done something really stupid, Mom," I tell her, sniffing.

"It'll be all right. Tell me all about it, darling."

I take a moment to calm down before admitting the worst of it: I came to Las Vegas with Dad. I met a man and got taken in by him. She purses her lips as she realizes I've been lying to her.

"Your father was wrong to take you with him. It's not good for you. You should have stayed here, at home."

"I know. I'm sorry."

"Who is this man?" she asks suspiciously.

I grimace but don't say anything. Do I really have to tell her everything? What if she starts to hate me too? I can't stand the thought of disappointing her. But when I look into her eyes, I don't have a choice.

"Levi Ivanovich," I admit miserably.

Her mouth opens in surprise. The name is clearly familiar to her. She says nothing at first, then shakes her head and sighs. Her movements are frenetic as she begins to sign again, frowning.

"This is all your father's fault! He dragged you into this business, didn't he? What did he offer in return?"

"Money."

"Is it money you need? We've got money, for God's sake! You only had to ask!"

'I know, but I don't want to ask, Mom. That's the whole point. I don't want to be dependent on you anymore. I want to manage for myself."

She doesn't reply immediately, and her expression grows resigned. She must guess why I need money, but she knows me too well to try to talk about it now. Instead, she asks me the question I feared the most.

"Do you love this man?"

I sit quite still, my eyes full of tears. My mind fills with images of Levi: his playful smile, the gentleness of his hands when he disinfected my knee, the taste of his mouth against mine, the feel of his legs wound around mine when he's asleep. The way he calls me *my love*.

I look down and nod miserably. Yes. Yes, I'm in love with Levi Ivanovich. I knew that already, of course. But admitting it to another person is different. It makes it seem real.

"Is he good to you?" my mother interrogates me. "That's all I care about."

"It doesn't matter. He doesn't feel the same toward me."

There's no point in discussing it. What's done is done. I thought I deserved a second chance, but I was wrong. Levi and I aren't made for each other. I'm a Capulet, and he's a Montague. Sorry, Shakespeare. In my world, Juliet is a mercenary floozy, and Romeo is a manipulative shit.

If any scenario deserves a tragic ending, this one does.

"Come home," my mother begs. "You need to be with me. We'll find solutions to your problems. I love you, darling."

My heart doesn't like this idea, for the simple reason that it hates the thought of being far away from Levi. But I do desperately want to go. To feel like I'm home again. To be back in my own bed, my garden, my room. With people who speak my language, who understand me . . .

I'd give a lot for a hug from my mother right now.

I dry my tears and nod resignedly. There's nothing more for me to do here, anyway. Nothing to hold me back.

"All right. I'll come home."

◆ ◆ ◆

I've bought a plane ticket to Italy for this afternoon. I've made up my mind. I just need to do two things: collect my belongings and talk to my father.

When I reach the hotel entrance, my head still spinning, the day's play has already started. I know for sure that Levi's playing this morning, but Tito isn't. I'm worried I'll bump into Thomas in the suite, but I have to take the risk. I can't leave without my passport.

"Rose!"

I jump as though caught red-handed, then see Li Mei, still wearing the same clothes as yesterday, trotting toward me. She looks tired, and I realize she must have come straight from the hospital. Has she already heard the truth about me?

"No offense, but you look as though you've just had the worst night of your life," she says, wrinkling her nose.

*I have.*

"Are you OK?"

"I'm great. Do you know if Thomas is in the suite?"

"No. He's playing this morning. I'm on my way there too."

Perfect. That leaves me time to pack before they get back.

"How's Lucky doing?" I ask, genuinely concerned.

She tells me he's doing fine. Hearing her friendly tone, I conclude she hasn't heard what's happened. Not yet. I take the opportunity to give her a hug, which surprises her. Then I draw back and smile.

"I'll see you soon, OK?"

"Er . . . we live together."

"I'm going home," I say, taking her hand.

Li Mei's eyes widen in astonishment. She asks me why, and whether it's because Levi and I fought again. I don't want her to hate me, not my one and only friend, so I answer vaguely.

"I've fucked up. I thought I could sort things out, but I was wrong. Staying here . . . would be too hard. I've been away from home too long. I want to be with my family."

She wants to stop me, I can tell, but she can't find a reason to keep me here. The sadness in her face touches me. It seems sincere. Unlike Levi, she genuinely likes me.

"You're right," she says. "Family's important. I realized that too late. Make the most of it. We'll see each other again, though, won't we? Promise?"

*I'd like to, but you'll probably hate me once you know the truth.*

"Of course. Say bye to Lucky for me. And Thomas . . . He's grouchy, but I can't help liking him anyway."

"I will."

I go then, not wanting to make her late for the tournament. I'm relieved to find our suite empty and silent. The traces of Levi's and my violent argument are still there—books scattered on the living room floor, my ring, Levi's chopped-up clothes all over the bedroom . . .

The bed's still made, as though nobody's slept there. I don't linger, just quickly pile my clothes into my suitcase. I change out of my torn dress into a pair of jeans and leave it lying on the floor when I leave.

Once I'm in the corridor, I'm just a few steps from Tito's room. I haven't even planned what to say to him. I'm too angry, too disappointed, too shocked. I want to tell him how used I feel. I want to say I'm abandoning my ambition to make him proud, no matter what that costs me.

But most of all, I want him to swear to me that he didn't try to physically harm Levi. I still refuse to believe he was behind that.

I knock on the door, my heart pounding. When it opens, I quickly rearrange my face into its usual mask. Tito doesn't look particularly amazed to see me. He steps aside to let me in.

"What a pleasant surprise."

I walk in, dragging my suitcase behind me, and stop in the middle of the room. As I fold my arms, my father sits down on the sofa, where he's been eating breakfast.

"To what do I owe the pleasure?"

"Levi knows everything," I blurt out.

He doesn't seem bothered by this revelation, but simply bites into a brioche and opens the newspaper in front of him. "I know."

I can't believe it. Has Levi already confronted him? I want to ask how he knows, but that's not the most important issue right now. I watch him, fear gnawing at my stomach, and ask coldly, "Did you have anything to do with it?"

Still chewing his food, he asks what I'm talking about.

"You know exactly what I'm talking about."

"It wasn't *my* car."

"Answer the question."

He swallows, and finally looks at me. He doesn't speak, but his silence tells me everything. An awful shudder runs down my back. My hands form tight fists as I absorb the shock. I feel like I might throw up every drink I knocked back last night.

This whole situation is too big for me. I'm not up to it. I never was.

"You're sick," I breathe.

That doesn't seem to wound him. "It's your fault, you know. I had to do something, given that you weren't doing anything at all."

"And you thought that something was running him over?" I shout, suddenly furious. "What the hell were you thinking?"

He rolls his eyes, as if to say my reaction is excessive. He's frightening me. "Such harsh words. I'd never have killed him, so stop panicking. I just wanted to scare him. He's fine, isn't he?"

I stare at him, not believing my ears. I knew my father had his faults, but I didn't think he was this crazy. I have it all wrong. All this time, I was seeking approval from someone completely incapable of loving anyone except himself.

"Lucky's in the hospital because of you," I say, fighting back tears of rage.

"Who?"

*Oh my God.* He's played opposite Lucky several times, and he doesn't even know his name. Because he doesn't give a damn.

Suddenly, the awful truth hits me: right from the start, I've been on the wrong side. Levi's the hero, of course. And I'm the antihero.

My father needs help. Money and power have gone to his head. He's prepared to order a man run over, just to avoid being beaten at poker.

I feel as though I'm suffocating. I put my hand to my mouth, on the verge of being sick.

"Don't look like that," says my father teasingly. "At least now you won't have to pretend anymore. You can move in here until the end of the tournament. I've already got everything I need anyway."

What does that mean, *everything he needs*? I can't even begin to grasp what he's implying. I shake my head repeatedly. "I can't."

"You can't what?"

"You have to quit the tournament." The words tumble out of my mouth of their own accord.

Tito stiffens, then turns toward me very slowly. His eyes seem to pin me down. He always intimidated me, even when I was little. But things are different now. He's lost my respect.

I can't believe that this man is my father.

"What did you say?" he asks me.

"It's dishonest. You're cheating in every way you can!"

He bursts out laughing. His laughter has nothing to do with amusement; it's cold as ice. I know the worst is still to come.

"And if I don't?"

"I'll go to the police and tell them what you did."

I'm as surprised by this statement as he is. I hadn't intended to say it, but deep down, I know it's true. I don't want to be an accomplice to something like this. I'm giving him a chance to back out and save himself.

But if he doesn't take it, I'm not going to stand here and do nothing.

Tito's expression as he looks at me is cold and disdainful, almost disgusted. The heart of the little girl inside me breaks to see it.

"I don't think you will," he says.

I frown. That was the last reply I expected.

He continues confidently. "Because if you do that, I'll have to expose your darling fiancé's secret to the whole world. I don't think he'd like that, would he?"

I freeze and feel myself turning pale. *No. No, no, no.* Can it be that he knows about Jacob's death? How could he possibly have found out something like that? I don't say anything, feeling trapped. I detest Levi, but I promised to take his secrets with me to the grave. If my father has managed to get hold of them . . . it'll be a disaster.

I try in vain to think of a way to stop him. I'd rather Levi lost the tournament than ended up in prison. So I bite my lip in shame and beg.

"Please . . . you can't do that."

Tito tuts in disapproval.

"You're too weak, Rose. It's very exasperating. I tried to harden you up, but I was wasting my time. First poker, now this. You're full of good intentions, but the moment a good-looking guy pays you a bit of attention, you open your legs. Disappointing."

I feel as though he's slapped me. It's almost the same thing Levi said last night. As if I give myself to whoever comes along, for the sake of some money and a bit of sweet talk. Is that really all they see in me?

I resist the temptation to slap him, too, and my cheeks burn with humiliation. Better to let him think whatever he wants. Once I'm back in Venice, my mother and I will leave and go somewhere together, far away from him.

"So . . . what's your decision? You stay here until the end of the tournament and help me, and, in exchange, I keep this little secret to myself?"

I swallow, feeling like nothing more than an empty shell.

"OK."

# Chapter 26

## Levi

***June***
***Las Vegas, USA***

When I get back to the suite after a long day of poker, I sense immediately that Rose has been there. My instinct is proved right when I go into our room and find her dresser and side of the closet empty. Even the ring, which was on the floor in the corridor, is gone.

I stand in the middle of the room for a few minutes, not knowing what to do with myself. I feel completely empty. I stayed up all night, playing cards alone in the living room, not even taking the time to clear up the mess we made.

I haven't got the strength to do anything at all.

Glimpsing Tito's face out of the corner of my eye today was enough to make me want to throw up. He looked relaxed, triumphant almost. Strange. Why would he be triumphant if his plan had just blown up in his face?

Could it be that Rose actually did rat on me? I decide to take a cold shower to clear my head. I wonder what she's doing. Is she asleep in the next-door suite? I guess we're officially enemies from now on.

I don't like that idea. I'd rather not have to see her strutting around for the next few days.

After my shower, I head to the kitchen to make myself something to eat. I notice two peppers sitting in the fruit bowl, and I'm about to take one when I see they have Post-it notes stuck to them, labeled in Rose's writing: *green pepper* on one, *red pepper* on the other. I see she's done the same with the apples.

I pull off all the Post-its and throw them in the bin. I've lost my appetite. I'm about to go back to my room, but when I walk past the living room, I see the others sitting around the low table. The conversation breaks off when I join them, and they all turn to look at me.

"What's going on?" I ask tonelessly.

Lucky looks as though he's about to cry. His eyes are full of pity as he gazes at me. Li Mei bites her lip pensively. I can guess what's happened.

"You told them?"

Thomas shrugs. "I had to."

I nod. Lucky launches into a tearful tirade about how he should have seen this coming; he's failed in his duty as a friend; he even ordered friendship bracelets for all five of us, and so on.

Li Mei is sitting next to him, not saying anything, but I can see from her pursed lips that there's plenty she'd like to say. She looks at me, and I raise an eyebrow, inviting her to go ahead.

"It's . . . disappointing," she says sadly.

"Yes, it is."

"Do you think . . . she was pretending the whole time?"

"I know she was."

She doesn't seem totally convinced. That annoys me. I don't want to have to ask myself that question again. There's no way I'm going to let myself harbor doubts—they only lead to false hope.

"Did you have feelings for her?"

Her question comes from out of nowhere. All three of them look at me. I hate showing my emotions, but I have nothing to hide from these three. So I thrust my hands deeper into my pockets and nod.

The worst part of it is, I've *still* got feelings for her. They didn't disappear when she did, unfortunately. That would have been too easy.

"Did she explain why she did what she did?" Li Mei asks.

"Tito's her father. That's reason enough, isn't it?"

To my surprise, it's Thomas who answers, "Not necessarily."

Am I dreaming, or is he taking her side? I glance at him questioningly, but he doesn't elaborate. I tell them that Rose needed money and attention from a daddy who didn't praise her drawings when she was little. A total cliché.

"She's probably with Tito right now," I say.

Li Mei shakes her head.

"I bumped into her earlier, when she came to get her things."

My heart pounds in my chest. I manage to keep myself from asking how Rose looked, what she was wearing, how she was doing. *That girl wound you around her little finger and broke your heart, you absolute imbecile!*

"She told me she was going home."

"What?" Lucky exclaims. "Home where?"

"Her home. Italy."

I hide my surprise—and deep disappointment—as best I can. Is that why I didn't see her with Tito today? I assumed she was keeping a low profile, but that wasn't it.

"When?"

"This afternoon. She's probably on the plane by now."

I should be relieved. I won't have to see her anymore. That's what I wanted, isn't it? I clench my teeth in annoyance. I must have been kidding myself when I decided that . . . because the very thought of never seeing her face again makes me feel terrible.

Why is she leaving? Doesn't she want to help her father win the jackpot? It doesn't make any sense. The final is soon. Leaving now would be a waste.

And anyway, she has no fucking right to do this. It's too easy. She takes my heart, tears it in two with her bare hands, and runs off when I tell her I refuse to take any more? Not fair. She should at least stay until enough time's passed for me to start hating her.

"It's for the best," I say abruptly, trying to silence my own thoughts.

Nobody else says a thing.

◆ ◆ ◆

We don't talk about it anymore after that. Rose's name is banned in our suite. The atmosphere is strange, almost incomplete, as though something were missing. Or someone. It's like our little gang can't be the same now that she's gone.

I shut myself in my room and practice every evening. I know they're talking about me behind my back, but I let them do it. Nobody's heard any news about Rose. Tito's always alone when we see him, proof that Li Mei was right.

She's really gone.

Lucky is knocked out just before the semifinals. Only Li Mei, Thomas, and I are still in the race. Lucky doesn't let it bother him. In fact, he seems to enjoy lapping up the sympathy from his ex. She's been much gentler and more patient with him since the accident.

I still can't stand the sight of Tito. His smile makes me want to throw up.

One day, when I return after several hours of play, I find Li Mei and Lucky on the sofa, watching something on the computer. I move to join them before realizing the figures on the screen are Rose and me. I stop short, confused.

"What are you doing?"

They jump simultaneously. When Lucky sees me, he gives Li Mei a violent nudge, and she slams the computer shut, not even trying to be subtle.

"We're . . . watching porn," she blurts out in a panic.

I raise one eyebrow and scowl at them. I definitely recognized our outfits and the plain white backdrop. I guess our video interview for *Glamour* must have come out. I'd completely forgotten about it.

"You've come back at the perfect time!" she continues, jumping up to fetch her cell phone. "I've made you the best playlist ever. I'll send it to you now."

"A playlist? Why?"

She gives me an innocent look that doesn't fool me for a second. "Just because. To help you sleep."

Lucky nods vigorously and jumps up to fetch a bulging plastic bag, which he hands to me. "I want to lend you a few of my DVDs too."

"Lucky, I'm not in the mood for porn right now."

"It's not porn!" he exclaims indignantly.

Now that I think about it, that should have been obvious. Porn's not Lucky's usual fare.

I don't know what to say, so I thank them and go to my room, shutting the door behind me like I do every evening. I open the bag and find the Bridget Jones trilogy, no surprises there, along with *Romeo + Juliet*, *Pride and Prejudice*, and *Titanic*. I put them aside wearily.

I sit on my bed and open up Li Mei's playlist. I don't usually listen to music much, but I guess it can't hurt, and I could do with some distraction.

I glance over the titles, none of which rings any bells with me: "The Story of Us," "White Horse," "Back to December," "We Are Never Ever Getting Back Together," "Picture to Burn," "I Knew You Were Trouble" . . . all by the same artist, strangely.

I ignore the titles, which sound ominous, and listen to a few tracks out of curiosity. I stop after the fifth. As I suspected, they're all about breakups.

I guess Lucky and Li Mei are trying to tell me something.

I'm about to go to bed when my phone vibrates. It's Li Mei, asking if I'm asleep yet.

I know we're not supposed to talk about this, but I think you should watch the video.

It takes me a while to realize what she's talking about.

I was there, Li Mei. I know perfectly well what happened that day, and what we said.

Are you sure? I don't think you saw everything. Especially the way she looked at you when you were talking to the camera.

I freeze, my heart pounding.

That doesn't mean anything. She was acting. It was all a lie.

Did she tell you that? Or is that just what you've assumed?

. . .

Levi, there's no way she can have faked that. I think we might be wrong about her. OK, she messed up, but Rose is a human being. And what if she fell in love along the way too? What if she'd decided to take your side but you didn't give her time to explain?

I stare at her message for what feels like ages, my teeth clenched. I so want to believe her. That's the danger. Hope is growing inside me. Li Mei's right. I never really gave Rose a chance to explain. She did tell me she'd changed sides, but I refused to believe her, because I was too scared, too angry, hurt, and disappointed. I didn't want to listen to her. I just wanted to hurt her.

What if I was wrong?

The video isn't hard to find on YouTube. I swallow nervously and press Play. Seeing us on the screen, side by side, smiling adoringly at each other, hurts a lot. Still, I manage to watch it through to the end. I see us exchanging compliments, laughing, and hugging one another affectionately.

Lovingly.

Because yes, we do look like a real couple.

*You've got this amazing charisma that makes people want to follow you to the ends of the earth . . . Oh, and I love your smile,* says the on-screen Rose, with a shy look.

Li Mei was right. My pulse quickens, and my arms suddenly grow covered in goose bumps as I watch Rose's furtive glances. The glances she only allows herself when I'm looking the other way. She does it unselfconsciously, unaware of the camera that's following her every movement.

*God, I miss her. My life's as boring as hell without her, and she's only been gone a few days. I'd never noticed that before, but I guess you only appreciate things once you lose them.*

Could it be that . . . Rose felt the same way I did?

It's completely crazy, but I'm starting to have second thoughts. It's as though I want to torture myself. I jump up from my bed. I have to find Thomas and ask him to find Rose, wherever she is, even if she's in Italy.

I rush out of my bedroom, adrenaline flooding through me, and come face-to-face with Thomas. We both jump and stare at one another open-mouthed.

"I was just looking for you," I say, trying to keep my expression neutral.

"Me too."

"Oh. OK. Me first: I want you to find Rose. A phone number in Italy, an address, anything. Some way for me to contact her."

Thomas doesn't seem surprised. The same couldn't be said of me when he replies. "I've already found her."

I stare at him in disbelief, sure I must have heard him wrong. "Huh?"

"I've found her."

"That was . . . fast."

He glares at me and explains that he's been looking for her for a few days now, without telling me. He'd found her willingness to give up and leave strange too.

"So?"

"So she's here."

"'Here'?" I repeat stupidly.

"Downstairs. Now. At the poker tables, to be precise."

It takes me a while to digest this information. Rose didn't go home. He explains that she's been at the hotel all along, right under my nose. I never saw her for the simple reason that she's been spending all her time at the bar.

And apparently, she's been gambling again.

*Has she had a relapse?*

I thank Thomas and head down to the casino. She isn't hard to find. My throat tightens when I see her sitting at a poker table. She's as beautiful as ever, dressed in a tight, pale-colored dress and black high heels.

She downs her drink in one gulp, vodka by the looks of things, and places a large bet in the center of the table. That makes the other players laugh, young men probably out for a stag night.

"Excuse me?" I call a waiter as he passes by. "How long has she been here?"

I point at Rose. He doesn't need to think for long. "Since this morning, I'd say."

*Shit.*

"How many drinks has she had?"

He laughs at my question. "I don't have enough fingers to count that high!"

It's worse than I thought. I'd have been happier if she'd gone home to her mother. Where's Tito? Shouldn't he be protecting his daughter from her demons?

As if by magic, he appears at my side. I stiffen, my hands balling into fists.

"Are you lost?"

"You should take her away from here," I say curtly, before lying through my teeth. "I can't stand the sight of her. Get her out."

Tito looks at me, then laughs to himself. I guess I must be worse at lying than I used to be, because he sees right through me. He leans toward me and says in a low, confidential tone, "You still want her? I tell you what: if you pull out of the tournament, I'll give her to you."

He nearly gets my fist in his face, right then and there. And he knows it, which just makes him smile even more. How can he say something like that? She's his daughter! He brought her here.

The most shocking thing of all is that I'm surprised by any of this. After all, this man betrayed my father and tried to run me over. He's far more dangerous than I'd first thought, and he deserves to rot in prison for a very long time.

*I'll make sure he does.*

I cast a last regretful glance at Rose. I can't accept that in the blink of an eye she's become a stranger in my life, someone I'll mention in years to come as a vague memory, a wound from the past that I'm trying to heal.

I just wish she'd stayed. That she'd forced me to listen to her. That she'd fought for me.

If there's still a chance I've made a mistake, I'm determined to do all I can to find that out. But in the meantime, Tito mustn't know the truth. And so I lie, casually.

"No thanks. It's like Taylor Swift says, 'We are never ever getting back together.'"

# Chapter 27

## Rose

***June***
***Las Vegas, USA***

I've relapsed.

I know it, though I don't admit it to myself in so many words. My mother hasn't stopped calling to ask why I canceled my flight, but I don't answer. I feel trapped. Tito said he wants me to help him, but he hasn't asked me to do anything. I get the sense he just wants to keep an eye on me.

Or maybe he's making me stay just to torment me.

That's exactly the kind of thing he'd do.

I'm doing my best to avoid him. I barely sleep in my new room. I spend my nights at the hotel casino or in the bar, depending on my mood. Naturally, I've already lost three-quarters of the money I managed to earn working for Levi.

That first evening, I decided to play a few rounds to release the tension and forget what had just happened. "A few rounds" turned into "all night." It helped calm the tsunami of negative emotions that was threatening to drown me, at least for a few hours.

Then the next day, it all started again.

The first withdrawal symptoms. I recognized them a mile off. It's like meeting an old friend. A habit, a ritual of emptiness I'd missed. It felt good to go back to something I knew. After two days, the negative effects started to appear.

Stress, anxiety, frustration, withdrawal.

At least I haven't bumped into Levi or any of the others yet, thank God. They probably all hate me, and they're right to. I heard that Lucky got knocked out, and so close to the semifinals too. I felt bad for him.

"You're home early," my father says as I come through the door into the suite, my head still fuzzy from the alcohol.

I take a drag of my cigarette. He tells me to put it out, but I ignore him and keep smoking, not looking at him. Tito always claimed to hate the idea of my coming to a casino because of my addiction, but he's been strangely silent these last few days. I guess he really has abandoned me this time.

Levi was apparently the final straw.

"I have something for you," he says.

I stop short, trying to ignore the signs of a migraine coming on. My father gets up, holding a package in his hand. He tells me to open it.

"A present?" I say mockingly. "Thanks, but no thanks."

"I was a little hard on you," he admits, his voice soft. "I'm sorry. You've done some good work. I'm proud of you."

I blink in astonishment. A strange feeling starts to swell inside my chest. I couldn't say exactly what it is. My father has never said anything like that to me before. For one thing, he never apologizes. And I spent my whole life waiting for him to say those four little words, "I'm proud of you," but he never did.

Until today.

"You walked into a trap, it's true, but that can happen to anyone," he says. "Let's forget about it."

He nods at the package, indicating I should open it. I stub out my cigarette in the nearest ashtray and take the velvet box in my trembling hands. Jewelry, by the look of things. Without meaning to, I remember the moment Levi slipped the ring onto my finger. My chest tightens.

The ring that I keep carefully wrapped inside a pair of socks at the bottom of my suitcase.

"Oh wow . . ."

It's a long gold chain with the most sublime pendant, a heart-shaped aventurine. The stone is translucent, shot through with marbled streaks that give it a unique, luminous green luster. Tiny diamonds twinkle all around it—it's a real beauty.

I feel torn. Should I accept the necklace as the apology it's intended to be, or refuse it because I promised myself never to take anything from my father again? He's done terrible things that I could never justify, but perhaps it's possible that he can change?

I answer politely. "It's wonderful."

"Glad you like it."

He helps me fasten it around my neck and gives me a peck on the forehead before disappearing into his room. I stand there a few minutes, feeling shaken. I put my hand up to the reassuring shape of the stone. It's the first real grown-up gift he's ever given me.

I splash my face with water in the bathroom, then pull on a pair of camel-colored trousers and an ivory satin top. Before I leave, I put on my sunglasses to hide my eyes, which are still red from too much alcohol. I need to get something to eat.

I make sure the corridor's empty, not wanting to bump into Levi, and head for the lift. I wait impatiently for a few minutes, and when it arrives, I get in and hit the button for the ground floor. As the doors start to close, I lean back against the wall.

At the very last moment, a hand shoots through the gap between the doors, and they open to a figure I know only too well. I freeze.

Levi's right in front of me, dressed all in black, like some kind of avenging angel. Gorgeous. His eyes are fixed on mine, or rather on my sunglasses. I remain still, my heart beating crazily. Seeing him hurts so much, too much. I can't breathe.

At first, I think he's going to get out again, but he doesn't. He comes right in, hands in pockets, and turns so he stands with his back to me. The tension is palpable.

"Nice necklace."

I nearly jump in surprise to hear him speak to me. Oh God, I've missed his voice so much. I need to get a grip on myself. I ignore him. Acting as though he didn't exist is my best weapon, unfortunately.

"Though . . . I'd personally have gone for a rutilated quartz stone for you. That stone isn't your color."

I almost laugh. What does he know about colors? That being said . . . he's right. Rutilated quartz does suit me much better, with its beige and brown tones. But I'd rather die than admit that.

Suddenly, he presses the emergency stop button. The lift trembles slightly, catching me off guard. I'm about to ask what he's doing when he turns to face me, his intense gaze trying desperately to meet mine. I keep my mask firmly in place, terrified at the prospect of what he might say.

"I thought you'd gone back to Italy," he says, his voice not giving anything away.

I give him a mocking smile. "I changed my mind. Sorry to disappoint you."

For a few seconds, he simply observes me carefully. My arms break out in goose bumps, to my annoyance. I have to get out of here.

"Have you started gambling again?"

I can't work out where he's going with this. What's his problem?

I take off my glasses to look at him properly, raising one eyebrow. "What do you want from me, Levi? Be quick. I haven't got all day."

His face is still impassive. I was clearly an excellent teacher. I'm very surprised when he says, "I'd like us to talk."

"Haven't we already said everything we had to say?"

He shakes his head, and this time I imagine I detect a hint of shame and regret in his expression. He seems to have difficulty getting his next words out.

"I didn't give you a chance to speak that night. I was too angry . . . but I should have."

"I don't see what difference that would have made."

"A big one maybe," he sighs. "I need to know once and for all. Did you mean it when you said you'd changed sides?"

I gaze at him in confusion. Why ask me that now, after everything that's happened? I'm tempted to lie, but something in his expression forces me to be honest for the first time in my life.

"Yes."

There. I've said it. My legs are trembling under me. Levi closes his eyes and shakes his head ever so slightly. He sighs deeply before opening his eyes again. He appears to be thinking something through. When he looks at me again, his expression is determined.

"I lied," he says.

My brain seems to empty completely. I'm afraid of what he might mean.

He goes on, his face calm now. "When I said I used you, I lied. It's true that when I discovered who you were, I didn't say anything. But it was because I wanted to see what you were planning. I wanted to stop you, maybe even get you to change your mind."

All I can hear is the frantic beating of my heart.

"But things didn't turn out the way I thought they would," he adds. "I started to hope . . . that you'd choose me."

I melt inside. I swallow hard, my feet rooted to one spot. Levi is telling me that he cares about me. Isn't he? Or am I dreaming? Is this just another one of his games? It's very possible. I can't trust him. I can't let myself suffer even more.

"Rose," he murmurs. He slowly moves closer, stopping just a few centimeters from my face. "I'm prepared to forget everything. Forgive everything. I just want you to answer yes or no to one question, OK?"

I feel a desperate urge to cry. Because this is what I've dreamed of hearing, but also because I'm not sure I can believe him. I hold his anxious, silent gaze and note with astonishment that he's let his mask fall. He's standing there in front of me, the entirety of him laid bare.

"Rose Alfieri . . . do you love me?"

His breath is no more than the faintest of caresses on my lips, but still my legs are threatening to give way, and my chest feels as though it's about to explode. He's asking me if I love him. I want to tell him I do, but I'm so afraid he'll use that against me. It's much easier to pretend to be a stone-hearted bitch. And even if I did admit it now, what difference would it make?

Tito and his blackmail have me prisoner.

"No."

I thought he'd close up again and hurl insults at me when I said that, or show his true colors by admitting everything he'd said was all a trick.

Instead, a sad smile appears on his lips. He lifts one hand and caresses my cheek tenderly.

"Do you know what your biggest mistake was?"

The silence between us is broken only by my pounding heart.

"Teaching me to detect lies," he whispers, his finger running down my neck. "You're breathing heavily . . . like your heart rate has gone up. And you're completely tense . . . as though readying yourself for a confrontation."

My pulse quickens even more at the touch of his finger. I shouldn't have taught him all those things . . . I look at him without blinking as he lowers his head and whispers to me.

"I think you love me, Rose. Very much."

I've had enough. I can't stand this. I give him a gentle push to free myself, but he takes my wrist. I look at him, knowing I'm completely trapped. His next words are my ruin.

"Ask me if I love you . . . and see if I lie."

I can't do that. I'm too weak to withstand those words, that look. All of it.

"I don't want to."

"I warned you, remember?" He cuts me off in a reproachful voice. "I told you not to get involved with me. The lady doesn't listen to advice, does she? And now you have to pay the price. So tell me . . . what are you planning to do? Run away? You're good at that."

I'm suffocating. I'm not prepared for another fight, not if he's planning to hit me where I'm vulnerable again. I feel a terrible urge to kiss him, to touch him and tell him I'm sorry, that he means more to me than anyone else in the world. But I'm not ready, damn it.

"If this is another one of your games, it's not funny," I warn him furiously, pulling my wrist out of his grip.

"I'm not playing a game."

"You'll excuse me if I have my doubts. I can never tell with you! You trick everyone; you're always one step ahead. How do you expect me to confide in someone I can't even trust?"

This time I've gone too far. I can see the anger in his expression.

"You've got a lot of nerve saying that to me, Rose. You of all people!"

It's true. And that's exactly what worries me. If we're constantly playing games, unable to trust one other, what's the point? I don't want to be with a man I don't trust to tell the truth, and I don't want him to spend his life second-guessing my feelings.

"It seems we're just not made for one another," I say.

His smile is icy on his beautiful mouth.

"So it's running away, then. Not too surprising but still disappointing. Rose goes back to her old ways because she's scared of the dark, like a little girl terrified of the monsters under her bed."

"Go to hell."

"No, *you* go to hell," he hisses. "You're a coward, Rose. You make fun of Lucky, but you're worse than he is. If you still don't believe me even after I've told you my most intimate secrets . . . there's nothing else I can do."

He doesn't give me time to reply. He presses the emergency stop button again, and the lift starts to move. I feel terrible. He's right; I'm a complete coward.

"I've had enough," Levi adds in a low voice as the doors finally open on the ground floor. "I'm not going to run after you anymore."

Then he disappears without another word.

I lean against the wall to keep from collapsing, my knees are so weak. The problem isn't whether I believe him. That was just an excuse. I saw the sincerity in his eyes.

Levi Ivanovich feels the same way about me as I do about him.

The problem, the real problem, is Tito. I don't want to imagine what will happen if I decide to go back to Levi. My father will probably do something drastic in revenge. It's unthinkable.

I'd rather have Levi hate me than have him go to prison. He'll curse me . . . but at least he'll be free, and he'll be with his mother again, like he's always wanted.

My family has hurt them enough already.

I won't curse them a second time.

◆ ◆ ◆

I'm not going to eat after all. I've lost my appetite.

I go straight back upstairs and take off the stupid necklace, which suddenly feels too heavy around my neck. I can't believe I let my father buy me back. It was a bribe, pure and simple. He's good at that sort of thing.

I take a shower and go straight to bed. I fall into a heavy, dreamless sleep that lasts three hours, until I'm woken in the early afternoon by a series of loud bangs on the door. I ignore them, thinking that Tito will open it, or that our impromptu visitors will give up and go away, but the noise continues.

I finally get up and open the door, still half-asleep. I stiffen when I see three security guards.

"Hello. Are you Rose Alfieri?"

"Er . . . yes."

"Can you confirm that the person in this picture is you?"

I screw up my eyes and inspect the photo they hand me. It's black and white. It looks like it must have been taken by a security camera. It shows me waiting for the lift, earlier this morning.

"Yes, that's me. What's going on?"

"I'm going to have to ask you to come with us."

My heart does a somersault. I ask them why, but the man who first spoke to me just frowns and says something I can hardly believe I'm hearing.

"You've been accused of theft."

# Chapter 28

## Levi

***June***
***Las Vegas, USA***

"Theft?" I repeat, dumbfounded.

Thomas nods. I still can't believe it. After my conversation with Rose, I went back to the tournament for a few hours. I'd just returned to the suite when Thomas came in and announced that Rose has been arrested by hotel security. She's accused of stealing a six-thousand-dollar necklace. *Well, as long as it wasn't something big,* I think bitterly, shocked by the accusation.

"D'you think she did it?" Lucky asks.

I shake my head immediately. Rose has her faults, but she isn't a thief. And yet I saw the jewels around her neck myself. I don't know what to think.

"She should have gone home, like she planned . . ."

I look at Li Mei, who's staring down at her nails. I know she misses Rose. She's still here out of loyalty to me, nothing else. I ask Thomas to repeat what he's just told me.

"A guest reported that she'd lost a necklace with a red quartz. She says there's only one in existence like that, because she had it made for her. Rose was caught on the security cameras, wearing it, but when they arrested her, the necklace was nowhere to be found . . ."

"Wait a second," I interrupt him. "You said it was a red agate?"

"Yes."

*It wasn't her*. I'm overcome by a wave of relief, which I try to hide from the others.

"Then they've made a mistake. I saw her, and the stone she was wearing wasn't red."

They all look at me in silence. It takes a second, but I eventually realize why they're not totally convinced.

Li Mei makes a face and murmurs, "I don't want to offend you or anything, but you're not the first person I'd turn to when it comes to the matter of colors."

"I know. But also, it wasn't an agate."

"OK, I believe you," Thomas says. "But the problem is, you're the only witness because she went back up to her suite right after she was with you. She didn't meet anyone else."

Oh. Another heavy silence falls. If Rose went straight back after we talked, then yes, I'm the only person who can confirm her innocence.

I already know what I want to do, but I ask the others what they think. "Should we help her?"

Li Mei shrugs and looks doubtful.

Lucky says hesitantly, "I don't know, Levi . . . I love her, but she tricked us all."

"We have to help her." All eyes turn to Thomas in amazement when he says this. All eyes, that is, but mine. I just smile. I knew it. Thomas plays it cool, but I knew he had a soft spot for Rose. Like we all do.

"She's a liar," Lucky points out.

"What about us? Aren't we liars?" protests Li Mei. "We weren't straight with her, either, as I recall. At least, not at the start. She didn't owe us anything. Sure, she could have told us the truth later, but imagine how hard that would have been for her, knowing how much we hate her father."

Lucky seems to agree with her point, because he lowers his eyes and says nothing else.

I jump in. "So?"

"So Rose is one of the gang now," Thomas says. "And we don't leave anyone behind."

I laugh in spite of myself, feeling pleasantly surprised. It seems Rose is one of us, whether she wants to be or not.

"Great," I say. "Then let's go!"

◆ ◆ ◆

I'm shown into a bare room, where I find two security guards, a man in a suit, two police officers . . . and Rose, sitting at a table in morose silence. Her face doesn't give anything away. She doesn't look up at me, but her shoulders tense, proof that she knows I'm there. They tell me to sit down opposite her.

The man in the suite introduces himself as the hotel manager.

"You're Levi Ivanovich, one of the Main Event poker players," he says, crossing his arms. "I recognize you."

"That's right."

"And Ms. Alfieri is . . . your wife, right?"

"Fiancée," I correct him.

Rose doesn't speak; she just sits there scowling, her jaw set.

"OK. Your fiancée was seen with a six-thousand-dollar necklace around her neck, a unique piece that belongs to one of our guests. This guest assures us that her necklace has disappeared. But when we asked your fiancée where the necklace is, she couldn't tell us. It's nowhere to be found."

I resist the temptation to glance over at Rose. The fact that we're meant to be engaged makes my job more difficult. They might think I'm defending her because we're in love.

"You also appear on the CCTV images," the man goes on. "In the corridor, then in the lift. But you didn't leave the lift together."

"No, we had . . . a little misunderstanding. I'm not a great fan of my future father-in-law." I lower my voice as if I'm letting him in on a secret. That gets his attention.

"You mean Tito Ferragni? Is that why Ms. Alfieri's staying in his suite?"

"Exactly. She and I had a little lovers' tiff, nothing serious. Tito and I are rivals, hence the argument."

He nods understandingly, clearly intrigued. Eventually, he clears his throat and lets one of the security guards take up the questioning. The balding man comes over and explains that although the police were called, they've decided to keep things quiet for now.

"You're the only person to have seen your fiancée wearing the necklace. Can you describe it?"

I do my best, and he seems satisfied. He shows me the black-and-white image captured from the CCTV camera and asks if this is the necklace I'm referring to. I nod.

"OK. You said there was a stone in the center. Can you tell me what color it was?"

Rose looks up quickly. I was anticipating this question, but not so soon in the conversation, and I haven't got an answer ready. I just know it wasn't red.

"Your fiancée claims that the necklace she was wearing isn't the one reported lost. The stone is a different color, apparently. Your testimony could be extremely helpful."

"It was red, wasn't it?" the other security guard asks, looking daggers at Rose.

I look at him and reply calmly. "You're trying to influence me, sir."

"Just tell us what you saw," he grumbles. "What color was it?"

Silence. I think for a long time, then shrug. I have no choice but to tell the truth. I can't name a color at random and risk contradicting Rose's story.

"I don't know."

"Lying won't get us anywhere. If you're charged as an accomplice . . ."

"I'd love to see you try that. But regardless, I'm unfortunately not lying."

Rose interrupts curtly. "Shut up, you idiot."

I smile a little, without even looking at her. I understand her concern, but it's needless. I know what I have to say. I also know it's for the best. Even though deep down, I'm afraid.

I try to calm my pounding heart as I admit, "I can't answer your question for the simple reason that I have no idea what the color red looks like. Or any other color for that matter."

There's an uncomfortable silence. The men exchange glances as Rose stares at me, unable to believe her ears. She tells them I'm joking; the hotel manager sighs, thinking I'm trying to make them all look stupid.

"It's not a joke. I was born with achromatopsia," I explain, trying to convince them. "The only colors I see are different shades of gray."

"You're lying."

"I can give you my doctor's number if you like. He only speaks Russian, though, and he's not particularly friendly."

Some of the men frown. They look more serious now. I have their attention. My heart beats faster when the blond man asks the obvious question.

"You can't see colors, but you play poker? How does that work?"

"I don't see what one has to do with the other," I say. "Have you heard of Jay Lonewolf Morales? He's got achromatopsia, but he's still a painter."

I sense Rose giving me a meaningful look, but I ignore her. I can't allow myself to look at her now. The men confer in low voices, at a loss for how to proceed. I guess they're disappointed that my testimony didn't give them the proof they wanted.

Unfortunately, it also didn't prove her innocence. There'll have to be an investigation. I hadn't thought of that, and I don't like the idea.

"Just because I don't see colors in the same way as other people doesn't mean I can't see them at all," I say.

They turn back to me, intrigued. "What's that?"

It's a risk, but it's one I'm prepared to take. I can't let those hours that Rose spent making color charts for me go to waste.

Her eyes don't leave my face as I explain, crossing my legs nonchalantly.

"With practice, I've learned to associate colors with everyday objects whose colors I know. I'm able to identify a whole spectrum of different nuances of gray. For example, the gray color of grass isn't the same as the gray of your trousers, and since I know grass is green, I know that your trousers aren't green. They do look very much like the color of the sky in summer, though, and as everyone knows, the sky is blue. I therefore deduce that your trousers are blue. They're probably jeans, in fact. I could confirm that if I were to feel the texture of the cloth, but I don't make a habit of touching strangers—no offense intended."

Nobody speaks. I think I've succeeded in making them think twice.

"OK . . . so what *nuance* was the necklace you saw?" the bald guard insists doggedly.

I remain silent for a few long seconds, letting the suspense build. There's still time to stop this. What if I get it wrong? I think of Thomas, who told me a million times that this plan was too risky . . . and I plow on.

I look at Rose for the first time since I came in. Her eyes register a mixture of shock and anxiety. She's wearing the same shirt as she was on the day she blushed for the first time, after I told her she was beautiful. After she left that day, I asked Thomas what color her clothes were.

"It was that color," I say now, calmly, pointing at her shirt. "Emerald green."

I hold my breath, terrified I've said the wrong thing, but Rose's eyes don't change as the blond security guard lets out a deep sigh.

"Your fiancée did claim that the stone on her necklace was an aventurine. So, it was green."

*Oh thank Christ.* I hide my surprise and nod, quietly proud of myself. Rose was right to insist that I should learn the chart. It wasn't as pointless as I thought.

"How are we supposed to believe you?" the second security guard butts in. "This whole thing could be a scam. You could be lying, and we'd never know."

"I could be lying whether I see colors or not. That's a ridiculous argument."

He doesn't like my tone; I can tell. His colleague signals to him to be quiet and thanks me for my assistance. He leads me out, and once we're in the corridor, I ask him what's going to happen to Rose.

"I'm afraid we'll need to . . ."

"Excuse me?"

We turn toward the sight of an elegant brunette woman striding toward us. The security guard seems to recognize her, because he gives her a wave and asks if everything's all right. She grimaces as she pulls something out of her bag. I raise my eyebrows in amazement when I see the necklace that was reported missing.

"I'm afraid there's been a mistake . . . I found my necklace!"

The guard can't believe his eyes. He questions her, but I'm not listening anymore.

The whole thing could be a coincidence, but my father taught me to question everything. This woman accuses Rose of stealing a necklace that is in fact very different from Rose's, and then she finds the lost necklace, as if by magic . . . just after I've come to give evidence?

I look around me uneasily, and my gaze falls on the source of my discomfort: Tito, deep in conversation with somebody over by the fountain. The whole time he talks, he stares at me. I watch him, not knowing what I'm looking for, but . . .

He smiles and gives me a knowing wink.

*That bastard.*

"I have to go."

I head off toward the lifts and soon join the others in the suite, my hands still trembling and my heart beating. I'm kicking myself for being such an idiot. Tito was obviously behind the whole thing. I bet he was the one who gave her the bloody necklace in the first place.

And he made it disappear just before the police came to find Rose. He got his own daughter arrested, but why? What was the point of it all, if he ultimately intended for her to go free?

I ask Thomas this after I tell him the whole story, and his reply confirms my worst suspicions.

"To get at you."

I laugh incredulously, running my hands through my hair. I didn't even begin to see it coming. I rushed in blindly because Rose needed help, which was exactly what he predicted I'd do.

He knew my secret. He knew I couldn't see colors, somehow. Through Rose, perhaps—though when I consider this possibility, I don't believe that for a second. He concocted this cunning little plan, knowing full well that I'd do anything to clear her name . . . and that in doing so, I'd have no choice but to expose my handicap. After all these years, Tito knows me well enough to know I wouldn't want people to find out—not because I'm embarrassed, but because I would hate for the world to see me differently. I don't want my adversaries to play against me knowing that I'm struggling. I want them to think I do this effortlessly.

But what's done is done. I regret nothing.

"I'm ready to bet that by tomorrow, everyone in the tournament will know."

He's right. That asshole used his daughter as bait to reel me in, and I can't believe I let him do it. It was a moment of weakness, but it won't happen again.

"It doesn't matter. Let them talk! It's time I stopped hiding, anyway."

Thomas nods. "And what do we do about Rose?"

Whether she loves me or not, Rose is on our side.

Now we just have to convince her to help us destroy Tito once and for all.

# Chapter 29

## Rose

***June***
***Las Vegas, USA***

The word is well and truly out.

Ever since the security guards let me go free of charges, nobody's talked about anything else.

"Levi Ivanovich is color-blind."

"Jacob's son can only see in gray."

"How can he win if he can't see colors? I bet he cheats."

Some people are curious; others take pity on him; and a few idiots say he must be lying. This is exactly why Levi wanted to hide his achromatopsia. And it's all my fault. His reputation is taking a hit just before the semifinals, and all because I was stupid enough to fall into my father's trap.

He really got me, that bastard. An apology, a necklace, and an "I'm proud of you"—I should have seen through it all. It's not like I don't know him. He was obviously counting on my feeling blind love for him; he knew what I'd always dreamed of hearing, and he used it against me.

To hurt Levi.

Tito doesn't give a damn about me. Once more, he's thinking only of the Ivanovich family. I'm just a means to an end, for him. I assumed the secret he was using to blackmail me was the truth about Jacob's murder, but that was naive of me. There's no way he could possibly have known about that.

When I realized he'd used me to get to Levi, part of me was amused. I was sure he'd miscalculated regarding the situation involving the necklace, because there was no way Levi would come to my rescue. Not after everything that happened between us, and especially not after our conversation in the lift.

It seems I underestimated him.

Levi admitted to his achromatopsia in that room, knowing full well what the effect of dropping this bombshell would be, and all just to try to prove me innocent. He had no way of knowing whether what he was trying would even work. He'd never have attempted it if he didn't care for me.

His feelings are sincere. I still can't quite believe it, honestly. But I'd be crazy to keep running away now. The hardest part will be going back to face him. Am I strong enough to do it? Isn't it too late?

I wait outside the door of the tournament room, hoping to intercept him before he starts his day's play, but security closes the doors before I can find him.

I just hope Levi won't do something stupid in there if Tito provokes him.

"What are you doing here?"

I spin around to find Thomas standing behind me, his hair pulled back in a low bun. My mouth opens in surprise. I assume he hates me—even more than he already did, that is.

"I could ask you the same question. Shouldn't you be playing?"

"I was knocked out two days ago."

I didn't know. I doubt he cares all that much, but I don't know how to react, so I nod. "Oh. I'm sorry."

"Li Mei's still in, though."

That doesn't surprise me. Li Mei's a dark horse. I thought she didn't know how to hide her emotions when she was playing, but that was before I knew it was all an act. She's a pretty amazing player actually.

"I'll tell her you're looking for her," Thomas says.

"No need. I was just leaving anyway."

"Where are you going?"

What does he care? I shrug. I have no idea. To collect my things, for a start, because there's no way I'm sleeping in the same suite as my father anymore.

Perhaps I really should go back to Venice this time.

The thing is, I don't want to. Not until I've seen Levi again.

Just one last time.

"Does it even matter?" I say.

I turn to go, and he doesn't stop me.

◆ ◆ ◆

I leave a note for Tito on the kitchen counter before I leave. Nothing very poetic, just a simple *Fuck you.*

I take refuge at the bar, my natural habitat, where I can watch the semifinal for free on my phone. My heart leaps when I catch sight of Levi, more gorgeous than ever in his vintage shades.

Tito flashes everyone a supposedly charming smile that makes me want to bang my head against the wall. There are twenty-seven players left, divided between three tables. As I drink, I analyze Levi's game. He was already good when I met him at the Venetian, but he's improved noticeably over the last few weeks. I wouldn't go so far as to say it's all thanks to me . . . but some of it is. He's much better at controlling his gestures and facial expressions now. He analyzes other people's faces too. Sometimes, I can tell that he's trying to calculate the probabilities.

He and Tito are by far the best players, but there are other good ones, too, including Li Mei. She'll make it to the last stage; I'd bet my life on it.

A few hours later, I'm proved right. Ten players make it to the final, which will take place in a few days. Tito has the biggest stack of chips, but only just. Levi's doing all right. He has enough to survive two big hits, maybe three. No more than that.

By the time the day's last round ends, I'm already tipsy. My head's spinning, but I don't let it show. I'm craving a game, too, but I try to keep myself in check. I have hardly any money left. If I place a bet and lose everything, I won't even have enough to buy my plane ticket home.

On the other hand . . . this is a good chance to win back everything I've lost over the last few days, isn't it? I can't go back to Venice with my tail between my legs. I promised my mother I would get better and clear my debts.

I'll do it just once. Just this evening. The moment I've won back what I lost, I'll stop. I swear.

It's this line of thinking that leads me to find myself at a blackjack table at one o'clock in the morning. I didn't manage to tear myself away earlier, when I could have. But why stop when it's going so well? I'm cleaning up! It's so easy. So satisfying. So energizing.

I *never* want to stop.

I soon move over to the poker tables. There again, I win most of my rounds. I drop my chips several times, making myself laugh. I've ordered another drink, but that was a few minutes ago, and the waiter still hasn't come back.

Oh, here he is!

"Here you are, madam," he says, holding out my martini.

I'm about to thank him when a familiar voice interrupts me, stopping me in my tracks.

"The same for me, please."

I freeze, and my whole body starts to tremble. Levi sits down opposite me at the table, taking off his jacket with a gesture that manages to be both casual and elegant. I watch him, trying to ignore the butterflies in my stomach.

The waiter puts my glass on the table and leaves. Levi's eyes haven't left my face. I don't know what to say. The first thought that comes into my head when I see him is *God, I've missed you*, even though he hasn't been far away. We saw each other yesterday—twice.

He raises an eyebrow and takes out his chips.

"Another game?" he says.

I feel a sense of déjà vu.

I don't reply, but I signal to the croupier, who deals our cards. I get an ace and a three of spades. I make the first bet without really thinking, my blood coursing through my veins. I feel lucky this evening, completely invincible.

Levi follows without a second's hesitation, his piercing gaze fixed on me. The first flop is dealt: an eight of hearts, then a seven and eight of clubs. I hide my annoyance. I have very little chance of winning now. I don't know what's in Levi's hand, of course, but it's starting out badly.

He doesn't look very worried, but then again, he hides his emotions well. When a three of hearts is dealt, I hesitate. I watch him, my expression playful, and ask, "What do you think?"

He moistens his lips, deep in thought. "I think I'm going to win."

I laugh confidently. "You always say that."

"And I'm often right."

*That's true, but not when the opponent is me.*

"I'd give myself . . . about an eighty percent chance of winning," he says. "You should fold."

"You know me. I believe in miracles," I say with a cold smile.

He smiles back, which is enough to set my poor heart on fire. I hate him. I hate him so much. I hate him for being here, seeing my weakness. I hate the fact that he came to my rescue and that he confessed how he feels. I hate how he makes my heart race, and I hate the way he makes me feel things I don't want to feel.

That's why I go all in, keeping my head high. One part of me is determined to beat him, even as another part of me prays he'll fold. He thinks for a long time, glancing between his cards and me.

"How about we make a wager, to spice things up a bit?" he suggests invitingly.

This doesn't sound good. "What sort of wager?"

"You tell me. What do you want, if you win?"

*You.*

I feel my cheeks go warm. I'm relieved he can't see me blush. All I want is for him to forgive me. I can't tell him that, obviously.

"A new Carlotta."

He smiles and agrees.

"And if you win?" I ask, curious to hear his answer.

I imagine he'll ask for something indecent, just to annoy me. Then I think, he's going to ask for information about Tito. That's all he's ever been interested in, isn't it? But nothing prepares me for what he actually says, his expression serious now.

"If I win . . . I want you to promise never to gamble again. Not in a casino, not online."

I sit there, petrified.

"And I mean *never*," he insists.

I wasn't expecting that. OK, so he's not here to have fun. He's here to mother me, because he pities me. For some reason that makes me furious, but it also makes me want to cry. I'd told him I was fine, and that he shouldn't worry. Clearly, I lied—to him and my mother both. Yet again, he's trying to save me.

"You could ask for something a lot more interesting, you know?"

"That's the only thing I want. Is that a problem?"

Yes. It's a huge problem. Because I don't know if I'll be able to keep my promise, and I'd hate myself if I broke it; if I let him down.

"Not at all. It's a deal."

I can be so stupid sometimes . . .

My pulse quickens as the croupier takes the last card and places it in the center of the table: a ten of spades. The sight of it is like a cold shower.

I've lost everything. Just like that, in the blink of an eye. Levi watches me without even glancing at the card, wanting to see my reaction. He makes no move to take the chips, even though they're all his now.

My eyes prickle. I've spent hours winning this money, promising myself I'll go home rich. I wanted to stop lots of times, my conscience screaming that enough was enough, but I carried on. Wanting to win more.

Like always.

But of course, no one can win them all. You always come up against someone better than you. And this evening, for me, Levi is that someone.

"Rose."

His voice is tender. I clench my teeth, afraid I'll say something that I'll regret. When I look at him again, his head is tilted at me.

"A deal's a deal," he murmurs.

I'd almost forgotten. Not only has he taken all my money; he's also made me promise to stop gambling—*forever*. I'm panicking. I didn't think this through properly. There's no way I can promise something like that. I say, in a strangled voice, "I can't."

"You're Rose Alfieri. There's nothing you can't do."

My hands start to shake. My mind's blank of every thought but the fact that I'm completely broke. I came here to earn money, for the sole aim of paying off my debts. Instead, I'll be going home empty-handed. I detest myself.

I haven't recovered. I was in remission, but I've relapsed. Because I'm *weak, weak, weak*.

"Rose," Levi says again.

I get up, breathing hard. I'm about to beg him to give me back my chips, not to make me do this, when I suddenly feel a reassuring hand on my shoulder.

Li Mei appears, followed by Lucky, who smiles timidly at me. Thomas is suddenly on my left, and he nods his head in polite greeting. I want to ask them what they're doing here, but Li Mei's too quick for me.

"You didn't think you'd get rid of us that easily, did you?"

"You'll never find another group of crazies like us, no matter how hard you look," Lucky adds, wiping the tears from my cheeks.

I didn't even know I was crying, but now I can't stop. Li Mei puts her arm around my shoulders, and, bizarre as it may seem, Thomas lets her do the same to him.

I'm devastated. Everything hurts, and yet I have the strangest feeling that things are going to be all right. Because it turns out, I'm not alone. I have friends. I have a gang of oddballs who accept me as I am and who, despite all my mistakes, have shown up to keep me from destroying myself.

I hide my face in my hands, crying even harder. Li Mei takes me in her arms and holds me very tight.

"Group hug?" Lucky suggests, embracing us both.

I hear a sigh to my left, probably Thomas's, followed by a laugh I'd recognize anywhere. Then suddenly two more bodies join in. They're surrounding me, holding me so close I can hardly breathe.

I feel understood, loved, supported.

"OK, who hasn't had a shower in ages?" asks Li Mei, sniffing in disgust. "And which one of you has got their head between my breasts?"

"Not me, unfortunately," says Lucky.

"I think it's me," I manage a laugh. "Sorry."

"That's all right, then."

When I emerge, my eyes meet Levi's above me.

"Thank you," I murmur through my tears. It's not much, but I know he understands. Thank you for yesterday. Thank you for this evening. Thank you for not giving up on me even though I don't make things easy.

He nods, a hint of a smile on his lips.

"What now?" asks Lucky.

Thomas grimaces, trying to untangle himself from the hug. "Now we all take a step back. Li Mei's right; we all stink."

"But what are we actually going to do?" Lucky insists.

We all look to Levi. His eyes rest on each of the others in turn, before meeting mine. He holds out his hand to me in a determined gesture.

"Allies?" he says quietly. "For real this time."

Everyone turns to me and holds their breath.

I think of Tito, of his intrigues, and the humiliation I felt when the police arrested me like a criminal . . . and I grasp Levi's hand, smiling conspiratorially.

"Allies."

# Chapter 30

## Levi

***July***
***Las Vegas, USA***

Rose has moved back into the suite. Even though she's gone back to her old room instead of sleeping with me, I'm still able to breathe more easily. Now that I've got her back, I realize just how much I missed her.

Li Mei and Lucky still share a bed. Everything's like it was before, almost.

Last night, saying I needed to sleep, I left them all in the living room explaining everything to each other and catching up on what's been going on over the last few days. But I could hear them through my bedroom walls: first, Rose apologizing, then my friends telling her it's water under the bridge, and she's part of the team now. Most importantly, she promised that she really will do everything she can to stop gambling.

That's why I've decided to fire her. There's no way she's coaching me on how to play poker if that brings back her old demons.

I practice in my room with Li Mei and Thomas all day while Lucky keeps Rose amused by making her watch romantic comedies.

"We have something to tell you," Lucky says once we've all gathered in the living room for dinner.

Rose frowns.

"It sounds like you're about to break up with me."

"I'm not; I promise. This is for keeps, baby," says Lucky, making finger guns and pointing them at her with a seductive wink. Li Mei rolls her eyes, and they all turn to me, waiting patiently. I look Rose straight in the eyes and explain gently.

"We're planning to bring Tito down."

I didn't know how to tell her. She must have suspected something, though probably not the extent of our plans. I don't just want him to lose the tournament. I want him to go to prison for his crimes.

I'm sure Rose guesses what I'm thinking. I'd rather tell her than do it all behind her back. And yet, as much as she may hate him, he's still her father.

"You don't have to help us. If you'd prefer, we won't talk about it in front of you. I just wanted you to know."

I also don't want her to think I don't trust her. I know she won't rat on us to Tito anymore. Rose thinks about it, then nods.

"What are you planning?"

The others seem surprised. Not me. Tito made a huge mistake when he reported his daughter to the police: he had her love and her unending loyalty, and instead of cherishing them, he ground them into the dirt. And those feelings are never eternal or unconditional. If you don't feed them, they can't survive.

Plus Rose hates being trampled on, no matter who's doing the trampling.

"He's planning to cheat again," I say.

"In the final? In front of everyone, even the cameras?" she asks indignantly. "He must be completely crazy!"

"He isn't stupid," Thomas interjects. "He's planning a sophisticated cheat, using infrared contact lenses and invisible writing on the cards."

Rose opens her mouth in astonishment. She says it's impossible, that this isn't some kind of thriller, that these things don't happen in real life. At least she makes us all laugh.

"Just to win a poker game?" she says. "Seriously?"

"Not just a poker game. Twelve million dollars."

That convinces her. Tito isn't the first to cheat in a poker tournament at this level, and he won't be the last. He's a good player, and he's rich, cunning, and knows the right people. There's every reason for him to cheat if he's not confident that he can win honestly.

"How do you know?"

"We've been keeping an eye on him for weeks now. One of his cronies, a croupier here, was . . . sympathetic to our cause."

"How much did you give him?" says Rose mockingly.

"Way too much," says Thomas with a sigh.

We explain everything to her, and she listens attentively as we try to work out a plan. She suggests alerting the casino, but I reject this, explaining that denouncing him now is the last thing we want.

"The tournament would be canceled, and we wouldn't be able to win."

"Even if we do it after we've won?" asks Lucky.

"It amounts to the same thing," says Rose, understanding now. "It's not just Levi's victory that would be undermined, but the whole tournament. We don't know how long Tito's been cheating, but it's probably since the beginning. Which means that some players may have been eliminated when they shouldn't have been."

Exactly. So the aim is to stop Tito from cheating rather than call him out.

"Simon, the croupier, is reliable. Now we just need to decide what we do next."

We order food and eat around the low table, making our plans. It's as though nothing ever happened. Rose smiles and jokes with everyone; everyone, except me.

We're cordial to one another, but the atmosphere is tense, with neither of us daring to make the first move. Still, we have to talk about it sometime.

She knows how I feel about her, and I know, despite her lie in the lift, that she feels the same way. The situation is fraught and complex, like something out of a Shakespeare play, but I want to give myself a shot at this. I've spent too long pushing away all the good things that have come my way, thinking I haven't deserved them.

I'm tired. I want Rose. Maybe I don't deserve her, either, but I've decided to be selfish in this. If I'm going to hell anyway, why hold back?

Except it's never the right moment. Every time I manage to get her alone, either I get cold feet or someone interrupts us. So I have to make do with the briefest of interactions—my hand brushing hers as we both move to pick something up at the same time, or hesitant smiles exchanged from opposite ends of the table.

Every day is torture. I hardly recognize myself.

"What are you waiting for?" Li Mei complains one evening when she finds me playing cards alone on my bedroom floor.

I grunt in a way that's meant to mean "leave me alone," but Lucky comes in, too, and shuts the door behind him.

"I agree. What the hell are you playing at?"

"I have an important poker final tomorrow, remember? That's what I'm playing at."

"It looks more like you're chickening out. This isn't like you. You usually do what you need to do without worrying about the details."

I clench my jaw. "Exactly—this is different. This time, I don't want to mess up."

Lucky gazes sympathetically at me. He's all ears. This kind of drama is right up his alley. The moment anyone starts discussing their love life, he's there.

Li Mei says her piece, too, telling me not to drag my feet if I don't want to risk Rose's changing her mind.

"And after this, what?" I retort. "The tournament ends, and what happens next? She lives in Venice, and I live in Saint Petersburg."

"So what? Love doesn't recognize borders."

"My mother will be out of prison soon. I need to catch up on lost time with her. And I have to think about the Rasputin. I haven't got time for . . ."

"Blah blah blah, pathetic excuses," Li Mei murmurs. "Long-distance relationships do exist. Take Lucky and me."

"OK, let's talk about that." I smile maliciously. "What are you planning to do, anyway? Lucky's studying in Los Angeles, and you've got the Rasputin in China. How's that meant to work, exactly?"

They look at each other and shrug. They don't appear to be as concerned as I am.

"There's such a thing as phone sex, you know? We have Skype and Snapchat now. And if everything goes as planned, we'll be so loaded, we can take a plane every month to see each other if we want to."

I make a disgusted face, but deep down I think they're sweet. At least they're trying to find ways around their problems. Li Mei's right; I've just been making excuses. I can't let Rose get away. There's no way she's going back to Italy before I've at least tried to win her back.

"I don't know how to tell her," I admit miserably. "I've already tried, but . . . I don't think it was very effective."

Li Mei shakes her head despairingly. "You act like you've never done this before."

"I *haven't* ever done this before. The only girlfriend I've ever had was while I was still at school."

They stare at me in astonishment.

"Levi . . . you're twenty-seven!"

"Yes, I know how old I am, thank you. So what? Sex I can handle; it's just relationships I haven't been too hot on . . . I haven't really had time to focus on them these last ten years."

"My God."

I scowl at them. It's not as unusual as all that. They're making a huge fuss over nothing. But it occurs to me now that I know nothing about Rose's romantic past. Has she got much experience? What kind of man does she go for?

"You've got a lot to learn, then," says Lucky, putting his hands on his hips. "You need to watch . . ."

"Don't you dare say *Bridget Jones*!"

*"Bridget Jones."*

I smile sarcastically, making Li Mei snort with laughter. Lucky starts to chatter to himself excitedly. He leaves the room, telling me to wait. I'm almost certain he's gone to get his computer so that he can spend the rest of the evening torturing me.

"I thought he was too young and sentimental for you?" I say to Li Mei, who sighs and smiles weakly.

"He is. But . . . I still love him. I can't help it. So I've decided to roll with it. Who knows; maybe it's just what I need."

I nod pensively. She's right. The heart has its reasons. Mine wants Rose despite all the obstacles, and who am I to argue with it? If I don't try, I could regret it for the rest of my life.

◆ ◆ ◆

We spend the next two days preparing.

Tito has no idea what's about to hit him. I pity him—OK, I don't. I can't wait to see his face when the penny drops. The only thing worrying me is Rose. She's helping, and acting as though it's not affecting her, but I know her better than the others do.

It does affect her, whether she wants it to or not.

I feel guilty, of course. I don't want to be the person who destroys her family. That would make me a pretty terrible partner, wouldn't it? But then again . . . Rose and I have never had a very conventional relationship.

"Ready for tomorrow?"

Rose jumps. She's alone in the kitchen, searching the cupboards for something to eat. She stops and leans against the counter, her arms folded.

"I should be asking you that. You're the one who's going to be there."

I remain still, keeping my hands in my pockets. Rose, Thomas, and Lucky are planning to watch the final on the TV in the living room. I wish Rose were going to be in there with me, but I guess this is for the best. At least I won't be distracted.

"No matter what Tito says . . . don't let him provoke you," she says quietly. "He'll do it on purpose to unsettle you."

I know that already, but I nod seriously, not taking my eyes off hers. She's absolutely sublime. I wonder what she'd look like wearing nothing but one of my T-shirts. The thought alone is enough to send a thrill through my whole body.

This is the moment.

"Rose."

She raises an inquiring eyebrow. I see from her expression that she knows this is the time, too, and that she wants to get things out in the open once and for all, just like I do. I still don't know how to start, so I improvise.

"What's going on, between us?"

She opens her mouth but doesn't say anything. She looks lost. I just want to hear her say it. I want to hear the words from her mouth. Only then will I be able to find a way around whatever obstacle comes between us.

"What's going to happen in two days' time?" I continue, trying not to fixate on the way she's biting her lip. "I win the tournament, then what? You go home . . . I go home . . . and that's it?"

"Is that what you want?"

"No. Is it what you want?"

"No."

My pulse quickens as the tension mounts. I take a step toward her, still not taking my eyes off hers. I'm terrified, but I manage to get the words out.

"Everything I told you in the lift that day was true. I know we've said some terrible things to each other, things I didn't even think and that I only said because I knew they'd hurt you. The truth is, I'm an asshole. I don't cope well with pain. I always want to fight back because I'm scared that people will take advantage of me again. And you . . . you were different. I wanted it to be real, and that seemed to hurt me even more."

She swallows but still doesn't say anything. I pray silently that nobody comes and interrupts my speech now that I'm finally on a roll.

"Except I was wrong. Because what actually hurt most was . . . your leaving. I never want to go through that again. And I know this is all happening fast, I know we don't know each other very well. I know there are circumstances that mean we can't be together, but I don't care. I've never wanted anything so badly in my life. So I need to know if you feel the same . . . or if this is all in my head."

I take another step closer, reducing the space between our two bodies. I see her breathing faster, and that makes it even harder to control my instincts. All I want is to take her in my arms and put my mouth on hers. I don't want to sleep alone anymore. I want her arms around my waist when I have nightmares, her fingers in my hair when I wake up, her tongue on every other part of my body.

I'm afraid she won't believe me. She told me the other day that she couldn't trust me, and I understand her anxiety. But she must be able to see that the mask is off now, mustn't she?

"I know you're sincere," she begins in a hesitant murmur as if reading my mind. "But, Levi, I'm a total mess. My daily life is a world away from glitzy Las Vegas. I'm ill. I'm in debt, my father is a megalomaniac, and I'm unemployed. Worst of all, I'm the daughter of the man who took everything from you. What if you ended up hating me despite your best intentions? What if every day that God gave us, you saw my father when you looked at me? I wouldn't blame you . . . but I wouldn't be able to stand it."

How could she think all of that? I move closer still, daring to put my hands on her divine hips. I feel my heart pounding.

"I've never hated you for being Tito's daughter," I whisper, my mouth brushing hers. "Never. Rose . . . I just want to know one thing: Do you want me, yes or no? Nothing else matters."

There's a long pause while she gazes at me, so long that I start to lose confidence. I'm already steeling myself to leave her for the last time, when I feel her arms wrap around my waist and pull me to her.

"It's real," she whispers. "You, me, us. It's always been real."

The next moment, my lips meet hers.

# Chapter 31

## Rose

***July***
***Las Vegas, USA***

Levi carries me to the bedroom, his hands under my bottom and my legs wrapped tightly around his waist. I'm still trembling from the confession I've just made, and my heart's ready to burst.

"I've missed you so much," he breathes, closing the door behind us.

Unlike the first two times, wild urgency has given way to gentleness. I sense the difference straightaway: we're no longer rivals competing against one another. We're finding our way together now, but the passion is just as strong.

His lips are soft, and his tongue is warm against mine. I kiss his neck, licking his Adam's apple on the way down, and carefully unbutton his shirt.

It falls to the floor, as do my dress and his trousers. My whole body is on fire at the thought of what's to come. Levi admires me, standing there in my matching bra and panties, breathing fast.

"If you only knew the thoughts going through my mind right now . . ."

I just smile and walk backward to the bed. He stays where he is, his eyes running up and down my near-naked body as I climb onto the mattress. I ask him why he's not following me, feeling suddenly shy.

"I'm memorizing the scene for later. As a souvenir."

I want to tell him we don't need souvenirs anymore, because I'm not planning on leaving him ever again.

"Why don't you take a picture of me?"

He disappears for a second, then reappears with his camera and kneels on the bed. I lie down, and he adjusts my hair, spreading it artfully over the pillow. I've never done this before, but I don't care. It's only Levi.

I pose in my underwear as he takes photographs of me lying down, sitting; sometimes in provocative poses, sometimes modest ones. I ask him if I'm beautiful, and he replies, "The most beautiful," so I lower his camera and kiss him.

Little by little, I remove my underwear, letting one bra strap fall, then the other. His hands touch me, bringing out goose bumps across my chest. When I undo the clasp, my bra slips down along my stomach.

I take Levi's hand and put it on my breast, panting. His eyes gaze piercingly into mine over the camera, and my body warms to the touch of his loving fingers on my nipple.

"More," I beg him. "I need more."

He doesn't make me wait. Setting the camera aside, he leans down and kisses my nipple reverently. His tongue licks it and traces light circular movements around it, making me moan. The sensation is divine. When he starts to suck it, I tremble even more and tense my thighs.

My chest is moist by the time he's finished with it. He gives one last lick, then blows gently over each breast. *My God.*

"Let me immortalize the expression on your face," he says, picking up the camera again.

He photographs me as I lie with my arms over my head, trying to catch my breath. My breasts are moist and burning hot, almost painful. His mouth glistens with saliva.

"Turn over, *lyubimaya*."

I do as he asks, and he slides my panties down. I hear him taking off his boxers, too, and feel his hand on my bare back. His fingers trace along my spine all the way down to my buttocks. I shiver, nearly bursting with excitement.

I'm longing to touch him and try to reach around to do so, but Levi grabs my hand and clicks his tongue at me.

"No, leave this to me."

"Quick," I moan.

"Get on your knees."

I do and hear him tearing open a condom packet. The sound makes me tremble with impatience. I expect him to penetrate me right away, but he makes the suspense last. I close my eyes, savoring the incredibly intense sensations made by his hand caressing my back and then my bottom.

Suddenly, his finger begins to stroke my clitoris. I moan and give a little start, but his other hand is on my buttocks, holding me still.

"Don't move."

Levi's fingers make small, circular movements that drive me completely wild, and then he puts two fingers inside me. Pleasure slowly begins to well up. I stay as calm as I can, but I can't help moving my hips gently under his hand.

"Faster, please," I beg him.

He quickens the pace, and then he's partly under me and adding the pleasure of his mouth. I can't help swearing.

*"Oh Dio mio."*

His tongue licks me, and I moan even more loudly, feeling like my heart could explode. His fingers find that sensitive spot that guarantees orgasm every time. The next minute, I climax like a tsunami.

I've never felt anything so good. My cheeks are red with excitement. I lower my head, my hair hanging over my face, and sigh with exhaustion as Levi kisses my buttocks.

"Sorry, but it's far from over . . ."

He pulls me toward him, and a second later I feel him pushing himself inside me. Even though I've just climaxed, I feel excitement growing again in the pit of my stomach. My arms are trembling, but I hold firm.

Levi groans as he enters me completely, his hands on my hips.

"Rest on your elbows; it'll be less tiring."

I do, and his fingers sink into my short hair and pull, a delicious sensation. Every thrust of his hips makes me moan, and I keep my eyes firmly closed.

He covers my back with a thousand little kisses, then leans over me, bringing his whole torso into contact with my body. His arm curls around my waist to support me, then to caress me again between the legs.

I'm struggling to support my own weight, afraid I might collapse before I come.

"Tell me what you want," he murmurs, nibbling my neck.

"I want to see you."

No sooner said than done—he gently pulls me up and turns me to face him. I open my eyes as I sit on him, our bodies entwined.

His gaze is like an electric shock. I tremble under his delicate hands, moved by the intimacy of our position. My heart, intoxicated by him, flutters in my chest. His cheeks are red and burning hot, making him even more beautiful.

I move against him, my arms tight around his neck, and he holds me in the same way.

"Levi?"

He kisses me before I can say anything more. We stay like that for several long minutes, until, unable to hold back any longer, he lays me down on my back and penetrates me forcefully.

We reach orgasm at the same moment.

Levi collapses against me, his cheek against mine, and kisses my ear.

"What did you want to tell me?" he whispers.

I try to catch my breath. My skin feels sticky as I plunge my fingers into his dark hair. I feel completely serene.

"I've decided to fall madly in love with you. If you want to run away, now's the time. After that, it'll be too late."

He doesn't move for a few seconds, but I can feel his heart beating faster. Finally, he turns his head toward mine and strokes my cheek.

His expression mirrors mine, contented and carefree.

"I'm happy right where I am."

◆ ◆ ◆

"I'm not sure I could ever go without this now." I sigh and rest my cheek on my knees, which are drawn up to my chest. Levi is washing my back with slow, gentle movements, sitting behind me in the bath. Settled between his long legs, I blow on the foam to make it fly in the air like snow.

"What, the sex?"

I close my eyes, feeling totally relaxed. I feel him trace invisible letters on my shoulder blades, tickling me.

"Everything. The sex, but also moments like this. It's so sad . . . I feel like we haven't experienced anything together yet, but we're going to have to go our separate ways soon."

I can't explain it. We only met a short while ago, and even though things have moved fast, we don't really know each other. I know he killed his father by accident and that his mother took the blame, but I don't know what his favorite food is, or what sort of films he watches when he's sick.

He doesn't reply for a long time. I start to wonder if he's going to say anything at all, but then he wraps his arms around my stomach and draws me closer to him. The foam moves in waves around us, making me smile. I lie back against him, my head on his shoulder, as he joins our hands together over my stomach.

"I feel the same," he says into my hair. "But . . . we don't have to part ways. You could come with me to Russia."

My heart leaps. I know he can't suggest coming with me to Venice. His mother is about to get out of prison, and he needs to be with her and make up for lost time. Give her the life she's dreamed of.

I'm sorely tempted. I don't want to say goodbye. But . . .

"I miss my mother," I admit quietly. "I've been traveling too long. I'm tired of running away. I want to be back in my own home, my own bed, my own sheets . . ."

He nods in understanding. I know he doesn't resent me for it. He plays with my fingers and asks me what my mother is like.

"She's amazing," I say with a big smile. "She was born deaf, so it hasn't always been easy to communicate. But now we couldn't be closer."

"I wonder how she could have fallen for a man like Tito. I suppose he was different back then, when he was young."

"Not really . . . he was always a bad boy. She gave in to him because she was too kind, that's all. Then, when she got pregnant, she was trapped. They didn't marry for love."

He holds me more tightly, bringing our hands up between my breasts. "I'm sorry."

I shrug. To be honest, it doesn't affect me much. I ask him if he thinks his mother would like me. That makes him laugh. I turn around to scowl at him, annoyed.

"What's that supposed to mean?"

"She'd adore you; don't get me wrong," he says. "But I think she'd be quite . . . surprised."

"Why?"

"I don't think she's expecting her son to marry a girl like you. Not that there's anything wrong with you," he adds quickly, seeing my murderous look. "But you're very free, very uninhibited, very independent, very . . . passionate."

I'm silent for a few moments, something inside me warming at his words. I think of the ring hidden in my suitcase and say teasingly, "Nobody's said anything about anyone getting married."

He kisses my cheek in reply. My feet wrestle playfully with his at the end of the bathtub. I ask him what he plans to do once his mother's home. He tells me he wants to sell the Rasputin and set out with her for some country where the sun always shines.

"Somewhere where my mother can rest, and I can . . . maybe . . . take up photography again."

I hide my happy, astonished smile, but he must have seen it because he laughs softly.

"For how long?" I ask.

"Forever."

*Oh.*

"You know . . . ," I tell him, "the weather in Italy's pretty good . . . I'm just saying. And Spain and France are right next door. You'd love Paris. They haven't got any casinos, but they've got great cabarets."

"I know." He smiles. "A good friend of mine works at the Moulin Rouge. I'll take you there."

"Show-off."

He runs his finger under my chin and turns my face to kiss me. I find his tongue with mine, and we sigh.

"Stop worrying," he whispers. "We'll see each other again soon; I promise. In the meantime, it turns out it's possible to make love over Skype . . . according to Lucky and Li Mei."

Oh my God. I can't help laughing. I don't even want to know how he ended up in that conversation.

"And we're still here now, aren't we? So let's enjoy it while we can."

He's right. We're both going home for a while, but that doesn't mean forever. I'm just afraid that the distance will affect our relationship, which is still so new. What if he realizes that his feelings for me were just part of the surreal atmosphere that is Las Vegas?

What if he gets home and decides there's no place for me in his real life?

"Stop it. Stop brooding and kiss me," he scolds.

I'm only too happy to obey.

# Chapter 32

## Levi

***July***
***Las Vegas, USA***

This is it: the big day.

Ten players still remain in the game, including Tito, Li Mei, and me. The WSOP final round should last no longer than six hours, but that's still a lot, especially with a month and a half of intense poker already behind us. Yet I'm not stressed. Dressed in black trousers and a beige shirt, I feel nothing but excitement as I join the others in the lobby.

"Is everything ready?" I ask my teammates.

Thomas nods, though he's clearly feeling tense. They all are, even Rose, who's at my side. I'm the exception. And yet this is what I've been dreaming of for the last ten years. The do-or-die moment when I finally bring Tito down once and for all.

"How are you feeling?" asks Rose.

I look down at her, and she takes my hand discreetly in hers. I'm about to reply when I see something glinting on her finger. It's the salt-and-pepper ring I gave her . . .

She kept it, and she's decided to start wearing it again. The gesture warms my heart, and I smile reassuringly at her. "Very confident."

Our plan is risky. The slightest hitch could mean it fails, but I have faith in it.

"Here he is," Thomas says.

All eyes turn toward Tito as he saunters into the lobby. He smiles at the other competitors, then seems to notice us. His eyes meet mine before settling on his daughter and our joined hands.

Rose stiffens at my side. At first I think he's going to pass by without saying anything, but he must feel supremely confident, because he stops right in front of us.

"Today's the day that really matters," he says, holding out his hand to me. "Let's make it an honorable game, shall we?"

Li Mei gives him a look of pure disgust. Nobody says anything as I hold his gaze, keeping my hand by my side.

"You should check the definition of *honorable* in the dictionary, because I don't think we see it the same way."

He smiles and withdraws his hand. He looks down at Rose again with an expression of false disappointment.

"When you finally realize he's using you to get at me, we'll discuss this again, OK?"

"That's your specialty, not his," she retorts coldly.

We're about to move away when Tito addresses us again.

"It's a shame Simon fell ill last night. So strange—food poisoning, apparently."

I stop in my tracks, and so do all the others. Li Mei looks at me, her eyes wide. Lucky and Rose look horrified too.

I turn to Tito, keeping my expression neutral. I want to ask what he's done, but I already know the answer from his triumphant smile. He got wind of our plan and made sure Simon was out of action today. It doesn't matter to him which croupier we have, as the cards are already marked with invisible ink. In Tito's mind, I'm fucked, since I would have been counting on Simon to distract Tito from my game.

*"Buona fortuna!"* he says in Italian, pretending to wish us luck. With those sarcastic words, he walks away.

We exchange looks in silence. It's Thomas who finally speaks.

"Don't stress. It'll be fine."

A member of the staff interrupts to tell us it's time to take our seats. Rose grabs hold of my tie and pulls me toward her, giving me a threatening look.

"Levi, listen to me. If our plan fails, to hell with honor. You beat him. Have you got that? We can't let Tito win."

I smile and promise to do my best; then I kiss her tenderly on the mouth. I signal to Thomas that he should stay with her, and follow Li Mei toward the tournament room, which is nothing like the crowded spaces we've been used to. It's a private room with a wide table against a blue background, surrounded by cameras. There are chairs along the sides, in shadow, and technicians are hurrying about. The cameras must already be rolling as we come in.

It's as though someone just shouted, "Action!": it's five o'clock, and the final table of the Main Event is starting with a bang. I'm sitting next to Li Mei and opposite Tito. The croupier arrives shortly after us, and my pulse quickens when I see that Tito wasn't lying: it isn't Simon. Li Mei conceals her anxiety to perfection, playing her usual role. Each player is introduced as if we're on a game show, in true Las Vegas style.

As the croupier shuffles the cards and deals them out, my eyes are fixed on Tito. A triumphant smile spreads across my face at the precise moment when he realizes I've tricked him. I relish the moment, watching his eyes widen in astonishment.

Right away, he looks over at me and understands.

*"Buona fortuna!"* I mouth silently.

The strange thing is, the only person I'm thinking about at that exact moment is my father. For the first time in years, my heart isn't full of resentment. It's at peace.

*Look at me, Dad. Watch me outdo you.*

◆ ◆ ◆

## Rose

I've never been so stressed in my whole life. Thomas, Lucky, and I are sitting hunched on the sofa in the suite, watching the game live on ESPN.

Officially, our man, Simon, was supposed to have prevented Tito from seeing the backs of Levi's cards, dealt from a deck that Tito had arranged to be marked. But since Tito has made sure Simon isn't there, my fake fiancé's cards are going to be easily readable by Tito—at least, that's what Tito thinks.

I can pinpoint the exact second when he realizes he's been duped. The truth is, Levi knew all along that Tito was going to get rid of Simon. In fact, he was counting on it. The croupier was just a red herring, a cover. Our real plan was always to switch out the marked deck before play began.

Tito had based his planned victory on knowing he could cheat, but now he's there with his infrared contact lenses . . . and cards that aren't marked. He'll have to play it straight, just like everyone else.

"He's scared stiff," Lucky observes. "Serves him right . . . But I still don't get how this is supposed to make Levi win."

"That wasn't the goal," I say, shaking my head. "Levi refuses to cheat. He wants to win fair and square. The aim was to make the game squeaky clean, and now it is!"

The first round starts slowly. Li Mei wins it. Tito seems shaken, and I can tell he's struggling to adjust to the new situation; it's probably been a long time since he played without cheating. Levi doesn't pay him any attention; he just plays as he always does, with concentration and rigor.

The hours pass as if in slow motion. My nerves are in tatters. They're both playing well, but as the number of players decreases, my anxiety mounts. It's not long before only five people are left around the table, and Li Mei has taken a few big hits and lost a lot of money. I don't think she'll last long. Sure enough, she goes out in fourth position.

"She fought well," Lucky says.

Thomas and I nod. There are three finalists left now. One of them is Wittelsbach, the German with the *Jurassic Park* T-shirt from a few weeks ago. He's good, but not experienced enough to beat Levi and Tito.

A new round begins. The end is getting nearer. Levi gets an ace of clubs and a ten of diamonds. Wittelsbach has a king of clubs and a queen of hearts in his hand. He has a far smaller stack of chips than Levi, which puts him at a disadvantage, but he's very confident, and calls straightaway.

"A snap call," Lucky murmurs, referring to the kind of calls that players make quickly, and seemingly without thinking them through.

He's right: Wittelsbach doesn't appear to think before going "all-in dark preflop," so called because the player goes all-in even before knowing what the flop is. Tito folds first, with an ace of diamonds and a three of clubs. Levi calls, with a 50 percent chance of winning.

"He's crazy."

"He's got the advantage."

"Only by a little." I grimace. My heart's pounding. I know he wants to get rid of Wittelsbach as fast as possible, but still. The whole room buzzes with excitement, and even the presenters seem intrigued.

Then the flop comes . . . an eight of hearts, a seven of clubs, and a king of diamonds.

"Shit."

Wittelsbach smiles triumphantly. He's ahead, with an 87 percent chance of taking it all. Levi doesn't react, just continues to rest his chin in his hand. I can't believe my eyes. He's losing, and not even to Tito!

Impossible. What can he be thinking?

The stress is visible on both of their faces when the fourth card is revealed: a jack of diamonds. Levi's chances rise only a few percent. It's not enough. I bite my lip, feeling pessimistic.

I can almost hear him saying to me, *I thought you believed in miracles?* Whether I believe in them or not, the last card is like a bomb going off: a nine of spades.

Levi has won everything with a flush. He closes his eyes, the relief he feels evident on his face. Even he wasn't certain that it would work out this way. Wittelsbach shakes hands with Levi and leaves the table with dignity as Levi collects his winnings.

"Tito isn't doing badly, in spite of our plan," Lucky grumbles, rubbing his hands on his jeans. "It's close."

Thomas reassures him, saying that even if Tito wins now, it's too late. The wheels of Levi's revenge are already in motion. I ask him what he means.

"Levi always has at least three different plans, just to cover himself. Whatever happens, Tito has no idea what's coming to him; that's all."

I focus on the television again, puzzled, as Tito returns to his seat at the table, his eyes fixed on Levi.

There are only a few minutes left, and two players in the game.

◆ ◆ ◆

## Levi

With over twenty million dollars in my pocket, I have the advantage now in terms of chips, thanks to Wittelsbach. Tito knows it, but he doesn't seem particularly worried. Not yet. It's all I can do not to burst out laughing.

He thinks he's already won, just because he's more experienced than I am. Just because he got rid of the croupier I'd bribed. He thinks I'm caught in a trap.

He doesn't know me very well.

I guess he underestimates my desire to win. I refuse to cheat against him, it's true, because that kind of victory would taste less sweet. But outside the tournament, it's no holds barred. There's only one thing I want now—for the tournament to end, and for him to face the consequences of his actions.

The longer we play, the more I win, and his smile begins to evaporate. His game grows clumsy as stress makes him rush his decisions, and he makes juvenile errors. After cheating for so long, he's lost his touch.

He's avoiding my gaze now, as though he's worried I'll break his concentration. As the minutes pass, I feel more and more energized.

I suppress a smile when I see my next hand: a five of spades and a five of diamonds. It's a good hand. Luck must be on my side.

As if to contradict that assumption, Tito looks straight at me and makes his move.

"All in."

◆ ◆ ◆

## Rose

Tito's gone all-in before the flop.

His hand is an ace and a two of spades. It doesn't put him at an advantage. Levi's hand is better for the moment. I just hope it stays that way. It all depends on the flop . . .

"It's now or never," Li Mei says.

It's true. This is it, the last round. The last chance for Levi to destroy Tito. Everyone in the room is starting to lose their composure. Levi gets up to stand with Li Mei in the shadows, a hesitant smile playing on his lips. I sense that he's anxious but excited too.

I smile like an idiot, my hands clammy.

"Christ, I'm sweating like a pig," Lucky complains. "I'm scared."

I am, too, but I don't say so. I clench my fists in silence. On the TV, Tito takes a sip of water, looking wary.

The two players are called back to their seats so the flop can be dealt. With a swift movement of her hands, the croupier reveals the first three cards: a king of hearts, a jack, and a ten of clubs. I breathe a sigh of relief, still sweating. The advantage is still Levi's.

"He hasn't won yet," Thomas reminds me.

"Watch out for a double-up that could lead to a river counterfeit," I murmur to myself.

A double-up on the ten really would be exciting, but in the end, it's a three of hearts. Lucky lets out a happy yelp, causing me to dissolve into nervous laughter. Levi now has an 84 percent chance of winning.

It's almost in the bag. Tito knows it, and his expression is dark and menacing.

"He's going to do it," Thomas whispers. "He's going to win; I'm sure of it."

I'm about to tell him not to jinx it, but I don't have time. The croupier turns over another card . . .

It's a ten of spades.

# Chapter 33

## Levi

***July***
***Las Vegas, USA***

I stay absolutely still, my eyes glued to the final card. I don't feel anything. People around me are exploding into cheers, but I'm frozen to my seat.

I've just won twelve million dollars.

I'm a millionaire . . . and the poker world champion.

"You did it!" Li Mei shrieks, throwing her arms around my neck. "Levi, you did it!"

I can still hardly believe it. I get up slowly and put my arms around her, my hands trembling a little. I've imagined this moment a thousand times. I always thought I'd feel a wave of relief . . . and pride . . . Or at least a sense of satisfaction at the thought of having kept the promise I made to myself six years ago.

I don't feel any of that.

I'm just . . . sad. Empty. I think of my father, and all I want to do is cry. Does this moment of victory make it all worthwhile? I'm not so sure now that it's here.

I extend my hand toward Tito, knowing full well he won't shake it. I smile cruelly as he scowls at me in front of the cameras; he's doing a very good job of making a fool of himself, with no help from me.

"You knew," he growls.

I know what he's talking about. Yes, I knew he'd have the croupier changed. Yes, I knew he'd cheat. Despite it all, I managed to beat him. I hope he feels like a piece of shit right now.

"You can say goodbye to Rose," he hisses, "because you won't be seeing her again after this."

I burst out laughing. Even Li Mei raises an eyebrow and smiles. Does he still think he has some kind of control over her? It's hilarious.

"With all due respect, dear father-in-law, I don't see how you'll be able to stop me from seeing your daughter. Not from where you're heading."

He doesn't grasp my meaning, but I don't care. He'll understand soon enough. As I expected, Rose is waiting for me outside the room, with Thomas and Lucky. I give them a smile intended to convey both pride and calm, as if I knew all along how it would end.

Rose runs over and bounds into my arms with a cry of joy. She nearly bowls me over, but I hold on to her as she wraps her legs around my waist.

"How was I?" I ask, sensing the cameras all around me.

"Totally sexy," she breathes, and kisses me. I return her kiss willingly, taking it as my reward.

"Your fiancé's loaded now, you know."

She raises an eyebrow. "Of course he is. I know how to pick a winner."

Rose pays absolutely no attention to her father, even though he's standing nearby. I put her down but keep hold of her hand, and the others in our group come over to congratulate me. All of a sudden, the reality of the situation hits home.

I won. I actually won. Me, a *handicapped dolt*, as my father used to put it so beautifully. I'll be able to use this money to give my mother the peace and happiness she deserves. As for Tito, it shouldn't be long before he's made to pay for his sins.

Right on time, revenge joins the party, sealing my victory. A worried-looking man rushes up to Tito. He says something urgent to him in Italian. I don't need to understand the language to know what the message is.

I look at Thomas, who nods silently in reply. Rose sees this and looks over at Tito with a frown. I know she hears what they're saying, because she gradually turns pale.

Tito's expression also darkens, and he turns abruptly to me, his eyes wide.

"What have you done, you little shit?"

I keep one hand nonchalantly in my pocket, assuming an expression of innocence incarnate.

"Who, me?"

I don't have time to say more. He explodes and leaps toward me, grabbing my shirt collar. The force of his movement throws me back against the wall. I don't fight back, aware of the cameras swooping in.

"Smile—you're on camera," I whisper, so that only he can hear.

"This is my whole life you've just fucked up!" he bellows, a vein in his forehead throbbing dangerously. "My career! My legacy! You dirty . . ."

I can't believe my ears. He has the nerve to say that to me? He was the one who ruined *my* life! All I did was expose his crimes. He should have been smarter; that's all.

Someone comes over to pull him away, but before they succeed, I hiss one last thing through clenched teeth.

"In that case, we're even. Rot in hell, asshole."

I give him a wink and a wolfish smile. Rose watches us in silence, her arms folded. Her father curses to himself, running one hand through his hair in frustration, and takes her by the wrist.

He says something to her in Italian, but she pulls her hand away and completely ignores him. Seeing him alone, the journalists immediately pounce. They've been waiting for six hours now—six hours beyond the moment the *New York Times* published an article about what it refers to as the "Ferragni Scandal."

I guess they have a few questions to put to him.

"I have no idea what's going on," says Lucky.

"Check out the *New York Times* social media feeds," Thomas advises him.

The journalists are trying to get something out of Tito, but he's denying all the allegations and shouting about defamation. Eventually, he shoots a murderous look at me and disappears.

At my side, Rose is still silent. She already knows what's happening. Li Mei reads Lucky's phone over his shoulder.

"'Tito Ferragni, founder of the Italian streaming platform Speakup, is accused of evidence tampering, interfering with witnesses, and money laundering.' Shit. Is this true?"

She turns to me, shocked. I nod. They read the rest—but I already know everything that's in the article. The bribes and money laundering were already common knowledge. The evidence tampering, on the other hand . . .

Seven years ago, an employee of Tito's named Muzio died in an accident at work. He was about to get out of a lift when the car broke away and fell down the chute, apparently because there was air in the cylinders. Speakup was clearly at fault because Tito hadn't had the company perform regular safety inspections.

This hasn't been generally known until now. Tito obviously did everything he could to keep the affair quiet, to the point of tampering with evidence and bribing witnesses. It was simply a stroke of good luck that led me to finally uncover this secret, after years of digging.

This article is all the Italian police will need to begin an investigation. He won't have time to hide all the evidence before he gets home. Tito's in a real fix, and so is his business. He'll be sentenced to several years in prison; the exact number will depend on how well he's able to defend himself in court in Italy. Plus the police are already looking for the guy who tried to run me and Lucky over.

"Whoa, that gives me goose bumps," Lucky murmurs.

I look worriedly at Rose, who still hasn't moved. I'm afraid she'll resent me. Despite all he's done, Tito's still her father, and a scandal like this is bound to have repercussions for her family. I even thought about not going through with it, but in the end, I realized the risk to them was low: Tito has always been smart enough to keep his wife and daughter out of the media spotlight, so nobody knows who they are. I'm also rich enough now to look after them both if need be.

Tito should be the only one made to suffer from his new situation. Especially because Rose and her mother have loved and supported him all these years without ever receiving anything in return.

"Hey . . ."

I move to put my hand on her arm, but she pulls away.

"I need to get some air."

I let her go.

◆ ◆ ◆

Rose is nowhere to be seen for the rest of the day.

After a few interviews and photographs, I sit down alone next to the pool to enjoy the peace and the sunshine. I hoped Rose might join me, but there's no sign of her.

Li Mei offers to look for her, but I tell her to leave Rose in peace. She needs time, and I understand that.

"So, is it really over?" Lucky asks as the four of us gather in the suite for dinner.

Thomas has opened a bottle of champagne to toast the occasion. After years of planning and preparing, we're finally rich and free.

"It's really over," I assure him with a smile. I still find that hard to believe, but I guess that's normal. It's going to take me a while to adjust.

Now that I'm no longer single-mindedly pursuing that goal, what am I going to do with my life?

"Shit . . . we're all millionaires? Seriously?"

"I'm not all that surprised," Li Mei comments. "My name means *silver*. Being rich has been in my DNA all along."

"What are you all going to do with the money?" asks Thomas.

I told them I'd share the twelve million between the four of us, and I intend to keep my promise. I also promised Rose a share if I won, back when we were in Macau. I hope she'll accept it. There's a very good chance I wouldn't have succeeded without her help.

"Pay for my studies, to start off with, and my little sister Jasmine's too," says Lucky without hesitating. "Then buy a huge house for my parents."

"Will I seem terribly shallow if I say *shoes*?" Li Mei grimaces.

"No more so than usual."

"Cool. What about you, Thomas?"

My friend shrugs pensively. Nobody knows anything about his family or his past, not even me.

"I haven't decided yet."

Nobody asks me what I'm going to do; they already know.

We eat and drink until we can't eat or drink any more. Lucky has to go back to Los Angeles tomorrow; he's been away from his family way too long. Li Mei doesn't take her eyes off him all evening, and they're the first to disappear into their bedroom.

"It appears I'm going to need earplugs again tonight," Thomas sighs. "Don't you guys ever give it a rest?"

"Envious?" I tease him, with a lascivious smile.

"No," he lies.

I'm about to ask him what's stopping him from finding someone himself when I hear the beep of the suite door opening. Thomas downs the rest of his beer and wishes me good night before disappearing. I stay on the sofa, my legs stretched out and my cheeks hot.

Rose appears, a plastic bag in her hand. She looks devastated, but she manages a sad smile.

"I brought Chinese, but I see you've already eaten . . . I should've guessed."

I can tell by her face that she's been drinking. I hold out my arm, inviting her to come over. She drops the bag and comes to sit on my knee.

"Do you hate me for it?"

She shakes her head immediately. "No. You did the right thing. He deserved it. It just . . . hurts. I feel guilty, I guess. I hope my mother will be OK."

"Of course she'll be OK. I'll make sure none of this touches her, or you, Rose. I promise."

She nods, playing with my fingers. She brings one to her mouth and gives it a little kiss, then does the same with the others. A shiver runs all through me.

There's something weighing on us both, and although we don't mention it, we both know what it is. Lucky's leaving tomorrow, and it won't be long before Li Mei and Thomas do the same. As for me, I . . . need to go and be with my mother. And Rose needs to be with hers.

We can't stay here indefinitely. Sooner or later, we'll have to say goodbye.

"You played brilliantly today. I was impressed," she says.

"Wow. That means a lot. Thank you."

"How do you feel? Now that you've got your revenge . . . relieved? Calm?"

"Not really. It's stupid, isn't it? I . . . I think you were right. Revenge doesn't really work that way. I'm glad Tito's paying for his crimes, of course, but when I think about my past, I still feel the same pain. And part of me regrets spending ten years of my life obsessed with him."

She rests her head on my shoulder, and I know she understands exactly what I mean.

"That's true. But don't forget that ten years is only a smaller piece of a whole lifetime. Now you can look to the future: you'll have your mother by your side, and no worries. As for the other things . . . the trauma, the guilt . . . you can work on them. Luckily, your beautiful and brilliant girlfriend studied psychology."

"Model, painter, *and* psychologist? I've hit the jackpot."

"Well . . . everyone's got their talents. I'm a multitasker; you're a millionaire. We're a good match."

I burst out laughing and lean in to nibble her neck. She kisses me, tenderly at first, then passionately. I hoist her onto my shoulder and carry her into our bedroom, where we make love until she collapses on top of me and then falls asleep like an angel.

# Chapter 34

## Rose

***July***
***Las Vegas, USA***

Tito left in the night without warning. I guess he wants to get home as quickly as possible to hide the traces of his crimes. I've warned my mother about everything, of course, even though we haven't spoken much recently.

I was avoiding her because I was running away from my problems, but now I'm determined to face up to them.

I'm sorry about the last time we spoke . . .I was scared.

I know. It's OK. But we need to talk about it, Rose.

I promise her I'll listen to her this time. When I ask what she's planning to do about Dad, she tells me not to worry. They're already divorcing, anyway, so his troubles won't have too much impact on us.

And this young man?

He's going back to Russia ☹

It is serious?

Maybe.

Then I need to meet him.

I smile and type that she should slow down. Levi and I have known each other for only two months. There's no need to get ahead of ourselves.

Still, the idea isn't so bad. I imagine Levi sitting at the table in our garden, wearing those shades of his, and my heart melts.

I tell my mother I have to go, then get up and join the others by the door, where Lucky's standing next to a huge black suitcase. He said he didn't want us to come with him to the airport, because he doesn't like dramatic, tearful goodbyes, "except in films."

The guys reach out to shake hands, but Lucky forces them into a hug, which makes me smile. Am I dreaming, or is he . . . crying?

"Lucky, you do this to us every year." Li Mei sighs. "We'll see each other soon."

"And we've even got a WhatsApp group chat," I remind him. "You can talk to us every day if you want to."

Thomas gives me a warning look and murmurs, "Don't give him ideas."

Lucky seems reassured, though. He thanks Levi, who promises to transfer the money as soon as he can, then kisses Li Mei on the mouth.

"See you all . . . in a year, then, no longer! We could go on holiday together? Santorini looks like it's gorgeous in the summer. We can do a special *Mamma Mia 2* pilgrimage!"

Li Mei interrupts his plan making, telling him he has to go or he'll miss his plane. A moment later, we're closing the door behind him. Silence falls in the suite. Li Mei disappears into her room, saying she has things to do, but I think she just needs to be alone.

Levi spends the day teaching me to cook some traditional Russian dishes. He also teaches me a few Russian words besides *lyubimaya*. He's especially insistent on one phrase in particular: *Ya tebya lyublyu*. I love you.

I try whispering it to him that night as he's moving between my thighs, and it makes him come immediately.

*"Ti amo anch'io,"* he murmurs back. I love you too. *"Sono pazzo di te."* I'm crazy about you.

I laugh in surprise. "Am I dreaming, or has someone been teaching you Italian?"

"I may have downloaded a few apps . . . It's important to speak lots of languages. Now I'll be quadrilingual."

Puzzled, I ask him which languages he speaks.

"Russian, obviously. English. And Italian, soon."

"So what's the fourth, Professor?" I tease.

There's an indecent glint in his eye as he lifts the sheets to expose my naked body.

"Stay right where you are, and I'll show you."

◆ ◆ ◆

Li Mei jumps ship two days later.

She has to go back to the second Rasputin in Macau, which she left over a month ago. She confides to me that she wants to patch things up with her parents too. When I ask if she thinks it'll work, she shrugs.

"I don't know. It won't be easy. They're very proud and very stubborn. But if they love me, in time they'll forgive me."

"Are you going to give them money?"

"Of course. They deserve it a lot more than I do," she says with a sad smile. "Will you come and visit me?"

I swear on the soul of Jimmy Choo that I will, and she's much happier after that. This time, we all go to the airport. Levi embraces her longer than the rest of us do, whispering things into her ear that I can't understand.

I think he's worried about her. In a way, Levi is a kind of father to all these broken people, like Peter Pan and his Lost Boys. Before this, they've had the pretext of the tournament to get together every year. But from now on . . . it's every man for himself.

Still, I'm perfectly confident that their friendship will survive the distance. That evening, I suggest to Levi that we organize an annual reunion. That way, we'll have to see each other at least once a year. He loves the idea, and we put it to a vote on the WhatsApp group: measure approved unanimously.

We speak so often that in some ways it's as though they're still here. I sometimes feel I've known them forever, and that feeling energizes me, but scares me too.

"Tito's been arrested," Thomas announces one morning, phone in hand.

I freeze in amazement. That was faster than I'd ever imagined. The evidence against him must have been overwhelming. The Italian police acted fast, that's for sure. My mother hasn't said anything . . . but I guess she's trying not to worry me.

"How many years will he get?" I ask in a low voice.

"If we add up all the charges against him . . . about eight years, I'd say. But he'll obviously get off with less. They always do."

*Oh. Fuck.* Eight years in prison. That's a long time. But then again, Levi's mother survived ten years in a Russian prison.

"Financial crimes are some of the least justifiable offenses, so there's often a heavy punishment."

I don't really know what I'm feeling. I've tried to avoid thinking about it, but now it's real. My father is going to appear in court and will probably lose his business. Who will take it over from him? My mother? Definitely not me!

"Your father's got good lawyers," Levi reassures me. "And plenty of influence. His sentence won't be as long as that."

At this point, I don't know if that's good news or bad news.

◆ ◆ ◆

It's been a week now since the tournament finished. This morning, I wake up in Levi's arms, as usual, and I just know. I feel it. Today's the day. All good things come to an end.

I'm having breakfast by the pool when Levi joins me, wearing only his swimming trunks. Everything's normal, but as silence falls between us, I know I was right. He just doesn't know how to tell me.

So I play the game. I make the most of the day. I talk him into going shopping, and he takes me for lunch at a classy seafood restaurant. On the way back, we walk past the Little Vegas Chapel, where lots of stars got married: Johnny Depp, Frank Sinatra . . . Marilyn Monroe.

"Shall we go have a look?" Levi asks, laughing.

"Isn't a fake engagement commitment enough for you, *amore mio*?" I joke, but I follow him inside.

We go through the heart-shaped entrance, curious to see more. Inside, a crazy-looking couple are having their photo taken by a petite blonde woman with a huge smile, presumably the maid of honor.

I laugh when I see the bride, a girl with faded pink hair. One of her hands clutches a bottle of champagne and the other is around her fiancé's neck.

"Zoe Camara, do you take this man, Jason Delaunay, to be your lawfully wedded husband?" asks the Elvis impersonator who's officiating.

"I doooo!" she cries, then continues in broken English, clearly tipsy. "I take you, your nerdy cats, and your stupid butt tattoo . . ."

Levi sniggers and murmurs into my ear, "D'you think they'll regret this once they're sober?"

I look at them, feeling unexpectedly moved. The Jason in question also says, "I do," though not before objecting to the insult to his cats, then gives his new wife a prolonged kiss. The maid of honor starts to cry her eyes out but is soon comforted by a guy who must be her boyfriend. Though they're not speaking English, I get the sense she's blaming her tears on her hormones. One glance at her stomach tells me she's pregnant.

"No," I say quietly. "I think they know exactly what they're doing." And deep down, I envy them.

I swallow my jealousy and take Levi's hand in mine as we walk back outside. I don't say anything the rest of the way home, and as soon as we get into the suite, I head straight for the shower before he's even put his bag down.

I stay in there for a good half hour, just buying myself time and letting the room fill with steam. I'm not too surprised when I feel Levi's arms wrap themselves around me, just under my breasts. He kisses my neck tenderly, and I can tell he's already apologizing for what he's about to say.

I revel in the embrace, keeping my eyes on the wall.

"I know what you've been doing all day . . . ," he murmurs. "But we need to talk about it . . ."

I don't say anything, just let him kiss my neck, then my back. When he turns me around to look him in the eye, all my resolution dissolves. His eyes are gentle and beseeching, and his voice is full of regret as he whispers, "Rose . . . I have to go home, really soon."

I was expecting it to hurt, but not this much. Not this intensely. I nod and bite my lip. His hands stroke my wet hair reassuringly under the falling water.

"And so do you," he continues. "Your mother's expecting you."

"I know."

I also know he doesn't want to leave any more than I do, but I'm annoyed that he can hide it so much better than I can. He takes my face in his hands, as gently as if picking up a small chick, and kisses me.

I return his kiss, my hands resting on his naked back. His whole body is pressed to mine, hard and wet.

"This isn't the end of us, Rose Alfieri." He smiles against my mouth. "It's just the start. I promise you that."

◆ ◆ ◆

Thomas has decided to stay on a little longer. My mother reserves a plane ticket for me, and Levi buys his at almost the same moment. It reminds me of the end of summer camp, with everyone going back to their normal lives. The worst feeling in the world.

I'm going home with two overstuffed suitcases and a head full of memories. It turns out to be very hard to leave the suite where I've lived through so many precious moments—and less precious ones too. I don't say a word while Thomas drives us to the airport. Levi keeps a tight hold of my hand.

When we arrive at the airport, Thomas is the first to speak.

"No hugs please. I've had enough of them this week. One more and I'll puke all over you."

"Don't worry; I wouldn't' dream of it!" I reply with pretend disgust.

Levi shakes his head and rolls his eyes.

I start to walk away. "See you, Chris Hemsworth!" I shout over my shoulder, just to annoy him.

A few seconds later, I hear footsteps and turn around to see Thomas walking up behind me, looking fiercely determined. At first I think he's going to start yelling at me, but at the last moment . . . he pulls me into a bear hug.

I stand completely still, in shock. Am I dreaming? No, Thomas really is giving me a hug. And, contrary to what he just said, he seems happy to be doing so. I put my hands on his back, grateful for the gesture. Despite our rocky start, Thomas and I like each other more than either of us would ever admit.

He's a guy you can rely on.

"You're a pain in the ass," he says, drawing away.

With those beautiful words, he sets off again in the opposite direction. My laugh gradually dies on my lips as I realize what this means. It's just Levi and me now. We check in and go through customs in silence. When it's time for us to go to our separate gates, Levi pulls gently on my hands so I'll stop walking.

We stand facing one another, both of us uneasy.

"Call me when you get there," he says.

"You too."

Silence.

"Don't forget your promise," he reminds me. "No casinos. No online gambling. Don't drink too much, either, and go easy on the cigarettes. They're not good for you."

I roll my eyes and groan.

"Yes, Mom. Anything else?"

He pulls me toward him so hard, I bounce back off his chest. His nose brushes mine as he seizes the back of my neck with one hand and kisses me roughly. I wrap my arms around his neck as our tongues intertwine.

Our kiss has the taste of regret, of the anxiety and melancholy of something unfinished, and also barely begun. He hasn't left yet, but I already miss him.

"Keep that safe," he says, tapping the engagement ring I've been wearing all this time.

"And you, take good care of your mother. Make the most of this time with her, OK?"

He nods, then buries his face in my neck, his face hidden by my short hair. Our embrace reminds me of the one we shared for our *Glamour* shoot. I don't know how I'll let him go. I feel as though I'm . . . home. Safe. I don't want to ever leave.

After a few minutes, I prepare myself to pull away, but he holds me even tighter, whispering against my skin, "Not yet. Just a little longer."

I stroke his hair as if I were stroking the hair of a child. As my flight time gets closer, I finally make him release me. His face is impassive once more, as though he's put the mask back in place.

I can tell he doesn't want me to see his true feelings.

"I have to go," I say.

I kiss him once more, then wave to him as I back away. He waves in return, his lips tight. His expression breaks my heart, so I turn around, hoping he won't see the tears in my eyes.

I feel alone in the world once again.

# Chapter 35

## Levi

***August***
***Saint Petersburg, Russia***

I'm a bag of nerves.

Stupid, isn't it? This isn't a job interview, or a first date. I'm just going to collect my mother from prison. Nothing scary. And yet my hands are sweating in the taxi. There's a bouquet of flowers on the empty seat next to me; peonies, her favorite.

The moment I've been anticipating for ten years has finally come, and the truth is I'm terrified. My mother knew me as a teenager, but she knows nothing about the adult I am now, except what I allow her to see on my monthly visits.

What if the reality disappoints her, and she doesn't like the man I've become? I'm already worried about how she'll react when I tell her I play poker—that I'm the world champion, in fact. And that I've fallen madly in love with the daughter of the man who stole my father from us.

*Shit, now I'm panicking again.*

I'm not the only person waiting outside the prison. I guess they're freeing more than one prisoner today. I tell the taxi driver to park and wait; then I get out, flowers in hand. I check my clothes one last time:

white trousers and T-shirt—nothing controversial, nothing that screams *reprobate.*

My phone vibrates, and I see a message from Rose that makes me smile.

GOOD LUCK TODAY!

She remembered.

It's been a month since we parted. To tell the truth, the first couple of days were fine. It didn't seem real yet, and I still felt like I'd see her again the next day. Then, after the realization really hit me . . . it was as though I'd fallen down a hole. I miss her way too much.

I've never had emotions like this before. Seriously, I embarrass myself. But I don't question her choice; I know she needed to go back to Italy, back to her roots, her mother, and a stable, loving home.

Over the last few weeks, the Rasputin's taken up most of my time. I've started the process of selling it and of sorting out my finances so that I can leave.

I finally feel as though I'm moving in the right direction. I still find it hard to believe the rivalry between Tito and me is over. I almost expect him to knock on my door and challenge me to a duel one of these days.

The nightmares haven't stopped, and now I haven't got Rose to calm me down. But I often call her in the middle of the night, and she always answers. She tells me all about her day, and I soon relax. We spend hours making completely crazy plans for our future together.

My phone bill's never been so high.

By the way, have you planned
what you'll say after she reads
in the paper that her son's
engaged to a pregnant former
stripper?

First of all, nobody heard your little tirade that night, thank God. And no . . . I haven't thought what to say about you—and about us.

You'd better start thinking, then.

But it's too late for that now, because the prison doors are opening, and my heart is going crazy. I put my phone in my pocket and clutch the bouquet, taking deep breaths in an unsuccessful attempt to slow my heartbeat. I'm like a kid with stage fright.

I'm almost afraid I won't recognize her. A stupid thought because I saw her just four months ago, and she always looks the same. My chest tightens when I finally catch sight of her.

My mother stops just outside the door and looks up to the sky, her arms hanging by her sides. She's wearing jeans and a sweater, and she's holding a cloth bag that must contain all her possessions. She looks a little lost. I don't approach her right away.

I'd rather wait for her to come to me. I want to give her time alone to take in her freedom, the fresh air, the landscape. After what seems like an eternity, she glances around, looking for me.

When she sees me, I freeze like a child who's been caught stealing sweets. She walks toward me, smiling, and opens her arms. My response is immediate: I burst into tears. I cry silently as the distance between us shrinks, then pull her into an embrace.

I haven't held my mother in my arms in ten years. Not since that fatal day when I wouldn't let her go, and she smiled and said everything would be all right. A whirlwind of emotions tears through me, good and bad. It's like I'm a teenager again, and not a grown-up with a terrible thirst for revenge.

"Mom," I sob. "I'm sorry . . . I'm sorry."

She holds me tight, despite the vast difference in our heights, and strokes my hair just like Rose did. I hide my face in her hair, overcome.

"You're so tall . . . and handsome!"

Of course, that's the first thing she finds to say to me. I smile even as I'm crying. When I draw back, she wipes away my tears, not bothering with her own, and takes my bouquet.

"Oh, they smell incredible."

I look her over carefully, resisting the temptation to comment on her pale skin, her sunken cheeks, and thin arms. Whatever she's gone through in there, it's over now. For good. I'll spend the rest of my life making up for having put her in that situation, even though she always says it was her fault, not mine.

I ask how she's doing, and we exchange a few banalities. The whole thing feels totally surreal. I don't think I've come to terms with it yet: it's like I'm just picking her up at the station after a long journey. I'm almost afraid they'll come and take her away again, saying there's been some mistake.

I suggest we leave right away, so we go back to the taxi, and I give the driver the address of a restaurant nearby.

"What do you want to eat?" I ask shyly. "Something you've been wanting for years, something you haven't had for ages."

She doesn't hesitate; she's clearly been planning this moment.

"A burger and fries."

I can't help laughing in surprise. It's so . . . ordinary.

"Perfect. Then let's go."

Our plan is to live together for a little while, for as long as she wants, or at least until she's sick of me. We know she'll be monitored for a while, so we can't leave the country just yet. But it's only a short delay. We've got lots to talk about, lots to catch up on, lots to learn about each other.

"Can we . . . can we take a selfie together?" I ask when we arrive at the restaurant. "To send to my friends."

"A what?" asks my mother, smiling.

I explain what that is, and she agrees, tidying her hair. My mother always looks very well put together. I bet that was true even in prison.

We take a photo at the table, with our burgers, and I send it to the WhatsApp group "Ocean's Eleven"—the group name chosen by Rose, naturally.

"What are your friends like?"

My mother picks up her burger in both hands and takes a huge bite, closing her eyes to savor it. I've never seen so much pleasure on someone's face.

It makes me sad and happy at the same time.

"Strange, but amazing. Tommy works as a bodyguard in Sweden and the US. Li Mei runs the Chinese Rasputin. Lucky's studying architecture in Los Angeles, and Rose . . . Rose studies psychology. She models for art students, and paints. She's wonderful. And very intelligent too. But I don't tell her that because her ego's strong enough as it is."

I stop talking, realizing she's watching me in silence, a gentle smile on her lips. I ask if I said something funny, but she shakes her head.

"My son is a man now; that's all. It's strange."

"OK . . ."

"Does she live nearby, this Rose?"

I pick up a fry to hide my feelings. "Not really, no."

"I see . . . How did you meet?"

This is it. She's given me the perfect chance to tell her everything. The poker, Tito, Rose, my victory. She'll know it all soon enough anyway, and I'd rather she heard it from me.

"Mom . . . I have something to tell you. Please don't be angry."

"If you tell me you're married with two kids, I warn you I might have a heart attack."

*No, just a sham engagement.*

"It's nothing like that," I say. "The thing is, I've hidden this from you, but . . . I'm a professional poker player."

My heart misses a few beats as I wait for her reaction. She raises her eyebrows in surprise and purses her lips. Not a good sign. Before she can say anything, I tell her about wanting to beat Tito.

She tries to interrupt, her cheeks red with anger, but I press on. I skip over the most sordid details, like Rose's spying on me and my role in Tito's arrest. She listens but won't look me in the eye.

"But it's over now," I say. "I did it to prove I could. To take revenge. And because I wanted money, to be honest."

"So that explains your mafia tattoos," she mutters. "I don't like them."

I smile and blush in embarrassment. "That's one of the reasons I got them, yes. But please believe me: poker's behind me now. Behind *us*."

"I don't want you to end up like him," she says, her voice beseeching. "I know you're not your father, and I might be being unfair, but I just . . ."

"I know, I know," I say, putting my hand on hers. "I feel the same way."

My mother nods, calmer now, and wipes her eyes. She says she wants to get to know everything about my life, including whatever else I'm hiding from her. She didn't react much to the fact that Rose is Tito's daughter. When she asks if I plan to see Rose again, I nod.

"That's part of my plan, yes."

"In that case, you need to do things properly," she insists. "And I need to meet her. Does she speak Russian?"

I grimace. The few words I've managed to teach Rose won't be much use in a conversation with my mother.

"About as well as I speak Italian, I guess."

She asks more questions about my pretend fiancée, and we spend the next two hours talking about everything and nothing; about my life, my work, my love life. And then about her plans for the future.

Before she went to prison, my mother worked as a nanny. When I ask if she wants to go back to doing that, she suddenly looks sad.

"No parent will want to trust a former convict with their child. And they'd be right not to."

There's nothing I can say to that. She's right. I know my mother would never hurt a fly, but they don't. I wouldn't leave my baby with someone I wasn't sure I could trust either.

I ask her what she'd like to do instead. "Tell me your dreams, even the craziest ones, and I'll make them come true."

She laughs, clearly not believing a word. I tell her I mean it.

"Mom, the only reason I've worked to get all this money is so I can spend it on you. I know it'll be hard for you to get back to normal life, but we'll manage it. You love cooking! Why not open a little restaurant? Or maybe you'd rather travel? You don't have to work. You can do whatever you like. Go and bask on a beach in the Maldives, cocktail in hand; get yourself a massage . . . You'd love it there."

"Slow down, slow down," she interrupts, looking overwhelmed. "That's . . . too much all at once. I have no idea what I want to do yet, other than sleep in a soft, warm bed."

"Sorry . . . I'm just a bit excited."

"I know. Me too."

I smile at her and try to rein myself in. We don't say anything while I finish my meal. I know she's watching me, but I let her do it without saying anything.

Abruptly, she says, "Do you still not sleep well? You have bags under your eyes."

I shake my head, not looking up. She asks if I'm still seeing the psychologist her brother recommended. I tell her I stopped a few months ago. Silence falls again, and this time it lasts longer. I look at her empty plate: she devoured her food in an instant.

I suddenly want to cry again. She must notice this, because she leans toward me and takes my face in her hands, forcing me to look at her.

"Levi, my darling. You have to stop," she whispers. "You have to stop blaming yourself. About your father, and about me. It was an accident. Do you hear me? You defended yourself. You defended me.

That doesn't make you a bad person." I want to pull away, but she insists, "Going to prison was the best decision I ever made."

"I should have paid for my mistake. It was my responsibility."

"You were a child!" she retorts in a low voice, not letting me continue. "Having to live with this for the rest of your life is punishment enough if you ask me. You'll understand when you have a child of your own . . . You'll understand that no mother could let her baby go to prison if she had the power to stop it. It's in the past now. We're together again. I don't want to discuss it anymore, OK?"

I nod, and she caresses my cheek and gives me another smile. After a few seconds' silence, she says, "Actually, I do like the idea of traveling a little."

That's enough to get me smiling again. I suggest we leave in a few months. I say we can go anywhere, as long as it's warm and beautiful. She suggests South America and Australia. I can picture it already. There's just one tiny detail . . .

"Would you mind if someone else joins us?"

I know she's guessed what I mean, but she acts like she has no idea. "Not at all."

"Great. That means we'll need to make a little detour through Venice, OK?"

She raises an eyebrow. "Venice? Why Venice?"

I smile mysteriously, unable to hide my happiness.

"I left something *very* important there."

# Epilogue

## Rose

***December***
***Venice, Italy***

Levi Ivanovich is a dirty liar.

*We'll see each other soon.* Yeah right. It's been exactly six months since we left each other in the Las Vegas airport. Since then, I've had time to

- grow my hair (it's nearly down to my shoulders now, and my mother has promised to cut it this week);
- start seeing my psychologist again (she thinks Levi is a dirty liar too . . . or at least, in my head she does);
- find a job in a little pottery shop;
- decide to start studying again (but at an art school this time!).

A lot can happen in six months. As soon as I got back, my mother and I had the longest, most in-depth conversation we'd ever had. I don't have one single secret from her now.

We focused on creating a healthy, happy environment for me, to help me conquer my addiction—for good this time! I'm proud to say

I haven't played poker or gambled at all in six months. I've kept the promise I made to Levi and our friends. My debts are paid, to my great relief, even the interest.

I've been drinking less, too, though that's been harder to do than I expected. My mother always tells me, "You need to learn patience." That's still difficult for me. As for smoking . . . I'm not sure I'll ever be able to quit. Levi will just have to put up with it.

Besides, he's in no position to criticize! He's completely abandoned me, the traitor. Calling me every other day? No problem. But coming to Venice for the weekend . . . not a chance. The guy's a millionaire; he has no excuse.

"He needs time with his mother," Li Mei always tells me when I call her to complain.

I know it's true, and I do understand. I'm stupid and ungrateful to be jealous. He hasn't seen his mother for ten years, so of course he wants to be with her. But I can't help it . . . I miss him terribly. Time seems to be passing in slow motion. I need to see him, touch him, kiss him.

Time and distance haven't changed my feelings. Quite the opposite—I'm dying to see him again. When I told my mother that, she smiled and signed her advice.

"Hold on to that feeling. It's rare."

I know what she was thinking when she said that. She's never been able to feel anything like that because she was coerced into a marriage where there was no love. But she's free now, divorced and single, and I hope she'll be able to relive her youth. She still thinks about my father, more out of loyalty and habit than anything else, which is understandable. I think about him, too, sometimes.

I've only visited him once since he was arrested. Seeing him look so helpless made me feel guilty, and I had to remind myself that he was there because of his own crimes.

"I'm going to try to forgive you, if I can," I told him. "But I think it's going to take time."

He didn't reply. I think I saw regret in his eyes, but I can't be sure. It's time to let go of my fantasy of a perfect father. Mine will never be that, and I have to accept it and move on.

As for Levi . . . well, unlike me, he has *not* kept his promise. That's why, as I'm walking through Venice, I ignore his first call, and then his second. There aren't many people in the streets. The tourists never come at this time of year, mainly because it's always rainy and windy.

But today, the air is unusually warm. I'm wearing only a pair of trousers and a light jacket over a long-sleeved top. I sit on the steps of the Ponte del Parucheta—the Parucheta Bridge—and pull out my sketchbook.

I've been painting nonstop ever since I got the idea to apply to study at the New Academy of Fine Arts in Milan. But this morning, all I need is a pencil to sketch the narrow canal and empty gondolas on the white page. Over time, I've managed to start drawing all sorts of things, not just self-portraits. Something's finally clicked.

I feel myself relaxing, until my mobile rings yet again. I groan and decide to answer.

"What do you want?"

"And good morning to you, too, *amore mio*."

The bastard. He always uses Italian words when I'm angry. I'm sure he knows I can't resist them. When he's the one who's angry, he calls me *Bambina*, because he knows I hate it.

"I'd love to spend the next hour trying to get you to tell me why you're sulking, but I haven't got time," he says mockingly. "What are you up to?"

"I'm throwing darts at a photo of you."

"No, you're not. You haven't got any photos of me. I, on the other hand . . . have plenty of you, and very beautiful they are too."

I scowl at the canal, and suddenly remember our wild, tender nights in our room in Caesar's Palace. It seems like an eternity ago. Since then, we've had Skype sex, as Li Mei and Lucky recommended—and it was good . . . *very* good—but nothing like the real thing. The truth is . . . every day I worry that he'll get bored and forget about me.

"There are plenty of photos of you online, you know," I tell him. "All I have to do is search for them."

"I see. You're having fun, then. Fantastic."

"Why are you calling, Levi?"

He doesn't answer straightaway. When he does, his voice sounds reproachful.

"You lied to me."

I'm immediately on my guard. "Me? When?"

"You told me the weather in Italy was always good. That's not true."

Honestly. Is that why he's avoiding coming here? Really? I answer angrily, my cheeks burning.

"So don't come, then, if it isn't sunny enough for you!"

I hear him snicker. Then his voice suddenly seems to have an echo as he says, "Too late."

Someone sits down next to me on the steps, and my eyes widen as I see Levi, still holding his phone to his ear, smiling at me. Oh God. I almost drop my phone in amazement. How did he manage this? How did he know where to find me?

"What are you doing here?" I splutter.

His eyes stray down to my mouth, and he leans over to kiss me tenderly. I've hardly had time to enjoy the taste of his lips before he pulls away again.

"I missed you."

I can hardly believe my eyes. I lift my hand and poke his cheek with my finger to confirm he's really there. That makes him smile, and he tries to nibble my finger, but I pull it away.

"You're really here."

"I heard my girlfriend was getting impatient," he explains, resting his elbows on his knees. "So I wanted to apologize to your face. Do you forgive me?"

Of course I forgive everything. Because he's here, in real life, *finally*! I resist the temptation to jump on him, and instead look up at him as casually as I can.

"You took your time . . . It's been six months."

"I know. I'm sorry. I was busy."

I immediately feel awful for being selfish, so I ask how his mother's doing. He rewards me with a smile.

"Really well. She's making the most of her freedom. Soon, we're going to set off and travel, for who knows how long, starting with Bali."

I already knew they were planning to travel, but I didn't know it would happen so soon. I ask him where they plan to go after Bali, and he reels off a list of countries, some I've been to, others I'd love to visit one day.

"But I thought I'd stop off here before we go," he adds, looking at me with an intensity that immediately makes my heart beat faster. "Because you told me it would be warm. And now look at the sky. This is not what you promised, Rose."

"It's warm in the summer, you idiot! Not in the middle of December!"

He bursts out laughing, and I can't resist any longer. I take his face in my hands and press my lips to his. He responds immediately, as though he's been longing for this, too, and sighs with pleasure. His hands move over my back, possessively, and draw me to him.

We kiss for a long time, until he eventually draws back and murmurs, "I don't want to freak you out . . . but it was your mother who told me where you were."

I blink.

"Wait, what? How?"

"She wrote down where I should go. I learned a few signs before coming here so I could talk to her properly, but it's obvious I need to learn more . . ."

He's so adorable. I'm starting to panic, though. That means I'll have to formally introduce them; things are getting serious. Levi must see the anxiety in my eyes, because he takes my hand and pulls me up gently, saying, "Relax. Nothing's official, OK?"

"OK . . . and how long will you stay?"

"A few days, if you'll have me."

I just smile in reply. We go home together, hand in hand, catching up on what's been happening in each other's lives. Even though we call all the time, we still have lots to talk about.

As we walk in the front door, I hear voices. Who could it be? My mother and I hardly ever have guests. Levi rests his hand on my back reassuringly as I open the door and head into the living room.

"I swear it's true!" I hear laughter. "I was what, twenty? Worst Tinder hook-up ever. The guy arranged to meet me in a hotel room, and what do I see when I go in? Two other guys on the bed, holding cameras."

*Wait a minute* . . . I know that voice.

"Hang on there. Was this a hook-up or a job interview for a porn film?" asks another voice I'd recognize anywhere.

I walk faster, and when I open the door of the living room, the scene that meets me stops me in my tracks. Thomas, Li Mei, and Lucky are sitting around the table, laughing hysterically. They don't notice me straightaway, but Levi kisses my forehead and whispers, "Surprise."

It's Thomas who looks up first and sees me. He nudges Li Mei, who leaps up and rushes over to hug me. I hold her tight, closing my eyes.

This is the last thing I expected. All my friends sitting at my table, in the middle of Venice! I laugh incredulously. Lucky hugs me, too, and Thomas gives me one of his rare smiles. Apparently, the hug he gave me at the airport was a once-in-a-lifetime opportunity. But I'm not about to complain.

"What are you all doing here?"

"Haven't you told her?" Li Mei asks Levi in surprise.

"Not yet."

I turn to him, not knowing what to expect, but he just puts his arm around my shoulders. I insist he tell me, so he says with a sigh, "Let's just say, we're going to impose on you for at least a week. And then, if you'd like to . . . you can come to Bali with me and my mother."

*What?* I look at him, trying to hide my astonishment. The idea takes me aback, but there's nothing keeping me here except my mother. My classes won't start for another year, and in the meantime, I'm as free as a bird . . .

"Why not?" I say, smiling enigmatically. "After all, you know how much I love traveling."

Lucky sighs and says how romantic this is. Li Mei tells him to make a note of it for the erotic historical novel he's planning to write. Only Thomas looks unconvinced as he grumbles at Levi, "You've changed, dude. What's got into you?"

Levi isn't annoyed by this observation. Far from it. He leans over to kiss me, whispering, "There's a Russian saying, 'If you live among roses, you take on their perfume.'"

I smile at the metaphor and the play on my name. I guess he's right. Since we've been together, despite our far-from-perfect characters, we've achieved the impossible: we've healed our wounds and tamed our worst desires.

I'm still not convinced that some people are all bad or all good. I don't know what the elements are that make up an honest life. I only know that I think life is like the world Levi sees every day.

A blend of both black and white.

Sometimes people are good; sometimes people are bad. Sometimes, two broken people meet and come to love one another. Levi saw the good in me when I'd lost sight of it; I was able to comfort the broken, guilt-ridden child who haunted his dreams.

Somehow, in the mirrors of each other's eyes, we recognized one another. Falling in love began as a survival instinct. But it became far more than that.

It's become a way of breathing.

Because Levi has seen the worst of me, and I've seen the worst of him.

Now it's time for us to share the best.

Together.

# Acknowledgments

If I had to sum up the incredible adventure that has been my life since I started writing, the numbers would look something like this:

- Five years since the writing of my first novel, *Let's Fall in Love*.
- Six books published.
- Twelve fictional characters who've made a big impact on my life, and maybe on yours too.
- And finally, thousands of readers who've been reading my stories since day one.

Ten years ago, I dreamed of a life like this without imagining it was possible. I can still hardly believe how lucky I am to be living my passion. The list above is just numbers, and I know you can't count happiness, but it still makes me so happy. I spent the years 2020 and 2021 stressed, ill, and overworked, writing not one but three novels, one after another. Despite everything, it was the best thing that could ever have happened to me.

I wouldn't change it for the world.

The adventure has been made possible, first and foremost, by my publisher, Hugo Roman. Thank you to Hugues for giving me my first break in 2016, and to Arthur for having so much faith in me over the years. Thank you to my editor, Sylvie, as always, for following me down all the paths where my ideas led. And thank you, of course, to the whole team at Hugo for always looking after me.

I would also like to thank Johan, Marie (#Spidey in my phone), and Marie (Alhinho) for having been the first to read *The Ace of Hearts* (I wasn't too annoying this time, was I?). Your feedback was invaluable. You're the best, always. Special mention to the beautiful Dana Delon for answering all my questions about Russia (big kisses from Paris!).

Thank you to my parents, of course—Hulk and Sandrillon—and my brothers, Nénette (who'll hate me forever for calling him that in print) and Rorodu6 (no, I won't give your Snap) for always supporting me, and to Moh for answering my endless questions about poker (I owe you a game!). I love you.

I couldn't end without thanking Levi Stewart (*Fangirl*) and Levi Ackerman (*Attack on Titan*) for being the inspiration for my Levi Ivanovich, an amazing man for all his faults.

And a huge thank-you, of course, to all of you reading this book. Your enthusiasm, support, and messages motivate me more and more every day and warm my heart. It's true that we writers write stories for ourselves, but the experience I really treasure is sharing them with you. Without that unique interaction, none of this would be possible. I hope to carry on creating stories and characters that will touch your hearts.

# About the Author

Morgane Moncomble was born in 1996 in Argenteuil, France. Following the publication of her debut novel, *Viens, on s'aime*, in 2016, Morgane established herself as one of the leading romance authors of her generation. *Ace of Hearts* is her first to be translated into English.

# About the Translator

*Photo © 2024 Dionne Freeman*

A translator from French and Italian, Jennifer Higgins is based in Oxfordshire in the UK. She has translated fiction, drama, and poetry by such authors as Rachilde, Maria Orsini Natale, Clara Schulmann, and Emmanuelle Pagano. Her work has been long-listed for the International Booker Prize, and she recently produced the first English translation of Jean Lorrain's 1906 play *Ennoïa*. For more information, visit http://jenniferhiggins.wixsite.com/translator.